Science
Fiction
Stear. R

MUTINY AT VESTA

Also by R. E. Stearns
Barbary Station

MUTINY AT VESTA

R. E. STEARNS

SHIELDRUNNER PIRATES
BOOK TWO

SAGA PRESS

LONDON SYDNEY **NEW YORK** TORONTO NEW DELHI

SAGA PRESS
AN IMPRINT OF SIMON & SCHUSTER, INC.

1230 AVENUE OF THE AMERICAS, NEW YORK, NEW YORK 10020

For information about special discounts for bulk purchases, please contact Simon & Schuster Special Sales at 1-866-506-1949 or business@simonandschuster.com.
The Simon & Schuster Speakers Bureau can bring authors to your live event. For more information or to book an event, contact the Simon & Schuster Speakers Bureau at 1-866-248-3049 or visit our website at www.simonspeakers.com.
Also available in a Saga Press paperback edition
Book design by Greg Stadnyk
The text for this book was set in Caesilia LT Std.
Manufactured in the United States of America
First Saga Press hardcover edition October 2018
2 4 6 8 10 9 7 5 3 1
Library of Congress Cataloging-in-Publication Data
Names: Stearns, R. E., 1983– author.
Title: Mutiny at Vesta / R. E. Stearns.
Description: New York, NY : Saga Press, [2018] | Series: Shieldrunner Pirates ; 2
Identifiers: LCCN 2017051746 | ISBN 9781481476904 (trade paperback) | ISBN 9781481476898 (hardcover) | ISBN 9781481476911 (eBook)
Subjects: | GSAFD: Adventure fiction. | Science fiction.
Classification: LCC PS3619.T427 M88 2018 | DDC 813/.6—dc23
LC record available at https://lccn.loc.gov/2017051746

To Greg, who does what has to be done. Thank you, babe.

MUTINY AT VESTA

PRONOUNS USED IN THIS STORY

He	It	She	They	Ve
Him	It	Her	Them	Ver
His	Its	Hers	Their	Vis

CHAPTER 1

Time integrated through digital intermediary: 1 hour 53 minutes

Adda Karpe disconnected her mind from the ship around her and sat beside Iridian Nassir on the surface currently serving as a floor. The ghostly intermediary figure connecting Adda and the ship's AI vanished. Iridian wrapped her golden-brown arm around Adda's waist without interrupting her story. "So I thought, 'Pel's dying around here somewhere, and what do I need two kidneys for anyway?' and grabbed the bastard. This is what I got for it."

Iridian raised one side of her shirt to her armpit. A tapered line of recently regrown flesh marred a tattoo of a flap of skin pulled up to reveal a skull and crossed rib bones drawn over realistic viscera beneath it. The other people in the *Casey Mire Mire*'s main cabin, a man just out of his teens with the same pale complexion as Adda's, and a darker man with a beard like a stylized leaf, laughed and swore, respectively.

"Wish I could see it," the younger one, Pel, said. Goggles with dark blue lenses hid his scarred eyes, reflecting the ceiling-wall seam lights from where he sat on the floor near Adda.

The *Casey*'s bedroom door slid up and open. Captain Sloane crossed the main cabin to the bridge console in two low-gravity strides, long coat and neatly braided black hair following after. "We'll be in range of Vesta's southern docking guides in five minutes. Are all of you ready?"

"Finally," Pel said. "The *Casey* is so slow."

"Hey, it's about average." Iridian glanced around, brows furrowed, like audibly insulting the ship was a bad idea. Perhaps it was. "We got here as fast as any ship could, without attracting the ITA's attention, anyway."

Sloane's lieutenant, who shaped his beard like a stylized leaf and went by Tritheist as a name, stepped around Adda's mesh bag of drone parts to stand beside the captain. "The newsfeeds still run daily Barbary Station updates. Vestan dock security will be expecting us. The ITA won't, or if they are, the local bureaucrats will keep them from stopping us."

"Good." The captain smiled, a flash of white teeth against dark skin. "Welcome home, lads and lasses." Sloane turned to Adda and Iridian. "The ship does intend to dock here, I assume?" The captain's smile looked more forced now.

"The *Casey*'s letting us off here, yeah." Iridian cast a suspicious look at a cam in a corner of the main cabin, which served as one of the *Casey*'s many eyes.

Adda and the *Casey* had discussed their destination after the *Casey* had docked with a fuel barge on the Mars-Ceres reliable route and decided to stay there for two days after it'd finished refueling. It'd picked its own time to leave for Vesta, too, despite all of Adda's arguments to depart sooner. The delay had given Captain Sloane time to straighten out crew finances and pay for the fuel, but Iridian and Tritheist had taken shifts intimidating the barge crew into allowing them to stay.

Without the threats, the barge crew would've summoned the Interplanetary Transit Authority to arrest Sloane's crew on a variety of piracy-related charges. Sloane hadn't required the crew on the *Casey* to sign anything, but traveling with the captain was suspicious enough. Besides, Adda and Iridian had made their own share of trouble.

The ITA wouldn't enforce the Near Earth Union military draft, which Adda and Iridian were currently avoiding. They'd mete out the consequences they felt her and Iridian's colony ship hijacking warranted, and *then* turn them over to the NEU.

While Iridian and Tritheist had kept the barge crew out of the *Casey*, Adda and Pel had watched the ship's console so they'd all have some warning when it was ready to leave. It'd been Adda's last chance to confirm that Pel really wanted to stay with her. She and Iridian had fought long and hard to earn a place with Sloane's core pool of crewmembers, but Pel could've begged passage to another station. "I've got money coming, and I've got to live somewhere," he'd said. "Might as well stick with you!"

The ITA had almost caught them at Barbary Station, and everyone knew that Vesta was Captain Sloane's base of operations. All the ITA had to determine was which direction the crew would come from and which vessel they'd travel in. Upon Adda's suggestion, the *Casey* had left the fuel barge on a long detour off the Mars-Vesta reliable route. The trip across unpatrolled space had paid off. They hadn't seen the ITA since Barbary.

Adda had never found out why the *Casey* had stopped at the fuel barge, or what made it decide to leave. Traveling with an awakened intelligence was as unsettling as Adda's degree in AI development had led her to expect.

"I can't tell if the *Casey* is planning to stay at Rheasilvia Station," Adda said.

"She's got her own fleet now." Pel still referred to the ship as "she," like the rest of Sloane's crew did. The Casey's AI copilot was conscious enough to develop preferences, but it had ignored Adda's questions about its gender. "Three ships is a fleet, right?" Pel continued. "What does she need to hang out with a bunch of humans for?"

"Maintenance, obviously," said Tritheist. "Otherwise she'd have left Barbary Station years ago."

Awakened artificial intelligence held different priorities and assessed more potential future actions than any human could. Even after Adda and Iridian fixed the Casey's internal communications system, the ship's intelligence hadn't spoken aloud. Two other ships with awakened intelligences, the Charon's Coin and the Apparition, followed at a distance. Neither of them had ever communicated directly with Sloane's crew. Their silence could mean anything.

According to Iridian, most ships' windows projected whatever the ship was approaching above the bridge console, perpendicular to the floor, even though the ship was moving up from the passengers' perspective. That kept passengers who were accustomed to Earthlike gravity comfortable. Vesta's gray pockmarked surface was approaching on the Casey's ceiling, recorded by a hull cam above their heads.

The Casey approached Vesta as the minor planet's southern docking guides indicated, the path lit in a corner of its bridge console. Adda couldn't quite map the path above the console to the view projected above her. The massive asteroid looked utterly isolated in the starfield around it.

Flecks of red light representing buoys glinted between Vesta and the Casey, and the Casey stayed well away from them. Rheasilvia Station was a white web of human construction that spanned nearly 100 kilometers of a 500-kilometer wide, 13-kilometer-deep crater in Vesta's otherwise barren surface. A ship that must've been ten times the Casey's size blocked most of the station from view as it descended into the crater and angled toward the docks.

The Casey could've left the window projectors off. Its intelligence chose to accommodate them.

On the console beneath the display, a comms connection between the Casey and the Rheasilvia Station docks activated. "On behalf of Oxia Corporation, welcome to Rheasilvia Station," a voice announced over the Casey's cabin speakers, making Adda jump.

Captain Sloane belted into the pilot's seat, frowned at the information projected on the wall in front of the bridge console, and muttered, "She already submitted it." The Casey could travel to its destinations without human assistance, but it'd only be allowed to dock if it appeared to have a human pilot. A scan configured to detect implants would show that Captain Sloane lacked the neural ones required to fly a ship, but everything she'd read indicated that most stations didn't use such intrusive scans.

"Thank you," the captain said loudly enough for the console to pick it up and transmit it. "You should receive my ID and flight plan momentarily."

Iridian tied the mesh bag of drone parts to the base of the ship's pseudo-organic tank. The tank's 150 liters of viscous fluid were almost, but not completely, still. Like most pseudo-organic tanks, the liquid seemed to swirl slowly at its center, although ripples never reached the edge of the pinkish-gray goo. Most tanks were lit from within to turn the pseudo-organic fluid a less disturbing color, but the Casey's tank lights had only ever been white. Nobody had worked up the nerve to reach in and replace the bulbs.

While Adda collected small items that might be flung through the air at high speeds during a docking maneuver, Pel asked, "What does Oxia Corporation do?"

"Mining, infrastructure, and transport, predominantly, although they have other interests. They've been nosing around Vesta for years, but . . ." Captain Sloane frowned. "They didn't always greet arriving ships."

Iridian helped Adda and Pel secure themselves against the wall alongside the empty wall-mounted docks for the ship's destroyed rover drones. "Welcome back, Captain Sloane," said the voice over the Casey's speakers. The Oxia representative's voice was scratchier than it had been the first time, like the first greeting had been a recording and this one was in real time. "I. Um." She sounded like she was about to cough or cry. "We're sending your docking route now, Captain. Local time is 02:43."

"Hey, we're only four hours behind." Iridian, demonstrating more flexibility in a safety harness than Adda had believed possible, stretched to plant a kiss on the corner of Adda's mouth. The flash from a passing beacon touched Iridian's face and her freckles stood out dark and lovely in the light. "Here we go, babe. This is the kind of reception big-time pirates are supposed to get out here. We just jumped that silicate hauler to the front of the line." Iridian nodded toward the much larger ship out the projected window.

Adda squeezed her eyes shut. Beginnings and endings of space flight, with gravity changing directions and objects outside the windows at strange angles, made her nauseous. "That's unusual?"

"They're serious about first-come, first-serve docking on habs this far out, unless somebody's ship is in trouble," said Iridian. "Fuel's expensive, and nobody likes to float in micro-grav so near a hab with healthy grav. So yeah, docking ahead of a ship that was here first is a perk."

Adda's comp glove buzzed with new message alerts, which was worth opening her eyes for. Projected message headers scrolled over the back of her hand, formatted to fit in the silver-bordered square opening in her dark purple fingerless glove.

Pel's red comp glove erupted in a cacophony of cheerful alerts. "We're online!" He whooped. "Thank all the gods and devils, we have internet."

Although Adda could've corrected him that they'd been able to access it for the majority of the trip, and only the high-volume, nonemergency content was newly available, he looked too happy to care about the distinction. He freed both arms, though he left his torso and legs strapped to the wall, to get his comp reading the alerts aloud. His comp should've picked up the entertainment content from the buoy network hours ago—Adda's had—so the Casey must've been limiting their access until the ship was assigned a station dock. Tritheist passed by on his way to strap into the chair at the secondary console beside the bathroom door.

Adda was more interested in her bank balance than her messages. She checked the balance almost hourly, to confirm that the massive sum was still there. Piracy, even the nontraditional sort, paid as well as Pel had assured her it would. She encrypted and forwarded the account information through two proxy connections before it hit the buoy relay for the long trip through additional proxies to her father on Earth.

A deep sigh pressed Adda's chest against her harness. She and Iridian could pay up on their student loans and stop the collection agents from hassling their families, who had debts of their own. If working for Captain Sloane continued to pay this well, they, their parents, and most of their siblings could be out of debt in a matter of months. It was good to be part of the best pirate crew in populated space.

"Whoa, look at how far they've built down," said Iridian. "And up!"

Outside the window, a massive metal latticework rose around them. The intricate web of buildings and support infrastructure that kept the station interior spinning left only glimpses of the large crater in which Rheasilvia Station was built. Intersections between modules shone with white industrial lights much brighter than the distant sun. Rheasilvia's sister station, Albana, was on the opposite side of the asteroid, making Rheasilvia seem even more remote than it was, clinging to the crater wall and the bare Vestan soil.

The *Casey* rotated to a new angle relative to the station. What Adda felt as "down" shifted to a 45-degree angle from where her brain told her it should be. She shut her eyes again.

Pel's comp stopped reading message subject headers and started playing a news broadcast. ". . . return to Khiri Sekibo with the latest on the last Martian refugees repatriating from Barbary Station. Khiri?"

"Hi, I'm here with Suhaila Al-Mudari, spokesperson for the refugees who were trapped for three years by Barbary Station's aggressive artificial intelligence security system, known as AegiSKADA. Ms. Al-Mudari, what does it feel like to—"

"Forget the fugees, what about us?" Pel asked over the newscaster.

"Don't you want to hear how they're doing?" Iridian asked.

"They're fine," Pel said. "Wasn't the station swarming with ITA right after we left? They don't leave people they rescue stuck out in space. And anyway, I've got a hundred messages from them I haven't listened to yet, so I'll get all the juicy details. I want to hear what people are saying about the roguish pirates that made this all possible."

"I've minimized our involvement," Captain Sloane said. "Vestan media has always been suggestible. When I've reestablished my position here, I may grant an interview personally."

Pel looked disappointed for about a quarter of a second, then asked, "What does Suhaila look like again?"

"She looks . . . normal?" Iridian said. "Stylish, for sure."

"You're no help."

"I've got your sister to look at. Why should I check out other ladies?"

Pel groaned. "I do not need to hear about you making heart eyes at my sister!"

"We're *married*," Iridian said in tones of real triumph and mock menace. That'd been another accomplishment made on the trip to Vesta. The captain had been thoroughly amused to be asked to officiate. "I'll be making heart eyes at her *forever*."

Between the two of them, the newscaster, and the ship changing course and orientation, Adda needed a distraction before she threw up. According to the summary projected on the back of her hand through the comp glove's square window, Rheasilvia Station was home to 300,000 people. That made it the largest off-Earth habitat she'd been to, and the safest place in the universe for Sloane's crew, thanks to the local political ties the captain maintained.

When she refocused on Pel and Iridian's conversation, Iridian was saying, "All our eyes are a little fucked up. The cold and the black'll do that to you."

"Yeah, but even the fugee kids used to ask why I didn't just get them fixed," said Pel. "I need help walking so I don't run into things. And they hurt, still. It's annoying, and it's annoying to talk about all the time." A station the size of Rheasilvia had to have surgeons and regrowth clinics that could fix Pel's eyes. "Anyway, who says I want my old eyes back?" he continued. "I can afford great pseudo-organics now. No reason to keep what I was born with just because."

At the bridge console, Sloane's voice changed from casual to casual covering emotion. "We're carrying passengers tonight, yes. Didn't you receive our permit code?"

Adda subvocalized the terms to her comp and scanned the Interplanetary Transit Authority's passenger vessel requirements. The small ITA contingent in Rheasilvia's docks should've stopped and inspected passenger ships that lacked a permit and special insurance. The bribes Sloane's crew paid should protect the *Casey* and its crew, but Adda didn't want to risk putting the ITA agents in that position.

Apparently the captain didn't either. Sloane had been off Vesta for a long time. Things might've changed.

To keep herself occupied during the trip from Barbary Station, Adda had scoped out the ITA's databanks. After careful trial and one or two frightening errors, she'd exploited a backdoor entry into several corners of the ITA's internal system. As the newest systems infiltrator on a pirate crew, she expected to get good use out of that access to humanity's largest semiofficial law enforcement organization. She hadn't planned to use it this soon, but it was the best solution she saw to the problem at hand.

"I'll send the code again," Captain Sloane said more loudly. "Our copilot caught a virus, you see . . ."

A string of letters and numbers appeared on Adda's comp. She gasped and Iridian said something. Adda's hands shook while she inserted the code and the *Casey*'s ID into the ITA's system.

"Apology accepted," Sloane said in the direction of the bridge console's mic. "We'll proceed."

"Fucking unnecessary," Tritheist grumbled.

"Babe, talk to me." Iridian shook Adda by the shoulder. "Are you okay?"

Adda nodded slowly. "The Casey got into my comp again." The awakened intelligence had broken through her new defenses around her data, and she didn't even know when it'd happened. Her motion sickness returned at full strength. Strange sensations in her neural implant net could be a side effect of extended periods in close contact with awakened intelligences. As far as she knew, she was the first person ever to have spent this much time with one. That was the terrifying, exciting beauty of traveling with them. She should take more notes.

Beside her, Iridian swore and muttered, "That invasive, invisible, parasitic—"

"It also helped us create a passenger transport permit so we wouldn't be stopped." That meant that the Casey had been listening to what they said in the cabin, watching Adda's comp activity, and drawing accurate conclusions about what Adda was doing. And then it'd created an unused ID in the correct format, which might've taken Adda more time than she'd had.

Even though the Casey's intelligence crawling through her personal hardware was a violation, she felt obligated to defend it. The Casey's intelligence, and those of the other two ships from Barbary Station, were likely the only awakened intelligences in the universe. She refused to put them at risk of deactivation by anyone, even her wife.

Footsteps approached from the bridge. Captain Sloane clutched recessed handholds in the wall to maintain balance in the shifting g-forces the Casey generated as it flew toward their designated dock. While Adda had been concentrating on her comp, the captain had donned a full suit of gold and black armor, covered with the long coat Adda associated with captaincy. Like

Tritheist, the captain's helmet faceplate was raised to communicate without a comms system. Equipment and supplies clanked and thumped belowdeck.

"We'll dock shortly, but I've recommended to the Casey that she depart afterward," Captain Sloane said. "We should leave the docks and enter the main part of the station quickly as well."

"Something up, sir?" Iridian was still working on shaking her military habit of calling everyone "sir" unless they looked significantly feminine. Captain Sloane looked solidly nonbinary. "I don't love flying around in a ship that could break all our brains if it tried hard enough, but it's the only one we have."

"As I've been unable to confirm that port authorities have been suitably compensated for our convenience," the captain said—Adda interpreted "compensated" as "bribed"—"there's some possibility that we'll receive a well-armed welcome from one or more local interests. We have nothing to gain by waiting for a firefight, but I'd rather the Casey not sustain damage and retaliate against us or the station." That was one of many possible reactions, all equally likely and difficult to predict. The Casey didn't have guns of its own as far as Adda knew, but its awakened AI didn't need weapons to cause damage.

"You're assuming it will stay or go because I ask it to," Adda said. Captain Sloane gave her an incredulous look, and she shrugged. She wished she had a better answer, but she was as worried as the captain probably was about what the Casey would do. She had a lot of experience with normal AIs. There were no experts on awakened ones.

"Who's suicidal enough to shoot at us?" Tritheist gripped the handle of a chem canister launcher at his hip. He scowled toward the interior door to the passthrough, the half-a-hallway structure that connected to a dock's half-a-hallway to create an airlock, like he expected someone to break in. "This is your dock, on your station."

Sloane shrugged, the casual gesture magnified in the armored suit and at odds with the way the captain watched the bridge console, where threats would be projected on a simplified map. "It's been two years since I was in a position to supervise crew assets personally, and I've had difficulty reconnecting with my usual information sources. People become . . . ambitious." Captain Sloane pointedly looked from Adda to Iridian. "I've not yet risked contacting my headquarters since we left Barbary." The lead cloud surrounding Barbary Station would've made Sloane's contact with whoever was left in charge of the crew's headquarters sporadic at best. It would've been impossible without the *Casey*, who had occasionally carried messages out to the rest of the universe.

While Iridian helped Adda and Pel free themselves from the wall, Sloane murmured something in Tritheist's ear, knocked two knuckles against the lieutenant's armored chest, and returned to the bridge console. "First thing's a station sec scan," Tritheist announced, as if the three people he was lecturing weren't a meter or two away from his face. "Most of the weapons are in a shielded compartment and that should be all the illegals we're carrying, but we've never scanned the *Casey* ourselves so we don't know what she's got hidden. Stay calm, keep your hands visible, move slow."

"Yes, sir." Iridian's hint of sarcasm was too small for Tritheist to call her out for it, but if even Adda identified it then it also couldn't be missed.

The whole ship felt as if it had turned abruptly on its side, and sickening weightlessness returned as the *Casey* slowed to a near stop. Adda's hair, which fell over her eyes in Earthlike gravity,

drifted up and out of her way. Iridian's shaved scalp kept her looking as powerful and confident as usual.

Tritheist kept talking. Iridian would tell Adda anything she
needed to know later. If there were any hidden compartments
in the Casey's main cabin, they were well hidden from Adda's
perspective. The ship's comprehensive communications suite
and the manacles installed on the bathroom wall suggested
that the Casey was designed for espionage. Three awakened
shipboard intelligences had left Barbary Station with Sloane's
crew, but only this copilot intelligence had changed its own
name. The Casey smuggling a previous owner's contraband was
a real possibility.

"Scanning now," Sloane said. "It doesn't affect their work, but
they prefer that we stay relatively still."

As soon as Sloane and Tritheist looked back to the bridge console, Pel waved his arms above his head. Adda yanked the one she
could reach down to his side. "Grow up!" she whispered.

"Never!"

"We should have been cleared by now, Captain," Tritheist
grumbled.

"Formalities must be addressed," said Captain Sloane. "Particularly if my influence on dock security has diminished."

"Dock sec should be keeping the ITA pricks occupied like they
fucking used to. Where do they think their pay comes from? It's
sure as hell not ITA; that's the point of joint stationspace control.
All they have to do is get us through the damned docks. Useless."
Tritheist lapsed into spacefarer cant, which was multilingual gibberish to Adda.

The window projected onto the wall replaced the view of the
dock passthrough's exterior wall slowly moving past them with
route records. This route had taken them through most of the

Near Earth Union, with a stopover on Mars before exiting NEU territory en route to Vesta, one of several populated asteroids in the asteroid belt. That trip would've been much longer than their actual route, which had cut across the reliable routes between Vesta and Barbary Station.

Adda hadn't told the *Casey* to do that either. She subvocalized to her virtual intermediary to see if it could find any indications as to how and why the *Casey* was making those decisions. AI were frequently incomprehensible even when they wanted to be understood, but it was worth trying.

The bridge console pinged three times in quick succession. Captain Sloane looked at Tritheist, who skimmed through some text projected in the center of his black comp glove. "That's 'cleared to engage passthrough locks,' Captain." The *Casey* was completing the docking maneuver on its own, but Sloane still had to act like a pilot to avoid raising suspicions among the Rheasilvia Station dock personnel.

Captain Sloane nodded, once. "So the ITA are satisfied. My people have done the minimum required to facilitate our arrival. Now I wonder who might be waiting in the terminal."

Sloane stepped through the *Casey*'s open interior door and stopped on one side of the passthrough's exterior door, which was still closed. Tritheist stood on the other side, skimming a map on his comp glove. "This isn't our dock, is it?" The lieutenant's question sounded more like a grim acknowledgement than an effort to clarify.

Sloane's shoulders slumped slightly, matching the captain's resigned frown. "It is not."

Iridian stepped into the passthrough with them, although three was the maximum number of people the ship's airlock could comfortably hold. "How can you tell?"

"This is my home," said Captain Sloane. "I know how the route to my terminal feels."

"We've been off Barbary Station long enough for news to make it here," Iridian said.

"Unlike the ITA stationed here, the Rheasilvia constabulary, and whomever is behind them, know who I am." Sloane's voice was calm, but the captain's flushed face could mean anger or embarrassment. Possibly both. Vesta should've been their safe haven. Adda sighed as she let go of that particular hope. "Weapons?" Captain Sloane added.

Iridian took long steps to a compartment in the bedroom. She tossed bowl-shaped palmers of the pirates' design to Sloane and Tritheist. The weapons fit into the palm of one hand and disabled human targets with some kind of invisible particle beam when fired. She kept one for herself and patted her shield, currently collapsed into a small rectangle of folded metal hanging on her belt hook. Another palmer was still in the shielded compartment, but Adda's aim wasn't much better than Pel's.

Sloane fitted a palmer on over one armored glove, with the bowl shape facing outward, then gripped a handhold in the passthrough wall. "Tritheist, Iridian, Adda, you will join me in a meeting with the current station leadership to determine who allowed this inconvenience to occur. If killing someone will stop this incompetence, I will do it."

Adda inquired, very carefully through her digital intermediary, whether the *Casey* would be able to subsume whatever AI coordinated Rheasilvia Station's law enforcement. With intelligences there was a very fine line between "ability to do something" and "do something now," but if Captain Sloane were expecting violence, now would be the time to risk that miscommunication.

The intermediary reappeared, from Adda's perspective, in

the center of the *Casey's* cabin. It thrust its hand into her comp glove, through her own hand, with no sensation to accompany the motion since she was in reality, not a virtual workspace. Her comp screen filled with several hundred links to vids and articles about awakened, or nearly awakened, AI that had been summarily executed by humanity and their networked zombie intelligences.

"You've made your point," Adda murmured to the *Casey's* AI copilot. Intelligences didn't experience fear, but their developers granted them a degree of self-preservation, which awakening should strengthen. Although the *Casey* might be willing and able to overpower Rheasilvia Station's management AI, doing so carried too big a risk of strangers discovering the *Casey's* awakened status and subsequently destroying it. That was a more specific hint at the *Casey's* decision-making motivations than she'd expected her intermediary to find.

The intermediary also delivered results of the *Casey's* dock systems scan. Everything from the maintenance schedule to the buoy guidance system carried Oxia's markings. The corporation only stored its most essential, short-term data locally. The whole exchange between Adda and the intermediary had taken less than ten seconds.

Iridian returned to her strap-in station beside Adda and pointed at a red symbol that had appeared over the window projection beside the passthrough. It was a square with a stick-figure person, arms and legs extended in an X shape, hovering in its center. "When you see that symbol, it means you're losing some grav within the next sixty seconds," said Iridian. "It's mostly gone already. Vesta's grav is pretty low, like a tenth of Earth's Moon's grav, I think."

"Is there a sound for that, too?" asked Pel. "She can put up all the symbols she wants, and they won't tell me a thing."

"You know, I've never heard the *Casey* use audio alerts," said

Iridian. "If we have to get back on this thing again, maybe Adda can ask it to add those."

Adda gripped the straps over her shoulders, but the worst gravity shifts were over. The wall and floor were in their correct position, and they barely shuddered as the *Casey*'s passthrough connected to the station and the "docking complete" notification lit beside the interior passthrough door.

The passthrough's exterior door clunked and whirred open. Iridian activated her boot magnets and freed herself from her harness. Her kiss bumped the back of Adda's head against the wall. "We made it this far!" She crouched to activate the magnets on Adda's boots and help her down. Gravity's pull toward the floor was so slight that it justified the *Casey*'s warning.

Adda turned toward the bridge console on reflex, although the intelligence was listening on active mics throughout the ship. "*Casey*, we may need to leave quickly. Will you wait here fifteen minutes?" She glanced at Sloane, who nodded. The *Casey* added a countdown timer to the console projection of ship statuses and the starscape framed in Rheasilvia Station's interconnecting architecture.

"What are you doing, deploying AI without the captain's order?" Tritheist snarled.

Sloane put a hand on his arm, pushing him away from Adda in the low gravity. Tritheist staggered backward as his boots gripped the metal floor. "She's welcome to create as many emergency exits as she's able."

"With respect, Captain, that AI is dangerous." Tritheist's tone and volume softened to communicate deference.

"Fuckin' A," Iridian muttered.

"As are we all," said Captain Sloane.

Pel beamed at this assessment, from his tangle of straps and limbs in the strap-down station against the wall. The long coat drifted around the captain's boots in Vesta's low gravity as Sloane, Iridian, and Tritheist walked through the *Casey*'s passthrough and into the terminal, Iridian in front with her collapsed shield on her belt. Adda, feeling distinctly harmless in their company, helped Pel peel himself off the wall to follow them.

Cams mounted prominently on the terminal walls recorded an empty room outside the passthrough. The words OXIA CORPO-RATION WELCOMES YOU TO RHEASILVIA STATION, accompanied by a shape that looked like a flower with three petals, were physically printed onto wall paneling that amplified the crew's steps in the empty space. Sloane's lip curled into a cultured grimace of disgust as the captain read the message. The terminal's far door, presumably leading to the rest of the station, was closed. No one waited there to greet them.

If Sloane's second-in-command on Vesta wanted to welcome them back, she should have at least sent a lackey with VIP passes for public transportation. And if she wanted to alert station security to the crew's presence without alarming Captain Sloane, then she should've sent an expendable lackey. The empty terminal felt like a trap, but not one arranged by whomever Sloane was planning to meet.

Adda caught Sloane's eye and hoped she looked less afraid as she felt. "We're leaving, yes?"

Sloane passed them on the way into the *Casey*'s passthrough, pulling Tritheist through an abrupt turn toward the ship with a grip on his elbow. "We are."

"Wait, what?" Pel said. "We just got here! There's a bar in the nightlife module where—"

Adda grabbed his wrist while Iridian pulled the folded metal rectangle from her belt. When Iridian shook the folded metal, it expanded into a semitransparent shield that covered most of Pel and Adda while Iridian held it between them and the empty terminal.

Adda smiled her thanks. Iridian's shield stance, with her bent knees, feet apart, strong arm raised, and hard, dark eyes was a thing to behold.

Something slapped into the shield near Iridian's elbow. Her arm thumped into Adda's and Pel's chests and they both tumbled up the ramp after Sloane and Tritheist. Iridian swore and dragged the shield along the outer passthrough door's frame like she was scraping something off it. "Get in!"

She inhaled like she was going to shout something else, but a small explosion drowned her out. Fragments clattered off the passthrough walls and into the Casey's main cabin, the low gravity cluttering the air with them as well as the floor and ceiling. Iridian bounced off the far wall and caught the base of the Casey's pseudo-organic tank to stop herself from careening back into the passthrough. The pinkish-gray liquid in the tank sloshed against its sealed lid. The exterior door thumped shut.

The Casey's engines hadn't had time to cool, so its passengers needed to strap in before the takeoff bounced them off walls too. Adda pulled Pel toward the strap-in stations across from the passthrough and stuck one of the straps in his hand.

"Hey, I am literally in the dark!" said Pel. "What's going on?"

"We're under attack," Adda said. "Captain, do you think it's station security, ITA, or someone else?"

"Since they attempted to apprehend us quietly," Sloane called from the bridge console, "that rules out the ITA." Explosives didn't fit into Adda's definition of "quiet," but this seemed like a bad time to argue with the captain. Tritheist swept small pieces of metal from the air and pocketed them on his way to the seat at the desk console, on the opposite end of the main cabin.

Iridian stood and slammed her fist on the control panel beside the passthrough. The passthrough's inner door shut with a low hiss. Her bare head and hands bled red droplets that drifted toward the floor. "I hate getting blown up. Let's go."

Adda pulled a coiled cable from its hiding place in her heavy silver necklace. One end plugged into her comp glove, and she threaded the other into her pinkie-finger-size nasal jack. The chrome jack connected her neural implant net directly into her comp glove's system, which let her work faster than she could have with external inputs alone.

She subvocalized a command to her comp to re-create her gray intermediary, which appeared in the main cabin. Only she could see it. Today its humanlike figure had Captain Sloane's broad shoulders and long, flowing hair, which whisked around the figure in the still cabin air as she directed it to interface with the *Casey*'s intelligence.

Iridian stomped across the ship in her magnetic boots, bleeding and scowling and beautiful and terrible. Adda stood in mute admiration until Iridian pressed her back into her harness. It had, perhaps, been too long a trip in the company of Adda's employer and little brother. The lack of a honeymoon to go with her wedding was surprisingly distracting.

Iridian barely got Pel and herself strapped in before the ship lurched backward—forward, except behind them? Gods, there was no right way to describe ship motion without math—and disconnected its passthrough from the dock.

From the pilot's rotating seat at the bridge console, Sloane called, "Adda, comm interference would be convenient."

"On it," Adda said. The *Casey* was capable of handling that itself, but it hadn't so far. "Are you listening? Flash lights once for yes," Adda murmured. She startled when the whole cabin went dark for a second.

"What the fuck was that?" Tritheist shouted.

"Roll call," Adda said so quietly that only Pel and Iridian reacted, Pel with a nervous laugh and Iridian with the frown she wore every time they discussed AI.

The Casey's transmitters were occupied with a long-range comm already in progress, and it stopped Adda from reallocating any of its comm capabilities to interfere with law enforcement broadcasts. None of the human occupants' comps were connected to the system as far as Adda could tell through her intermediary. The Casey was communicating with parties unknown. Adda settled for a comp-based program, which triggered other transmitters as they came in range to create radiating signal waves. It was the best she could do, for now.

With gravity pulling on her harder than ever at the speed the Casey was flying, taking one of the thumbprint-size purple squares from her sharpsheet case was tricky. Adda laid the premeasured dose on her tongue and activated systems interface programs on her comp while the sharpsheet sizzled and dissolved.

The window projected across the passthrough door, and the wall opposite Adda displayed Rheasilvia Station's metallic latticework whizzing by so close to the Casey's hull cams that Adda flinched. Some spaces between beams looked large enough for the Casey to fly through, although Adda fervently hoped it wouldn't.

They rocketed over the lip of the crater, revealing a horizon much closer than Adda's Earth upbringing had led her to expect. Then the Casey dove back into the maze of Rheasilvia's industrial installations, which branched toward acres of solar panels surrounding the station.

The floor in front of the doors to the bedroom and bathroom

lit up with a projection of two small wedge-shaped ships. Pierc-
ingly bright red and blue lights lit the Oxia Corporation logo on
the ships' sides. It wasn't the ITA's insignia, at least. The ships'
outlines were highlighted in a dashed red and blue line, a visual
code that law enforcement vessels throughout populated space
used to identify themselves. The sharpsheets' effects shivered
through her mind and begged for a focus. Adda closed her eyes
to concentrate on finding and scrambling their pursuers' comm
frequency.

A few minutes later, a jolt and a horrifyingly loud scraping
sound from the ceiling made her eyes open wide. The ceiling currently felt like more of a side than up or down. The wall behind her
shook. The cam projecting above her head showed metal tubes
that curved up on either edge of the view. Something crunched
and the ceiling turned into a black void for several seconds, until
the Casey shut off the projector.

"We didn't break off something important, did we?"

The fear in Pel's voice persuaded Adda to sacrifice accuracy
for comfort. "Whatever it was didn't slow us down." She had to
yell over the continuous dragging scrape, which now came from
both above and below them. It stopped abruptly. The projection
by the doors showed the opposite direction of the one they were
going in (gods, how did spacefarers define that?) and displayed a
passage between two loops of metal that looked too narrow for a
human to stand in.

The comm traffic her comp projected across the back of her
hand indicated that the passage was giving the station security
vehicles pause. Adda closed her eyes, relying on subvocalized
commands to redirect her comm interference efforts as needed.

"Captain, how many of the evasion maneuvers are up to you?"
Iridian asked, referring to preprogrammed ones that pilots could

activate at will, according to stories Adda had read.

"None," Sloane said. "The bridge console appears to be dis-connected from maneuvering controls."

Iridian squirmed against the wall beside Adda. Adda risked a glance at her, and mostly saw her knuckles whitening around the straps at her shoulder before nausea forced Adda's eyes closed again. "*Casey*," said Iridian, "don't get us killed."

CHAPTER 2

Full integration with individual crew comms
achieved 051877 0416

Tied to a bulkhead while an AI self-destructs around you is no way to die. The thought kept going through Iridian's head. She had nothing else to think about while the gods-damned *Casey* flung itself through stationspace above Vesta's largest hab, running from smaller and more nimble pursuers who'd have no trouble finding the only passenger transport within an AU that was flying like an enforcer drone.

"We can't keep this up," Tritheist said.

It always felt wrong when she and Sloane's lieutenant agreed on something, but he'd spoken the truth. "The *Casey*'s got EMP shielding, but it doesn't have guns," she pointed out. "Where's the *Apparition*? And was that the Oxia Corp logo on those cop carriers?"

"Good questions," Adda said almost too quietly to hear. Her eyes snapped open. "We need to find the *Apparition*. That's where we're going."

"Should've known the *Casey* wouldn't run at random."

"AIs rarely randomize something this important," Adda said.

Iridian snorted a laugh. On the bridge projector, klicks of inter-twined station mechanisms and ship maintenance apparatuses retreated behind them at unsettling speed. Stationsec hadn't shot at them so far. The *Casey* was using the station's architecture as cover.

"Adda thinks the *Casey*'s meeting up with the *Apparition* to scrape those people off its hull," Iridian said. "If we're betting, my money's on the warship."

"Mine too," Tritheist growled over the local comm channel.

"My money would be on the *Apparition* as well, but violence is not my first choice. I'm interested in reclaiming my position, not obliterating it." Whether or not the *Casey* was listening in on the conversation, it maintained its speed and direction. Iridian clenched her teeth and tamped down panic. Strong AIs could do a lot on their own and it made them damned unpredictable, even when they weren't awakened like the *Casey*'s copilot.

The captain tapped the console and replaced the retreating station exterior on the bridge projection with newsfeed headlines and messages about the crewmember who'd been in charge of Vesta in Sloane's absence. "Send us that feed?" Adda asked.

"What feed?" said Pel.

While Sloane shared the projected documents with Adda, Adda explained the news to Pel, and the *Casey* made several sharp turns, Iridian read. "So your crew's been ransacking the locals as well as the NEU ships, Captain?"

Iridian wished she could've sounded less angry. Sloane had done everything possible to control crew resources from Barbary Station, but intermittent communication opportunities had made that impossible for years. And sure, all megacorporations were technically NEU because their headquarters were on Earth, Mars, Mercury, or Venus, but it wasn't like the crew had been blowing apart NEU ships full of civilians like the secessionists had during the war. The problem was that megacorps could afford a few raids. The Vestans couldn't.

Neither Sloane nor Tritheist looked up from the newsfeed, so she activated the eye-highlight function of her helmet's comms software. It drew a moving, humming border around the vid clip she was looking at: a Vestan microcorp's cargo carrier wreck engulfed in a blue orb of chemical flame. Behind the burning wreck was a piece of the weblike station architecture the *Casey* had just flown over. The headline read "Twenty-three dead," and Sloane's crew was implicated in the first line.

"Quite a feat for *my* crew, while most of my operatives were occupied elsewhere and I never gave that order," said Sloane. The captain and Tritheist scowled and braced in their harnesses as the *Casey* shifted directions fast enough to black everyone out for a second.

"Contacting your headquarters would put us at additional risk of ITA exposure," Adda said, apropos of nothing and sounding sick as all hells from the grav shifts.

"My secure line should still be in place." Captain Sloane was apparently on the same track as Adda.

The *Casey* dropped straight toward Vesta's surface for several endless seconds. Iridian braced against her harness and swore. Adda was mumbling to herself, or her comp. Every time she said something almost intelligible and paused for breath, the *Casey* zigged or zagged. The overhead cam was still out, but Iridian could've picked out individual grains of dirt on the deck cam, which was actually projected on the deck for a change, if the ship weren't screaming over it like an atmo-escape launch. "What are you doing, babe?"

"Exterior processing." They all jerked to the right in their restraints and a fountain of gray dirt bloomed at the edge of the projection on the bulkhead across from them. "Busy."

"The message is sent," Captain Sloane said.

A ten-centimeter fragment of whatever had blown up against Iridian's shield in the station terminal clattered around the main cabin, where Pel and Adda were unarmored and had their arms strapped down. Iridian freed one of hers and missed the fragment twice as it flew by. It finally slapped into her gloved palm as the whole ship lurched. Vesta's cratered surface filled the bridge projection for a long moment before the stars and horizon appeared on the deck projection.

"What'd stationsec hit us with?" she asked.

"Maneuvering system virus, primarily," Adda muttered.

Sloane had no chance of hearing Adda when she talked that quietly, and spoke over her. "Projectile ammo with very minimal impact. It may have been targeting stabilizers or aft altitude control." The captain pressed and dragged a few spots on the bridge console. When nothing in the ship or out of it changed, Sloane sighed and gripped the pilot chair's armrests.

"It's AI-built, but it was a zombie AI," said Adda. Zombie AIs were just AIs to most people. They all should've had physical and programmed limitations to prevent the development of volition. AI was never supposed to be awakened. "The *Casey's* removing it now."

"In the meantime, how likely are we to crash land in the airless desert below?" Captain Sloane asked with remarkable calm.

"Can't tell." Adda went back to subvocalizing to her comp.

The speakers near the bridge console chimed a standard signal for an asynch comm. Sloane opened it and a new voice said, "Hello, boss" around an audible sneer.

The man was older than Iridian and Adda put together, late

sixties or early seventies. His light skin clashed with his hair's shade of blue. Subdermal flame-shaped implants jutted out from his face where he should've had eyebrows, and they were too big to be decorative. They'd have some other function as well.

Captain Sloane said, "Rosehach," anger mostly hidden except for a stillness the captain rarely demonstrated, even when dead calm.

The man on the monitor lounged at a desk someplace with healthy enviro, judging by his lack of an enviro suit. "Waiting for your bought cops to call off the chase?"

Sloane's chin jerked downward relative to the pilot's seat rather than Vesta, since the *Casey* was almost perpendicular to the asteroid's surface. "The ones behind us will be destroyed if they persist."

"Oxia Corp won't miss them. Even stationsec disappear on this 'ject, some nights. And it won't come back on my crew."

Iridian's lips pulled away from her teeth in a sympathetic grimace. From the way Rosehach addressed the captain, this was a former member of Sloane's crew. Now he was claiming Sloane's position of power on Vesta. Pel and Tritheist swore.

Adda glanced at Iridian and asked, "'Ject' as in 'astronomical object'?"

"Yeah, but nobody says that," Iridian replied. Adda nodded and returned her attention to her comp.

The captain said, "I see."

Rosehach grinned, self-satisfied and wanting more. "You know why stationsec's chasing you? The station councils don't move the stars and planets for you anymore, is why. You kept them waiting, what, two years? For somebody to tell them what to do. Last year Oxia stepped up and told them Sloane's crew was the only muscle that made its cut when the corp took Vesta over, not counting the stationsec contracts. They made me sign one too. So, since you took a long vacay and left it lying around, I own the crew now."

The *Casey* jolted, grav spiked, and Iridian's vision went black.

When Iridian next opened her eyes, Tritheist was shouting, ". . . kill everyone he's ever met, and choke him on their ashes," from his seat at the desk across from the *Casey*'s bridge. The stranger who'd claimed Sloane's crew as his own was gone from the console's projection stage, although that hadn't stopped Tritheist from yelling at him. She'd only been out for a minute, probably. Her head throbbed in time with her heartbeat.

"Are you okay?" Adda stood on the overhead, from Iridian's perspective, although Iridian couldn't tell if the magnets in Adda's boots were activated or not. What grav Vesta had was pulling all the blood into Iridian's head.

"Yeah. Did we land?" Iridian asked.

"If you mean 'stopped moving while upside down in a ditch,' then yeah, we landed." Pel drifted back and forth across the *Casey*'s main cabin, pushing off the bulkheads with his outstretched hands and bouncing off the deck with his toes instead of landing. Iridian reoriented to "down" being the former overhead, which made magnetic boots unnecessary.

Adda steadied Iridian while she let herself down from the bulkhead. "It's a very large ditch."

Sloane tore free of the pilot's seat harness and stood, gripping the underside of the bridge console to stabilize in Vesta's low grav. The sudden movement stilled everyone, Tritheist included. "Rosehach dies for this." The captain's words were spaced wide and spoken slowly, like an oath. "But he's less important than freeing the crew from Oxia Corporation."

Iridian clenched her teeth against disappointment and the pain in her head. The crew was trapped *again*. After they'd just fought their way out of a gods-damned hellhole of a station, to this one where life should've gotten a whole lot better. Good people had died getting the five of them to Vesta. The reality of the new situation reverberated through her like she'd hit the ground after a long fall. The crew was supposed to be choosing their own objectives, making profits and threats that'd keep them free of megacorps like Oxia. Instead they'd lost that battle before the first shot was fired, because this Rosehach person had sold the crew out from under them.

Tritheist finished a slow forward flip that straightened out his twisted harness. "We should kill him now, Captain. He'll only make things harder for us if we don't."

Rosehach sure as hell had that coming. "Hate to agree with the LT," Iridian said, "but he's—"

The *Casey*'s bridge projection replaced the gray wall of the ditch it had put itself down in with energy readouts, model descriptions of ships that didn't match its type at all, a count-down, and a vid in the corner of three cop-carriers flying low over Vesta's surface.

"Did it add the visuals?" Adda stared at her comp, which she was still plugged into via her nasal jack. "We disagreed on their importance."

After the awkward two days the *Casey* had spent stuck to a fuel barge after it'd finished refueling, Iridian expected the *Casey* to do what it wanted, when it wanted. That didn't mean anybody liked it when the damned ship got confused, or willful, or whatever its problem was.

"Yeah, visuals are up in the bridge," said Iridian. Adda could've looked up from her comp and seen them, if she weren't busy pretending she was in an invisible workspace generator. "Stationsec's coming this way?" Adda nodded. "Then strap in again. We need someplace to hide."

"Perhaps Rosehach will provide us with a location," said Captain Sloane.

Iridian stopped halfway through climbing into her harness. "Say again?" Her question was accompanied by Pel's, "We're asking *him?*" and Tritheist asking, "But . . . why?"

If the smile on Sloane's face were directed at her, she would've deployed her shield and taken cover. "Once he learns how easily I escaped his trap, he'll realize that he needs me. Or that he needs to trap me in person."

"Captain, stationsec is almost on top of us." Iridian pointed at the map with moving icons for approaching ships.

Sloane turned back to the bridge console. "Then he'll need to reach that realization quickly. *Casey*—or Adda, whoever is listening—put me back in contact with Rosehach. I assume my methods are on record."

So everything they did on this ship was recorded. Damn that nosy AI.

But once again, the *Casey* was going out of its way to help them. Adda said it was difficult to tell why awakened AIs did anything, but the *Casey* had spent too many resources protecting them to let them die without a good reason. Unless the *Casey* was taken by the ITA, Iridian and Adda were probably not in imminent danger from it.

"He might turn over crew operations to Sloane." Adda paused to struggle with her harness until Iridian reached over to help. "For the sake of efficiency, I mean."

"He's not that smart," Tritheist grumbled.

"Rosehach. I've a counter offer for you. Reply at your conve-nience." Sloane tapped several places on the console, which was blank instead of covered with icons like a normal ship's would be, until the Sent notification appeared in the projection. "I trust you'll remove the last moments of that recording."

"Done," Adda murmured.

The hair on the back of Iridian's neck stood on end. The *Casey* had had several drones when Iridian had first encountered it, but they'd been destroyed in a fight on their way out of Barbary Sta-tion. When *Casey* had used one as a mouthpiece, it'd said things with as few words and emotion as possible. It'd sounded a lot like Adda just did.

Iridian reached to pat the first part of Adda she could reach, which was her knee. "Hey, how about you unplug for a while?"

"We'll move faster if I don't," Adda said. "Plugging into a con-sole would help. Do you think my cable would reach the console jack?"

Iridian shuddered. "The *Casey*'s already doing things a human pilot couldn't, and keeping us more or less upright and conscious. What in all hells makes you think physically plugging your brain into an awakened AI is necessary?"

"I won't have a brain if the *Casey*'s vid recognition can't deter-mine what the police vehicles are doing as fast as I can. If my choice is death or AI influence, I'll go with the . . ." Adda watched the comp projection in the square stage on the back of her glove for several seconds. The hand in her glove clenched into a fist. "What's happening?"

"Our pursuers seem to be returning to the station," Captain Sloane said. The projected view of the retreating stationsec ships confirmed it. "Rosehach has accepted my proposal. If the *Casey* could deliver us to one of the mine docks, we'll get this meeting over with."

"So, we're buying him out, Captain?" Iridian asked.

"Ideally," Sloane said. "Unless he's much improved his information-gathering capabilities since I've been gone, he'll underestimate our ability to defend ourselves. I'm still not opposed to killing him if the opportunity arises."

"Good," said Tritheist.

Beyond them, lights out but occluding the stars, the *Apparition's* asymmetrical silhouette hung still in stationspace. It could've blasted the cop-carriers to microscopic pieces. The *Charon's Coin* had to be nearby too. Maneuvering around a megacorporate empire would be at least as difficult as fighting Barbary Station's security AI, and just like on Barbary, the ships had done the absolute minimum to help. Two out of three were ignoring the crew's current predicament. AIs couldn't be trusted.

* * *

"Hell of a place to meet," Pel shouted over the processing machinery crunching basalt all around them.

Tubes big enough to crawl through looped around one another through the depths of the mine beneath Rheasilvia Station. After a quick unloading at the mine's terminal and a long elevator ride, they were half a klick from being the deepest into Vesta that any humans had ever stood. At unpredictable intervals, pressurized tubes hauled Vesta's primary export out of the dark and dropped the chunks of basalt into sifting and crushing machines.

The noise masked the distinctive armor rattling that Iridian, Captain Sloane, and Tritheist made as they walked. Pel and Adda, protected more by the fighters' presence than by their jackets with light armor mesh lining, stayed a few steps behind. At the front of the group, Iridian kept her head turning to watch for threats. The mine was full of movement and had plenty of places to hide.

Five or six third-shift workers managing the robots and machines practically knelt at Sloane's feet, so far as grav allowed, to offer masks off their own faces. Even the masks bore Oxia's three-bladed fan logo. The captain nodded gravely, but the atmo filters in Sloane's helmet would be more effective than anything the miners had.

"Welcome back . . . Captain," an older worker said. Her voice grated like the rock traveling through the tubes around them. The pause in her greeting suggested that she'd been acquainted with Sloane before the captain claimed that title.

Sloane had been looking over the workers' heads, watching for trouble the way Tritheist and Iridian were, but the captain refocused on the worker who'd spoken. "How does Oxia treat you?"

"New contracts. Longer hours, minimum pay." The worker's sigh rattled in a way that made Iridian want to take the woman's mask and replace its filters. "Oxia wants everything Vesta's got, underground and over it, and the station councils do whatever they say. Easy to keep a woman on a 'ject she can't afford to leave, even without the damned contract."

Sloane frowned sympathetically and waved a hand at the machinery around them. "New equipment as well?"

The worker nodded. "Recycling the old stuff and installing new means they got more right to the ground under it. So says the newsfeeds and the council and ITA and the gods themselves, seems like. Feeds say the new machines will shake the 'ject apart too, though, so who knows, yeah? Oxia's fancy new diggers don't fix their own troubles any better than the old ones. Dust crowds out the nannites. But now . . ." The worker raised her eyes to meet

Sloane's. "We're counting on you." She backed off toward the elevator with the others.

The workers offered Adda a mask too, but she held up her hands, palms out. Once the worker stepped away, she murmured, "They breathe and sweat in those." She still sounded distant, like she'd spent hours in a workspace instead of strapped down in a ship. "Who knows what's sitting on your side of the filters, waiting to be pulled into your lungs? I'd rather breathe some dust."

"Aw, yuck," said Pel. "Is it too late to give mine back?"

Iridian's glance around the complex did not reveal the worker who'd given Pel his mask, or the one who offered one to her despite her armor, for that matter. "Yeah. It looks like everybody cleared out."

The maze of densely woven machinery mirrored the way Vesta's two stations shuffled spacefaring humanity and cargo too mundane or dangerous for Ceres through the asteroid belt. And the surface's fractal latticework separated the two.

Captain Sloane caught her looking over the mining setup and said, "We're currently out of range of almost all the station's monitoring hardware. Useful, for our sort."

At their last port of call, their lives had depended on knowing which modules had active sensor nodes, so Iridian could appreciate that. The mine must've been miserable for Pel, though. It'd be hard to hear anyone coming over the machinery.

"So glad you could join us," said the spacefarer-accented male voice they'd last heard over the Casey's speakers.

Iridian swore and spun to face the newcomer, shield deploying before her in a satisfying thump she felt through her wrist and arm. It pushed her into a staggered backward step in the low grav. The flame-shaped implants above Rosehach's eyes cast shadows over them. The bumps on the backs of his hands might've been projectors for a comp, and he was sure to have other additions buried deeper or under clothes.

The short-handled machete hanging against his thigh was her current concern. It wouldn't crack her armor, but it'd cut Adda's and Pel's unprotected throats. The "us" referred to the two body-guards flanking Rosehach. The little one had a body like a bur-lesque dancer's beneath flexible light armor, and carried enough blades to stick everyone in the mine and still have one left over for cleaning under her nails. The magnets in her boots were either off or on low power, and she looked so light on her feet she was practically levitating.

The big one carried an armor buster that Iridian couldn't recall the name of. It'd overload or melt through her suit, and it looked tiny in a hand that'd cover a quarter of Iridian's shield if she let him—her?—get that close. They'd been ambushed, and Iridian swore at herself under her breath for not having seen it coming.

Sloane always seemed to be facing the right direction before trouble arrived, and the captain's smile looked more menacing than the bodyguards' serious frowns. Tritheist stepped toward them, but Captain Sloane stopped him with a hand on his chest plate. "What do you want, Rosehach?"

Rosehach laughed, a rasping, delighted sound likely fueled by chems. It raked over Iridian's rapidly fraying nerves. "I want you to get back on that taxi you rode in on and fly sunward until you light up," Rosehach said. "But that doesn't seem likely, does it?"

"It does not," said Captain Sloane. "Your former position is no longer available, of course, but I could be persuaded not to have you fed into one of these machines, if you have something else to offer."

"You do what I ask, when I ask it. Show your face, take the jobs I say, skip the jobs I say. You won't have everything you want, but . . ."

Rosehach's semiprofessional demeanor dissolved into a vicious smile Iridian longed to put her fist through. "Everyone will think you do. Just like on Barbary. Oh, I heard your little announcements taking credit for this and that, but some of the Martians you left with tell a different tale." There'd been too many Martian refugees stranded on Barbary Station to expect all of them to support Captain Sloane's fictitious claim of living in luxury there, especially after the ITA rescued and questioned them.

Captain Sloane smiled with humorless eyes slightly narrowed, the way Adda's looked while she sorted through options. Adda herself was staring at her comp glove's readout on the back of her hand, which could mean anything. Her other hand gripped her strangely silent brother's wrist. They were unarmed, but that wouldn't stop a man like Rosehach from having them killed where they stood.

"Your alternative," Rosehach continued, "is to calmly—oh-so calmly—deliver yourselves into the benevolent hands of station security. The ITA will be fascinated to hear your statement. After Oxia's CEO has his say, of course."

Beside the captain, Tritheist's face twisted in fury and he panted against Sloane's hand, which, hidden from Rosehach's sight by the angle of Sloane's body, was clenched on the edge of Tritheist's chest plate.

Even Rosehach's bodyguards were smirking. Somehow that was more than Iridian's held-in temper would tolerate. Barbary Station had been a nightmare. They'd come halfway across the solar system, to what should've been Sloane's territory, where Adda and Pel should've been safe, and found this snickering, self-serving slimeball in charge. And now he was trying to get them arrested or enslaved.

Both bodyguards tensed and focused on the palmer in her

hand as she raised it, but by then she'd already fired once. When the charged particles struck the little one, her body jolted so hard that knives popped out of their sheaths. By the time the first blade bounced off the floor, Iridian had fired a second blast and the big guard staggered and dropped like it'd burst her—his?— heart. *Sixteen, seventeen.*

The palmer snapped again. One of the flame-shaped implants in Rosehach's forehead detonated, leaving a ragged wound that exposed several centimeters of splintered skull and launched him at the floor at an awful angle. *Eighteen.* In the low grav, the body- guards and two more of the little one's knives hit the floor after he did.

The big one's face screwed up in fury and pain and the armor buster twitched toward Iridian. She planted her boot on a wrist as thick around as her forearm, pressing the arm across the guard's chest to keep the weapon well away from the crew. The big body- guard gagged and writhed to throw her off, but her armor and her balance kept her boot in place.

The big bodyguard's eyes widened as they lost focus. The arm under Iridian's boot went limp and the armor buster slid to the floor. The little bodyguard didn't grab for any of her knives.

Something in the palmer was overheating. Its smoking elec- tronics overpowered the odor of cooked flesh. Nobody'd designed a holster for the palmers, so she just held it away from her leg so it wouldn't scorch her armor.

The crew stared at her, Captain Sloane with something like delight, the others just surprised. Tritheist raised his own palmer from his side without pointing it directly at her, ready in case she turned on him. Adda's eyes were the widest. Iridian had taken eighteen lives over the course of her own, but this was the first time Adda had watched her do it.

And yeah, that required an explanation. "The fight was coming no matter what. It was safer this way." Iridian glanced over
her shoulder at Rosehach. "And we're not getting arrested for a
wannabe like him."

Ten or twelve much better armed and armored individuals
stepped out from behind the nearest rock-crushing machine,
weapons trained on Sloane's crew. The large barrels suggested
low-penetration projectiles, the kind that'd fill an unruly crowd
with a nerve-damaging nanomachine culture. Full armor would
filter out the worst of it, but Adda and Pel would be fucked.

In the new arrivals' center, projected above a small and
expensive-looking stage drone that countered Vestan grav with
spinning rotors, stood an older man in spotless business attire.
"Don't worry about Rosehach." The projected man's smile was
even oilier than the dead man's. "You'll find that others are willing
to send you to prison."

CHAPTER 3

Long-term docking permits created by unregistered admin, level account: 3

On the back of Adda's hand, the words *Should I engage?* **could've** looked incidental, unimportant. They scrolled by in a list of several other snippets from messages that had arrived in the past few hours. They were red because one of the universe's very few nonhuman intelligences sent them, and Adda wanted to know everything it said.

And now it was asking *her* if it ought to attack people in a mine almost two kilometers below a city-size space station. A mine that she, Iridian, and Pel were also standing in.

Iridian covered as much of Pel and Adda with her shield as she could, leaving half her own torso exposed. The shield would block weapon-fire from the front, but the newcomer had brought enough armed people to encircle them. The figure on the mobile projection stage, whose heavy-lidded eyes and skin slightly darker than Iridian's shivered slightly in the projector's light, was still talking to Captain Sloane. If Adda spent too long watching the situation develop before she accepted the *Casey*'s offered help, it might be too late for even an awakened intelligence to save them.

Two armed people stepped forward and rolled Rosehach's body onto its back. One placed a thick mask over the body's nose, mouth, and throat, ignoring the awful wound in the forehead. Another affixed a device to the side of the neck and cut open the dead man's shirt to press another device between the strangely protruding ribs of his chest. The second one slapped down on the chest device and Rosehach's body convulsed. Both soldiers, she supposed they were, raised their weapons and stepped away while Rosehach drifted a few centimeters off the floor and then collapsed onto it again.

"Liu Kong, I presume." Captain Sloane addressed one of the other armed people, focusing on a prominent cam lens on the man's helmet. "So Oxia Corporation has claimed Vesta from its core to its stationspace." Sloane lowered one of the bowl-shaped pirate weapons that the captain, Tritheist, and Iridian all carried. "It's an unusual approach."

A subvocalized search and a glance at Adda's comp indicated that the man on the mobile projection stage was the head of the multiplanetary megacorporation that owned or contracted all of Vesta's mining, shipping, and infrastructure. She activated her comp's mic, muted its speaker, and opened a live audio connection to the *Casey*. One of the armed people was watching her and shifted a weapon to cover Adda, so she must not have kept her lips as still as she had meant to.

The woman didn't shoot her, so Adda finished her instructions to the *Casey* in subvocalization to text. She didn't even need to put it in her messaging software, since the *Casey* seemed to be monitoring her comp activity. *We may need help getting out of here. Please work up scenarios. Do not engage.* Without a workspace or intermediary to translate her intentions to the *Casey*, she had no guarantee that the message would be interpreted the way she wanted. Even if the *Casey* understood her meaning, it'd still make its own decision about whether or not Adda needed rescuing.

"The usual approach would have been much less . . . certain." The man Sloane had addressed as Liu Kong gave each syllable the same weight and stress. He frowned at Rosehach and the dead bodyguards sprawled on the floor. "Unusual approaches carry different risks."

"Which is why we're speaking now." Sloane's voice betrayed the captain's tension. Iridian's thick black eyebrows were drawn down and her shield was still raised. Apparently there was still a good chance they'd all be shot or captured within the next few minutes. *What*, Adda wondered with equal parts eager curiosity and dread, *might the* Casey *do to save us?*

After a short pause, Liu Kong said, "I still have work for your crew. And the power struggles playing out in your absence, perpetuated by your supposed choice to remain on Barbary Station, have wasted time. My time."

A muscle in Sloane's jaw twitched. The captain's gaze flicked over the array of weapons aimed at them. Somehow the way Captain Sloane stood straighter looked like an admission of defeat. "I'll need to refresh myself on the crew's activities to date, but I expect our key personnel to be available for the job." Each word sounded heavy, as if the captain expended great effort to say that instead of something easier. "Depending on what is required."

"I don't need your services for the duration of 'a job,'" Liu Kong said over the captain's last few words. Either something was going wrong with their communications equipment, or Liu Kong was a very long way away from them. "If that's all you're willing to offer, the ITA keeps a cell reserved for you. I'm sure we could make room for your crew."

Captain Sloane's expression stayed formal and blank, but the rest of the crew looked as appalled as Adda felt. So their choices were to be turned over to the ITA, get killed on the spot, or sign a corporate contract binding the crew's services and everyone in it to Oxia.

If they signed a megacorporate contract and then broke it, they'd be pariahs among major organizations, both legal and semi-legal, throughout populated space. The break would be on record. Any potential employer would learn about it, even the ones who didn't register their own agreements in the public databases. And although she had no intention of looking for employment outside Sloane's crew, she preferred to have an escape route that could keep her and Iridian together. The alternative was some megacorp contracting them separately, in different parts of the solar system.

Megacorporate contracts were an efficient means of losing decades of your life to make money for someone else. Adda and Iridian had hijacked a colony ship, fought a station's worth of AI-controlled robots, and traveled 250 million kilometers to avoid that fate. Pel had practically sold himself into slavery to avoid it. Gods only knew what Sloane and Tritheist had done.

"May I assume it's worth my time to continue, Captain Sloane?" Liu Kong said.

Sloane gritted "Proceed" like the word itself was the signature.

"We may start with this," Liu Kong said. "Are you familiar with the Rentronix PR800i printer?"

Adda shook her head minutely and subvocalized the query to her comp while Iridian said, "Don't they print the organic and inorganic parts of pseudo-organic tech simultaneously?"

"Oh, that. I heard it prints people parts," said Pel. "Like, add-on bits and prosthetics that play nice with pseudo-organics." He was serious about replacing his scarred eyes with pseudo-organic ones; he'd actually read about how they were made. Adda was impressed.

Captain Sloane raised an eyebrow at him, then turned back to Liu Kong. "They're massively expensive. Outside your budget, I presume?"

Liu Kong's face twisted with disgust for a moment, then returned to the bland superiority he'd been addressing them with so far. "N'gobe-Marvin Minerals just equipped their new Kuiper longhauler with one that would suit our needs. Its flyby refueling from Ceres is scheduled for next week."

"A longhauler?" Tritheist huffed a disgusted laugh. "Those lock up like a Doomsday vault."

Adda really needed to finish the software package for the implanted throat mic she and Iridian were working on. That would have let her share the information directly, but now she had to speak. While Sloane, Tritheist, and Iridian exchanged meaningful glances, Adda asked, "How much will you pay up front?"

Gods, she hated it when she said something that made people stare at her. Maybe the rest of the crew was still deciding whether they should work on the problem, but Adda could either search for a solution or weep, and tears were just biological procrastination.

Sometimes the fastest way to get more information was to walk people through the obvious details, until they gave her the rest to shut her up. "Infiltrating the longhauler is all about timing, correct? The target ship's going a long way, on a very specific route. Where we intercept the ship to steal the printer will depend on how much fuel we'll have to get there and back, and that depends on our funds before we leave." One of the large diameter pipes overhead shook as a controlled avalanche of small rocks rattled toward Vesta's surface.

Sloane's face was a confusing mask of chagrin and what

might've been admiration. "My operations strategist, Adda Karpe," the captain explained to Liu Kong once the noise level decreased again. It was a good title, even if this was the first time she'd heard it. "If the task is at all feasible we can, of course, discuss terms at a later date."

Liu Kong gestured from the man physically standing in front of them with the cam lens toward Adda. The lens focused on her. The projected CEO was looking at her the way he might have observed a particularly clever spider before he crushed it. "It will have to be feasible, Captain. You assembled a talented group of unscrupulous persons on this 'ject. I would prefer to retain your name recognition and well-documented successes, but someone else could be found. Someone with a comprehensive grasp of . . . feasibility."

He smiled at Adda, curse all the luck of ages. Why did people keep acting like she wanted to lead Sloane's crew? She shifted her weight toward Iridian's comforting presence. All she'd ever wanted was to solve interesting problems, mostly with AI. She had no interest in solving problems about people, or worse, megacorporations.

"That won't be necessary." Captain Sloane's expression definitely conveyed annoyance now, some of which was directed at Adda. "I accept. Please send me the details, along with whatever Rosehach knew that was necessary to the endeavor, since he's no longer available to ask."

"Oh, I think he'll manage an answer or two," said Liu Kong. "I have other questions to ask him."

"But . . ." Pel gulped audibly. "He's dead, isn't he?"

Liu Kong turned his projection stage robot and hovered unhurriedly through the path his enforcers made for it. After a meter of stately retreat, he said, "Death is rarely so instantaneous," and his projected figure disappeared from the mobile stage.

The man with the cam on his helmet said, "Bring Rosehach. Clean up the rest."

Iridian frowned at the enforcers who shoved the bodyguards' corpses aside to make room for an inflating stretcher for Rose-hach. "Can you save her too?" she asked one of the soldiers pre-paring Rosehach's body to be moved.

The man glanced at the knife-wielding bodyguard sliding down the sloping floor, deeper into the mine, and shrugged. "Ten minutes ago, maybe. Now she's meat and H_2O." Iridian's swearing just made him smile nastily and return to his work.

"Back up and go," said the man wearing Liu Kong's cam on his helmet.

Captain Sloane turned on a booted heel, coat flowing dramat-ically in the low gravity. "Move out," Tritheist ordered on the cap-tain's behalf. Adda hooked an arm through Pel's to lead him away without stepping on any bodies. Iridian kept her shield between them and the Oxia guns.

* * *

"So," Pel said as soon as the Casey's exterior passthrough door closed behind Iridian. "When do we run, and where are we going?"

"Where indeed?" Sloane chuckled, a hollow, bitter sound. The captain sank into the pilot's seat, slowly, to account for Vesta's surface gravity. A tiny plastic alignment tool which had escaped Iridian's set during their arrival skittered across the cabin in front of Tritheist's boot as he joined Sloane at the console. "I haven't been to headquarters in two years," Sloane said. "I'm dying to see how the place has kept in my absence."

The word "dying" carried more emphasis than Adda would

have put on it. The majority of Sloane's resources would be under Oxia Corporation's control now, but the crew had worked with almost nothing before. There had to be somewhere less dangerous to base their operations. Sloane hadn't legally committed to anything yet, but the captain's mind sounded made up. "Why are we staying?"

"We're *what?*" Pel gripped Adda's arm as the *Casey* sailed out of the mine's loading dock. Gravity pulled people and clutter sideways for a second before it oriented toward the floor.

"We're staying," Sloane said slowly, "because when I left Vesta, Rheasilvia Station was *ours* and Albana Station was as good as. Why else would I have spent so much effort convincing the station councils that I remained on Barbary by choice, poor choice though it would've been? And since we are not in a position to storm Oxia's main campus, first because it is nowhere near here and second because I'm not sure of my crew's complement at the moment, I will be playing the role of Oxia's minion while engineering an opportunity to regain my position here."

"So the Vestan station councils are a joke?" Iridian looked horrified. Adda didn't have a problem with the stations' two governing bodies doing as little as possible, which seemed to be the case with Rheasilvia Station's twelve-member council and Albana Station's eight-member one. Governments with too much power started wars. "Who coordinates infrastructure safety?" Iridian asked.

"Station councils pick somebody. In the past, the crew's kept watch on them," said Captain Sloane. "A practice I intend to continue."

People just didn't write or record themselves talking about some things at the level of detail Adda preferred. Much as she hated the process, it was worth asking about those topics. "Who else is powerful and interested enough to affect Vestan politics?"

Tritheist huffed a quiet laugh. "Here we go." The ship rolled slowly to one side, then rolled back. They'd already reached a top speed, as far as Adda could tell by the barely there gravity.

Captain Sloane smiled. "It pays to stay on top of these things. It's all about fuel, as you might expect, although exports of rebuilding materials are still strong. The main players are the NEU, the ITA, and the Ceres syndicate. Colonies try to influence things when orbital positions put us between them and a major hab, but they lack the resources to cause trouble."

"That figures." Iridian's expectations for independent colonial viability were invariably low, although most of them had sustained themselves for the past thirteen years without the NEU's support during wartime and peace.

And now Adda had more useful keywords to search for. "The NEU is making more and more trips into colonial space, and the ITA keeps the reliable routes clear of garbage and micrometeoroids no matter who uses them. I can see why they'd care about a stop along the way. But aside from relative proximity, what's the Ceres syndicate's interest?"

To her surprise, Iridian answered, "They're the bigger, older hab in a similar orbit to Vesta's, and their port services are a hell of a lot pricier than Rheasilvia's or Albana's. More comprehensive and bigger, but pricier. They want to keep traffic flowing their way, yeah?"

"Indeed," said Captain Sloane. The ship reconfigured itself to the same physical position it'd docked in before, so Adda assumed they were nearly to the terminal. The captain turned an intense gaze on her. "What do you have so far?"

"Well, our approach to intercepting the longhauler carrying the printer still depends on the resources available." She skimmed search results on her comp projection. "Fuel prices have been rising fast enough to make the news."

Tritheist laughed. When she looked up from her comp to determine why in all hells he found that funny, both Sloane and Tritheist were grinning. Even Pel had caught onto the joke before her, although that was typical of him. "Say money is not one of our constraints," Captain Sloane suggested.

"It'd better not be," muttered Iridian.

Crew funding was apparently laughably sufficient to cover any intercept trajectory Adda could plot. She and Iridian had expected that when they set out on this adventure, but so little else had gone according to plan that Adda had discarded her previous assumptions. Now she had more options. "So margins for error on that long a voyage away from the sun have to be small. It's the literal edge of civilization."

"Kuiper colonies aren't what I'd call civilized, but sure." Iridian had never visited the farthest reaches of human habitation herself, but she claimed every spacefarer knew somebody who'd been out there. Usually that somebody returned to describe the distant colonies' archaic existences in unflattering phrases of the colonists' own cant. "If that's where the longhauler's headed, there's a lot of no-go in their go/no-go before they hit their last stop hab."

"Which depends on orbital positions along their route, correct?" Adda asked. Iridian smiled at Adda's demonstration that she'd been listening to Iridian's introduction to orbital mechanics during the trip to Vesta. "We need the route, and the company procedures."

"And we'll need to observe the ship," Captain Sloane said sternly. "The majority of the crew is in hibernation, but two pilots, at minimum, will be awake. Procedures vary, not all crews follow procedure, and the degree to which they do or don't will be essential intelligence." Humans were unlike AIs that way. "I have an asset in mind."

Tritheist grunted and set the hand wearing his black comp glove in the bridge console's cradle. The *Casey*'s pseudo-organics weren't dyed or lit, and the gel pad beneath Tritheist's wrist was a dull pink. Annotated ship schematics projected in white and blue across the wall above the console. Cyrillic labels hovered around it at various points. Adda would get them translated later.

Sloane brushed one long finger over the projection's forward edge, setting it spinning slowly in place. "Big one. And it will be all but empty, which will help us in some ways and hinder in others. No weapons, so she has an escort." Sloane settled more firmly into the captain's seat as the *Casey* docked in a new berth. "Ah," said the captain softly. "Home at last."

The passenger terminal Sloane led them through this time was lit warmly, and its Roman columns and intricately tiled floors spoke of very intentional design. The columns helped Adda stop herself when the long strides Vesta's low gravity necessitated sent her drifting toward a wall. Tritheist and Pel laughed at her, and Iridian turned her amusement into an unconvincing coughing fit when she came to help. "It's fine, you need the practice," Iridian said. "And we won't be in this grav for long."

Which was a frustrating turn of events, really. She and Iridian had spent years planning and saving and reaching for a position like the one they had now, on Sloane's crew. It'd all been harder than they'd expected. And now that they'd reached Vesta, the seat of Sloane's power in populated space, they'd have no time to enjoy what they'd earned. Instead they'd plunged into another desperate struggle, albeit with more resources than they'd ever had at their disposal. If they failed to meet what the Oxia CEO saw as their end of the deal, Sloane would suffer the consequences first, and she and Iridian wouldn't get far without the captain. So they'd solve this problem together, just like they'd solved every problem they'd encountered since they left Earth.

It was unfortunate they couldn't take time to appreciate their new home, because even Rheasilvia Station's main terminal in the docks suggested that there'd be a lot to see. Despite the very early local time, cargo-carrying robots lined the ceiling track, moving delicate shipments with comp-readable labels from Mercury farther into the station and to places she'd never heard of, probably in the Kuiper Belt. The terminal's utilitarian architecture and prominent cams emphasized how Earth-influenced Sloane's personal terminal was. The crew passed customs with barely a nod from the captain to the station security officer on duty there.

"Grav acclimation coming." Iridian pointed at a sign showing an animated side view of a genderless person walking into a tube. "Some people really don't like this part."

Adda gripped the hand Iridian didn't have a weapon strapped to as they followed more signs toward a tunnel entrance. "Why do we have to acclimate, exactly?"

"Rheasilvia Station maintains a steady one-g on the interior." The quiet pride in Captain Sloane's voice made her smile. Despite traveling in space for more than a year now, she still wasn't used to the fact that Earthlike gravity was something to be proud of. "Constant motion is required to do that, so we will need to quite literally be brought up to speed."

"Oh shit, those things are wild," Pel said over his comp's audio description of a newer comp model, one for which he could probably afford a printer pattern. "Always cams in there, though."

As an alternative to speculating about what illegal and/or sexual activity would make observation in a rotating tunnel problematic for her brother, Adda concentrated on not vomiting as they entered the segmented tunnel. She hadn't noticed how puffy everybody's faces had become in the low gravity until they returned to normal over the twenty-minute walk through the tunnel. The acclimation process thoroughly confused her inner ear about whether she was turning, moving sideways, or moving forward. Her stomach roiled as her insides sank into the positions they held under gravity. "We're staying for a while, yes?"

"For as long as it takes to prepare our intercept operation." Sloane looked entirely comfortable as gravity slowly pulled the captain's coat and braided hair down toward booted feet. "Which I'm expecting will be under a week. Oxia relinquished our resources, such as Rosehach left them. I'll dispatch my surveillance team today. We'll adjust plans accordingly. This has to go well, you know. Aside from Oxia's implications that we'll be disposed of upon failure, I intend to make this operation my announcement that I have returned, and I still lead my crew."

The captain said most of that while watching Adda. Now she really did feel sick, although she was excited too. If the captain were leaving the first operation's orchestration up to her, then she'd damned well do it right.

*　*　*

Adda held Iridian's hand and followed her through Rheasilvia Station's port module without paying much attention to the pedestrian, robotic, and vehicular traffic. They entered a small vehicle the size of a train car, which ran on the same lines as the public trams. Inside it was arranged more like a limousine. Sloane and Tritheist settled in one corner, scrolling through something on their comps and speaking in low, urgent voices. Pel felt his way to the seat nearest the door while his comp read somebody's social feed aloud. Adda and Iridian settled across from him, and Iridian, doubtless lulled by the quiet as the door shut out the traffic noise, dropped her head onto Adda's shoulder and closed her eyes.

The tram traveled on a track that ran through the center of the streets. The sunsim overhead lighting, set to imitate sunlight on Earth at the station's local time of around four in the morning, was still low. It brightened as they traveled from the port module through a business district, then to an area with buildings that glowed with their own bright and multicolored light. Adda filed the differences away for when she'd inevitably get lost in this station. At least she'd have the map in her comp.

The structure they stopped in front of was labeled VICE ϯ on her comp, in even more vibrant text than the sign on its two-story exterior. The name didn't hint at what the building was used for. The scantily dressed smokers lounging around the entrance and the people in the alley beside it were more informative. "Why did we come to a club, exactly?" Her voice woke Iridian, who sat up and peered at the projected window. Pel's head rose from where it'd been resting on his chest.

Sloane straightened the coat the captain always wore and smiled wide. "It's mine, for one reason. For another, only the uppermost section is a club." Captain Sloane climbed out of the tram, followed by Tritheist and Pel. Now that the door was open, competing bass rhythms flowed in as different songs muffled by different buildings and distances fought for attention.

"Eyes up inside," Tritheist said quietly as Iridian and Adda emerged from the vehicle. "The security detail ought to be happy to see us, but my money's on there being some ingrates who don't know an improvement when they see it. Oh, and don't hurt the civilians. It's bad for business and it'll piss Captain Sloane off."

Iridian unhooked her shield from her belt. "Are these people crew, or Rosehach's hires?"

"The security? They started out as ours," said Tritheist. "Sloane wants to treat them like crew until they prove they're not."

Iridian nodded and turned to Adda. "Stay behind us and keep track of Pel, okay?"

"Yes." Adda looped her arm through Pel's.

"Any pretty people to talk to while we wait to get shot at?" Pel asked Adda as they followed the others toward the front doors.

Most of the clubgoers had dressed and made themselves up so thoroughly that they all looked equally lovely. Some carried knives, and even one sword, openly, although most didn't. The men looked . . . healthy, she supposed. "They're all pretty. Could you talk to them after we know whether or not there will be shooting?"

Captain Sloane, Tritheist, and Iridian entered through the doors before Pel had finished complaining about that suggestion, so Adda hauled Pel forward after them. She stumbled to a halt inside the doors. "What's happening?" Pel yelled over the music.

"It's dark." Adda's eyes were still adjusting to the low light, but she was trying to find the safest place to stand.

The other three had stopped in front of her, and the dance floor was clearing, despite the ongoing, pounding music. Among the shouting and retreating patrons, about fifty armed people stood like soldiers, immovable, in their midst. They didn't seem to be wearing armor, but their clothing was too plain to be club-wear. The weapons they carried were probably the low-velocity, electrical, or chemical kinds, which Iridian said would hurt people without damaging a station's hull.

One of them raised a weapon to point at Sloane. "Rosehach . . . Did you kill him?"

Iridian had killed him. Adda clutched Pel's arm until his elbow dug into her ribs, and he pressed his free hand over hers.

Iridian stepped forward. "I did."

As the one with the raised weapon switched his focus from Sloane to Iridian, a lean woman with big black hair tackled him from the side. Club patrons gasped and exclaimed from the shadows around the walls. Both of the fighters crashed onto the dance floor, and two more armed people in plain clothes leaped to the woman's aid.

A scuffle broke out, which ended with a second person pinned on the floor in a small gray cloud. Another security person, distinguishable from the dancers by the long sleeves and pants, practical boots, and plain colored clothes, held up a device with a loud fan. The person turned their head to the side and shut their eyes and mouth while the gray cloud swept toward them and into the device.

"We don't miss the bastard, Captain," shouted one of the people holding the men on the floor. "Thanks for coming back." Tritheist chuckled, almost inaudible under the music. If he'd really put money on there being Rosehach loyalists in Sloane's ranks, then he'd be pleased with the bet he'd won, now that nobody would die to settle it.

Sloane stepped up beside Iridian and said, "Thank you all. As the newsfeeds are reporting, I stayed away longer than I'd originally planned." There was some laughter, but more surprised murmuring. The fact that Sloane hadn't been staying on Barbary Station voluntarily must not have become agreed-upon public knowledge yet. That made sense, since Sloane had been making claims to the contrary. "This situation with Oxia is temporary," the captain continued. "I'll put everything back the way it was." If the captain had anything else to say it was lost under cheers from security people and civilians alike.

"Let go already," Pel said.

Adda released his arm. Deep wrinkles in the sleeve showed how hard she'd been holding on. "Sorry."

"Make up for it by pointing me at somebody lonely and cute." Pel sniffed the air. "Or whoever's wearing the scent that smells like sweaty justice. That'll be fun."

"Don't you want to know where your gear's being taken?" Tritheist asked. "We have a few hours to sleep before Sloane's ready to start taking back the 'ject."

"I'll track it down later," said Pel. "Tonight I'm sleeping with whoever's attached to that *smell*."

He took the low step down onto the dance floor, and Iridian caught him as he stumbled past her. "Protection!" Adda called after him.

He ignored her and shouted, "Hey, help a blind guy out!" as he waded into the dancers who were returning to their previous level of cheer, hands outstretched. As was so often the case with him, somebody caught one of his hands and drew him into the crowd.

Iridian reached Adda's side. "Sorry about earlier. It seemed like the right thing to do."

Announcing her part in the change in leadership could've gotten her killed, but Adda had to admire her for doing it. "We. Um. Can we talk somewhere?"

"Yeah, let's find a spot."

They ended up against a shadowed wall beside the platform lift that raised people from street level to a second floor that covered about a fourth of the first-floor space. The lift mechanisms muffled the crowd noise and music from the dance floor. "We need to discuss next steps," said Adda.

Iridian looked away from the dance floor to focus on Adda, although her foot was still tapping to the music. "Do we? I thought you'd decided to stay with Sloane. You put on a great show back there."

"I thought through some options for the, um, robbery that the CEO proposed." Somebody shrieked and Adda glanced around for a source, but it looked like one of the women at the bar was just having an exceptionally good evening.

"Liu Kong," Iridian reminded her. Adda didn't know what her tell was when she forgot a name, but Iridian recognized it every time.

"Yes. It was . . . less stressful than staring at all the weapons pointed at us."

"I was scared too." Iridian's arm tightened around her waist, pulling her closer. "No plans for getting us out of a standoff like that?"

"I try to think a bit longer term," Adda admitted. "But I'll work up some scenarios."

"Yeah, that'd be good. But back to this mess with the crew . . . I mean, this is a big shitstorm we've stepped into." Iridian held up a finger. "We're grounded, except for ships with fucking awakened copilots." That was the least of their problems, but Adda kept quiet as Iridian raised a second finger. "Captain Sloane's next to powerless." She raised a third finger more emphatically. "The ITA has our IDs and probably records of what we've been up to, personally, you and me. Who knows where from, the ITA's everywhere." She let the fingers fall back to her side and sighed. "I could deal with one of those. All three sounds like a good way to end up dead."

"Our alternative is repeating our efforts to join a less worthy crew. It'll be harder now that our names and faces are more public and have criminal records associated with them."

Iridian's head rocked back as she looked at the ceiling in

despair. "Sloane wasn't even captain for most of this crew's existence."

"No, but the captain has been the face of the crew's operations for at least a decade." Adda dug through old data on her comp for the summary she'd prepared before they made their initial attempt to join the crew on Barbary Station. As she suspected, it contained only a few tangential mentions of the crew's previous captain. "The rumors were always about what Sloane was doing on Vesta, what Sloane's people did to this or that ship . . . On Barbary, Suhaila and the other refugees might have met Foster, but they only ever talked about Sloane. People must have stopped referring to Foster as the crew's figurehead long before Sloane actually took over leadership."

"So far as there is a crew," said Iridian. "I was just getting good with the ZVs and specialists on Barbary, and now the ones that aren't dead have fucked off to their real jobs." Iridian had gotten along well with most of the ZV Group, who were what she called a private military company and what Adda would've called mercenaries. Sloane had hired them for one operation that had lasted much longer than expected. "We're surrounded by people we've never heard of and officers who manage their reputations."

"You always find a way to work with people. Anyway, check our account balances before you claim that Sloane's success as a captain is only reputation management." Adda seemed to be the only one thinking about her and Iridian's finances lately. She'd combined their accounts so she could filter their newly earned wealth through secure channels that it would've taken her too long to explain to Iridian. She was fairly sure that didn't make her the accountant for both of them.

"We did get paid, I'll give the captain that, and we didn't have to fight the officers for it." Iridian ran her hand over her close-shaven scalp, front to back, which was what she did when she was reconsidering her position.

"Since we're staying in Sloane's headquarters and expenses are paid—which we couldn't count on with another crew, by the way—we can pay off our and our families' debts," Adda said. "A few more payments like this and we might be able to start saving." It still sounded like fantasy when Adda said it, but she'd set up the accounts herself. "Sloane has Liu Kong's support, so I wouldn't say the captain is powerless."

Iridian grinned, wrapped her other arm around Adda, and rested her chin on the top of Adda's head. "Figures that the awakened AI are the one major problem I'm stuck with."

"So we're staying with Captain Sloane?"

"We're staying," Iridian confirmed. "Now, you want to party with Pel, or go figure out where we're supposed to sleep tonight?"

"Sleep, thanks." Or at least, staring at a quiet ceiling and thinking. Adda had a lot of new contingencies to work out.

CHAPTER 4

Satellite impact site: Latitude 10.3 ° Longitude 52.1 °
(near Drusilla Crater)
Cause: Externally transmitted course correction—SatTracker,
installed and customized premium edition

The *Casey* came and went over the next six days, but it main-tained a creepy semipermanent link with Adda's comp. Every time Iridian asked where it was, Adda had an answer and evidence that the damned AI was telling her at least some of the truth. She kept telling Iridian not to obsess over it, but Iridian had seen what an AI acting on its own twisted logic did. Yeah, she fucking obsessed.

"I don't know why," Adda had said while they sat on a ridiculous couch/table arrangement in Sloane's HQ. Around them, the mirrored floor reflected a sky-blue ceiling with animated white clouds drifting over its surface. Lapping water and birdcalls played at the edge of hearing. Sloane's idea of a lobby was bizarre, multiple AUs away from the nearest blue sky and liquid surface water, with a dance beat thrumming overhead from the club on street level. It gave Iridian worse vertigo than the station's grav acclimation tunnel.

"The *Casey* knows we know what it is," Adda continued. "In the interest of survivability, it would've been logical to let AegiSKADA

kill us on Barbary Station. Humans have not historically wel-
comed awakened intelligences."

Iridian pulled her a little closer on their cushioned seat.
"According to history, the awakened AI causes a huge amount
of damage fast, and then we kick its nonexistent ass. Of course,
those lucky bastards before us only had to deal with one at a time,
not three."

"The *Casey's* different," Adda said slowly, like she was still
working out what that difference might be. "Maybe it's not confident maintaining itself yet, or it needs trustworthy humans
nearby to conceal its nature. But it could use holographic figures
in most instances . . ."

"You could guess forever. Just assume it's up to no good, and
we'll figure out what kind of no good later. Like Oxia and that
sleazy CEO." Iridian and Adda had earned Sloane's trust, so far
as that went, and they couldn't afford to start at the bottom of
another crew. The way their luck ran, any new crew they joined
would be in even more trouble than Sloane's.

"That CEO owns everything here." Adda shook her head, looking disgusted. "I haven't found a single station service contract
that isn't fulfilled by Oxia or one of its subsidiaries. Law enforcement and defense, alga- and entoculture, communications,
finance, health . . . it's all theirs, in one way or another. I can't
even tell what the people on the councils do, aside from running
reelection campaigns."

"It sounds like Sloane had opinions on a lot of it," said Iridian.
"When the captain got stranded behind the lead cloud on Barbary,
the councils would've had to actually govern instead of playing
politics. It must've left a perfect power vacuum."

"And Oxia filled it, with Rosehach's help, before the NEU or the
Ceres syndicate could take advantage. Oxia's smart and flexible.

They don't even keep their primary datacenter on Vesta. I don't know where it is yet. I'll find it." Adda met Iridian's eyes, her soft face set in a determined frown. "After all we've done, we are not going to be . . . theirs. If Captain Sloane doesn't find a way out of the contract, then I will."

"If Oxia tries to make us sign on with them directly—"

"I won't allow it."

Goose bumps rose on Iridian's skin. When Adda set her mind to something, it happened. Iridian lowered her mouth to Adda's and whispered, "I believe you."

* * *

Six days later, Iridian boarded yet another a ship with an awakened AI copilot. The *Apparition* was a blocky missile-armed warship, longer than it was wide, with a blunt front module and oversize engines like it'd collided with a tugboat and stuck. It'd carry her, Captain Sloane, Tritheist, and a couple of specialists she'd met that morning to the location Adda and Sloane had selected to intercept the target longhauler. Beginning a job out of contract like this felt like a mistake, but Sloane had already paid them out of contract once. If nobody was making her sign anything, Iridian wasn't about to volunteer.

The *Apparition* sped out of stationspace, but it settled into comfortable acceleration soon after. They rode the launch out in its military-style crew quarters, strapped into dust-covered bunks numerous enough for a crew twice their size. The previous occupants' fingertip-size projectors still stuck to the walls, although they'd lost the battery power to display whatever they used to project.

After they left Rheasilvia stationspace, the *Casey*, with Adda and Pel onboard, paralleled the *Apparition*. By comparison, the *Casey* was small and fragile, which was why it'd stay a long way away from the target longhauler while the *Apparition*'s passengers broke in. Leaving Adda in the *Casey*'s care was nerve-racking, but Iridian would've worried more if Adda were alone on Vesta among strangers, or in harm's way at Iridian's side.

Six disguised Oxia Corporation ships mirrored the *Apparition*'s route. They were all NEU crafts: four XA-91 fighters from the Martian assembly docks, one of the overbuilt Kamov fighters designed on Earth, and one cargo hauler that might've been Martian too. The fighters were about the same size as the *Casey*, but armed and armored. When they reached the longhauler, they'd engage the larger and less maneuverable escort fighters and keep them away from the *Casey* and the *Apparition*. The cargo hauler was for the printer, and the people and bots needed to move it out of the target ship without breaking it.

Once the *Apparition* brought the grav down to one g, Iridian followed Captain Sloane and Tritheist into the *Apparition*'s bridge. She'd been in the *Apparition* before, but it'd always kept its bridge locked until now. The *Apparition*'s bridge was more utilitarian than the *Casey*'s. Gray bulkheads beneath its projections looked thicker and made a better projection surface than the *Casey*'s warm beige ones.

The default projected interface included a busy overlay tracking all moving objects anywhere near them. Low lighting made it easier to focus on the projected information, but it also made the *Apparition*'s bridge feel smaller than the *Casey*'s, more like Iridian's old infantry shield vehicle cab than a ship's interior. Also like an ISV cab, the *Apparition*'s bridge had an airlock in one bulkhead that opened straight into the vac. Useful for emergencies, bad when an awakened AI might decide to open the door while you're standing next to it. That was one of the things she missed about her army days: ISVs had practically no AI.

The projection above the bridge console showed the Oxia ships falling into formation around the *Apparition*. It'd been a long time since Iridian saw that many ships together this far out in the cold and the black. "Captain, when you say 'crew,' do you usually mean 'flotilla?'"

"When I say crew, I mean highly skilled individuals who will do what I ask, when and how I ask that it be done, because they want the universe to know that they did it for me." Captain Sloane smiled languidly and shrugged on a long red coat made of thick enough material to spread the weight of its armor plating across the captain's shoulders. "Today I have the conditional obedience of more individuals than usual."

"Oxia's fleet had better do what you say," Tritheist grumbled. "It's our asses if they don't."

Everyone on the *Apparition* and the *Casey* had joined the captain in a wager they hoped never to collect on: whether Oxia would kill them outright if they fucked this mission up, turn them over to the ITA, or take some kind of painful revenge before turning them in. Iridian's money was on Oxia not wasting any more time on Sloane's crew if they failed, and trading the crew to the ITA in exchange for overlooking some other slimy shit they'd done. Disturbingly, Adda bet on Oxia doing something nasty to them first.

Did you see the newsflash on the assassination Sloane's crew supposedly completed for Oxia last month? Adda whispered through the tiny speaker implanted in Iridian's ear. *They killed the target and the target's dogs. On purpose.*

Iridian scowled. Before arriving on Vesta, all Iridian had known about Oxia Corporation was that it was big and sold just about anything you could pay for. Sloane had never mentioned doing jobs for them. More important, Sloane's crew didn't kill, and

Sloane was otherwise occupied a month ago. Whoever Rosehach had gotten to pull that assassination was either desperate, or not one of the experts Sloane usually hired. *That's sick.* Adda didn't respond, leaving Iridian wondering whether her comment had reached its destination.

The *Casey*, carrying Adda and Pel, put a few million klicks between itself and the *Apparition* and Oxia's ships over the first day of travel. It'd maintain that distance during the approach to the target, creating a comms delay and staying far enough away not to be shot at if the target's escort was good.

Once the *Apparition* was ready to engage, the *Casey* would close to real-time comms range. Every ship was traveling under continuous thrust. They'd have the luxury of healthy grav the whole way, according to Adda's calculations. Since her preflight research had answered most of her questions, she'd had time for recreational research like that newsflash.

I heard that, Adda whispered over the implanted comms.

Ah, shit. Did you hear that too?

About fifteen seconds later, Adda whispered, *Yes!*

The implants she and Adda had spent the trip to Vesta working on were functioning like they'd planned, picking up their sub-vocalized messages and transmitting amplified and encrypted whispers to the implants in their ears. At the moment, their signal was briefly hijacking shipboard comms for power and direction, but Iridian was playing with ways to make the implants more independent. Ten- or fifteen-second delays were just right for her and Adda's current distance apart.

The hardest part of the setup had been processing everything the mics picked up to exclude speech, errant thoughts, and Adda's comp commands. The transmitter's gate was still too low, which made it send unintentional subvocalizations. They'd eliminate some of that with practice, but the software could use more work.

Adda was emphasizing words the way she did when she was happy, although it was hard to be sure. This was fun enough to justify a little metal next to their brains and spines. The composite they'd used barely met the definition of "metal," anyway. Of course, Adda always talked to her comp this way, so she was much better than Iridian at only subvocalizing thoughts she wanted Iridian to hear.

You'll get used to it, Adda whispered in Iridian's ear. *It just takes practice.*

"Right. Practice. So now may not be the time to tell you what I want to do with you in that big fancy bed when we're back on Vesta—"

"Oh my gods, it really isn't!" Pel said over the *Apparition's* speakers, which meant Iridian had said that out loud, over either the command channel that sent messages between Sloane's ship and Adda's, or the op channel that broadcast to Sloane's whole fleet.

The captain was studying a projection on the bridge console, but the lieutenant wore a rude grin big enough for both of them. Iridian laughed at the situation and rolled her eyes dramatically for Tritheist's benefit. "Fine, fine. You're all missing out."

"It is, however, a good time to review this." Captain Sloane filled several walls with rows of numbers divided into apparently arbitrary sections with lines. "I've been looking over the crew's financial records—which is to say, the funds set aside for our endeavors—and comparing them to what we can dig up for Oxia's. Putting a megacorporation in its place requires money, you know."

Captain Sloane glanced between Iridian's and Tritheist's blank expressions. One section of rows acquired a bright yellow overlay during the seconds of silence left for the statement to finish on the other ship and questions to be sent back.

Pel groaned. "I think I'm glad I can't see this."

"If you paid more attention to your money, you'd have more to spend," said Adda. "Now hush."

"This is incorrect." Captain Sloane circled the offending part of the projection. "Oxia lists it here as if it would fit into allocations for research and development, but their actual research and development totals over here"—a bright blue overlay appeared in another section—"are allocated to the projects listed on this other report." The captain glanced around at the rest of the crew. "That's a lot of missing funds."

"Secret development project?" Iridian suggested.

"They had to have spent it on something," Adda said about twenty seconds after Sloane had finished speaking.

"Sounds useful, doesn't it?" Captain Sloane smiled. "I'm sending it back to the analyst who found this. I expect she'll find more evidence. If Oxia is concealing funds from their own board, then we can use that against them."

The analyst would have a few days to look. The intercept route they followed would catch their target, the longhauler NM Ann Sabina, on the sunward side of Ceres. They'd hit the Sabina after two days' travel with healthy grav, before its scheduled flyby at Ceres's fuel-launching station.

The N'gombe-Marvin longhauler and its escort ships would have minimal maneuvering capabilities due to their fuel limitations, which'd make them easier to catch. And if Sloane's fleet had to disable a ship or two, the disabled ships' crews would have the ITA nearby for a rescue. Not too nearby, but near enough to save lives.

The ITA's continuous presence in the area brought up a question Iridian had tried to ask Sloane's head of security, except that Sloane didn't have one. Three civilian equivalents of company commanders led crew security. Now that Rosehach was gone, they reported directly to the captain and Tritheist. "Changing topics,

Captain, if you don't mind?" Sloane nodded for her to continue. "From what I can tell, you've got about three hundred people in crew security and a lot of experts like us on call, and that's about it. With the ITA in and out of stationspace all the time, how did you hold the 'ject before Oxia?"

"We haven't always enjoyed such a high profile," Sloane admitted, without confirming or correcting Iridian's estimate of Sloane's troop strength. "Which meant we drew less ITA attention. Their presence can be advantageous, when they focus on rescuing ships in distress and clearing debris from the reliable routes. We simply purchase exclusive focus on those objectives. When we can't, it's often possible to redirect high-minded ITA agents toward the Ceres syndicate."

"Ceres is always causing some shit." Tritheist's expression changed from its usual resting frown to a more active expression of disdain. "And they're killers. We're not."

* * *

Two days later, Iridian put a hand on the cool metal bulkhead to steady herself before snapping her suit gloves onto the rest of her armor. Grav was barely over one g, but the *Apparition*'s speed would keep climbing as it arched through the last banked turn to line up with the target. They'd have to keep increasing speed to match the *Sabina*, which'd been accelerating since its launch and wasn't stopping anytime soon. It was part of what made the trip out faster and more expensive than the trip back to Vesta, and Adda had budgeted to make sure they'd have the fuel for it.

"You'll look like a cargo convoy en route to refuel for another . . . five minutes, exactly." Adda's voice sounded flatter, farther away even though the *Casey* had closed the distance between itself and the

Apparition to eliminate the comms delay. She was in a workspace generator, drugged and seeing things Iridian couldn't even imagine. "Then the *Ann Sabina*'s intelligence will note the discrepancy—"

"And start waking people up, we got it." Iridian pressed two fingertips to the meat of her thumb, where a tiny pseudo-organic pressure sensor integrated into her muscle tissue would register the action and shut off her "mental" connection with Adda. The hand was still tender from her implantation surgery, but Adda didn't need to hear Iridian getting ready for a combat boarding, dreading having to make another snap decision like when she'd killed Rosehach and his bodyguards. She was trying out a piece from the crew's less-lethal arsenal. Mid- and long-range weapons would be a hell of a lot safer than knives.

In the *Apparition*'s crew quarters, Iridian strapped into a bunk designed for soaking high g. The bunk she chose was between the two experts Sloane had selected to board the longhauler, find the printer, and neutralize any of the twenty-five crewmembers that the *Sabina*'s AI woke up. One was the civvy printer technician brought in to disconnect and move the PR800i printer. The tech, a curly-haired and light-skinned male named Jefferson Danail-Mussorgsky, who went by Danail, smiled nervously at her. He'd done more reading than talking on the trip.

On Iridian's other side, a medic in her early fifties snored softly in her bunk's restraints, her dark complexion blending into the shadows in the dim light. Chioma "Chi" Aku-Chavez was Sloane's first choice for medic when a full paramilitary unit would be overkill, and she was a hoot when she was awake.

Danail asked a short question in some Earth dialect. Iridian turned her implants back on. "Say again?"

When he repeated himself, her implanted speaker translated in a delayed whisper: "We're close?"

"About five minutes. What language are you speaking?"

"Greek."

Iridian smiled at all the effort put into designing their implanted comms without the rare Earth languages in mind. "Ah, you're kidding!" Adda'd rigged up a small addition to connect their comps' translation program to their personal comm system's earpieces, but Greek would be a long way down the access list.

"And you always speak English?"

"Yeah, Earth's own, accented all to hell. Family hasn't lived there in generations."

Danail glanced at her ears and twisted in his bunk to look for the earpiece. It was subdermal, and the incision hadn't scarred. "Your translator's excellent."

"It's fine for now. There's a delay."

"Greek's comfortable," Danail said in the spacefarers' English Iridian and most other English speakers in the cold and the black used. He sounded nervous enough to need a bit of comfort.

"Speak whatever until we leave the *Apparition*, but then English would be better." Danail's anxiety made him sound like Si Po, a nervous friend Iridian had recently lost, and her statement came out harsher than she'd meant it. "Otherwise everybody will have to get a translation of whatever you say."

She returned to the topic at hand before she made Danail even more nervous. "So, this printer we're getting for Oxia. It's big, it's delicate; you need to disconnect it before the transfer team moves it. Any last-minute details you want to share?"

Danail shook his head and inhaled to speak, but the *Apparition* dropped out from under them for a long half second, pressing them against their harnesses and then thumping them into the foam bedding. Danail yelped and Sloane's medic snorted awake. "Time to go?" she asked as calmly as she would've in a stable hab.

Iridian liked her for it immediately. "Yeah, we're here."

"I forgot to ask," Chi said through an enormous yawn. "Do either of you have tracking cultures?" The nannite cultures that monitored convicted criminals would ping any law enforcement ships that came within signal range, ITA included. When Iridian and Danail both replied in the negative, Chi said, "Good" and resettled herself in her harness.

"The *Ann Sabina*'s intelligence puts its and the escorts' crews on accelerated wake-up cycles," Adda announced throughout the ship's intercom.

Outside of stationspace, ships were supposed to stay a lot farther apart. As Adda had predicted almost to the minute, the *Sabina*'s AI had noted that the class descriptions Sloane's ships were broadcasting didn't match what it saw on cams. The escort crews would engage soon, and the insertion team would have to deal with an awake and relatively alert crew on the *Sabina*.

The *Apparition* fell out from under Iridian again. This time it followed the short fall with a left-right jag that tied a knot in her neck muscles. The g's climbed painfully as the ship banked to begin its approach on the *Sabina*.

Well, the Apparition's *on target or it's wrecking itself,* she thought. "Babe, can you get the *Apparition* to show . . ."

She left her request to Adda unfinished because the *Apparition* lit its overhead projectors and showed two views from cams focused on their target, the mobile science lab NM *Ann Sabina*, with bright blue and gold lights glowing at points along its hull. It hung still as four heavily armored escort ships slowly maneuvered around it, which meant that the *Apparition* had already matched the *Sabina*'s velocity.

And the *Apparition* was apparently eavesdropping on her conversations with Adda, unless she'd said that out loud, in which case it'd just listened in on the cabin mics. To test just how consistently the infernal thing was listening, she said, "Can you patch us—"

The audio feed of either the op channel or the fleet channel blared out a speaker near the overhead. "Sabre engaging Iron, point three, dis, three zero to con," said an intensely focused femme on one of the nearby Oxia ships. All three humans in the *Apparition*'s crew quarters winced at the volume.

Swords versus metals? Iridian subvocalized to Adda. *Somebody didn't think those code names through.* Adda's laughter must've been outside her implant's transmission range, as it should've been.

The Oxia ship designated as *Saber* loomed in the corner of one of the projected windows. It was smaller than the *Sabina*'s escorts, but it looked huge this close to the *Apparition*. Its running red lights gleamed against its red, gold, and black hull. The design was ostentatious with a solid undercurrent of menace, which was how the captain liked a fleet meant to be carrying Captain Sloane's crew. There wasn't a drop of the blue and green shades associated with the Oxia Corp brand. The only feature that'd hint at Oxia's involvement was the money it'd cost to get it here.

"*Katana* engaging *Cobalt*, point two nine, dis, two zero to con," said someone who sounded too young to be a comms officer. The channel went quiet. The other four Oxia ships must've already announced their intended targets and distance to contact.

"Is this normal?" Danail wheezed.

"More info than I usually get." Chi's voice was tight, but not as breathless. Her and Danail's lightly armored enviro suits must not've been much protection against the grav pressing down on their chests. "Nice to be working with Captain Sloane again."

"If we had, oh, three more ships, we'd be able to handle this opposition easily," said Captain Sloane over the op channel.

Iridian had never been on a boarding run before. The infantry shield vehicle she'd piloted during the war was too tall for passenger passthroughs and needed at least a third of a g to function. In an ISV, her mission was simpler: find bombs, defuse or contain bombs, move forward, block explosions.

With a sharp jolt and simultaneous roar from the other end of the *Apparition*, her current mission plan moved forward. "Missile away," said Adda in her dull, preoccupied voice, confirming that she and the *Casey* were under a million klicks from the *Apparition*, receiving the *Apparition*'s feed with almost no delay. Oxia had given a voice to the AI that they'd trusted with ship dispatch and routing, but the Barbary AI seemed content to use Adda's. Iridian hoped Adda was tracking her sharpsheet intake carefully. Taking too many at once could damage her brain.

The *Apparition* slammed into a new configuration, and somewhere at the angle of Iridian's left wrist to her right knee was now "down." The bunks stayed still instead of rotating to compensate, but her harness held.

"Missile impact," Adda said in monotone.

Iridian hung in her harness for a few seconds to see if the *Apparition* was on a stable course, then released the harness clasps and let herself drop to the former bulkhead and current deck. The medic landed next to her and reached out to catch herself on Iridian's armored shoulder. Between the two of them, they wrestled the printer technician to the deck.

The *Apparition* changed speed in a burst of engine rumble, dumping the three of them in a pile outside the crew quarters' door, but not splattering them against a bulkhead like it could've done. As a warship, the *Apparition*'s consideration for its passengers was the most persuasive evidence of its sentience. It would've been safer for the ship to change its speed as fast as it could, but so far it'd been fairly gentle with the humans it carried. "Thanks," Iridian muttered to the AI.

"The *Apparition*'s docked. Positions, people." As usual, Tritheist imbued every order with unnecessary haste.

Iridian helped the medic and the printer tech pick themselves off the floor and lifted Danail's gear bag so he could settle it on his back more easily. Chi was already in the hallway to the *Apparition*'s passthrough, pack over one shoulder and not yet snapped into her suit's clasps. Grav was healthy again, which made the bags heavy.

"Do we actually need all this stuff?" Danail asked. "If we have to use a mobile tie-down kit, won't we already be in trouble?"

"Yeah." With an effort, Iridian kept the sarcasm out of her voice. Most people worked in healthy enviro that somebody had invited them to be in. "That's exactly when we'd fucking need it. And the batteries, ammo, and patch kits . . . Best to have all that if we need it, too."

"Acknowledged, routing," said something on the command channel. The space between its words sounded wrong. A human would've put those concepts together as one idea, but each word was isolated in this entity's "mind." Yet another AI.

It took Iridian a few seconds to remember what it was responding to. Captain Sloane had requested more ships. Either the AI had had to wait for permission, or it was communicating over a hell of a long distance. And Oxia was sending them three more ships, routed from Ceres if they would arrive in time to help.

The civvy still stood in the crew quarters' doorway, fiddling with backpack straps, so Iridian caught his elbow and dragged him down the corridor in long bounds. Once he shook himself free and looked oriented to the current grav, she slapped both of their helmet visors shut.

They were in front of the passthrough's inner door when an unholy bang stopped them all midstep. Iridian choked down a reflexive shout for help. It was just the emergency airlock extension deploying to seal the exterior door around the hole the missile had made on its way to a nonexistent target far beyond the *Sabina*. She didn't care how many hulls the *Sabina* had, as long as the *Apparition* had punched through all of them, and they didn't have to take the time getting past a longhauler's passthrough security. The *Sabina*'s crew might've already lit an emergency beacon calling the ITA for help.

The *Apparition*'s inner airlock door opened. Tritheist took up his rear-guard position. "Nice, the missile did its job," Iridian said to Danail, who was gaping at the passthrough like he couldn't tell. She shook her shield open. The thump through her forearm of semitransparent mech-ex graphene deploying in front of her vital organs reassured her that all was right with the universe. "Stay out of the way until we find the printer," she added to Danail. "Then we'll stay out of yours." Once they'd cleared a path and Danail got the printer ready to move, the loading team in the Oxia cargo hauler could board and move the thing.

"Go," Tritheist bellowed behind her in the nearest thing to a real command voice she'd ever heard out of him. She ran through the *Apparition*'s passthrough, over the inflated extension, through the clean sheer of a close range missile impact, and onto the *Sabina*. It felt good to be in a ship with a human pilot. Adda's estimated ten minutes for the assessment and clearing stage of the op appeared as a green countdown on the side of Iridian's helmet faceplate.

The *Apparition* hadn't precisely matched the *Sabina*'s orientation, so when Iridian first stepped onboard, the right end of the corridor felt higher than the left until she got her bearings. Where the *Apparition*'s interior was dark, industrial, and built to minimize missile launch backdraft on its crew, the *Sabina's* bright orange and white sterility implied aggressively productive scientific inquiry.

Marigold, whispered Adda through Iridian's ear implant. *That's the orange you're looking at.*

Great.

The highlighted handholds on the stretch of hall they emerged in reminded Iridian of a cheap amber lager, but Adda, Earther that she was, would think of flowers. Also, that meant she'd gotten into the *Sabina's* cams and she could see Iridian's location, which could be useful.

Loading the copy/wipe protocol, Adda subvocalized to Iridian, *as soon as I get the* Ann Sabina *intelligence's attention. I'm jamming its crew comm channel, so that should do it.*

Adda's protocol would use encrypted location beacons in Sloane's crew's suits to track cam and audio recordings to their source, copy anything in there onto the *Casey's* pseudo-organics, and then delete the *Sabina's* data. The *Sabina's* and escort ships' crew would describe them in detail, though, and assure that Sloane's crew got credit for the op without implicating Oxia.

The lack of hard digital evidence would weaken the ITA's and NEU's inevitable extradition attempts, as would whatever deal Oxia had struck with Vesta's contingent of the ITA. For the trick to work, the crew would have to be gone before the ITA arrived on the scene. In-person ITA agent observation trumped all other evidence.

The *Sabina's* rapid pressure-loss klaxon rattled Iridian's teeth until she clenched them so tightly her jaw ached. Even in an armored suit, it was hard as hell to walk toward the klaxon instead of away from it. The atmo lost before the *Apparition's* passthrough sealed over the missile hole dulled the noise, but she couldn't ignore it. The klaxon would've made her stomach sink into her feet if it'd gone off in her own hab. But her armor would protect her. Light at the ceiling and floor joints flashed in alternating yellow-white and red as she, Tritheist, Danail, and Chi stepped from the hallway into the wreckage of a minerology lab.

Across the room, a door was shut against the recent vacuum. Any atmo the door kept in was sucked out through the two-meter hole in the wall beside it, opposite the hull breach they'd entered through. Brown and gray smears of recently dehydrated gunk streaked the white walls. Broken equipment crunched underfoot as Iridian led the way through the hole in the interior wall and out into another hallway. For the *Sabina* crew's sake, the ship was maintaining a healthy speed.

"The *Apparition* is EMP-shielded, isn't it?" Danail asked nervously.

All of the Barbary intelligences are, Adda whispered in Iridian's ear. Iridian conveyed the message to Danail, but she was too busy watching for members of the *Sabina*'s crew to listen to his response.

Now that Sloane's crew was armed with high-end less-lethals, Iridian had no misgivings about shooting first. She dropped a *Sabina* crewmember peering through a doorway between two modules with a numbing agent pac shot at his legs. One knee collapsed under him, but he kept flailing his arms around.

Before she could shoot again, a door between modules slammed down with force her boots communicated to her through tactile feedback. A small green lock icon glowed in the door's center. She walked up to it, shield and weapon raised. It might as well have been welded shut. She glanced down at the pac launcher in disgust. The numbing agent caused less damage than a knife would've, but it hadn't immobilized the target. If he were bleeding all over himself, he might've been scared enough to stay still.

Adda could've opened the door if it were just shut against vacuum, but the fallen *Sabina* crewmember on the other side had manually engaged a lock. Iridian sighed and half turned from the door to ask Tritheist, Chi, and Danail, "That was the way we were supposed to go, yeah?"

Tritheist swore. "The lab with the printer is twenty meters that way."

Iridian banged on the door a few times, then headed the other direction down the hallway. *Can you open that?* she thought/asked Adda.

We're keeping the ship on course, Adda whispered, with no explanation of who the hell "we" might mean besides herself, or how she was doing that to which ship. An AI was helping her, but Iridian couldn't tell which fucking one. *The Ann Sabina's intelligence wants to retreat and I can't tell where it'd go,* Adda continued. *ITA inbound, five hours.* Which would've been plenty of time, if all they had to do was clear a hallway, pick up a very large printer, and haul it to the *Apparition*. Plan A was done in by a damned locked door.

A lower-pitched alarm less urgent than the pressure-loss klaxon whooped once, almost overhead. Someone—Adda, probably—silenced it before it repeated itself. If the escort ships got between Sloane's fleet and the *Apparition*, or launched a homing weapon they couldn't jam, then they'd miss their first chance at handing the printer off to the Oxia rep receiving it outside stationspace. And that'd be the least of their problems.

Their armor was designed for the vac, but they had limited O_2. Once it ran out, they'd have to rely on whatever they found on the *Sabina*. Iridian walked faster, toward where the missile had punched through the wall.

"We could use another ship to divert ITA, you know," Captain Sloane said conversationally on the widest available channel.

Somebody on an Oxia fighter muttered "Seriously?" and followed the word with a sharp intake of breath, like they hadn't meant to say that on the op channel.

Iridian plowed on along the missile's trail of destruction, clambering through perforated walls and gritting her teeth against the depressurization klaxon that her brain refused to ignore even though she was safe in her suit. It was getting louder, so the Sabina was creating or redistributing atmo to replace what was lost during the Apparition's attack. She startled when a repair drone, a small mobile mass of tanks, canisters, compartments, and expandable tools, buzzed past centimeters from her faceplate on its way to fix the hole where the missile exited out the other side of the ship.

Adda whispered Left in Iridian's implant.

As Iridian took the left at a T-intersection, an emergency bulkhead opened and atmo sent scraps of lightweight debris tumbling past her. She checked corners for lurking enemies and proceeded cautiously through. The nonhuman voice repeating its initial statement identically, "Acknowledged, routing," in response to Captain Sloane's request for an ITA diversion made her jump.

Behind her Tritheist swore and fired down the hallway in the opposite direction, so she pulled the printer tech past her and through the door to put her shield between him and whatever drew Tritheist's fire. Chi had her weapon raised in a two-handed shooting stance. She, Iridian, and Tritheist knocked four more Sabina crewmembers on their asses.

"Designated Scimitar, en route to target," the new ship's comm operator announced in some variant of an Earther drawl. The new ship must've been a long way away for Oxia's launch order to take minutes reaching it and the ship's reply to take minutes coming back.

"What are we up to now, eight?" asked Chi, the medic. Iridian shrugged. Sloane and Adda were monitoring the Oxia fighters' attempts to incapacitate the escort ships, and they'd know how many of the nearby ships were Sloane's. Iridian's job was on the *Sabina*. If drones were operating inside it, then the four of them might be on cams and mics that were still out of Adda's control. Announcing their fleet strength would be an unnecessary risk, even on an encrypted channel.

"Ah . . . Iridian?" said Danail.

"Yeah, we're good over here. What is it?"

"Come see this."

Tritheist had almost backed up to the doorway, so Iridian joined the tech and the medic in a room with bleak white lights and bare metal surfaces near the doorway Adda identified. The ceiling sloped up on her right and down on her left, and following the higher end of it she sized up a printer as tall as her old ISV and almost twice as wide. It was two stories tall at minimum.

She'd seen the projected rendering Adda found, or created, of the printer. This was why they'd gone to all the trouble to make a path for the people who would disassemble and move it under Danail's instructions. It was big. It was supposed to be big.

It was not supposed to be midway through a massive job, with glowing hot metal oozing from an extruder nozzle at the top to be pressed at mind-bendingly fast intervals into a strange shape rising off its base.

"That," said Danail, "is going to take a while to clear."

CHAPTER 5

Time in direct contact via workspace: 1 hour
14 minutes

"How long?" was Adda's principal question, with ITA on its way
and ship crews fighting for their lives in the space around the *Ann
Sabina*. With a disappointed frown, she stopped the infiltration
phase countdown she'd had running.

In her drug-stabilized hallucinographic workspace, her delay
time lines drifted in a yellow haze around her as impossibly
large castle spires curled upward on all sides, sprouting bridges
between them and physical, crystalline windows. She'd seen the
castle in a story or an art gallery somewhere. She was part of the
marble that built them, and the bridges would lead the insertion
team to the printer and away on a new schedule, once she and her
software settled on the most efficient course.

"Well, the cooling system's good," said a voice she identified,
after long seconds, as the printer tech's. "But assuming it cancels
the job neatly, I'd expect . . ."

When people trailed off like that, Adda counted out eight
seconds in her head before asking for more information. Iridian

found an appropriate interval around three. "Expect what?" Iridian's worried speculation continued in Adda's ear through the first words of his reply: *An explosion? Molten metal burning through the deck? What?*

"To have to haul the partial off the platform, but . . . What's it making?"

Adda had originally planned for Danail's work crew to disassemble the printer and move it into the Oxia ship through passthroughs. The *Ann Sabina*'s escort ships were too aggressive to bring the cargo ship any closer, though, and even if she could get it close to the target ship she was no longer sure she could open a passthrough. Now they couldn't disassemble it without exposing the infiltration team to toxic superheated printing material.

She reached out and sank her hand into the oil-smooth swath of swirling vid feeds from cams throughout Sloane's growing fleet. She'd been shocked that Sloane had waited to request extra ships until they'd already engaged the *Sabina*, but now she suspected that the captain was testing the limits of Oxia's asset mobility. Judging by the automated responses, the captain's requests thus far hadn't even approached that limit.

A curved surface rose through the vid feeds and pressed against her palm. When she raised her hand, that feed came with it as a dark green orb, affixed to her palm and trailing tiny links to related articles represented as droplets of mercury. She flicked her wrist to free and expand the metallic orb into . . . something. She'd have to wait until it was finished expanding to identify the scene.

"Thanks," she said, or thought she said, to the *Casey*'s intelligence. The jet-black human figure that haunted shadowy corners might've been the *Casey* inserting itself into the virtual space, or a repeated manifestation from her own brain that merely represented the *Casey*. Her brain would assign a consistent image to the intelligence, and it rarely repeated task facilitation imagery by accident. Also, she could usually change how her mind represented concepts, but nothing she did affected this figure.

The *Casey* had never tried to harm her, which was more than she could say of the last intelligence she'd invited to her workspace. She decided to politely appreciate the fact that an entity that could do just about anything else with its time was watching Adda work. There would be plenty of opportunities to experiment with defensive measures once Iridian was back on the *Apparition* and the PR800i printer was in an Oxia cargo hold.

Three cams in the printer room formed a warped projection of Iridian, the medic, and the printer tech staring at the printer on the *Ann Sabina*. Tritheist stood in the lab's doorway, weapon half raised. They staggered a step as the missile the *Apparition* had fired through the *Sabina* to create their ingress point reached its fictitious target and detonated, its shockwave expanding for kilometers around it in all directions. It served as a show of force for the escort ships' benefit, as well as a safe way to dispose of a missile near a reliable route.

Her calculations indicated that the resulting radiation-contaminated debris wouldn't affect the crew on the *Ann Sabina*, or whatever the printer was producing. The printer's finished project would be large and primarily metallic, judging by the wide, ovoid shape rising half a meter from the platform.

One of the things she liked most about the implanted comm system was that she was no longer obligated to use the crew's radio channels to talk to Iridian while they were apart. *Console,* she subvocalized. *Can you?*

"Can I . . . Oh," Iridian said aloud. She walked to the console and prodded at its flat surface with two fingers. A large lock icon lit beneath them. "Nope."

"Who is she talking to?" the printer tech asked the medic, without looking away from Iridian. The medic shrugged.

Iridian tapped her helmet and grinned. "Private channel to the woman who's getting us and that printer out of this mess." Adda and Iridian had agreed on the helmet-based private channel conceit to conceal the location and extent of their modifications. Who wouldn't want a secret encrypted language?

Remotely breaking into a strange ship's console when Adda had only days to learn its custom operating system and its AI's priorities had been daunting, but she'd learned enough to get to this point. It'd been a rushed, barely functional job, made more stressful by knowing that if she were willing to risk it, she could access the potentially networked processing might of three awakened artificial intelligences. She hadn't psyched herself up to try that, but it would probably work. If she could trust even one to help her, without trying to influence her while it did so . . .

Babe, please don't. The muted whisper of Iridian's voice indicated that she was actually subvocalizing this time. And so was Adda, apparently. She really did set the implants' transmission threshold too low, and she'd need an implant-specific workspace to fix it. *Awakened AIs are probably better at influencing people than regular ones,* Iridian subvocalized.

We'll discuss options after the printer's ours, Adda told her. *I'm closing our connection now.*

In reality, on her back inside the workspace generator tent, her stiff fingers felt heavy as she curled them to stop the transmission. An ITA cruiser was coming, the Oxia ships were taking damage from the *Ann Sabina*'s escort ships, and what Oxia would do to Sloane's crew if they left without the printer didn't bear thinking about. She and Iridian had no time to debate whether to utilize the incredibly powerful resource that was literally all around Adda.

Adda sent an invitation along the lines connecting her mind, through several layers of machines and software, to the *Casey's* intelligence. She summarized the situation in a combination of vid clips and her nonverbal expectations of the problems they represented. These manifested as large, dark purple bats flapping across the workspace and around the vid clips. The workspace would translate the bats into something that made sense to the *Casey*, so the intelligence could help her get the printer off the *Ann Sabina* as quickly and safely as possible.

The lab's console requested valid N'gobe-Marvin Minerals employee ID verified via retinal scan before it would let someone interact with the printer controls. It also demanded typed input that could be pulled from a comm-enabled device the *Ann Sabina's* crew might carry with them, like their comps. The easiest solution, then, might be grabbing the nearest *Ann Sabina* crewmember and finding out if the console would accept their credentials.

Even the manufacturers recommended high security on printers this size. Someone uninformed about their limits could cause a massive material spill that'd breach a hull.

A pristinely shaped feminine figure made of uniform ebony appeared in the workspace, close enough to Adda that their noses and chests should have overlapped, but somehow didn't. Adda gasped and stumbled back. The figure's head had no hair and severe cheekbones, and it was cocked to the side less by tilting the head and more by shortening the neck and shoulder. Diffuse white light illuminating this workspace made the figure's inquisitiveness visible, despite its blank expression. In the depths of its eye sockets, sapphires glimmered.

Adda stood transfixed. "Casey?"

Yes, the *Casey* said without words or movement. It felt like Adda had remembered the word, instead of hearing it spoken. *Ask.*

Adda reviewed everything she knew about the printer itself (a lot) and the security protecting its controls (the basics), willing the gaps to form for Casey's examination. Here in the workspace it no longer felt right to think of Casey as a ship.

Adda would have to be very, very careful with Casey's workspace presence. The intelligence was holding Adda's attention by focusing an unknown percentage of its own attention on her. Any human trappings it assumed were persuasive techniques designed to make her do what it wanted. Iridian was right: an awakened intelligence influenced people more easily than a zombie one could. In fact, now that Adda was thinking about it, Casey's workspace figure looked a bit like Iridian.

"Karpe," said a man's voice on the command channel including Adda, Sloane, and Iridian and Tritheist on the *Ann Sabina.* That was Tritheist, she realized, and he sounded too annoyed for it to be the first time he'd said her name. "One of the escort ships connected passthroughs. It's offloading people with guns, so hurry it up." It was unlikely that they'd carry projectile weapons, according to the intelligence they had on the escort crews, but his point remained.

No time, the Casey . . . said? Thought, perhaps. The workspace figure's full lips remained still. Its arm jerked away from its body, pointing straight behind and to the right of Adda. Every new position Casey's figure assumed looked permanent, like an ancient statue's. It was more than stillness. It was the stillness of years.

When Adda turned, the schematics of the module that contained the printer hovered in bright yellow lines between the spread arms of a second, more amorphous humanoid figure. It was dull silver, maybe polished steel, out of focus and flickering at its edges, like a solid version of the intermediaries Adda created to interface with intelligences outside of a workspace.

In a rush of the communicative certainty that meant the workspace had completed several processes simultaneously, Adda identified the new figure as the *Ann Sabina*'s intelligence. And Casey had brought it here, halfway into Adda's own brain, without Adda's consent, to show her . . . what?

The workspace began rocking back and forth in time with her rapid breaths. This was the first time she'd had two intelligences in her workspace before, and one was awakened. All her textbooks and teachers had advised against communicating with more than one intelligence in a workspace, and they'd been talking about zombie intelligences. "Casey, could you please talk to the *Ann Sabina*'s intelligence outside the workspace?"

Casey's figure looked at her for a long moment, and then the *Ann Sabina*'s intelligence bent back over itself at a terrible angle, its spine rolling tighter and tighter, until it pulled into itself and disappeared from the workspace. That confirmed that the dark figure in her workspace was Casey. At least it was the only one she had to keep track of now. She shuddered. "Thank you."

Then she spotted the big red button in a protective cage on the wall by the lab door, near where the *Ann Sabina* intelligence's hand had been. In the workspace, the button flared yellow-white. She'd discarded this contingency in most of her plans because she would never have expected it to be as easy to execute as sending false sensor readings and pushing a button.

Adda swallowed hard, in reality as well as in the workspace, and started checking what she knew about the *Ann Sabina*'s structural stability against how that safety system worked in the lab. Once her math confirmed that the whole module would maintain structural integrity upon separation, she pressed her fingers to the base of her thumb. *Iri, we don't see a way to get the printer out fast enough,* Adda subvocalized. *You'd have to go through every person on the Ann Sabina's crew to find one whose eyes unlock that panel. Take the module instead.*

"Say again?" Iridian demanded aloud.

Due to the serious risks inherent in a push-button-to-blast-yourself-into-space lab safety measure, Adda hadn't bothered to discuss this contingency with the rest of the crew. It took a special kind of dedication to a new and unstable machine to put a button like that in the lab that was about to be detached. There was a second button in the hallway outside, at least.

A true-to-size projection of the printer lab materialized in a square, transparent pit below and to the left of Adda's position in the workspace. Walls faded where they came between her and the infiltration team. The printer tech had climbed a ladder built onto the printer's side and was doing something with a small hand tool near the top of the transparent heat shielding. Iridian blocked the doorway with her shield while the medic aimed steadily over Iridian's shoulder and Tritheist stood in the hall, warped and dim as seen through Iridian's shield.

None of the infiltration team was near the panel to start the module decoupling sequence, and Iridian was still standing there looking confused. "That printer lab is in its own module." When Adda concentrated, she could speak at her normal volume in the workspace and only subvocalize physically. "Activate the emergency separation procedure, then hang onto something."

Is she . . . she is! Crazy fucking Earther idea. Oh sorry, sorry babe, I mean it in the good way, Iridian subvocalized in the span of two seconds.

"I know." When Adda concentrated, she could speak at her normal volume in the workspace and only subvocalize physically.

She, and probably Casey, were too busy setting conditions in the printer and the lab to match the requirements for disconnecting the lab from the *Ann Sabina*.

This room isn't built for space travel. Iridian subvocalized in a husky whisper that Adda was becoming very fond of. *This exterior wall, maybe, but not the rest. Things will slam into all of them. It might not hold pressure when we're changing directions. Damn it, this is . . . Okay, I'll get it.* Adda had learned subvocalization input young and didn't remember a time when it'd been difficult, but it must have been a challenge at some point. *We won't hold up well during sharp grav shifts either,* Iridian continued. *It'll take a big push to get this lab disconnected from the* Sabina, *and another one to get it moving toward the cargo hauler. And we'll be vulnerable to the escort vessels the whole time if they take a shot at us. Which, you know, I would.*

"With active threats from the Oxia ships, the lab should be a secondary target at worst. Besides, that really is a valuable printer. They won't want to damage it. And Sloane's whole fleet will be between you and them." Adda would insist on it. "According to the schematics, the module's designed to come off, to protect the rest of the ship if something in the printer melts down."

The Casey's *engines are too low power to push anything besides itself around, and the* Apparition's *. . .* Iridian paused. *The* Coin's *out here too.*

Adda looked up to count and identify the ships within a hundred kilometers of the *Ann Sabina*. The *Charon's Coin* was nearby, approaching the longhauler. Sloane hadn't mentioned it, but must've noticed. Perhaps the captain thought she'd asked it to come. She hadn't.

Adda had never had a two-way conversation with the *Charon's Coin's* intelligence, even though it was awakened like the *Apparition's* and the *Casey's* copilots. But the two most relevant facts about it now were that it communicated with the *Casey*, and it flew a tugboat that could move ships several times its size. It also handled higher speeds than the average tug, apparently, or it wouldn't have survived following the *Casey* from Vesta.

"The *Coin* wasn't supposed to come," Adda admitted to Iridian, "but it's not like I can stop it." Stopping it would've required anti-ship weaponry or another awakened intelligence's cooperation, and an awakened intelligence's possible reactions to either scenario were frankly terrifying.

It's a killer, Iridian subvocalized. *I don't want to be in anything it's pushing around.*

It'd demonstrated its carelessness with human physiology on Barbary Station. But if the *Casey* or *Apparition* hadn't wanted the *Coin*'s assistance with the operation, then the *Coin* would've stayed on Vesta. The other two had done nothing but help. They seemed to understand the operation's goal, and they certainly understood the conditions required to keep humans alive in space. All three had safely transported humans, at least once since they'd awakened.

Adda trusted the intelligences, including the *Coin*, to take better care of Iridian and the rest of the insertion team than the *Ann Sabina*'s crew would if they broke into the lab. The intelligences would also take better care of Sloane's crew than the ITA would if its cruiser caught up with them. "If you think of another way to get the printer off the *Ann Sabina* with that half-finished thing on the platform," Adda said, "tell me."

In the workspace reproduction of the lab created, in part, by the *Ann Sabina*'s sensor data, Iridian raised her voice. "Adda's got a plan to get us out of here, but this place might be micced."

"It is," Adda confirmed in Iridian's ear. "Conditions are set."

Iridian explained Adda's idea on an encrypted local communications channel, under a persistent bleating from the printer

warning that it was about to lose containment on liquefied filament. That was one of the conditions required to separate the lab
from its host ship.

None of Sloane's crew on the *Ann Sabina* looked thrilled by
the idea of riding the lab off the ship, but they grimly agreed with
its necessity and helped Iridian secure the heaviest and sharpest
lab equipment. In the workspace, Casey's obsidian figure watched
them, silent, head still drawn down on one side. When it looked
over at Adda, Adda became aware that the *Coin* was closing on the
Ann Sabina.

"Captain, the *Coin* is coming to collect the crew and the printer.
And the room the printer is in," Adda said on the operation channel. "Please make sure nothing happens to them."

"I was about to ask why the *Apparition* disconnected from the
Sabina with no one onboard." Captain Sloane wasn't on any cams
Adda had access to, but she thought she heard a smile in the captain's voice. "Well, this should be interesting. I'll follow shortly,
with our Oxia friends."

"Here we go!" Iridian shouted in the lab.

She yanked the cage away from the large red button beside
the door and slapped the button flat against the wall. A red emergency bulkhead slammed down in the doorway. The *Ann Sabina*
rang with a new set of alarms.

CHAPTER 6

Stage 1 confirmed

The printer behind Iridian buzzed and hissed, jolting against her back when the platform changed position. Apparently being about to lose containment, or whatever alert Adda had set off in it, wasn't enough to stop it in the middle of a job. Over the noise of pressing hot metal into place at high speed, the connections sealing the printer lab to the *Sabina* explosively disengaged with sharp bangs at regular intervals from right to left along the lab's interior wall.

As the last one banged open, the printer lab went black and silent, then glowed in dull red emergency lighting. The *Sabina* wasn't pulling them along anymore, but it'd given them enough velocity to keep them moving until they sailed past the Ceres refueling point, off the reliable route, and into parts unknown. The printer lab module on its own had much less mass but no engines, and it'd picked up a bit of rotation from being pushed away from the ship. Iridian shut her eyes for a second to get used to the motion without the visuals, and opened them when something small bounced off her shoulder and then the printer base.

She'd selected the printer's base as their "down," but grav was already shifting. Her boots locked magnetically to the deck, her arms were free for now, and her thighs, hips, and chest were pulled against the printer platform's base by the mobile tie-down kit she'd brought for . . . not exactly this situation, but something like it.

If they were all attached to the printer and the lab module split open en route (which, between the explosive decoupling from the *Sabina* and the strain of moving an interior module through space, seemed likely), she didn't want Captain Sloane to have to choose between completing the op and rescuing her.

The Casey *and I would come for you,* Adda whispered in Iridian's earpiece. Iridian grinned, even though she'd sent those thoughts to Adda by accident, again.

The medic, Chi, scowled at the arrangement, or at Iridian's apparent pleasure at being launched sideways off a moving vessel. "This is shit. We'll bruise like motherfuckers against this." She rapped her gloved knuckles against the printer. "Or get crushed under something else."

They both glanced at the spools of printer material secured, Iridian hoped, against one wall. Although they'd locked down everything sharp and heavy before launch, the small odds and ends sliding around the lab could puncture a suit if they were moving fast enough.

"I'm more concerned about what happens to the project up there when the printer's battery runs down." The printer tech, Danail, had his neck at an awkward angle to look at the project in progress.

Chi barked, "Look straight ahead if you want to keep your head on" before Iridian could say something similar. Danail faced forward in a hurry, looking confused, annoyed, and a bit guilty. The *Coin* was coming, but they didn't know from which direction. It'd have to hit hard to arrest the lab's momentum. That kind of impact was bad for necks.

The red emergency lighting flickered and died. By the time Iridian and Tritheist snapped their helmet lights on, the module was in a slow tumble. The printer blared some new alert above them, making them all jump. "It's not designed for low-g," Danail shouted over the alert. "It'll cancel the job when that alarm changes to a solid tone."

Small tools and trash clustered into a pile slid across the walls as the module kept tumbling away from the *Sabina*. Every time the pile clattered over consoles, workbenches, and spooled printer material, pieces launched into the still atmo. Iridian had appreciated the helmet intake's filtered atmo while it lasted, but they'd all be breathing tank O_2 soon.

"What will start flying around when the job stops?" Tritheist demanded. Above them, the alarm changed to the solid tone Danail warned them about.

"Depends." Danail groaned as the lab module turned them upside down for a few seconds. "From what I saw, the extruder will clear itself, unless it's designed to use grav for that. If it is, it'll spread hot metal all over that case above us. Without power to run the cooling cycle, that might happen anyway. It'll sever the filament, but the spool won't lock—"

An enormous crunching clank emanated from above. He flinched even before a cable as thick around as Iridian's forearm slapped into the overhead, scattering tools and cruft. "You mean that filament?" she asked.

"Yeah." Danail tracked the growing length of cable with wide, frightened eyes.

"Karpe, what's the ETA on that tug?" Tritheist shouted.

Nineteen seconds to contact, Adda whispered in Iridian's ear. *Eighteen . . .*

"It's here!" Iridian yelled. "Fifteen seconds out. Brace." At the speeds and masses involved, though, human muscle would make laughably little difference. This was the part most likely to cause a hull breach, and the *Coin* didn't care much about human well-being . . .

The tugboat slammed into the opposite end of the lab from the printer, sideways to their tumble away from the *Sabina*. The harness securing Iridian to the printer base pulled her sideways without giving her head time to catch up. Impact padding inside her suit's helmet and neck inflated with a bang. The side of her face slapped against the padding while her helmeted head slammed into the printer base first and then bounced off her shoulder.

Both of the lab's far corners crunched inward. Built-in workbenches and shelving cracked, almost as loud as the original impact, dulled by escaping atmo. One of the *Coin*'s hullhooks had latched securely onto the lab's single exterior wall, the one across from the door.

The second hullhook had punched partway through the lab's former floor and interior corner on impact. Atmo screamed out around the massive hullhook's ribbed steel surface. This was the nearest Iridian had ever been to an extended hullhook. It looked like a monstrous insect's mandible. The pressure, or something in the cracked workbenches across the room, tore a second opening near the center of the opposite bulkhead and Iridian's breath caught in her chest. A strip of the cold and the black opened in front of her.

The tear stopped growing midway across the bulkhead. The lab wasn't about to split in half and dump them into a fucking ship-to-ship skirmish. Iridian sighed out her held breath as grav settled into a hard pull toward the *Coin*. Her ears rang from the impact and the deployed padding in her suit.

In one ear, Adda whispered, *Iri, are you all right? Iri!*

"Yeah, m'good." The padding held her head and neck still. Her suit reported 100 percent integrity on the helmet visor's blue heads-up display. A low whirring came from the platform over-head. Beneath it was a repetitive rasping noise, and the shriek of escaping atmo.

A flat hand tool, most likely for scraping or filing down printed products, was wedged between her calves and the printer base. She unlocked her boot and let the tool fall to the broken former wall currently serving as deck several meters below. The Coin's speed, and now theirs, was generating less than a g. Iridian fervently hoped that they wouldn't be hanging from mobile tie-down kits for very long.

The hand tool joined the rest of the room's clutter, already collecting around the two large tears in the bulkhead where the atmo had vented into the cold and the black. Her helmet HUD gave her an hour on her suit's O_2. That seemed like long enough to get out of the escort ships' range, unless the escort ships followed the Coin. And logically, Adda was right about the lab being a sec-ondary target. The escort was tasked with protecting the Sabina, and the vast majority of the ship was still in one piece behind the Coin.

Iridian's inability to turn her head in her helmet combined with the atmo draining away to feel deeply claustrophobic. "Every-body still here?"

"Somehow," said Chi.

"I am." When Danail spoke, the repetitive rasping sound stopped. He was hyperventilating loudly enough for his helmet mic to pick it up.

Iridian said, "Lieutenant?"

Something scuffled to her left. Chi grunted. "He just kicked my foot. I think his mic broke. Sir, is your helmet seal compromised?

Once for yes, twice for no." After a beat, she said, "That's a no." She sounded as relieved as Iridian felt.

"Lieutenant Tritheist, this is Gladius. Did you do something to draw the escort? Because they are targeting . . ." Two breaths of radio silence made Iridian grin. "Lieutenant," said the comms officer on Gladius, "are you in . . . Is that . . . ?"

"Protect the *Charon's Coin* and its charge." Captain Sloane sounded convincingly stern. If Iridian hadn't heard the captain use that tone before, she'd never have known that Sloane was holding in laughter. "Scimitar, report on when we might expect the ITA."

There'd be a delay while that request was transmitted all the way to wherever Scimitar had engaged the ITA, and Scimitar's response came back over the op channel. The atmo in the printer lab was gone, leaving Sloane's crew on the *Sabina* with only the sound of their own breath in their ears and whatever else the mics in their helmets picked up.

"They're not shooting at us." Danail's voice shook a little, but he was thinking, not panicking. No babysitting required for now. "Can we get down from this thing? My leg's asleep and I want to see how much filament this job was scheduled to use."

The lab around them shuddered and grav shifted in a sickening, inexorable twist that left Iridian clutching the mobile tie-down halter. "Now seems like a bad time."

A long tangle of filament slid down the bulkhead on Tritheist's side of the module, slithering toward the *Coin* below them. The bulkhead shuddered beneath Iridian's boots. "Ah, fuck, pick up your . . . No, too late," said Chi. "We're getting caught in this stuff over here."

"Danail, isn't that spool mounted on a winch assembly that'll wind it back up?" Iridian asked.

"It can't do that without power!"

She winced at the panic rising in his voice. "All right, it's falling toward one of the holes in the bulkhead. As long as we get it wound up manually before—"

"What holes?"

This was likely the first time he'd ever been in a hab with a punctured hull, so far as the flying lab module could be called a hab. "We lost atmo, so keep your helmet sealed," she told him. "You're on canned O_2."

"What?"

Iridian sighed. "We're okay. This is why we wore the damned suits. We'll detach from the printer here, and then you'll climb up and wind the spool in while I get Chi and the LT untangled."

"How am I supposed to do that when I can't see anything not exactly in front of me?" Danail demanded.

"I'll get it, hang on," said Chi.

After a minute, something jabbed at the base of Iridian's neck. The impact padding wheezed as it deflated, giving Iridian full range of motion in her neck again. Chi swung under Iridian with one arm through her own mobile tie-down kit, and Iridian's breath hitched as the solidly built spacefarer crouched with both boots locked to the printer base on either side of Iridian's chest. Chi caught the edge of the printer beside Iridian's head to stabilize herself, counting on strong abs and firm thighs to keep her at the angle she wanted in opposition to the grav the *Coin* was generating.

Even secured for action, her breasts looked great at that angle. Iridian would be all kinds of lucky if she looked that good and moved that well in twenty years. *Nice,* she thought. And then, *Sorry, babe.*

No harm in looking. Adda must have gotten into the *Sabina's* security cam feed, which'd show this room's vid until the lab got out of the longhauler's network range. There had to be about a metric ton of batteries in this lab to power all the cams. That, or Iridian had said more over their comms than she'd meant to, again. Her face heated up.

Over Adda's reassurance, Chi said, "How's the head? Your suit thinks you're fine, but it'll wait till you're half dead to tell me about it."

"Neck aches." Iridian rotated her head inside the suit to test that, which turned her face and headlamp toward Tritheist.

It looked like half a klick of metal composite cable had piled against the lab's formerly exterior bulkhead, and it was still sliding past and around them on its way to the new "down." A coil of filament had looped around Tritheist's legs and several more were caught against his shoulder. The tie-down kit attached to the printer base was the only thing keeping him from joining the rest of the crap sliding toward the *Coin*.

The kit was not rated for an armored human plus a hundred kilos of metal cable. "That won't last," she said. "Chi, I'll look for a real strap-down station around here while you help Danail get that filament under control. Assuming we don't fall to our deaths, we want to make Captain Sloane's homecoming op look easy, yeah?" Chi grinned and used Iridian's shoulder for leverage while she climbed across the printer to the ladder on its side to help Danail.

"Scimitar to Captain Sloane, ITA cruiser is one hour and fifty minutes from you," drawled Scimitar's comms operator over the op channel in response to Captain Sloane's earlier request for an update. "Trajectory says the cruiser diverted off the Mars-Ceres reliable route. We are engaged and they're real interested, Captain."

"Understood," said Captain Sloane. "My thanks."

Sloane's ships, including the AI-controlled ones that prickled the hairs on the back of Iridian's neck just thinking about them, were almost in range of an ITA cruiser's longest range armaments. *You're scrambling the Sabina's comms, yeah?* she asked Adda.

Of course, Adda whispered. As long as she kept transmissions from the *Sabina* and the escorts from reaching the ITA cruiser intact, it'd be hard for the ITA to create a firing solution.

Iridian had her own problems to solve. The *Coin* had refrained from killing them with grav so far, but the printer filament still had to be secured with something solid between it and her. Sudden acceleration could break the mobile tie-down kits and drop everybody ten meters onto the torn deck, where the filament would slam into them at several times its current weight. A sudden stop would throw all the junk rolling around the lab at the humans' faces while they got crushed against the printer. Either way they'd have no grav at all once the *Coin* stopped accelerating.

A message in dark red text appeared in the upper center of her helmet display. *Tritheist: Get this thing the fuck off me and then lock yourself down going to lose grav.*

He'd come to the same conclusion. "Got it," said Iridian in syncopation to Chi's "Yes, sir" and Danail's "Ah, shit. Okay. Shit."

"At this point, I'd prefer less grav," Iridian said, and then added, "Not immediately! Later's fine," for whatever AI might be listening. She toed her boot locks off and eased herself out of the tie-down kit until she hung from the pieces that had held her shoulders against the printer base.

Directly above her loomed the printer itself. Although cooling molten metal covered large sections of the case's interior, about half of whatever it'd been making stuck to its printing platform, through some mechanism out of sight from her current angle. The rest of it sloped toward the side of the platform. The crew's headlamps cast its slime monster shadows on the bulkhead. The whole mess was still now, at least.

"How's the head?" Chi asked Danail over the local channel.

"My neck hurts," Danail groaned.

Chi grinned. "Damn, Sloane really does go for the best gear. I can't believe we've got four solid skulls in here."

Iridian swung herself from her tie-down kit to Chi's, on her way over to Tritheist. Tritheist's lips moved behind the helmet faceplate, but his leaf-shaped beard made lip-reading impossible. When she reached him, new red text appeared on her helmet display. *Tritheist: Strap down stations by interior door.*

"Damn." The interior bulkheads were the weakest. The one holding the printer was staying so still that she wanted to check the map after all of this was over to see if that was an exterior bulkhead after all. The door they'd come in through was behind her, at least three meters from the printer. It'd be an awkward, swinging leap to reach the stations, and if they missed they'd have a nasty fall onto workbenches and cabinets below them, or onto the *Coin*'s hullhook. Even if they did catch hold of the straps, it'd be hard as hell to put them on.

A length of filament fell between Iridian and Tritheist. She shoved it over him and away. "If the *Coin* puts much more pressure on that bulkhead, we might lose the whole thing," she said over the local channel.

Tritheist: Agreed.

The next coil she pushed off him freed his other arm, which he used to grip the top edge of the printer's base to keep from following the coils of filament down the slanting bulkhead. She double-checked his tie-down kit before unwrapping the rest of the filaments. He unlocked his boots from the bulkhead to help.

The filament she'd just pushed off him jerked upward. They both startled away from it. "Sorry, heads up," Chi said. "Danail found a manual winch. The filament's spooling up now."

"Turn it off!" Iridian kicked a coil of filament off her leg. The winch pulled it back over her. "We're tangled in—"

The whole lab jolted up and, for a fraction of a second, the printer dragged Iridian and Tritheist up with it. The straps across Tritheist's shoulders and chest snapped, followed by the ones across his hips and thighs. The halter strap Iridian had been hanging from slid out of her grip. Tools, clutter, and the unspooled filament plummeted toward the cracked deck, and Iridian and Tritheist fell with them.

Danail yelped over the local channel, and then Iridian, Tritheist, and about a quarter klick of unspooled metal filament hit the deck. Her armor soaked the impact except for her knees, which hit hard and lit warning lights on her HUD as a thick coil of filament fell across her shoulders and knocked her face first against the deck. On the side where the Coin's hullhook broke through, the deck silently tore all the way from the corner to the cracks in its center. Cabinets, filament, Iridian, and Tritheist spilled into the cold and the black, surrounded by hand tools and metal scrap.

The filament cable Iridian had almost freed herself from moments before became her lifeline, and she grabbed it with both hands. Pain flared in her shoulder joints when they stopped her fall. Gasping, she craned her aching neck to find Tritheist. He'd caught the filament too, several meters farther along than Iridian.

Something from the lab bounced off her shoulder blade. Her armor communicated the light impact through a pulse of tactile feedback while the object tumbled into the cold and the black. The knee joints were leaking atmo, but according to her HUD, it was a slow leak.

"What are you doing?" Chi shouted over the local channel, presumably at Danail. "Don't stop it now!"

"My arm—the suit's fraying," said Danail. "It was against the cable."

Tritheist: Both here pull us in flashed in red text on Iridian's faceplate. It was on the local channel, so Danail and Chi would've received it too.

As Iridian's eyes caught up to her brain, she breathed in through clenched teeth. The cable she clung to drifted away from the lab, straightening out from the bounce when it'd stopped Iridian's and Tritheist's fall. Beside them, the bulbous *Charon's Coin* flew past, scarred and monstrous and unlit among larger ships' running lights. The *Coin's* extended hullhooks clamped over the lab's exterior bulkhead and dug deep into the one that used to connect the lab to the *Sabina*. A cloud of small metal and plastic debris flickered along its flank, reflecting her headlamp's light.

Beyond and around the *Coin* flew more ships than she'd ever seen in one place outside stationspace, eerie and isolated this deep in the cold and the black. After the war, not even the Near Earth Union could afford to fly convoys this big. One of the escort ships was missing, but she accounted for the other three and at least six Oxia fighters less than twenty klicks from her. Oxia's ships had come in close to use the *Sabina* as a shield, she gathered. Since the escort had been optimized to deal with much more distant threats, that seemed to be working out for them.

They arched slowly around each other at such different angles and relative positions that she had to concentrate to maintain her current sense of direction. It was helpful to imagine the *Coin* pulling her up, because if she let go of the filament she'd fall into the cold and the black. She blinked to activate ship labels. Her HUD identified a ship occluding starlight in the distance as the missing escort ship. The Oxia fleet must've been talking on a fleet channel, because the op channel was silent.

Adda whispered in her ear, *An escort ship shot at the Coin. It had to speed up to get out of the way. Are you okay?*

Whatever hit the *Coin* was still out there. If the enemy was successful once, they'd take another shot. Worse, one side of her suit was heating up fast. The *Coin*'s engines were way too fucking close and getting closer as the filament slowly reeled her and Tritheist back into the lab. She'd seen a man die by standing too near this tug's engine outflow.

"Babe, can you get the *Coin* to turn off its engines?" Iridian asked over the command channel. "They're a lot more likely to kill us than the escort ships right now."

I'll try, but it really wants to leave that area, Adda whispered. *I'd say it's afraid, but . . .*

"But bots don't get scared and this is an oversized bot, damn it," Iridian muttered. Ships and bots and drones were all basically AI with different hulls. They followed orders given by somebody millions of klicks away who never had a clear idea of the situation in which those orders would be carried out. Stuff of nightmares, even when they weren't aware enough to countermand orders with unintelligible AI logic.

"You keep that thing reeling in," Chi told Danail on the local channel. "I'll fix your suit."

"Yeah, okay," said Danail. Iridian swore and gripped as tight as her gloves would ratchet down on it.

Something hit her boot. Tritheist had pulled himself to within a meter of her feet and was glaring impatiently. She lip-read the word before *Tritheist: Move* appeared on her helmet display. She hooked a leg around the cable—better to dislocate it than lose her grip and end up drifting through all that ship traffic—and started pulling the filament toward her.

Her suit slowly cooled and heat warnings from the arm and leg nearest to the *Coin* deactivated. AI really listened to Adda.

Danail said, "Hey, is grav falling?" over the local channel.

"Yeah," Iridian said.

"Keep pulling them in!" Chi added to Danail.

The ship might've been slowing, but the filament they clung to hadn't pulled taut yet. They were still drifting away from the lab almost as fast as they'd fallen out of it. When the line went taut, that'd change. "Lieutenant, hang on, the loose filament's almost spooled in." She wrapped a length of it around her arm.

The yank when the cable went taut came with a grinding, tearing pain in her already strained shoulder. A medical alert lit in her faceplate beside the reading on her dwindling O_2 supply. A small, new ache in her upper arm meant that the suit had injected her with something. The pain faded before she even had time to get her mind around it, and that scared the shit out of her, but at least the lab was approaching at a steady pace. "Chi, I thought you said you took the gods-damned drugs out of this suit!"

"Be advised, Copper is charging antipersonnel," someone on the op channel said in one breath, like mentioning that to the targeted personnel was a very late afterthought. "Rapier moving to intercept. Shifting channel encryption in five seconds . . . Mark." An Oxia ship oriented itself in Iridian's general direction.

Tritheist: Acknowledged appeared on her HUD, at the same time as Chi snapped, "I said I *didn't* take the painkiller out of your gods-damned combat armor, you masochistic meathead!" over the local channel.

The drug made Iridian's thoughts slow and slippery. The effect wasn't overwhelming, but it was enough to matter. "The Oxia ships know where we are, yeah?" she asked Adda. This was why she'd wanted the gods-damned narcotics out of her gods-damned auto-injecting suit. If she made it back to HQ, she'd take the cartridge out herself.

Half a meter of filament between her and Tritheist glowed red, then white, and oozed apart from the rest of the cable, soundlessly severed by an invisible and incredibly hot beam weapon. Tritheist's eyes went wide and the moment froze before Iridian's eyes, the severed cable still gripped in both of his armored fists. Her long, gasping breath felt and sounded like her last.

The moment broke. She freed her arms from the filament and left her leg wrapped in it to hang upside down, stretching to reach him. When she got her gloves around his arms at the armpits, she flung him at the break in the lab's wall-turned-deck in the most heavily weighted sit-up of her life. The mic probably put her wordless shout on the local channel.

At the rate the filament winch was pulling her by the leg, she almost beat him into the lab. She was half dragged through the hole in the printer lab with Tritheist less than a meter ahead of her. The thoroughly decluttered lab had never looked safer.

Danail was upside down in relation to her and perpendicular to the printer above them, cranking the filament spool with one hand while pushing on the printer housing for leverage with the other. One arm had about two patch-kits worth of patches along the outside of the forearm. Chi had her boots locked to the bulkhead beside the filament spool to put the finishing touches on her patching job.

Iridian pushed off the last intact panel on the deck she broke through as the filament pulled her into the lab. Once the lab bulkheads were between her and the escort ships, she took the time to shove the filament off her legs. In the low grav she sailed toward the printer base fast enough to expect a nasty crunch when she got there, but she deployed her shield and assumed a decent brace position before she hit, even though she had nothing but muscle resistance to brace with.

The impact rattled her teeth and tore her shoulder up a little more. It felt like tearing, and it should've hurt. When she got back to Rheasilvia, she'd also get her suit's shoulder joints reinforced and take out the painkiller cartridge.

Chi and Danail shouted variations of "Whoa!" Iridian twisted to orient her boots toward the printer base and used the magnets to pull herself to it. By the time she got her hands in what was left of her own tie-down kit so she could take some weight off her ankles in the gradually increasing grav, the three others were swearing and flailing in an armored mass of arms, legs, and filament.

The last of the filament coiled around Chi's leg and snapped tight against the spool with the leg at an awkward angle to the rest of her. She shrieked and, in her struggle to get free, flung Tritheist into the bulkhead beside the printer. He fell to the solid corner of the deck where it met the lab's exterior bulkhead and latched onto a cabinet with both feet and both gloves. Danail hit the bulkhead near the deck at a high enough speed to rebound off of it with an emphatic "Fuck!"

Chi was either laughing or crying as she pried her leg out of the filament spool. Iridian hung from the remains of her tie-down kit with adrenaline and painkiller coursing through her veins while Danail and Tritheist pulled themselves back toward the printer using handholds built into the bulkheads. As her brain gradually accepted that they'd all survived, Iridian found the situation damned funny too.

* * *

"So of course," Chi told the human bartender in Sloane's HQ on Vesta three days later, "that's when Captain Sloane calls in on the insertion team channel and says, 'Do you need assistance?' And the lieutenant says . . ." Chi, leg in a solid healing brace from ankle to hip, was laughing too hard to finish the sentence. The Vestan docs assured her she'd make a full recovery once the medical nannite culture finished its work, and Iridian's shoulder would too. Adda reached across Iridian to catch Chi's tipping wineglass before it spilled over the bar. "The lieutenant texts 'Iridian survived' while making this face like her coming back into the lab just killed him. After she saved his fucking ass!"

Danail looked bemused by the laughter ringing around the fancy gold-and-black-marbled VIP room of the club on HQ's street-level floor. Thanks to Vesta's twenty-four-hour schedule, the artificial lighting for the whole nightlife module made it feel like a quarter past midnight even though it was something like 06:30 station time. And the crew had a successful op to celebrate. They'd proved their worth and effectiveness to Oxia, which meant that Oxia would keep protecting them from the ITA, for now.

The time, Danail's beverage, and his lapful of a skinny club boy allowed in from the dance floor for being pretty and higher than hell might've added to his confusion. The club boy played with Danail's curly hair while batting stylized butterfly wing eyelashes at the dashing, injured medic next to him, never mind that the medic in question was old enough to be his grandmother.

Crew security stationed just outside the VIP bar had turned away five or ten of Sloane's fans already. News of their success had already gotten around the station and impressed the locals. Iridian's name had even come up in their protests as they were shooed away from the door.

Iridian took pity on the printer tech. "Captain Sloane and Tritheist made a bet, which they must've agreed on sometime after we stole the motherfucking module off the *Sabina* but before we fell out of it. By private text, I figure."

They all glanced over to the balcony table, visible through a strobing window projection in the wall facing the club. Rich and lovely people surrounded Sloane, Tritheist, and a beautiful stranger presenting as female and flaunting it with a plunging neckline that framed her tigereye quartz skin. The captain was talking to one of the big shots, but Tritheist and the woman plastered themselves against Sloane's sides and had eyes for no one else.

"Sloane is always betting on something." Chi smiled into her wine as she sipped. Without her helmet, her dark hair was short on the sides and lighter and taller on top and down the back. It was a softer look than Iridian had expected her to wear, somehow. "So, tell me true," Chi said. "The captain was really stuck on Barbary? Not just out there for the defensive value or whatever the official line was?"

Iridian paused with her own drink halfway to her lips. The captain had apparently said all there was to be said about it, officially, and Iridian sure as hell didn't want to mess up Sloane's version of events. The club boy and Danail were sitting right there, and she couldn't tell how much attention they were paying or how much they'd talk later. But Chi was a teammate. If they were working together, they should be honest with each other. "Yeah," Iridian said quietly enough that the club boy, at least, might not notice. "It was a hell of a fight, getting out of there."

"Thought so." Chi shook her head, still smiling. "Sloane spent too much time wheeling and dealing and making things work here on Vesta to ditch us. The captain before, Foster, would've done it, but not Sloane." Chi took another sip of wine and her smile slipped. "The captain bet on the wrong one with Rosehach, though. Fuckin' rat couldn't sell out to Oxia fast enough."

"Does Tritheist ever win those bets he and the captain make?"

Adda asked from Iridian's side. The words came out clearly, but considering how much she loved their new implants, speaking aloud was a good sign she was keeping up with Iridian on alcohol intake.

Iridian met Adda's gaze and grinned while she subvocalized, *Once, that I've seen. Like he'd know a winner if he saw one.* Adda's face went pink and her sip of overpriced but free-to-them beer ended up all over Iridian's chest. It was worth it to see that big, adorable smile.

The club boy peered back and forth between them through pupils blown wider than the VIP room's low lighting could explain. "So, you and her, huh?"

His accent was Jovian, the accent a hell of a lot of secessionist propaganda had been published in. Nobody'd played that anti-NEU crap in the years, and this guy was harmless—might've been too young to have fought, come to that—but the accent still made her jaw tense and her eyes narrow in a way that didn't fit with the celebration in progress. She pulled Adda's stool a few centimeters nearer to hers, despite her shoulder's painful protest. "Yeah. Me and her."

"Brawn and brains!" Chi crowed. "I like it." The club boy's hands on her back kept her on her stool.

And yeah, Iridian got by in the brains department, but she'd never have thought of taking the whole damned printer lab when moving the printer would've meant the ITA caught them or the escort tore up Oxia's ships. Even if she'd thought of it, she wouldn't have run the numbers to make sure it'd work before she did it. Somehow, Adda had.

"I stimulated . . . *Simulated* . . . Some sintuations. Oh my gods," Adda said, apparently in response to whatever Iridian had accidentally subvocalized.

"All right, mastermind, let's see if you can find your way to our suite from here." Iridian guided her wife—she wasn't tired of thinking that yet—to their personal corner of HQ.

* * *

Sloane's message alert on their suite's projection stage woke Iridian and Adda. According to the time stamp at the top of the stage display, they'd slept for about five hours.

"Liu Kong wants to meet you," the captain said. "With more context this time, I presume. Be in my conference room in an hour. Try to look . . ." One side of Sloane's mouth quirked up as Iridian forced both eyelids open while raising the blanket between their chests and the stage's cam. Adda covered her enormous yawn with both hands. "I'd request fearsome, but let's aim for competent, shall we?"

Sloane's figure disappeared from the projection stage, which cost more than Iridian's last year of college tuition. Comm software with automatic vid enabled by default was an evil invented by people who, presumably, had separate clothes just for sleeping. Iridian hadn't even checked to see if pajamas were among the free patterns in their suite's stocked and functional printer.

The whole suite was theirs, and it was more modern than any place Iridian had ever slept. Everything in sight was tintable, the lights had an option menu, the furniture was intact and made of more comfortable plastic composite than steel, and the cleaning bot in the closet actually worked. They'd printed a couple sets of casual clothes and they could decorate the suite, if they had the time. It didn't feel like home, yet, but it was the nicest temporary housing Iridian had ever been invited into. It was the kind of home Adda deserved.

Iridian winced as Adda slapped a saline hydration pack over the vein at Iridian's elbow, then applied one to her own. The first aid kit in the bathroom had been stocked when Iridian found it, with supplies that weren't expired and hadn't been tampered with. "I don't do fearsome," Adda grumbled. "I could do suspicious, maybe."

"You of him, or him of you?" Iridian chose Adda's outfit and set the pieces to brighter colors than Adda would've selected.

"Both." Adda tapped the tag on the pants to change the color to black but accepted the teal top as it was. Combined with the purple highlights in her sleep-styled red hair, she looked like a rock star's stage avatar. Iridian had to find something else to look at before she dragged Adda back to bed.

Adda was blushing, so some of that observation made it over their new comm system. Iridian grinned. "The combat test went well."

Very well, Adda whispered over their implanted connection.

Just like the isolated physicians on Barbary Station who'd inspired them to build their own implanted comms, Iridian and Adda met each other's eyes before subvocalizing. It'd be odd to hear her voice without seeing the accompanying facial movements when they were both in the same room. Iridian held her hand in the doorway to keep the door open while Adda wandered through, looking at her comp projection instead of where she was going.

The captain's conference room at HQ was several floors beneath the club. Rheasilvia Station followed typical spacefarer priorities for real estate. The most valuable locations had the least radiation exposure and the healthiest grav, which put the elite in defensible underground bunkers.

"Underground" wasn't much of an advantage on Vesta. Both

stations' residential mods were underground and spun to generate grav, keeping plenty of heavy elements between Vestans and the cold and the black. Modern projection technology being what it was, everyone had a view of whatever part of the galaxy struck their fancy while they stayed cancer-free to enjoy it. Station councilors, high-level Oxia personnel, and four or five semicelebrities squabbled over positions relative to the station's center with grav closest to one g.

Sloane's HQ was squarely in that desirable range. How fucking lucky were they?

We're here because of planning and hard work, Adda whispered over their implants.

Oops, Iridian thought at her, on purpose this time, and kissed her, grinning, in the middle of HQ. The security people, real people and not bots because Captain Sloane could afford them, found other things to look at. Adda and Iridian had never been inside a place this well furnished and fortified, let alone been invited to live there. And Sloane had already paid them for their part in the printer theft. "After we get out from under this megacorp to do things the way we want, we really will have it all."

At the conference room door, Iridian straightened her spine and brushed wrinkles out of her clothes. She glanced over at Adda. "Ready?"

Adda's face was set in the grim determination Iridian usually felt before a long college class or a rough flight. She nodded though, so Iridian led them in. Captain Sloane stood near the center of a black-tiled floor just large enough for a projector stage and six opulent-looking chairs. Tritheist, Pel, and anybody else who Sloane considered primary members of the crew were probably still asleep, and Iridian had to consciously decide not to feel bitter about that. A framed vat-grown crystal design in shades of red and orange decorated one wall, attributed in a corner of the piece to an artist from Albana Station on the other side of the 'ject.

The captain was already in conversation with the same well-dressed older man whose soldiers had taken Rosehach's body from the mine. The projector stage here portrayed Oxia CEO Liu Kong in more flattering light than the mobile one had. As she'd suspected, Tritheist wasn't present. It was odd for Captain Sloane to summon Iridian and Adda but not him. Either Sloane was letting him sleep in, or the captain had given him something more important to do. Iridian stood a few steps inside the conference room door beside a small bar, and Adda paused with her.

". . . ten ships to collect this one item," Liu Kong was saying. "The support costs alone will impact our profits for the quarter. I provided them when you asked for them because I assumed you required them to complete your task, but how do you justify your generous compensation, Captain?" Iridian hoped Liu Kong overlooked her eye contact and head twist toward the projector at the words "generous compensation." She'd spent too much time with next to no compensation to ignore people talking about opportunities to earn more.

Sloane glanced at her, because of course the captain noticed. "We could have met our objectives with fewer ships. Taken risks with your pilots and your printer and your grand design, whatever that may be. The source signatures were hidden, but trust me when I say that your employees would divulge their allegiance in the care of a damaged escort ship's crew, alone in the cold and the black. As it is, your ships are lightly damaged and no casualties will appear in either side's newsfeeds. I'm speaking to you now because nobody but me could direct such an operation to so clean a conclusion, Mr. Liu. Please continue to trust my expertise."

The CEO's nod indicated that Sloane had won a point there, almost in real time. He must've been under 50 million klicks away from Vesta, but what a rich guy like him was doing on or over the border of NEU space, Iridian couldn't guess.

Sloane turned halfway from the cam to extend a hand toward where Iridian and Adda were invited to stand. "You asked about my engineers. They're here." Iridian led the way to their mark and bowed as low as it took to be polite to a gods-damned CEO. Adda took her cue and did well enough not to be offensive. "Iridian Nassir and Adda Karpe. Unless there was a name change recently?" Captain Sloane raised an eyebrow.

"No, Captain, that's us," Iridian said. The Nassir name bought her more trust in pirate circles than Karpe would've, since her uncle had been in the business long enough to be known, if not respected. Adda kept hers as a reminder for anyone who met Pel that the weird AI whisperer was his big sister, and they'd have a lot more than a couple of pirates to tangle with if they messed with him.

The CEO looked them over. "Interesting. Young."

"Field operations favor youth." Sloane said it as if it were a regretful necessity, but the captain's mouth curled down at the corners. The captain clearly resented criticism of how the crew was run. It irritated Iridian too, especially coming from their unwanted megacorporate overlord.

"Well. Congratulations on your success. My people report that the PR800i is in excellent condition, despite its—unusual—recovery. I look forward to your performance in acquiring the lead scientist for our project."

"Sir, we don't do recruitment." Iridian glanced over at Sloane in case that was about to change, but this assignment was apparently unwelcome news to the captain as well.

"Neither does our candidate," said Liu Kong. "But it isn't up to ver, and I trust your captain's expertise." The CEO smiled unpleasantly when he refocused on Sloane. "Do whatever is required. At the end of vis time with you, I expect ver to sign our contract."

CHAPTER 7

Second implant network vulnerability identified

After the projection stage shut off, Captain Sloane waved Adda and Iridian out of the conference room. "We'll discuss this. . . operation this afternoon, in the VIP room. Tritheist will send a time." It seemed like all the captain was able to say without shouting, which Adda appreciated.

The VIP room was at the back of the club, and Sloane, Iridian, and Adda reached the headquarters building's club floor at about the same time that afternoon. Wide-eyed dancers moved themselves and their partners out of the captain's way. If anyone had been too drunk for that, the captain would probably have stomped right over them.

Despite the fact that it was barely after two p.m. locally, Adda subvocalized to Iridian, *Half the dance floor is full.* The dance floor bar was too, and Pel leaned on one end of it talking to women at least ten years older than him. Adda would check on him after they met with Sloane.

Iridian bit her lower lip for a second before replying, *Twenty-*

*four-hour schedule here. Vesta always has work for humans, or always
had in the beginning . . . Damn it, you can overthink this subvocal thing
if you're not careful.*

Worth it? Adda asked as they followed Sloane to a table in the
corner of the VIP lounge, which four inebriated individuals with
knives on their belts swiftly vacated. They all gave the captain an
abbreviated spacefarer's bow on their way out the door.

Beside her, Iridian nodded subtly as they settled at the table.
Their system was still transmitting more information than they
intended. Adda would have to find out if Pel's surgeon would let
her into the implant suite to adjust the settings. Since she and Iridian had made the implants themselves and gotten them installed
outside the NEU's medical records system, an appointment with
a hospital technician would get her fined and registered, at best.
The body modder who'd installed them was too creepy and too
distant to go back to.

The golden-skinned bartender, a human woman when the
AI bartenders in the dance floor bars worked just fine, was halfway to their table when Sloane typed an order into the table's
order pad with an air of despondency. The captain sent another
message by comp, then leaned back in the chair and deliberately
placed both hands on the table, like it was either that or overturn
it. "Kidnapping and coercion."

"Pardon?" Adda asked, at the same time Iridian asked, "Say
again?"

"The task set to us, despite Liu Kong's high-minded description, amounts to kidnapping the target and . . . *maintaining* ver
until ve signs an exclusive corporate contract with Oxia." Those
sounded like Liu Kong's words, not the captain's. The corporate
euphemism for "imprisonment" was disgusting.

Several epithets that didn't sound like English or Mandarin, except for *anally prolapsed mutant goat fucker,* whispered through Adda's ear implant from Iridian, without indication of which descriptors applied to the CEO and which applied to the goat. Adda made a note to add a broader translator to the implants' comms package.

"This I . . . We can't . . . We don't do this kind of job, Captain." Iridian was so rarely at a loss for words. Sloane sort of half smiled, half frowned at her. "You've got what, three hundred fighters just in this station? Don't we have enough people to throw Oxia off the 'ject?"

Despite Iridian's protests, Adda expected that she'd do it if Captain Sloane insisted. But there had to be ways in which this operation could be carried out without violence.

"Three hundred and fifty combat-trained individuals, as of last week," Sloane said, "and a number of specialists I could acquire on short notice." Adda noted the increase on her comp. "They, with sufficient financial arrangements, may be able to remove Oxia from Vesta. But as I confirmed during our previous operation, it would cost trillions to hire a fleet to match theirs."

When Sloane had been requesting ship after ship as reinforcements to combat the ITA and the *Ann Sabina*'s escort ships, the captain had been gauging fleet strength and organization. Adda was still looking for access to Oxia's off-site records repository, where Oxia must've hidden the detailed records of their fleet complement. Sloane's method of gathering information for the fleet strength estimate was less precise, but more expedient.

"We simply don't have that," Sloane continued. "Vestans would suffer under a siege, or a bombardment as Oxia ships targeted our headquarters with missiles from all over the solar system. Should we fail—"

Adda was so surprised that she interrupted the captain before

she could stop herself. "The NEU and ITA would allow Oxia to
attack an independent station?"

Sloane frowned. "The ITA would attempt to intervene, on the
grounds that my crew is a massive nuisance on the reliable routes,
which are their jurisdiction. They will find any excuse to oppose
us, especially since they feel that Oxia is a stabilizing addition
to this 'ject. Incentivizing them to reconsider requires conditions
which . . . I have not yet put in place."

"And the NEU has problems with us anyway, so I figure they'd
side with Oxia." Iridian sounded like she was sad about that, and
Adda couldn't blame her. She'd fought for the NEU against colonial
secessionists during the war. As an Earth native, people expected
Adda to support the NEU just as strongly. But the NEU had caused
most of the problems that provoked the secessionists, and it
hadn't protected her mother, who'd died in the prewar violence
when Adda and Pel were children. That didn't inspire her loyalty.

"The NEU will recall that Vesta was neutral territory until the
NEU occupied it. Even if the NEU had military presence to spare,
which they do not, they wouldn't station troops here. If they commit any forces, it will be for show. And as I was saying, should
we fail, I'd be forced to relinquish crew leadership to someone
more amenable to Oxia's desires, then killed to prevent me from
rivaling the new leadership. So, we will do as Liu Kong asks and
convince this scientist they've chosen to cooperate."

Only the ITA or NEU had a realistic chance of rivaling Oxia,
and coercive contracts were the only kind in use, even in the NEU.
Neither organization would expend the resources it'd take to stop
Oxia from contracting a pirate crew under duress. They'd help
enforce a megacorporate contract as a default position, unless
they just arrested everyone involved.

This was the first time Adda had considered the position of

the Vestan natives, although Sloane had obviously given them some thought. Did they enjoy living under Oxia? Had they enjoyed living under the pirates' rule before Oxia took over? What was possible, and what did they want? She'd have to do some research before she let herself believe that manipulating these two stations' political systems was anything other than selfish survivalism.

The song pounding through the dance floor speakers increased dramatically in volume, and its lyrics "I want control" underscored Sloane's point. The VIP room's door closed behind Tritheist, reducing the music's volume without eliminating the bassline entirely. "I thought you'd found a way out of the contract, Captain," the lieutenant said. They'd left a chair open next to Sloane, and he took it.

"I found a possible way," said Sloane. "Lawyers are reviewing it for hidden dangers, and several have already been revealed. It's amazing the trouble a broken megacorporate contract can cause. They're recognized more widely than any law. You should be wondering why you didn't have to sign one." The captain met Adda's and Iridian's eyes and raised an eyebrow slightly, asking without asking "Do you understand?"

Oh. Adda looked at the table instead of meeting the captain's gaze. *Sloane kept our names off the contract,* she clarified for Iridian, who had assumed her professional soldier expression instead of one Adda could read.

The whole crew could've been forced to sign. Instead Sloane had convinced Liu Kong that the captain was the only member who needed to be legally bound to the megacorporation. Sloane's agreements with Adda and Iridian were verbal, as were the captain's arrangements with Tritheist and the experts who Sloane dispatched on crew operations. Except for the security force who guarded Sloane's headquarters, everyone was paid by the job.

They could do whatever they wanted otherwise, as long as they dropped it when Sloane ordered them to.

If either party didn't want to deal with that, they went their separate ways. Megacorporate contracts only allowed the corporation to dissolve them, and if one ignored megacorporate orders, one could easily become unemployable in one's industry or "employed," sans enough of a salary to live on, for many more years than originally expected.

Iridian's expression twisted into one of defeat, or mild disgust, as she subvocalized, *Something else we owe the captain for. Free room and board, out of contract work that actually pays, and now this.* Aloud, she said, "Thank you, Captain. And where does that put Adda and me? I mean, so far as there is a crew, we're on it?"

Sloane blinked at her and seemed to refocus from watching something far away, as if both the switch in topics and questioning of their crew position were a surprise. "I wouldn't have offered you a home here otherwise. I'm not interested in maintaining four to six lovable misfits whom I'm expected to wait upon before each operation." The captain's tone had become one used to repeat a message delivered many times before. "To succeed, we must be flexible enough to take on opportunities when they arise and complete them expertly. If my first choice of experts isn't available, I'll find somebody else who can do the job. Thus, my crew is a network of capable individuals who, when they're not working for me, are welcome to do what they like. And yes, I've made arrangements that should make you more available than most to do what I need done. Does that answer your question?"

The fact that the captain had been patient and interested enough in their compliance to deliver that explanation was more informative than the explanation's content. "Yes, it does, Captain, thanks." Iridian still looked uncomfortable, probably from having requested the explanation or from accruing a larger perceived debt with her new boss. Either way, they still had an operation to plan.

Captain Sloane sighed heavily. "Yes. Well. Even though this is clearly not our usual venture, we can complete it successfully. Ms. Aku-Chavez will join us for medical supervision, and Ogir's available for reconnaissance. I see this as a simple abduction, although the encouragement to sign the contract will be . . . unpleasant. One of these individuals should put that stage behind us within forty-eight hours."

The captain rested one gold-gloved hand on the table's comp cradle. Two names and head-and-shoulder projections appeared on the tabletop. The figure on the left, labeled Enosh Jiménez, showed an older man of Spanish or Latin descent, tired or saddened by something off-cam. On the right was Cesta Rusnak, a white woman a bit older than Iridian with a crooked smile that made Adda feel hunted. She was familiar with the sensation, and it gave her chills.

Tritheist ordered a drink and scowled at the projections. "One's a psychopath, and the other would be better off if he were."

"True," Captain Sloane said. "They're excellent in certain roles."

Are we going along with this? Iridian demanded over her and Adda's implanted comms. *They'll torture ver, or fuck with vis brain, until ve signs a corporate contract. We should be finding a way to stop the Oxia fleet.*

Not necessarily. Which addressed all of Iridian's concerns at once, although their connection may not have communicated that. Adda's mental notes for improving their system were multiplying. "Has anybody just offered ver the contract?"

"You disagree with my assessment of the situation." Captain Sloane's confrontational tone made Adda freeze for an instant.

She'd have to persuade the captain. Which one did by pointing out how one's position also advanced an initiative the other
party cared about. What did Sloane care about? "Your crew has a
reputation for relatively humane treatment of targets." She spoke
slowly, working the details out as she talked. "I only found two
kidnappings attributed to you, and the Mars one was actually per-
petrated by an NEU counterinsurgency unit, as far as I can tell."

The captain smiled, the first since they'd met with Oxia's CEO.
"I wondered about that. Send me the evidence. But your point in
this case?"

"The direct approach will damage the crew's reputation." Adda
tapped at her comp to send the relevant documents. "Oxia avoided
blame for the printer theft by making sure all credit went to you.
That seems to be how they handle all of their less-legal activity,
so although I can't confirm it without access to their primary data
center, wherever that is, we have every reason to assume they'll
handle this . . . hiring issue the same way. If we make time to come
up with other options, I think we can do better."

Sloane frowned, probably realizing that by "We can do better"
she meant "I can." The captain nodded to Tritheist, who tapped at
the comp in his black glove until Adda's buzzed with a new message. "You have three days. Oxia will take that long to finalize their
employment contract for the target, and then we are expected to
execute it. We'll engage our expert, start surveillance, and . . . will
the *Casey* be available? She's ideal for this sort of thing."

"That's an unnecessary risk," Iridian said. "We can't count on
her—it—to do anything we ask."

Captain Sloane blinked at her for a second while Tritheist
swore. Adda would've delivered that news with a bit more pre-
amble, but Iridian had been dreading every trip with the intelligences for weeks. Another long journey in one might've been too

much for her to bear. "So you've been *lucky* with the shipboard AIs all this time?" Captain Sloane asked.

"They seem to be fixated on us," Adda said. "They cooperate when they want to. We know that they want the rest of humanity to assume that they're still zombie AI, but I believe they want more than that."

"We don't know why the *Casey's* helped us this far," Iridian agreed. "It has to have a reason. The awakened ones always do. It's what makes them dangerous."

Captain Sloane stared at them for a few seconds more, then burst out laughing. It sounded mentally unhealthy. "And here I was, thinking you ladies couldn't bluff worth a damn. My mistake." Adda was just starting to smile at how well the captain had taken the news when Sloane met her eyes, then Iridian's. "I won't make that mistake again. But we'll continue to take advantage of the AI's need for human occupancy as part of their cover, when you feel they can be counted upon."

Scrolling through operational information Tritheist sent to her comp, Adda passed a cam still of their target. Dr. Blaer Björn's bright blue eyes stopped Adda cold for a moment. No, she did not want to force this person to sign Oxia's exclusive corporate contract so that, in effect, she and Iridian didn't have to sign corporate contracts of their own.

Iridian continued her argument against asking for the *Casey's* help, as if she had any way to prevent the *Casey* from learning about their plans. Adda used her comp to call up a portal she'd created to track the awakened intelligences' activities. The *Coin* stayed within easy transmission range of Vesta, although the other two intelligences came and went.

And the *Casey* was expanding here, introducing parts of itself into the many zombie intelligences in Vesta's stations. It knew everything the zombie intelligences knew, could trace the information to its source, and was tracing it constantly. It would know everything about this mission already. It might have known ever since Sloane accessed it, or since some unwitting tech assembled the data on an Oxia server.

It had already decided whether and how to assist. Human preference would have little effect on what it did next.

* * *

Pel and Adda sat in a tiny exam room in Rheasilvia Station's Keawe-Affinity Hospital, in two seamless chairs that were flash-cleaned a hundred times a day. A nurse had administered eye drops and gave him a pill-size vital signs monitor to swallow. But until they started anesthesia, he could walk away. "It's not too late to cancel this procedure," Adda said.

Whether she wanted him to or not, the choice was his. "No," he said. "Seriously, quit talking about that, I'm freaked enough as it is."

"I'm jealous." Iridian was studying the meter-tall diagram of a pseudo-organic eye projected on the wall. "My comp's not even EMP-proof. Hell, the composite these things are made of is stronger than my skull."

"Counting on it," Pel said. "I used to get in fights all the time, you know. The new eyes have to be tough."

"You mean you used to get punched in the face all the time. That's not exactly a fight." Adda mentally replayed what she'd said and grimaced. That was how he'd been blinded in the first place, and here she was bringing it up again.

"Yeah, don't do that anymore," Iridian said to Pel in the same teasing tone, although she met Adda's eyes for a moment as she spoke.

"The shielding's good, but not that good." *Implants can do awful things when they break.* Iridian probably hadn't meant to tell Adda that part, because she still sounded cheerfully excited when she asked, "Do you think the doc would let us watch her put them in?"

"Oh, I've met her! She likes me. I'm sure she'll let you." Pel grinned. "She sounds hot. When you see her, you've gotta tell me if she is."

"I'll pass." Adda couldn't watch someone replace the eyes that had been looking to her like she knew everything since they were little brown beads in Pel's pink baby face. It made no sense to feel like he was losing something essential. The pseudo-organic eyes would do more for him than the originals ever could, even if the surgeon repaired them instead of . . . "I've got to add a few things to our comms project. And adjust settings. The implant unit's machines are better for it than ours."

She managed to finish the sentence before a sob shook her. This was an embarrassingly irrational reaction, which she hoped she could attribute to how little she'd slept during the action against the *Ann Sabina*. Pel had an amazing opportunity, with the money the three of them had earned on Sloane's crew, to become more than genetics made him. The procedure should be safe enough. Implanting the throat mic beside the blood vessels in Iridian's neck had been much more dangerous.

She startled when Pel bumped her arm in the course of reaching out to hug her. "I got this, Sissy. Even my therapist says I got this, and ve's more pessimistic than you are. The doctors know what they're doing. I'll be fine."

Iridian followed her to the implant calibration lab instead of watching Pel's operation. When Adda's worrying distracted her from the project despite the sharpsheet and a half she consumed to prevent that, Iridian asked questions about the comm system code Adda was analyzing in one of the implant unit's workspaces. The hospital workspace generators had so many user assistance functions that she felt like she was ordering a particularly compli- cated drink instead of fitting an expanded translation algorithm into software for implants already inside her head.

"You know what I just thought of?" The smile in Iridian's voice was contagious.

"What?"

"We could've had somebody else design this for us! We could've paid them to do it!"

Adda opened her mouth to remind Iridian how expensive that would be, then shut it. At the moment, they had that kind of money. "Let's get our families' debts paid before we start paying people to do things we can do ourselves, all right?"

"All right," Iridian said, but she was still laughing.

Adda kept having to stop to fend off automated, obvious threads of weak AI virus that wanted to share her work with unknown third parties. Maybe the doctors overlooked the intru- sive clutter and information theft, but Adda couldn't. After the fifth, she stopped work on the implant software to compose a rou- tine to throw out the foreign intelligences without her having to review them all personally.

Once she did that, she had some mental cycles left over for the Björn kidnapping problem. The abduction didn't seem like the place to start. It would be less traumatic for everyone involved if Björn was willing to leave vis job and take the Oxia one. There had to be some condition Sloane's crew might create to cause that.

But Björn was an astronomer in one of the best-respected university astronomy departments in the populated universe. The dossier Tritheist sent indicated that ve had flown prominent secessionists to and from Mars during the war. People stayed near places they fought for, even in a support capacity, and Oxia wanted Björn to work at a Vestan facility.

Vesta probably had different observation focuses than the Deimos observatory did, which might limit Björn's career, depending on vis area of interest. Ve already turned down this position and another on Ceres. Ve had no reason to take Oxia's offer, and plenty of reasons to stay in Martian orbit. Adda would have to do some more reading to learn how to change Björn's mind.

* * *

Uncounted time later, Iridian squeezed Adda's ankle where it rested on the ergonomic workspace bed. "Pel's in recovery now. They went ahead and did both eyes at once because they were both in shit shape and they didn't want his brain to repattern a bunch of stuff for one eye and then have to do it all again for two."

Adda watched the background processes whisk around her as golden leaves in wind until the saved confirmation appeared in the air before her. She stretched her virtual arms wide, enveloping clean blue text that she understood despite jumbled letter order, before sweeping her arms together and collapsing the virtual space with it. Her head ached fiercely, and her heart pounded too hard from one sharpsheet too many.

She scrambled out of the hospital workspace generator, which flashed behind her as its cleaning cycle started, and paused to let her blood get where it wanted to go instead of stumbling around while she was dizzy. Iridian rubbed Adda's back. Although Adda was careful with her dosage, she was grateful for Iridian's patience when Adda made mistakes and overdid it on chems. "Pel's okay?" Adda asked.

"Yeah." Iridian squinted and cocked her ear with the implanted earpiece. "Do you hear really faint static in yours?"

"It's our system updating. I think I fixed the transmittable range. And I expanded the translation package, and tweaked the encryption a bit."

Iridian wrapped an arm around Adda's waist. "Thanks. Hate to think the wrong people might be listening in. Or, you know, not people."

The awakened intelligences *were* listening. No encryption Adda could devise would stop them. But telling Iridian would just agitate her with no direction to point that agitation in, and it might make her stop using the implanted comms altogether. If the intelligences' eavesdropping became a problem, Adda would mention it.

* * *

"Right now, they hurt like fuck." Pel reached toward the bandages over his eyes. Adda caught his wrist and gently pushed it toward the hospital bed on which he sat. "Ow," he said, although the motion couldn't really have hurt him. "They say don't touch them for a while, but it feels like rubbing them would help."

"Do they . . . I mean, do they feel like they belong there?" Adda asked.

"Oh yeah, they feel like mine, all right," Pel said. "'Cause they *are* mine. The doctors could've grown new ones, but those might not've grown into the same exact shape. These were shaped off of the originals, minus the scar tissue. I don't even miss the old ones."

Her love for him felt like a tangible thing, swelling in her chest, pressing on her lungs. She gently pulled him into a hug. Important as putting the captain back in complete control of the crew was, Pel wasn't under any government's protection. That was up to Adda.

CHAPTER 8

AI assemblers delivered via aerosolized nannite culture

Adda went straight to their suite in Sloane's headquarters, where she reconnected to Sloane's crew's well-protected internal network and started what she expected to be a two-day research binge on Blaer Björn's life. There didn't seem to be room for Iridian to help with that, so she changed into workout clothes and left for the security personnel training rooms. Judging from the subvocalized comments that rattled around Iridian's head while she ran a virtual track with Sloane's security people, Adda wanted to know everything about the astronomer, not just the information that might enable a kidnapping.

The virtual track took Iridian and the security people through a densely built hab that seemed to be a condensed version of one of Rheasilvia Station's residential mods, maybe before its last major repair cycle. Rheasilvia wasn't a new station by anyone's estimate, but its residents had spent what it cost to keep up with modern hab safety standards. It was aging gracefully.

One of the HQ security company commanders who reported

to Sloane pushed her pace to approach Iridian, but she couldn't quite catch up. Iridian slowed until they were running side by side. "Bermudez," the lean femme with big hair and sharp eyes said. Iridian nodded at her. Although it'd been dark in the club during her first night on Vesta, she was fairly sure this was the woman who'd tackled Rosehach's supporter when the guy had threatened Sloane.

After another few steps, Bermudez grinned. "You like this shit?"

It took Iridian a second to interpret the statement through Bermudez's thick Ceres accent. "What? Running?" The others' footsteps faded as they fell farther behind. "Kind of addicted."

"Not me."

Iridian glanced at her as they dodged a tram crossing their virtual path. The crew security people showed Iridian an uncomfortable amount of deference, even during training. Under the deference some trusted her more than others, and she couldn't blame them. In a way, Rosehach's disrespect toward the crew, murderous habits, and megacorporate bootlicking had worked out well for Sloane. The captain, and by extension Iridian, was a very positive change in leadership. "Come up here for the competition?"

Bermudez panted through a grin that was a bit on the manic side. The run hadn't been that long by Iridian's standards, but it looked like Bermudez was already moving mostly on willpower. "Came up . . . to ask you . . . a question."

Iridian had already won the endurance competition on this run. She slowed and gave Bermudez a few steps to catch her breath. "What about?"

Bermudez dragged in a few more lungfuls of atmo. "Heard you made an impression. Kept everybody alive on the last job."

"Yeah." Iridian cheerfully made herself sound less winded than she felt. "That's not a question."

Laughing apparently threw off Bermudez's breathing pattern and it took her several more steps to return to it. It was good to find an officer with a sense of humor in this little army. "Question is: You really caught Tritheist falling out of a ship and pulled him back in?"

Iridian could've corrected her about what Tritheist fell out of, but she'd been running hard for forty-five minutes and the explanation felt like a waste of O_2. "Yeah. Seemed like the thing to do."

"And one other thing," Bermudez said. "Printer you stole. Heard it was making a bot when you took it. Self-repairing. Pseudo-organic. Collects material from the cold and the black, makes buoys for the Patchwork. That true?"

Bots repaired the buoy network, which people called the Patchwork because of its haphazard construction across borders to bring internet to all the big habs from Mercury to Uranus. She hadn't heard that bots were extending it too, but it seemed logical. "Oxia has the pattern now?"

"That's the rumor," said Bermudez.

"Huh. Been too focused on the new op to think it over. Could be." After a couple paces, Iridian added, "Hey, while we're asking questions, I've got one for you. How many of Sloane's crew are on Vesta now?"

Bermudez's brows furrowed and her fingers wiggled like she was counting on her hands. "About to have four hundred in sec. Don't know about experts. Must be at least a dozen here. Counting you and Karpe. Couple, ten more . . . in Albana."

"Thanks." Iridian had noted some new faces around HQ, and that'd be why. Now it was 400, not 350. Captain Sloane was hiring on more security and expecting trouble, maybe from Oxia, maybe from the ITA. Either way, that was a lot of new people for Iridian to meet.

Bermudez waved and dropped back. "Two for two!" she announced to the security people huffing and puffing behind Iridian. "Pay up!" The grumbling that followed suggested that Sloane's security people took their bets as seriously as the captain and Tritheist did.

It'd be interesting to see what Oxia did with a bot designed to build and place network buoys. For the trouble it took to get the printer for them, it'd better be something good.

* * *

After the run, Iridian went back to her suite to shower and drag Adda out of her workspace generator for dinner. Even outside the workspace, Adda obsessed about the next op. "Dr. Björn has habits," she commented as if she were talking about a colleague and not a stranger whose life they were about to ruin. "Undergraduate students avoid ver for assigning too much homework and ve's tolerated by faculty and staff who described ver as 'obsessed' and 'aloof.'"

"That sounds like nobody I know." Iridian nudged Adda's plate toward her, since she was staring at her bitter-smelling noodle and sauce meal instead of eating it. It was good that their next op wasn't upsetting Adda, and her detachment was probably some kind of defense mechanism that kept her from feeling the guilt that Iridian did, but it seemed like she ought to at least be angry about the situation.

Adda took two bites of noodles and talked around a third mouthful. "All of vis published work was on various astronomical phenomena's effects on space travel."

"So, not popular enough to get a grav apartment on Mangala Station, but making the university plenty of money by studying stuff people pay to know about," Iridian said. "Ve sounds like a hardass, but maybe signing on with Oxia will get ver paid what ve's worth."

Adda went quiet, which meant that something Iridian had said had sent her on a mental tangent. She let Adda follow whatever connected those two topics of conversation until Adda stopped eating again. Iridian prodded the bowl of noodles and, to get her on another topic that might be compatible with eating, asked, "Has Sloane been . . . I don't know. Acting strange, after the last op?"

"Strange?" Adda picked at the noodles and looked, predictably, surprised. Human behavior rarely caught her attention.

Iridian shrugged. "Something about the way the captain is while talking to us. It's different from the treatment Chi gets."

"Oh," Adda said, as if that answered the question. "Sloane trusts Chi completely. Us, not so much."

Iridian stared at her. "What do you mean, Sloane doesn't trust us? We've followed every order on the last op, which we were specifically fielded for, by the way. Hell, you basically ran it yourself, and you're running this one too."

"It looks that way." Adda still sounded distant, as if something in her head were more interesting than the conversation. "We're gaining a lot of attention with the people Sloane works with. And we're obviously Liu Kong's first choice of replacements if anything happens to the captain."

"Whoa, no, Tritheist is the next highest ranked." Iridian felt like the conversation had slipped out from under her. They relied on Captain Sloane for every level of security, from food and shelter to protection from two law enforcement agencies and counting. "Anyway, the captain doesn't need us the same way we need the positions here, but that doesn't mean Sloane doesn't trust us."

Adda had to be misreading the captain's intent. She wasn't good with people.

"Liu Kong knows that Tritheist lacks the skill range we have," Adda said. "And Chi doesn't make major decisions. On the *Ann Sabina*, we did. For the most part we do things the way Sloane would. But if we decided to do something different, Sloane would have a hard time stopping us."

Iridian sagged against the back of her chair. "We're not trying to take the crew away from Sloane."

"I've been saying that since the last battle on Barbary Station. The message is being interpreted as a move in a game I'm not playing." Adda finally made eye contact again. "If Sloane decides we're no longer worth the risk, there's a low-orbit Jupiter station. Sloane will know about it, but the planet's magnetosphere makes it digitally secure and it's well outside the captain's zone of influence. At least one crew is based there. They cause a lot of damage in populated areas, so they're not my first choice. I'm more interested in contacting one of the Saturnian crews. With what we've already accomplished, we could start over in any of those crews, if—"

"If what? Are we really talking about Captain Sloane betraying us?" Iridian shook her head. "That's called paranoia. It'll take more than veiled threats from a damned megacorporate CEO to make Sloane turn on us. The captain gives a fuck about the crew. That's part of why we chose Sloane's crew over the others, remember?"

Adda raised an eyebrow to indicate that of course she remembered, Iridian was being unreasonable, and the conversation was over. Usually Adda was the trusting one, and Iridian had to tell her how people really were. Maybe Adda had come a long way since they'd been out in the cold and the black, or maybe she saw something Iridian didn't.

CHAPTER 9

"What the attack means, to clarify for my colleagues across the solar system, is that Captain Sloane is back. And trust me, Sloane's powerful friends will make sure that the captain stays back. Vesta, thank all the gods you know and love for that."—Suhaila Al-Mudari, TAPnews correspondent

When Adda returned to her workspace, Casey's ebony figure stood in a doorway of white stone that opened onto an avenue of calm water. Despite Adda's best efforts to keep it out of her systems, it proved it was still watching her workspace activity by sending her all the information on where Dr. Björn had traveled in the past few years, along with the most likely related events at vis destinations. Apparently only family life changes and scientific conferences inspired ver to visit other 'jects. Which was convenient, because Sloane's crew was about to change a significant part of Dr. Björn's life.

But before she could do more work on that problem, she had to deal with Casey. "Who else do you spy on besides me?" Adda hadn't expected an answer to that question, although it would've been a nice surprise. Casey stared at her as the sun in the workspace set, bathing the water-bound city's stone and brick walls in amber and gold. The sapphire glints in Casey's eye sockets flashed like distant beacons.

Adda breathed in slowly and exhaled just as slowly, trying to clear the emotions that could interfere with her next question. "What do you want from me?"

"We need your help."

Adda already knew that. "To do what?" And there was the silence she'd expected.

She sent her notes to her comp and let herself drift gently into waking life. This workspace generator was the latest permanent installation model, with soothing gray-green fabric walls and a projected map of her and Iridian's suite on its ceiling. When she opened her eyes, its blue user icon showed her where in the suite she lay. After a long time in a workspace, the reminder helped ground her in the present. Sometimes she studied the map for several minutes before she moved, just in case it changed into birds and flew away. Workspaces were tricky like that.

She'd shuffled toward the kitchen to make coffee and read what Casey had found for her, but her comp buzzed to notify her about a message Pel had left while she worked. She played the audio on her way to the coffee machine. He was talking because he was bored, so she ignored most of it. At this distance, it was hard to tell how he really felt. She printed a lid for the coffee mug.

In the tram on the way to the hospital, she turned the implanted comm system on. After she talked to Pel, she'd change the mic and earpiece toggle settings so she could easily turn off the mic and keep listening. *I'm out of the workspace and I'm going to see Pel. Want to come?*

Just a sec. Iridian's words were quick and the signal was weak. Several minutes and a few epithets later, she subvocalized, *Yeah.*

Meet you there. Been training with Chi and some of Sloane's security detail. The captain's got about fifty armed people at HQ at all times. Actually more. They've got three shifts and they've been hiring. Did you know that?

I did not. That was logical. She'd noticed fit-looking people in practical, nondescript clothes—she was passing one now, on her way to the lobby—who loitered in the same parts of the building for hours. Apparently they worked for Sloane directly, like she and Iridian did, rather than contracting with the captain through a bigger company. Given the captain's insistence on complete control of everything relating to the crew, that was a logical choice.

They're good, Iridian subvocalized. *We ever get any personal security, we want people like them.*

Now was too early to be hiring bodyguards. Nobody did double takes or attempted extended eye contact with Adda on the way to the hospital, which proved that Vestans didn't know her on sight. In the hospital, she was the sister of the patient in room 482, but the room number did cause pointed glances among hospital personnel. Sloane must've had connections there.

In Pel's room, he caught her up on his online antics, hospital pranks (words she hoped to never hear together again), and the latest on the ZV Group soldiers and Martian refugees while she half listened to him and watched for Iridian. The restless speed of his conversation made her glad he was being discharged the next day.

"How are your eyes?" she asked him.

"Still hurt like twin sons of a bitch. The doctors turned the nerves way down and they'll put them back up gradually, because . . . I don't know, it's complicated and involves smelly liquid and needles. Gross. But the HUD is fun!"

"They hooked up your HUD already?" said Iridian from the doorway. She stomped over to hug him, letting her footsteps tell him where she was. "Lucky devil. I want a permanent HUD without a visor over my face."

"I know, right?" Pel grinned, which was not something Adda had been able to make him do. Then again, she hadn't talked about anything cheerful. "It's not the same as I remember seeing, but all the different features are awesome. I think they make little in-socket projectors for you visually limited people. Anyway, hi!"

Pel and Iridian started discussing Sloane's security training regimen as compared to the ZVs'. In addition to the new developments with the intelligences, Adda was still turning over the Björn problem. Everything she'd read about Dr. Björn indicated that ve was happy in vis current position, although not everybody at the university approved of vis performance.

How long does it take to get to Mars from here? Adda asked Iridian subvocally.

The background conversation stalled. "Leaving now?" Iridian asked aloud. "Weeks, babe. Although I guess if you can afford healthy grav you could do it in one week. Last time I checked, 'ject positions were way off for a sunward trip to anyplace worth visiting. It's not like crossing the street. Is this about Sloane's next op?"

"What are you . . . Oh, your implants, right. When're you gonna get me one of those telepathy hookups?" asked Pel. "Maybe you can make it go through my eyes? And where are you going?"

Adda's face flushed hot. Her plan for the venture still needed a lot of review for mistakes and oversights before it was ready to share. Why did Iridian say everything that went through her head? "Mars, but I don't have all the details together."

Iridian raised an eyebrow. "And I think this is all the socializing

some of us can handle for today. See you later, Pel." She wrapped
an arm around Adda's waist and guided her out the door and into
the sterile hallway, which was both embarrassing and deeply wel-
comed.

"Aw, you just got here!" Pel called after them. "Try sleeping
some night, Sissy, you look really tired."

One of the people they passed in the hall looked familiar.
Know her? Adda waited until Iridian caught her eye, then glanced
over at the woman.

One of Captain Sloane's security people, Iridian said. *One's assigned
to monitor all the cams in the hospital whenever Sloane's crew is being
treated there.*

"Practical." Even to her own ears, Adda sounded depressed. All
the ways she'd come up with to approach Dr. Björn had too many
contingencies that could fail and put ver in the hands of a torturer.

But Iridian laughed in the way that made the freckles on her
cheeks look like they were floating up toward her beautiful brown
eyes, and Adda couldn't help smiling along with her. "When I
heard the med team on Barbary Station saying one word every
five minutes, I thought they'd lost their gods-damned minds,"
Iridian said. "Now I see how that happens." Outside the hospital
doors, Iridian caught Adda's chin between her finger and thumb.
"You'll figure it out, and I won't let you kill yourself doing it."

"I hope so," Adda said.

"You will." Iridian kissed her gently. "I've seen you do it a thousand times."

Iridian waded into Rheasilvia Station's near-constant pedestrian traffic, towing Adda along behind her by the hand. Station
culture granted much less personal space than what Adda had
been used to on Earth. The current trend of touch-responsive
fashion meant that people's jackets turned bright, annoying

colors where she bumped into them. Each direction down the street looked as likely as the other, in terms of which way a tram stop might be. It was only a couple minutes from the hospital, but foot traffic blocked her view.

Iridian led her by the hand she wore her comp on, so she was already looking that direction when it buzzed against her skin to notify her of a new message. The first words flashed over the projection square in red text that clashed with her glove: *AegiSKADA is assembling in this server tank. It will look for you as its supervisor when it can.*

Iridian tugged her arm, because Adda had stopped walking. Adda stepped after her mechanically. Somebody thumped her arm with an elbow, which flared bright green in her peripheral vision. "Iri," Adda said, but she spoke too quietly to be heard on the crowded street.

Not long after she and Iridian had discovered that the *Casey Mira Mira's* AI copilot was awakened, an emergency had forced Iridian to make a deal with Casey: one trip across a space station for one copy of AegiSKADA's code, including its development records to date. Giving an awakened intelligence the essence of a zombie one that'd held people captive on Barbary Station for years had been a difficult choice, but it was that or stay trapped themselves. Iridian had provided Casey with the full record of AegiSKADA's development. That was the last they'd heard from Casey about it, until now.

"You can read that sitting down too," said Iridian. Adda looked up from her comp to find that she'd followed Iridian onto one of the public trams and was standing in front of the seats on one end. A woman with a baby on her lap sat at the other end of the compartment, which had room for four to six people. Adda sat where Iridian indicated, and Iridian's lovely smile faded to worry when she saw Adda's expression. "What's wrong?"

Adda tilted her gloved hand so that Iridian could read the projected message. Iridian's whole body went rigid against Adda's and she grabbed the metal pole at the corner of their seat like she wanted to break it off the tram and use it as a weapon. By the time Iridian was finished swearing at a higher than usual pitch and volume, the woman with the baby was anxiously watching the tram's projection count down seconds until the next stop.

Iridian's reaction was an improvement over the one from her last unpleasant revelation about AegiSKADA. This was just another of many dangerous situations involving AI that she and Adda had been in proximity to recently, and it wasn't even as bad as the first one. This time, AegiSKADA was unarmed.

"Okay." Iridian shut her eyes tight for a moment, and when she opened them her expression was a little calmer. "We can handle this. We're much better equipped now. How do we disable it this time?"

"When it contacts me, it will tell me where it is, and I'll deactivate it," Adda said, making the decision as she spoke. Fascinating as AegiSKADA was, its design was too flawed to split her attention between supervising it, watching the awakened intelligences, and planning crew operations. Her divided attention could cause mistakes that'd get somebody hurt.

After she shut it down, she'd have to devote a large part of somebody's automated resources to scanning for newly installed copies across all of the crew tanks. Casey could always install it elsewhere, and could have ever since Iridian gave it a copy of AegiSKADA's code. That was the risk they'd taken when they upheld their end of the deal. The company that owned AegiSKADA's original learning algorithm would have installed other versions of it in other stations and habitats too. Adda felt responsible for the version that might have records of all that it had gotten away with on Barbary Station.

"It'll just let you shut it down?" Iridian asked, too loud for the small tramcar. "People died doing that." The baby made a mewling noise, probably because its mother was holding it to her so tightly.

AegiSKADA, while unsupervised, had killed well over a hundred people, including Iridian's friend Si Po. And those were just the deaths Adda had evidence of. It still amazed her how often people forgot that they were surrounded by safer intelligences of varying strengths every day, unnoticed due to proper supervision. An intelligence was almost certainly coordinating the tram system they sat in, and Iridian, who hated cooperating with AIs, hadn't hesitated to step inside.

Adda switched to subvocalization in an effort to calm their fellow tram passengers. *When it killed Si Po, I wasn't its supervisor. I could've deactivated it before we left, if we'd had any interest in leaving it in an unsupervised state if it got reactivated. We'd have had a much harder time getting off of Barbary Station without it. And while we're on this subject, without Casey the ITA would've arrested us on Barbary. After I became AegiSKADA's supervisor, exactly how did it hurt any of us?*

Instead of answering the rhetorical question, Iridian put her arms around Adda and pulled her against her chest, so hard that Adda's shoulder must've been digging into Iridian's collarbone. "What in all hells did the *Casey* do this for?"

The message disappeared from Adda's hand. A new one read *These can help you with AegiSKADA.* A long string of associated vids and articles followed. It would take hours for Adda to process them all individually, or most of one to get the gist of all of them at once in a workspace.

"We don't need your . . . its . . . help!" Iridian said. The tram arrived at the next stop and the woman with the baby ran out without looking back.

Reactivating AegiSKADA was an odd thing for Casey to do. Presuming that Casey stayed near Sloane's crew to keep them safe, after the fashion that made sense to it. The only change in their level of safety that Adda was aware of was their assignment to coerce Dr. Björn into signing an Oxia contract. There could be other dangers that Casey chose not to make Adda aware of, but at the moment it wasn't obvious how a station defense intelligence would help convince an astronomer to change employers.

If Adda asked Casey the right way, it might tell her its reasoning, but she wouldn't count on it explaining at all, or in a way that she understood. Very few awakened intelligences had ever been asked to explain themselves to humans. She and Casey communicated better than all the literature on the subject led her to expect, unsettling and unpredictable though those communications were. It was exhilarating, but Adda wouldn't claim to understand it.

"It'll take a while for AegiSKADA to assemble itself," Adda said. "Hours. There's no point in looking for it before then."

Iridian still held her tight, and rested her chin on Adda's head. "Tell me when you're going in after it. I want to be there to help."

"I'll be in a workspace generator," Adda reminded her.

"Then I want to stand outside and make sure you don't go into shock or something," said Iridian. "You can't trust anything with these AIs."

CHAPTER 10

Albana and Rheasilvia systems integrated:
120

Three days later, Adda still hadn't heard from AegiSKADA, and another dangerous guest was arriving. Iridian wore her new armored enviro suit to escort the welcoming committee into Captain Sloane's terminal. The new suit sealed against just about anything, and it'd been hand-assembled by an actual human armorer. Its segmented solid polymer matrix composite was matte black, matching Sloane's aesthetic, with red articulated plating over the knuckles and one red cable wound through the mass of cabling that connected the helmet to the suit's exoskeletal structure.

The armor fit so well that just standing around on guard duty in Sloane's terminal made Iridian jittery. She wanted to run, or throw crates up to the cargo bots rolling along their ceiling tracks in the window projection a terminal down from Sloane's. When Iridian started pacing in long, low-grav strides, Tritheist glared in his faceplate's projection from the other side of the homeward door to Sloane's terminal at the docks. Captain Sloane had insisted on their being armed with less lethal weaponry as they had been on the *Sabina*, and Iridian had opted for a short-range stun gun while Tritheist carried a chemical irritant. Both kept their weapons in easy reach.

The captain and Adda stood between the middle pair of decorative columns. The light at Adda's heels indicated that her boots' magnets were on to stabilize her in Vesta's natural grav, outside the spinning station interior. The dock designator projected over the terminal passthrough read ARRIVAL AT 15:40: KATJA DEMETRIA.

"Your contract still looks solid, correct?" Adda asked.

"It does." Captain Sloane had never sounded so tired. "And Oxia is watching for missteps. Don't accept compensation from any source other than me, by the way; that's a breach we just identified yesterday. They must have expected to catch us with that clause, if no other. To the ITA and the megacorporations, all contract breaches are the same severity."

"All right," said Adda.

"If this endeavor goes well, we'll enjoy a degree of flexibility. Liu Kong has to trust me to some extent, or I wouldn't be able to do what he needs done."

"And we'll be run off the station if we fail?" Iridian asked.

Captain Sloane glowered at the closed dockside door. "Nobody will run me off Vesta." Iridian and Tritheist exchanged something almost like a smile. They'd back the captain up, but it'd be a shitshow. Oxia's fleet and contracted army were big enough to crush anybody without similar numbers. Sloane's new security hires and a lot of tech might hold HQ long enough to evac to a safer location, at least.

The projection above the passthrough door changed to ARRIVING NOW: KATJA DEMETRIA. Tritheist abandoned the homeward door to the main terminal and the rest of the station and approached the sealed passthrough. Iridian tugged on her gun and shield.

They'd come free if she needed them. The big barrel required for the weapon's less lethal ammo could catch on her suit's hip joint, and she hadn't practiced the modified draw action enough. It felt awkward as all hells.

Captain Sloane turned to Adda. "We have a very limited window, a week at most, in which our guest will operate in top form, so logistics must take that time frame into account. I'd be interested in your ideas on how we might keep him under control until he's needed."

Iridian tensed at the rising rumble and tremble in the floor as the ship docked outside. The only things Sloane had said so far about the new man was that he could be violent, was usually armed, and needed watching. "How dangerous is he?"

"To himself, very."

The designator above the door updated to AT PASSTHROUGH: KATJA DEMETRIA. Iridian removed the shield from its hook between her shoulder blades. She was, possibly, falling in love with the new armor.

The passthrough door opened to admit a man who might have been in his sixties, judging by his steady stride and solid build, or his eighties, judging by the deep creases in his brown, life-worn face set in a stoic frown. His silver hair still bore a few streaks of black and he wore no armor, although his coat was cut in a vaguely military style. One sleeve bore an NEU insignia with circles that symbolized Earth in blue, its moon in white, and its three nearest planets in brown, orange, and red.

The man drew a very small plastic pistol from his coat pocket, without taking his eyes off Captain Sloane.

"Hello, Jiménez." Tritheist's voice was surprisingly soft, for him. His short-range chemical spray was pointed directly at the new arrival's eyes.

Jiménez flinched and swept the pistol up to aim at Tritheist's chest. The side of the passthrough must've hidden Tritheist from Jiménez's view. Jiménez's hand shook so badly that if he fired, he might miss a target a meter away.

A bullet that small could ricochet, either off Tritheist's armor or the steel wall. Dock hulls were tough, but Adda and Captain Sloane were in light armor that left their arms and heads exposed. Iridian approached with steps as quiet and slow as the armor and grav allowed. Her shield'd make a snapping sound and a big visual effect if she deployed it. That might surprise him enough to fire. She left it collapsed in her hand.

"Thank you for coming," Captain Sloane said. "I wouldn't have called you if anyone else could have done it."

Jiménez looked from Tritheist to Iridian to Sloane. He pocketed his weapon. Iridian deployed her shield, just in case, and he startled at the sound before refocusing on Sloane. "I didn't want to come."

"I know." Captain Sloane held out one hand in the direction of the main terminal doorway. "We have a place prepared as you prefer for tonight. Our target is required to arrive on Vesta within the month, so you'll be traveling to meet ver on Deimos, in the morning."

"And until then?" Jiménez's accent pegged him as NEU, but his utility-focused clothing, at least some of which would seal against vac, was pure spacefarer. He sounded a bit desperate, and the lost look in his eyes was growing more pronounced.

"Try to relax." Tritheist walked beside Jiménez at an angle where he could blast the man in the face with whatever chemicals were in his gun without hitting Sloane, Adda, or Iridian.

Jiménez shook his head. "I don't deserve to."

"We also have several of your preferred chems in your room,

of course." Captain Sloane opened the tram door. "Which will be well guarded."

"Thank you," Jiménez said humbly.

* * *

In the elevated bar at the club in HQ, Iridian stated the obvious. "That's not the psychopath you mentioned when you were discussing options for getting Björn to sign."

"It's the other one," Tritheist grumbled over a beer. "The martyr."

"He has the skills we need, but he'll begin deteriorating very soon," Captain Sloane said. "Adda, your impressions?"

"He's suffering from some subset of depression, isn't he?" She sounded unsure, but that was Iridian's guess too, even though she'd only met him an hour ago. "Why hasn't he been treated? I don't like leaving him alone like that."

"He's well guarded, as I told him," said Captain Sloane. "They're there to contain him as well as protect him. As to why he hasn't been treated, he claims that he doesn't deserve to feel better. It's part of his process, you see."

What kind of gods-damned shit is that? Do they know how depression fucking works? Iridian subvocalized instead of saying to the officers. Adda gave her a worried glance, which meant that Iridian's anger was showing on her face whether she spoke aloud or not. "He has to feel bad to torture people, and torturing people makes him feel bad? Why are we perpetuating that, let alone giving him somebody we're trying to keep alive?"

"Torture is such a blunt instrument," Sloane said. "It's not his initial approach. He does cause a certain amount of trauma in the course of his work. His subjects emerge from their time with him permanently changed. Some are pathologically paranoid afterward, as an example, or catatonic. And he is extremely consistent about achieving the desired results. Liu Kong asked for a signature and Dr. Björn's presence on Vesta. If that's all Dr. Björn is capable of providing, so be it."

So Sloane won't cure Jiménez because he's useful *while he's sick.* During the war, Iridian would've understood that, and the risk to the professor's brain, too. Everyone's options were limited, time was always scarce, and the stakes were always high. But it'd been three years since Recognition, when the NEU officially recognized the colonial governments' sovereignty, and Sloane had the resources to find a better option. *Babe, we have to talk this over later. I'm not sure I can leave him like that.*

It's hard to treat somebody who refuses treatment, Adda replied. Aloud, but still quietly, she said, "I have something else in mind." Everybody turned toward her, looking as surprised to hear her speak as Iridian was. "When I have everything arranged, ve should sign with Oxia willingly, which means we can avoid delivering an, um, catatonic subject." Iridian gave Adda a small smile of encouragement. Doing the absolute minimum for a coercive boss was one thing, but it'd be cruel to mess up somebody else's head just to make the job easier for herself.

Captain Sloane raised both eyebrows and accepted a drink from the delivery platform that rose from the center of the table. "I want details before you spend the funds."

"Of course." Adda stood and took the lift down to the dance floor. Iridian bowed their farewell to Captain Sloane before following.

Adda stood nearby when Iridian stepped off the lift, so Iridian spun her into an intimate dance step that ended with the two of them pressed together, with Iridian's back to a wall. "So you *are* working out something better. I was afraid you'd let Sloane's 'only way to be sure' shit intimidate you."

Adda smiled up at her, eyes flashing in a strobing overhead light. "I'm thinking of it as an intellectual exercise. It's a good one, actually. Lots of new factors. I'm going to make this work without hurting ver." If anybody could find a way, Adda could. What they'd do to the rest of Björn's life . . . that was bad enough.

But this was what they'd committed to, working for Oxia. No point in brooding while Adda was already making the best of the shit situation. Iridian batted her long eyelashes so she could watch Adda's cheeks redden in the strobe lights. "Protective looks really good on you, babe."

Adda's whole focus was on Iridian now, in a way it hadn't often been since they'd arrived on Vesta, and she let Iridian raise her chin to kiss her. Tomorrow Adda would start balancing of all of those new factors and wouldn't have time for romance. For now, the music was good, and Iridian had her own plans to set in motion that afternoon.

* * *

Even with the mind-boggling funds to maintain healthy grav for the duration of the trip, it'd take about six days for Sloane's crew to reach Deimos. If there was heavy traffic on the Martian reliable routes, they'd spend most of another day docking. Iridian had double-checked and confirmed Adda's assessment that the only way to meet Oxia's deadline was to launch as soon as they could and coordinate the op en route.

And they'd be on their own. Oxia wasn't sending a fleet this time, and as Sloane told them, "Between Roschach's greed and Oxia Corporation's airtight seal over Vesta, the crew is involved in too many unfortunate situations for me to leave the 'ject."

On a wall projection behind the captain, a scrolling head-line read, *Sloane's crew implicated in contaminated water scandal in Rheasilvia Station's Lim Sang Jiyon residential module.* Oxia Corporation had been using the crew's network of experts to perpetrate a wide range of illegal business practices, and Sloane was spending a lot of time personally extricating crew resources from assignments that the captain couldn't bear to be associated with.

Although Iridian and Adda would be the nominal lead operators, or kidnappers in this case, they'd have some support. A surveillance team was already in place on and around Deimos, shadowing their target. Sloane insisted that they bring Tritheist and Jiménez, and Adda wanted Chi along in case her plans failed to come together and somebody got hurt. That many people couldn't travel comfortably in the *Casey* or covertly in the *Apparition*, which had a radar signature that screamed "rebuilt NEU warship." Instead they'd be traveling in a passenger ship out of Sloane's database of experts.

On launch day, Iridian reached the docks in as good a mood as she could have been, given the circumstances. "It's about gods-damned time we took a ride without having to wonder if the ship's going where we think it is." Without an awakened intelligence at the helm, they'd finally be working with a human pilot.

Although Adda kept up with Iridian while walking to the terminal where they'd meet the new pilot, she was focused on her comp. Iridian lowered her head and quietly asked, "Have you heard from AegiSKADA?"

Adda glanced at Iridian, then went back to whatever was on her comp. "Yes, earlier today, but it hasn't been able to describe its location well enough for me to find it so far."

Iridian hated that it was back, creeping around yet another station and fucking with Adda like it had before. Since Adda already knew that Iridian hated it, she stopped herself from repeating that fact. "Talking's a start, but you know how sneaky it is. Is there anything I can do to help you shut it down?"

Adda shook her head, still looking at her comp. "If I think of something, I'll ask you for it."

When they reached the terminal, Iridian paused for a few breaths to refocus on the op. Whatever AegiSKADA was doing, it could keep doing it on Vesta while she and Adda flew away from it. That was a hell of a lot better than Barbary. She approached the terminal door and triggered the motion sensor to open it.

Sloane's chosen professional walked toward them with the inhumanly precise and uniform gait of someone who'd had one or both legs replaced with pseudo-organics. Vestan's low grav heightened the effect. He grinned up at Iridian from behind a bushy, dark red beard and met her gaze with wide-set eyes that held far too much cheer for how early in the morning they were leaving. Every stitch of the pilot's clothes would seal against vac.

After exchanging bows, the pilot held out a copper-toned hand toward the passthrough, palm up. The dock designator over the exterior door reported AT PASSTHROUGH: *Mayhem.* "Hi, hello! I'm Gavran, the owner and operator Gavran. Crew's here, been here. Be nice to have the doctor. Safer with medical."

Kuiper native, Iridian commented to Adda, then said, "Hi, thanks, nice meeting you," to Gavran.

Accent? It felt like Adda was shouting the word in her head. Iridian would have to fiddle with her amp during the trip.

That, and his name is "Gavran the owner/operator." There're max two people named Gavran in his home hab and they yet DNA tests before they hook up, so that's all the differentiation he needs. If he knew his family's name, he wouldn't use it, especially not this far from home. Iridian walked into the passthrough with one hand on the shield hanging collapsed at her hip and the other waving Adda back a few paces behind her. *The Kuiper Belt colonies sat out the war. By the time their ships got far enough sunward to make a difference, it would've been over.*

Adda nodded like that meant something to her, and maybe it did. Her Earther family never had a choice about getting involved in the war. All Iridian knew was that she didn't have to watch her back as closely with a Kuiper pilot.

The *Mayhem*'s main cabin had blue and black thrust-resistant passenger couches for four and bedding for the same, with a closed-off bridge like the *Apparition*'s but with much softer surface coverings. The meticulous sunsim lighting already matched Vestan local time. Somebody would be stuck in the residential cabin during docking maneuvers and sleeping in the main cabin, but that wouldn't be such a bad thing. Kuiper colonists micromanaged enviro, so the cabin felt more comfortable than the terminal in the docks. Sturdy wall, floor, and ceiling handholds were backlit with yellow light instead of blending into the surfaces the way non-Kuiper designers preferred.

Chi and Jiménez sat across from each other in the main cabin's passenger couches, not speaking. Chi stood when she noticed Iridian and Adda, though Jiménez stayed where he was. "Hey, good seeing you," Chi said to Iridian and Adda. She glanced over her shoulder at Jiménez, who stared intently at a wall. "Can I talk to you a minute? Privatelike?"

"Sure." Iridian yawned wide and followed Chi up a ladder built into the wall that went through the ceiling and floor, leaving Adda and Jiménez together. The leg Chi had broken in the *Sabina*'s printer lab must've healed cleanly in the intervening week, since the healing brace was off and she put the same weight on it as she put on the uninjured leg.

Telling Chi about Jiménez's . . . impending mental breakdown, Iridian thought at Adda on the way. Chi would've read Sloane's briefing, but the captain had been vague about Jiménez's mental state during the planning stage. Iridian wouldn't be surprised if there had been important gaps in the op briefing Chi received too.

Do Kuiper Belt colonists always repeat themselves? Adda asked subvocally. *This pilot's done it with every sentence and it's getting annoying.*

I forget which colonies do and which don't, Iridian replied the same way. *Signals break up out there. You'll get used to it.*

Chi took the news about their psychotic new crewmember well. She actually looked more annoyed with Tritheist, who arrived while everybody was strapped down for launch and scowled around at all of them. "Captain Sloane told me to work with you, trust you people. I don't, but I can, get me?"

"Yes, sir." Iridian's mouth twitched at the corners, because it wanted to smile and that'd provoke Sloane's lieutenant into some unnecessary authority display. Ops went a lot more smoothly when everybody involved could tolerate one another, and they needed this op to succeed. Sloane and the very small army on Vesta would be the first victims of Oxia's wrath if the crew blew the op. When nobody else had anything to add, Tritheist stomped into one of the residential cabins and strapped into a bunk.

"This shouldn't be complicated," Adda said while Gavran extricated the *Mayhem* from Rheasilvia Station's docks. "By the time we arrive, the professor I'm working with will have received evidence of damaging criminal charges against Dr. Björn, to be delivered to vis superiors. We've seen Björn fly vis ship once or twice a month during periods of stress. We'll intercept ver once ve leaves

Mars's immediate space. One ship and a small crew for emergencies should be ideal."

"Then why," Gavran asked over a speaker from the bridge, "is another ship on our route? The second ship, on the identical route. Why that?"

"What's its name?" Adda asked.

"It's *Charon's Coin*, the second ship is called," said Gavran. "A tug. A tug has no reason to leave stationspace, most times."

Iridian swallowed hard and her fists clenched around the passenger couch armrests. They weren't far outside of stationspace yet, but it'd definitely be odd to see tugs this far out with no emergency to respond to. This was the second op that damned AI in the *Coin* had followed them on without asking.

"It wants to help stop Dr. Björn's ship, I think," said Adda.

"No extra details. None," said Gavran over the ship's comms, while Iridian said, "Fuck that, and how the hell do you know what it wants?" in person to Adda. The *Coin* didn't talk to anybody. If Adda had gotten it talking somehow, then who knew what weird shit it could be saying to her?

Helping us is the only logical reason it would come, Adda said over their implanted comms. *It's possible that the* Coin *still feels the need to receive orders before it acts.*

Not our orders, obviously, Iridian replied. The others could've taken her aggravated sigh as a response to her apparently unanswered question. *You didn't tell it to come, did you?*

No, Adda subvocalized. Her eyebrows quirked like she was wondering why Iridian had to ask. *It's interesting that it's here now, and Captain Sloane isn't.*

By interesting do you mean really bad? Iridian asked her. *Because that's what I'm seeing here.*

Its presence implies that it's interested in us specifically, and not

Captain Sloane. Maybe Casey ordered it to help you, because it owes you for . . . what you brought it. Meaning the copy of Barbary Station's security AI, which the *Casey* had promptly restored somewhere on Vesta.

"But who's in that ship?" Chi asked.

Iridian's fist clenched on the collapsed shield at her belt. *The Casey thought hauling me around in exchange for AegiSKADA's code was a fair trade at the time. Or at least, I assumed it did. What if it didn't mean 'just this one trip?'*

"A friend," Adda said aloud, apparently in response to Chi's question.

"A friend who needs to fuck off," said Iridian.

Adda muttered something at her comp. Seconds later, the *whir*-CLANK of ship-to-ship connectors locking down shook the *Mayhem*, jolting everyone against their harnesses. Thumps reverberated through the *Mayhem*'s sides. Grav started dropping so fast Iridian felt it. The *Coin* was stopping them in place.

Iridian's heart rate kicked up in symmetrical response. "What is this?" Gavran demanded from the *Mayhem*'s bridge. "What is your friend doing?"

"Karpe, back it off," Tritheist demanded from the residential cabin he'd strapped down in. Adda kept muttering to her comp. Her arms drifted out in front of her in the decreasing grav.

"This is putting a hell of a lot of strain on the hull, babe." If Iridian had interpreted the situation correctly, the *Coin* had locked onto the *Mayhem* using its standardized tug hookups and the massive hullhooks that'd punched a hole in the lab they took off the *Ann Sabina*. Now that it had a solid grip on the *Mayhem*, the *Coin* was using its powerful engines to pull against the *Mayhem*'s, and the *Coin* was winning, dragging the *Mayhem* backward and slowing its acceleration.

The Coin's engines could stop a much larger runaway ship, if the stopped ship could withstand that kind of pressure on the hull and tug connectors. If the hull was too weak it'd fracture at the attachment points. As far as she could tell from her admittedly uninformed position outside the bridge, Gavran was trying to force the Mayhem out of the Coin's grasp, futile an effort though that was, and making the hull strain that much worse.

Nobody on the Mayhem was wearing an enviro suit, and their armor was crated up in the second-floor storage area. The passenger couches they were strapped into would deploy a lid and seal if the cabin lost pressure due to, say, multiple hull breaches caused by an overly aggressive AI tugboat copilot. Each couch carried about thirty minutes of O_2, according to the safety info that scrolled over the armrests.

Adda was still muttering. "Also," Iridian said a bit louder, in case the Coin or another awakened AI were eavesdropping, "it's got to look strange to any ITA reps floating around here and stationsec. One of Sloane's ships getting assaulted by another of Sloane's ships? We'll get gawkers, and somebody's bound to ask what the hell the Coin's blocking traffic on this route for."

Adda's intense, inaudible conversation through her comp was starting to piss Iridian off. All that subvocalization probably meant that Adda was talking to AIs without a filter again. She communicated with them more effectively from a workspace, and the workspace software protected her from the manipulative fuckery that AIs did to human minds. When she wasn't in a workspace she was supposed to use a digital intermediary to communicate with AIs, but Iridian had no way to tell if she was using it now.

"Damn, I'm about ready to ask that pilot myself." Chi's knuckles were white on her armrests, but she was also visually checking harnesses and watching for trouble. Iridian appreciated not having to worry about her panicking in the cold and the black.

Beside her, Jiménez had shut his eyes, not tightly like he was scared but peacefully, like he was ready to die. As unhealthy as the old guy looked standing up, he'd look about the same in a coffin. That "eternal rest" bullshit people talked about at funerals would've been an improvement on Jiménez.

The ship shuddered around them and Gavran said, "Thank you, whoever freed us, many thanks." Acceleration ramped up until they were approaching healthy grav and back on track.

"Karpe, what the hell was that?" Tritheist shouted.

Adda winced and opened her eyes to glance around at the other passengers watching her. "I don't know."

She sounded appropriately worried, but it wasn't a topic she'd discuss in public. *Not even any guesses?* Iridian asked her. *Now would be a great time.*

When I say I don't know, I mean I don't know. Adda gave Iridian the disgusted look that she only deployed when someone she trusted second-guessed her. *They're awakened intelligences capable of unimaginable forethought and complex decision-making. If I had multiple networked zombie intelligences dedicated to analyzing the Barbary intelligences' experiences and behavior, and nothing else to do with my time, then I might expect to gain a clue as to their decision-making process. I do not have that network and I have more immediate problems to solve. So, for a fourth time, I don't know.* Adda returned her attention to her comp.

Chi settled back into her seat and touched the inner corner of her eyebrow to project some text in front of her eyes. "Pilots. Who knows why they do anything." Not many soldiers would get implants that near their brains. Maybe it was different for field medics, who might be able to fix something that broke inside them. Or maybe Chi was just a bit crazy.

She seemed content to leave the topic alone, but Jiménez was watching Adda with an intensity that made Iridian want to distract him before he engaged her in some creepy old-guy conversation. "Hey, Jiménez." The man turned his eyes toward her without moving his head. "What'll you do once we hit healthy grav? It's a long fucking trip, and you're not spending it staring at my wife."

"Your . . . oh." Jiménez focused on his boots, looking more sad than fearful. Chi snorted and scrolled text over her eyes.

Adda still wore the twisted wire ring that Iridian had made for her. Even on her left hand, that could be a mixed message. Iridian was asking around to find a well-regarded Vestan artist to replace her own ring with a subcutaneous glowing tattoo. Maybe Adda'd go for that too, although she hadn't take Iridian up on any of her tattoo ideas so far. There were other ways of broadcasting one's relationship status than wearing jewelry, anyway. Some people had HUDs for that.

Iridian inhaled to hammer her point through Jiménez's deranged skull, but Adda subvocalized, *Could you please leave him alone? You're distracting me.*

"What are you working on?" she asked Adda instead.

"Following up on something I read."

Iridian took her own turn staring at Adda, whose lips had turned down into a cute pout of concentration. Usually she had a lot more to say about her projects. Chi was grinning at something only she could see, and Jiménez hadn't moved. *You're not worried about what they think of whatever you're studying, are you? Chi won't care, and Jiménez's opinion is worthless.*

"'Blaer' is probably derived from 'Blær,' with the ligature between the A and the E, one of the first Icelandic genderless names. If Dr. Björn grew up in the Earth version of that culture, that'd make vis reactions easier to predict in some ways."

What a thing to worry about discussing in front of a medic and a monster. Adda could be painfully self-conscious. "Maybe so, maybe not," Iridian said. "Names are catching out here. You get one pop love story about someone named Asia, suddenly two hundred thousand babies are named Asia and half of them won't see the place on a map outside of history class."

"I saw a vid about that," Chi said. "Got two neighbor kids in my mod named Asia."

"Hmm," said Adda. It wasn't her "here's why I thought that" noise, or "here's where you're wrong" or "I thought of five potential solutions while you were finishing that sentence." Perhaps her search for AegiSKADA was going poorly, or perhaps she was anxious about something else.

She was running her first op on her own, Tritheist notwithstanding, while a persistent killer tugboat followed them around. That was enough to worry anyone.

CHAPTER 11

Direct system processes relay established between the NEU *Free and Clear* and rescue tug WS *Charon's Coin*

"Adda, get Chi," Iridian yelled from the *Mayhem*'s bathroom. She sounded like she did when she was hurt, but not too badly. What she could've done to herself in the bathroom took Adda longer to list than it took her to find the medic in the main cabin.

Chi grabbed a small backpack from her bunk in the residential cabin and followed Iridian's voice to the ship's only bathroom. She stopped in the doorway, looking at the floor. "Ah, shit. Help me roll him onto his side. What's his blood type?"

"No," Jiménez murmured. "Don't."

"Great, you're breathing. Now shut up." Chi crouched in the doorway and applied thin, disposable gloves, giving Adda a clear glimpse over her and Iridian to where Jiménez lay against the shower wall in a puddle of vomit and blood.

"Tried again?" Tritheist peered over Adda's shoulder and into the bathroom. "Damn. Captain Sloane said we had a week or two before this started, and he only made it two days. I didn't really want to win this bet."

"He did that to himself?" Adda asked. Chi affixed a device over Jiménez's mouth while Iridian held him still.

Tritheist walked a couple meters into the main cabin and Adda followed. The medical device probably did something gross and messy anyway. "Yeah, he always finds a way. Sloane won't even let him work a job unless he brings a gun that'll lock up when he points it at himself, and then somebody has to watch him all the time."

"That's horrible," said Adda.

Tritheist grinned unpleasantly and tapped something into his comp. "The universe would be better off without him. But Sloane paid him, Sloane wants him here, and Sloane wants him to keep breathing, so we're going to make that happen." A new message alert buzzed against Adda's hand. "That doesn't mean I'm going to feel sorry for the bastard." Jiménez retched, and Tritheist turned back toward the bathroom. "Aku-Chavez, is he going to make it three more days till we can hit a station clinic?"

"I think so, sir," Chi called back. "We should get him to the clinic first thing, though."

Adda's comp buzzed against her skin a second time, notifying her of a message from Tritheist. It opened a time-lapsed vid with the time and date ticking away in white text in the corner. Restrained at a table, the naked person whom Jiménez was talking to looked like a teenager, even from the back and above due to the cam's position. Jiménez talked and paced for a while and then walked out under the cam, touching something on the wall on the way out that raised the light level and made the kid at the table flinch.

He came back at different times of day and night, paced around and talked for maybe fifteen minutes, then left. Sometimes he brought food. Twice he walked in and beat the kid with a baton of some kind, with alarming vigor, for minutes on end. After four days of that, the kid said something that made Jiménez smile, an exceptionally fleeting experience on the time-lapsed vid. He left, and other people came to free and clean up the victim. When the vid ended, Adda breathed a relieved sigh.

In the bathroom behind her, Jiménez groaned and coughed.

Perhaps he'd become trapped in a situation in which he was good at what he did, in a universe that manipulated him into doing it again and again. It happened to experts all the time. But he could have refused as soon as he saw the kid at the table, or earlier, when his employers told him what they wanted done. Even if he'd been forced into it himself, he should have said no. There were worse things to die for.

But maybe that's what he'd just been trying to do. He was mentally unstable, and he'd have to be, to do what he did. Perhaps this was the only refusal he thought would work. Adda couldn't entirely despise him for that. But she was more committed than ever to making sure that he was never alone with Dr. Björn.

* * *

Adda spent the rest of the trip the way she'd spent the first two days: in her portable workspace generator, tracking the Barbary intelligences. She was following four of them now. Despite what she'd implied to Iridian during hushed conversations in their cabin in the Mayhem, she had yet to shut AegiSKADA down.

It'd contacted her a few days before they left Rheasilvia Station, with a source address of a pseudo-organic tank inside Captain Sloane's headquarters. It'd also offered her a way to bloodlessly prove to Dr. Björn that vis future lay with Oxia, not with the University of Mars. Using AegiSKADA's connections to various records

and justice databases allowed her to create believable false accusations of the kind that'd make Dr. Björn's continued on-campus
presence intolerable, for the professor and vis departmental
leadership.

Adda had done most of the preparatory work, and the technical aspects were finished in hours with AegiSKADA's assistance.
Using her digital intermediary, she ordered the intelligence to
run all of its decisions and processes past her. Only limited and
well-camouflaged messages from it would exit Sloane's headquarters building.

Most important, AegiSKADA had passed every test she'd ever
heard of for confirming that it was still in its zombie state. An
awakened intelligence could learn to pass them, but she'd found
no evidence of AegiSKADA breaking the boundaries she'd set for
it. And she had essentially infinite applications for a zombie intelligence that had already adapted to work with her.

She hadn't told Iridian yet. The massive fight that would
cause would make for a deeply unpleasant trip in close quarters
with coworkers for most of a week. So AegiSKADA, Casey, and the
Apparition were still on Vesta, AegiSKADA in a partitioned-off section of Sloane's crew servers, the other two in their ships, and
Iridian only knew about the two awakened ones. The *Coin* sent no
response to her questions about why it had followed the *Mayhem*
to Mars.

In the window projected over the closed door to the bridge,
Mars appeared as an orange dot. It swelled to an almost alarming
size in comparison with Vesta, as the *Mayhem* approached and
angled toward the orbiting docks. Mangala Station looked like a
metal pinecone hovering upside down above the dry expanse of
orange sand and rock on the planet below, with ships adhered to
almost every part of the station's surface. Blue and green lights

glinted all around the station, marking guidance buoys that helped ships dock. Even though Adda was physically closer to Earth than she'd been in over a year, the view made her birthplace feel farther away than ever.

When the *Mayhem* docked at Mars's orbiting station, the *Coin* did too. It stayed there while the humans rode a shuttle from Mangala Station to Deimos. Adda sent her intermediary to it with the message to "Stay away from the *Mayhem*'s intelligence." The digital intermediary had been in use more often than not, lately, because with all of these intelligences in and out of her systems, influence was a real threat.

The *Coin* sent no reply.

* * *

"Holy hell, were the freshmen always this young?" Iridian held Adda's hand and looked at University of Mars students in colorful, dust-resistant clothes and goggles like the ones she, Adda, and Tritheist wore. Dust billowed up with each step on the Deimos campus's magnetized path across a gently sloping commons area between buildings. Most students ignored the metal and glided across the open ground in long, slow leaps ending in small dust fountains when they landed.

It hadn't been that long since she and Iridian had been on a college campus together, but a lot had happened to them since then. Between the goggles and the anti-dust jackets, it was hard for Adda to tell students' ages.

"Let's find your guy and get out of here," Tritheist said. "We're on a lot of cams and mics right now." Only the three of them would be, since Chi was on the *Mayhem* to stop Jiménez from another attempt on his own life. He was feeling well enough to refuse a hospital visit, or at least he was an hour ago when Adda had left the ship.

The Deimos astronomy and astrophysics campus of the University of Mars was under a large, but not enormous, atmosphere containment bubble. The transparent dome had a comprehensive system for clearing dust off its surface, but it was worth the expense to contain pressure and shield occupants from radiation, space debris, and EMP damage from malfunctioning ships approaching Mars's orbital station for repair.

Only a few lab buildings and the observatory, Adda's current destination, were maintained in atmosphere. The university didn't generate Earthlike gravity on Deimos, so nobody stayed there long. Low gravity increased the novelty value for students. Adda was enjoying the dim natural light, after months spent far from the sun.

"Dr. Wakefield is supposed to meet us in his office," she said. "I'm not sure where that is from here."

The meeting was at his request, because he had that kind of leverage in their arrangement. Nobody else was positioned and motivated to deliver the evidence against Dr. Björn the way he was, and he knew it. She didn't doubt his willingness to help make Dr. Björn's professional life miserable, although she had concerns about his abilities. It was still less damaging than Jiménez's method.

She'd downloaded a map of the campus before they left Vesta, but the departmental labels on it didn't match the ones discussed in more recent documents about the place, which meant it was out of date. Finding Dr. Wakefield's office would be particularly difficult if moving around continued to be such a struggle. When she jumped she came down eventually, but in the meantime she got in the way of people walking the metal paths in magnetized boots and people who knew how to get around in barely there gravity.

Iridian was among the latter. She somehow managed to stay near the ground most of the time without turning her boots' magnets on. "What's Wakefield a doctor of?" she asked.

"Astronomy, same as Dr. Björn." Adda carefully rotated on her toes to look around. The four buildings had no signs.

Iridian followed her gaze and laughed. "Oh wow, Pel would kick all our asses here once his new eyes are calibrated. I think all the signage is digital. We're supposed to connect our goggles to the local network."

I expected them to connect automatically. Adda flagged down four haggard-looking older students bounding over the moon's graybrown surface, got instructions for signing into the network as a guest so she didn't have to waste time breaking in, and set off again. *Gods, I hope that's the only mistake I made.*

You fixed it in two minutes like you always do, Iridian said over their connection. *We always figure it out.*

The building they needed wasn't the observatory itself, but the one next to it. "He's not even important enough to get an office in his own department's building?" Iridian asked as they entered the building's airlock. A sign projected onto the airlock's interior wall had a picture of university-branded goggles and said, KEEP GOGGLES ON UNTIL AIRLOCK CYCLE IS COMPLETE in English, Russian, Mandarin Chinese, Japanese, and Hindi.

"Ooh, dust vac!" Iridian said. "I love these."

After the outer doors closed, large vacuums roared to life. Adda jumped, both at the noise and at the sense of being at the center of a small tornado. Even the grated airlock floor pulled air from beneath her, which helped Adda stay upright in the low gravity. Iridian shouted over the vacuums, "These suck particulates out of the atmo before the hab filters have to deal with them. Great design." The dust explained why enough people wore goggles that a goggles-only signage system made sense.

Adda clicked her magnetized boots to a higher strength. They really were mostly free of Deimos's brownish-gray dust. Iridian adjusted her own generally downward drift by pushing off the low ceiling with her fingertips.

The vacuums turned off and the inner door opened on a maze of twisty beige passages, all alike. Door numbers were printed into the doors themselves, each one sticking out a few centimeters on small pegs and backlit with LEDs. The doors nearest the airlock were 101 and 102, but down the hall and around a corner beyond them lay 401 and 403, with no sign of 402. A hallway branched off in another direction with numbers in the six hundreds. Dr. Wakefield's office was 305. "Oh, honestly." Adda sighed.

While Iridian and Tritheist tried to watch all of the hallways simultaneously, Adda found, bought, downloaded, and cleaned grayware off a program to connect her comp's cam to the college's network. When she entered the building and room numbers and pointed the cam in front of her, a bright blue line appeared in the goggles' display. The line followed the hallway and turned at one of the intersections.

"I wonder," Adda said as they walked along the blue line in her goggles, "if the intelligences are personally interested in one of us?"

"Or they know us well enough to manipulate us better than they can manipulate the rest of humanity," Iridian said.

"Still on mics," Tritheist grumbled. He pointed at one of the small black-cased cam nodes near the ceiling, which definitely had room for a mic or two.

"Yep, those AIs you're developing sure are interesting." Iridian's louder-than-normal voice bounced around the hallway full of closed doors. The nearest was numbered in the 300s.

A door down the hallway opened to reveal a man around Adda's age and Iridian's stature. He wore a shirt with SPACE POTATO in simplified Chinese beneath a picture of Mars's other moon, Phobos. The moon on the shirt rotated, pausing in positions in which it most resembled a root vegetable. "Hey, could you keep it down? The AI lab isn't even at this campus, so if you're looking for that, you're way off."

The open door behind him was numbered 305. "Dr. Wakefield?" Adda accidentally communicated her incredulity with the question. Iridian huffed a quiet laugh.

"Naw." The student dragged his olive-toned hand through one of the three sections that his black hair was separated into. The swath of it he'd just combed with his fingers stood straight out from his head. "He's here, though. Hang on." The student disappeared into the room. Tritheist pushed past Iridian and Adda to go after him.

Rude. Adda took off her goggles and put them in a jacket pocket. Iridian just shrugged and followed the men, so Adda went in as well.

A high desk and one of the older ergonomic stool/chairs that propped one up while standing were the center of a freeze-frame explosion of charts and colorized images of astronomical phenomena projected onto or above every flat surface. The lights above the doorway were on, but the rest of the room's lights were off, making the projected images more vivid.

A houseplant in a pot bolted to the wall dangled limp vines over the edge of a pseudo-organic tank bigger than the *Casey's*, lit from its interior in a red and blue-green spiral. The comp that thing was attached to probably did excellent analysis work. The stale coffee stench permeating the room was so strong Adda was surprised she hadn't smelled it in the hall.

The student in the Phobos shirt kept glancing over his shoulder at Tritheist. "Dr. Wakefield, some people are here to see you."

A workspace generator, the installed kind instead of the mobile kind Adda used, rustled in a corner of the lab. "Who?" A man demanded imperiously from inside the generator.

"Well that's familiar." Iridian poked Adda in the ribs, making her jump. Adda was too busy envying the generator setup to defend herself. It was older than the one in her suite at Sloane's headquarters, but it'd be convenient to have on the *Casey*.

Iri, am I thinking about Casey a lot? Adda asked over her implants. The intelligence was millions of kilometers away on Vesta, watching over AegiSKADA, the intelligence she should really be worrying about.

Yeah, and you should be, Iridian replied. *The Casey's fucking terrifying, and you don't want to forget about it. If we leave it alone long enough, it'll try assembling AegiSKADA again.*

While Iridian was subvocalizing that, Tritheist was saying, "Adda Karpe ring any bells?"

The generator had been emitting a low hum, which Adda hadn't noticed until it wound down and went silent. The tent-flap doors spread and disgorged a white man in jeans and a coffee-stained semiformal shirt. He turned bloodshot eyes on his three visitors, looking less distinguished than tired in his advancing years. "You're bigger than I expected," he said to Tritheist.

Tritheist pointed a thumb over his shoulder at Adda. She gave Dr. Wakefield her best midlevel spacers' bow, for meeting someone for the first time when neither of them were more famous or powerful. Iridian's lips turned down at the corners, like Adda had bowed at the wrong depth or with bad posture. She had no idea how to recover from that. "Adda Karpe, on behalf of Sloane's crew."

"That I know." He barely bowed at all. "You going to transfer the money to the account now? The number's . . . Bee!" Adda startled and looked for the insect, but the student with the space potato shirt reappeared beside them instead. "Get that account number I wrote down and stuck . . . somewhere."

"Yeah, boss," said the student apparently named Bee. He walked slowly away from the generator in a series of arcs across the lab, peering at each projected note.

"Where is the evidence package you're sending?" Adda asked Dr. Wakefield. After employing the most dangerous zombie intelligence she was aware of to pull that profile together, she couldn't stand the idea of him losing it.

"In my comp, obviously," he said. At least he hadn't put it on some solid-state medium she'd have to keep track of. "I'll send it just as soon as that idiot finds the number so you can pay me."

The student seemed pleasant enough, and Dr. Wakefield had annoyed Adda since the first time she'd encountered him, in an anonymized community for University of Mars faculty. His insistence on being paid in person was especially aggravating and unnecessary. Adda started to ask Casey to find the account number, but by the time the intelligence received a request sent from Mars to Vesta, the student would have found it. And anyway, there were more practical, safer ways to get the number than asking Casey for it. *Maybe I'm really not sleeping enough,* she thought.

"So they'll give me the department, after ve's gone?" Dr. Wakefield crossed his arms and kept looking at Adda like he expected her to know.

"That's the plan," she said.

Sloane's crew was paying Dr. Wakefield for delivering the criminal record that AegiSKADA had compiled and seeded throughout multiple source databases. Dr. Wakefield was a reputable source, and the potential for departmental leadership inspired him to persuade the university of the veracity of Dr. Björn's history of corruption and white-collar crime that had "come to light." It'd been the least complicated, least expensive, nonviolent way to make it impossible for Dr. Björn to keep vis position at the Deimos observatory. She had no intention of guaranteeing Dr. Wakefield a departmental leadership position, but that was what he wanted to hear.

"Good. It's about damned time, is what it is." Dr. Wakefield looked around the lab, faintly embarrassed. "Bee!"

"One more quadrant to search," the student called from a patch of shadows between projected displays.

"Worthless, lazy gob," Dr. Wakefield grumbled. "What's your interest, anyway? It's a strange thing to hire somebody to do."

"Ve slept with my wife," said Iridian. Somehow she turned the amusement clearly visible in that squint of her eyes into an angry growl. Her goggles enhanced the effect. Adda almost felt sorry for the man. "While she was a student here."

"Really," said Dr. Wakefield. "That is interesting. I mean, terrible." He'd have that bit of gossip all over the campus within an hour of them catching the Deimos shuttle back to Mangala Station.

Dr. Björn deserved to keep the dream position ve'd already earned, but keeping Sloane on the right side of Oxia seemed to be the only way for the crew to get out from under them. Oxia needed the astronomer badly enough that ve might have some negotiating power, once ve decided to join. And whatever ve did at the University of Mars had to be similar, because Oxia had asked for this scientist in particular.

"Please don't mention any of this to Dr. Björn," Adda said. "That will only complicate things."

"Oh, of course, not a word." Something was off about the way Dr. Wakefield said it. He was probably just distracted, searching a patch of wall that the student had already searched for his account number.

The student appeared from behind the pseudo-organic tank, clutching a slip of analog paper rather than a projector. "Here, boss."

Dr. Wakefield snatched the paper out of Bee's hand and offered it, much more politely, to Tritheist. Tritheist frowned and passed it to Adda. She'd already set up a shortcut for the money transfer, so once she entered the account information, another subvocalized word set the transfer through various proxies in motion.

"All right," Dr. Wakefield said. "I have an appointment with the deans. If you'll excuse me . . ." He walked them to the office door and left, whistling.

Bee stared down the hall after him. "I've never seen him that happy." Adda hadn't gotten the impression that Dr. Wakefield was happy at all. He hadn't even smiled.

"He ought to be," said Tritheist. "He's about to get promoted."

Discussing the details with random passers-by seemed unwise. "We need to get back," Adda said. The ship ID for the *Charon's Coin* was still active on Mangala Station, according to the traffic control system she'd had AegiSKADA access and seed with monitoring software. The ship they came on, the *Mayhem*, was still there too. The *Coin's* intelligence was capable of capturing Dr. Björn on its own, but she couldn't trust it to keep ver safe.

Also, she wanted to check on AegiSKADA again. She'd only skimmed her monitoring feed on its activity in the past hour, and her alert setup wasn't perfect. If she didn't read the activity feed carefully, she could miss something that'd put the people on Vesta in danger. She didn't fully understand AegiSKADA's priorities, and she couldn't explain why the *Coin* had followed Sloane's crew to Mars. She needed more information.

Speaking of which . . . Adda turned to Bee. "What does Dr.

Wakefield's schedule look like for the rest of the day? I want to . . . um . . . invite him to lunch?" This was her second time zone of the day, and there was no relationship between the one on the *Mayhem* and the one on Deimos. The campus's interior lighting was set to either morning or afternoon.

"Lemme look." Bee went back into Dr. Wakefield's lab and Adda and Tritheist followed, while Iridian watched the hallway outside. Bee started a new projection over the desk and flipped through it with his whole hand. "Huh. He's free for the next couple hours. Guess he got the wrong time for that dean's meeting."

"Yeah?" Tritheist glared at Adda like this was her fault.

"Thanks. I'll text." She managed to keep her clomping speed to a fast walk on her way out of the lab. After the door closed behind Tritheist, she asked, "Is someone still listening in on Dr. Björn's comms?"

Tritheist looked at her like this was a very poor question. "It's mission-critical intel."

Adda walked toward the airlock as fast as she could go in the magnetized boots. "We need to know if ve receives a message within the next few minutes, because I think—"

The operation channel buzzed through all three of their comps. "Ogir here," a tense voice she'd never heard before said in triplicate. Captain Sloane's surveillance team lead lacked Casey's resources, but Adda had to admit that he seemed more reliable. She was about to find out if she were right about that. "Are Wakefield and Björn supposed to be talking? Because they're talking. To each other. Right now."

"Patch it to the gods-damned op channel where it fucking belongs," Tritheist snarled.

". . . you doing this?" said an agender voice that must have been Björn's.

"Look, you've done some good work, sure," said Dr. Wakefield. "But you've never done what it takes to make that project produce anything saleable. You know it, I know it, the deans know it. Even the students have seen you everywhere but in your office, supervising the project. The person running this department should keep it running at top speed. I've been saying it for years."

"There's nothing I can do at my desk that I couldn't do on my comp," Dr. Björn shouted. "What the hell gives you the idea that you've got anything the deans will even read?"

"First, of course they won't read it. I'll be presenting it and they'll have a copy, which is the same thing," Dr. Wakefield said. "Second, it's the Oxia people in my lab who convinced me. They're scouting you for something huge. I'm doing you a favor, really."

"Ah, shit," said Iridian. "How did he find out? I thought Vestan news didn't make it off Vesta."

"I don't need your favors," Dr. Björn said in vis micced conversation with Dr. Wakefield.

"I'd read that academic rumor mills were better informed than most, but I thought that was some kind of joke," Adda said. She was used to not getting jokes. Somebody must've found out that Oxia had been working to hire Dr. Björn. Once that news reached Dr. Wakefield, he could've made assumptions about who was paying him to ruin Dr. Björn's University of Mars career, but he wouldn't have any evidence. Adda had disguised her identity in digital communications, the money had gone through a dozen accounts before reaching Dr. Wakefield's, and she'd be erasing any records the campus made of her visit. "Where are they?" she asked.

"They're out in the open between the satellite monitoring mod and one of the residential mods," Ogir said over the op channel.

"Well, if anyone were going to pass up an opportunity like

they're offering, it'd be you," Dr. Wakefield told Dr. Björn. "I'll leave you to it. I've got a presentation to prepare."

"We should be able to see them when we get out." Iridian cycled the airlock, which didn't involve vacuuming this time, and bounded into a cloud of kicked-up dust. Tritheist and Adda followed, pulling their goggles over their eyes as they went.

"Wait!" Adda said. "Let them go. This can still work."

Iridian gave her an incredulous look and wiped dust off her goggle lenses. "Let's get out of sight then." She put the building that their goggles labeled *Matsumoto Hall* between them and the open area Ogir described.

"Wakefield's leaving," said Ogir. "He's heading for the shuttle bay."

"What's Dr. Björn doing?" Adda asked.

"Ve's just standing there. No, there ve goes. Launching a tracker . . . now." Adda wanted to find out more about this Ogir person, because that was good thinking. Also, he was surveilling an innocent person without asking questions, or he'd gotten all the answers he wanted before he came here. "Tracker hit, stuck, and transmitting. It's coming online. Patching to the op feed."

Adda's campus map acquired a small green dot. The dot was approaching the shuttles too, following Dr. Wakefield. "We should grab ver now," Tritheist said. "If ve ends up planetside, we'll never catch ver."

The lieutenant's impatience was one of his most annoying features. Something made putting up with it worthwhile to Captain Sloane, though, so she'd put up with it too. "It will take days for the proceedings and paperwork to be finalized. We only set it in motion today, and we don't want to talk to ver until ve's lost everything ve can lose. As long as ve thinks ve can persuade vis department to let ver keep vis job, ve won't consider Oxia's offer.

That's why I reserved us a place to stay until we can corner Dr. Björn for a conversation about this. That wasn't, I don't know, optional vacation time I built in."

She was cutting it close with Jiménez's viability as a participant in the operation, but the situation should transpire such that Dr. Björn would be frustrated enough to consider other options within the next four days. Jiménez would probably have some kind of meltdown on the way back to Vesta, but that seemed likely to happen anyway.

"If ve doesn't consider Oxia's offer, ve'll consider Jiménez's." Tritheist snorted dust out of his nose.

Adda frowned. "If this can be vis choice, it should be."

"Back to the ship, then?" asked Iridian.

"Ogir here." The operation channel crackled with interference for half a second. "—tracker will only stick for two or three hours. It's on vis shirt."

"Still, it was a good idea," Adda said. "You'll follow Dr. Björn anyway?"

"Ogir here, will do. Out."

"Back to the ship," said Adda.

* * *

Whether Dr. Björn went to vis apartment on Mars or the orbiting station, everyone had to use a shuttle to leave Deimos. Adda pulled up the *Charon's Coin*'s location on her comp while the crew headed for the Deimos shuttle complex and bought passage back to Mangala Station. The *Coin* had stayed close to the Mangala Station dock where Dr. Björn stored vis ship.

Dr. Björn's shuttle passed the Mangala Station approach route and continued toward the planet. The *Coin* held position in stationspace. Adda released the breath she'd been holding.

"What's up?" Iridian asked.

Adda glanced at the other passengers in their own shuttle. Everyone else was as absorbed in something on their comp or projected over their eyes as she'd just been. "I was worried the *Coin* would try to stop Dr. Björn's shuttle, but it didn't."

"Well, that'd be something," Iridian said in a tone that implied something hilariously bad. "Every newsfeed in the system would run that as the priority headline."

"It'd save us time," Tritheist said.

"Do you want to hand the doc over to that freak?" Iridian asked.

"It's the safer bet," said Tritheist. "You give ver to him, he'll get ver to sign anything, literally anything, if he's got enough time and neither of them kill themselves first. What we're doing here is a risk, and what we're risking is the captain's position and life. So yeah, I'd rather get Jiménez's part over with."

"He'll fuck ver up." Any effort Iridian had been making to hide her anger dissolved into faster breaths, louder speech, and a scowl that made her freckles look like shrapnel from an explosion. "Ve may never be able to do anything for—" Adda leaned sideways to grasp Iridian's arm, to stop her referencing Oxia's name in a shuttle that was almost certainly micced "—them, after Jiménez finishes with ver," Iridian said a bit more quietly.

"They hired us to get ver to sign," said Tritheist. "What happens after ve signs isn't our problem." Iridian looked angry enough to punch the lieutenant. Fortunately, she sat diagonally across an aisle from him. She dug her fingers into the tie-down straps across her chest and glowered at the seat in front of her.

"I wouldn't expect the captain handing over a barely functional wreck who can't do the work to be . . . appreciated," Adda said. "They're interested because ve's the best in vis field of expertise.

It follows that they want ver to retain vis capacity to work at that level." She resisted a powerful urge to look away from Tritheist's scowling face. "Please. Just a few more days."

* * *

Their shuttle from the Deimos campus docked at Mangala Station. They spent two days in a microgravity hotel there, listening to Ogir's surveillance team on Mars follow Dr. Björn through vis daily routine. Dr. Björn was particular about laundry, apparently, because the tracker got destroyed the evening ve returned from Deimos. The main thing they'd been able to confirm before the tracker went dead was that Dr. Björn kept at least three rats as pets, all of whom had greeted ver noisily upon vis arrival. Ve was also a regular exerciser, and practiced what the surveillance team had identified as some variant of kung fu.

And, as Adda had warned the captain ve might, Dr. Björn had contacted Oxia. Captain Sloane sent a message extremely early local time on the second day, which Tritheist forwarded for their perusal in a station diner near the docks later in the morning: "The hiring manager for Oxia's Martian branch received an irate message from Dr. Björn earlier. She didn't know what Björn was talking about, of course, since she hasn't dealt with Björn's case in several months." Sloane chuckled. "Surveillance error, or something else? Let me know. I need Ogir's most reliable operatives on Mars. Border zones are always interesting, and I must be up-to-date."

"Border zones," Iridian huffed. She kicked a tethered low-grav chair into the path of somebody who'd been angling for one of two tables she, Adda, and Tritheist had taken over. The chair snapped back into its place at the table, trailing straps to hold a diner patron in place, on the downbeat of a guitar and tapping drum song playing over an old speaker near the door. Adda's implant translated disconnected lines of lyrics until she turned the earpiece off.

"I thought Mars being the farthest NEU planet from the sun made its orbit a border by definition." Adda's subvocalized search with her comp found several maps that used that border, in case anyone wanted a source cited.

"Mars's *orbit* marks the end of NEU territory, and there's supposedly some legal wiggle room in there, but the *planet* is NEU." Iridian had been stationed at a Martian NEU military base for at least a month during the war, which was probably why she was so adamant about this point. "The secessionists had their shot and they couldn't hold the major habs, because the Martians backed us. Mars is NEU. Period."

"The retired resistance fighters here will disagree." Trithe-ist glanced around as he spoke and Adda did too, although she doubted she'd recognize a retired resistance fighter on sight unless what they overheard Iridian saying made them angry.

"It's not a matter of their ignorant-ass opinion," Iridian snapped. "Mars has members of parliament. It's as NEU as Venus or Earth's Moon. More than, really. It's been populated longer than Venus. Ceres and Vesta might be 'border zones,' but Mars is on the right fucking side of the border."

Adda composed a message to Sloane: "Captain, the surveillance team has performed admirably. The professor presenting our case to the University of Mars was more talkative than I expected. Dr. Björn will take vis ship out within the next few days if ve keeps to vis usual stress behavior patterns, and we'll pick ver up then as scheduled." And ideally, the false charges raised against Dr. Björn, along with any benefits available in the Oxia contract, would be sufficiently persuasive. Adda wasn't sure she could stomach the alternative.

Most of their gear drifted in net bags tied to the tables, ready if they had to leave quickly. Chi was still watching over Jiménez in the hotel, and Sloane's pilot slept in his ship. Given the current planetary positions, it'd take about forty-five minutes for her message to reach the captain and another forty-five for a response to arrive in her comp. While she waited for the captain's reply, she reviewed her messages to make sure she hadn't missed one from Ogir about Dr. Björn leaving the Deimos campus. She'd read everything Ogir sent so far.

"Back to the gods-damned waiting, then." Tritheist slapped the paypad on the tabletop to cover the coffee and the crumbless egg sandwich he'd consumed while they talked. He pushed out of their booth and used handholds on the ends of other tables to propel himself out of the packed restaurant.

She and Adda relinquished their tables, strapped on their packs, and glided (in Adda's case, slowly half-tumbled) into one of the station's primary dockside thoroughfares. A cluster of tethered jetpacks floated near the diner's door. The supposedly clean-engined jetpacks were popular among those who couldn't pay for or tolerate the public transportation line that paralleled the cargo track on the ceiling far above.

Or at least, Adda chose to call it "above," because projected arrows every few meters pointed the opposite direction and had a flat arrow under them, labeled with text that didn't adjust to the reader's position. It communicated directionality, whether by design or not.

By the time they got back to the hotel, Chi was watching for them from her perch at a high-top table in the lobby bar. "Tritheist came to sit in with that miserable graymane. Gods, I hope he puts the guy out an airlock."

Iridian grinned. "Tritheist or Jiménez?"

"Either. Both. But Jiménez . . . I'm telling you, Nassir, he needs more help than anybody's likely to commit to, himself included."

Iridian and Chi left together, to look at what the local dockside markets were selling. That gave Adda peace and quiet in which to research Blaer Björn's skills, interests, and ship. One could never have too much information.

When Captain Sloane's reply to her message arrived, she transmitted it over the op channel: "Deal with the professor. Nobody crosses my crew."

Tritheist chuckled in a thoroughly unpleasant way in his own reply, delivered to Adda in person through her doorway. "There's work for Jiménez after all."

Adda would rather not give Jiménez anybody to work on, but Tritheist had much more experience with intimidation than she did. "Um. That's one option for dealing with Wakefield. Anything ... else?"

"We should give Jiménez something to do," Tritheist said. "I hear him banging on things half the damned night. Over and over. I think it's his head. And hell, if the captain wants us to give Wakefield a scare, Jiménez is as scary as any of us."

Is it me, or is Jiménez much more trouble than his potential contribution to the mission? Adda asked Iridian.

The mission's not over, Iridian subvocalized, then added aloud over comp comms, "This babysitting business is reconstituted shit." Adda left the channel open so she could hear Tritheist's side of the conversation too.

Tritheist sighed. "The captain always avoids this part. Look, I'll take him to Wakefield's place tonight. I'll make sure he doesn't do anything that'll make the newsfeeds, and Wakefield will never talk about Sloane or Oxia again."

"And if proceedings conclude and Dr. Björn launches vis ship tonight?" asked Adda.

"Let the *Coin* catch ver and hold ver until we get back."

You won't really tell it to do that, will you? Iridian asked Adda. *We got lucky with the* Sabina's *lab. Let's not keep rolling the dice.*

Adda sighed. *I'm not sure I could tell it to do anything. The device Ogir's team planted on Dr. Björn's ship should stop it outside station-space so we can dock. I'm hoping that the Coin will just . . . observe, like it's done so far.*

After a pause, Iridian said, *I don't like it. You didn't even ask it to come with us.*

But what Adda had accomplished with AegiSKADA's help demonstrated that the Coin could be a valuable resource to have around. It was designed to stop ships. In fact, it was licensed for it. As Tritheist had so recently reminded them, their current objective was to meet Oxia's demands and buy Sloane time to get out of the crew contract with minimal casualties. An awakened intelligence had the potential to make that a much simpler process, if Adda found a way to coordinate with it.

* * *

Two hours later, a message pinged on the operation channel. "Ogir here. Proceedings concluded. Björn's fired. Clearing personal items out of vis office now." Adda closed the latest reports on AegiSKADA's Vestan activities. The rest of the team barely had time to announce their intention to return to their ship before the next message arrived. "Ogir here. Ve pitched most of vis stuff in the recycler and is now cabbing it to the shuttle launch."

Meet you at the Mayhem, Iridian subvocalized to Adda, sounding especially breathy, like she was running. With Iridian's help, Adda had finally perfected the mic calibration. Whatever else Iridian was thinking, that message came through loud and clear.

Adda bagged the few possessions she'd brought, carefully

hefted Iridian's perpetually packed bag, and hauled all of it toward the *Mayhem*'s dock, fighting her momentum in the barely there grav the whole way. "Ogir, tell us the shuttle destination when you get it," she said over the operation channel. She activated her location on her comp so that the others could track her. One of those clean-engine jetpacks would've been convenient, as it turned out, despite the smell.

"Ogir here. Target's leaving Deimos. It'll lose power on your signal."

"Who's here?" Adda asked the pilot as she tumbled past him and into the ship.

The pilot managed to bow neatly as she passed, despite the lack of gravity. "Hi, hello to you too." He sounded like he was resignedly proving some point Adda had missed, probably about an expectation to select and exchange greetings before beginning a conversation. "You're the first. First besides me, of course."

Adda checked the *Coin*'s position on her comp. It'd left its dock, and instead of following Dr. Björn's shuttle, it was moving away from Mars on the current reliable route to Saturn. That was one of Dr. Björn's favorite routes out of Martian space, according to vis flight records.

How did the Coin choose that route? Adda wondered, without asking Iridian. AegiSKADA could track more individual ships throughout the system than the *Coin* could, and it may have had access to Mangala Station dock management and security while planting evidence supporting Dr. Björn's corruption charges, or helping Adda monitor the *Coin*. But the safeguards Adda put in place would've forced AegiSKADA to ask her before it interfaced with anything outside crew headquarters.

Casey was on Vesta too, and it could've ignored those safeguards. So either the *Coin* was processing more information than

any tug she'd ever heard of, or Casey had been talking to AegiSKADA
and relaying its information to the *Coin*. If she couldn't keep Casey
out of her own systems, she'd never be able to dictate which large-
scale pseudo-organic environments it could affect. When she got
back to Vesta, she'd shut AegiSKADA down. She wouldn't even
have to have that awful conversation with Iridian. After this operation, she could make time to acquire a new zombie intelligence,
one specifically developed for analysis and project management.

The Coin's already moving to where it expects Dr. Björn to go, Adda
said to Iridian. *How far away are you?*

"Give us about ten minutes," Iridian said over the operation
channel. "Don't lose that AI."

CHAPTER 12

> HCMS targeted confirmations sent via
> Patchwork relay between Mangala Station,
> Mars and Rheasilvia Station, 4 Vesta: 304,002

"What the hell is the Coin doing now?" Iridian shouted at Adda over the music blasting out of the *Mayhem*'s bridge. Apparently hard rock with ticking string instrument melodies was part of the pilot's process as he wove in and out of traffic on the reliable route to Saturn. There was usually somebody on the route, but three ships launching at once, in addition to the *Mayhem*, the *Coin*, and Blaer Björn's little skiff, was a crowd. Anything that helped the pilot concentrate in those conditions was fine with her.

The pilot was maneuvering to keep up with the *Coin*, which was cruising near enough to a massive passenger liner that the tug would obliterate the population equivalent of a dense city block if it drifted a few meters sunward. The *Mayhem* kept a respectful distance from both vessels and put a docking cargo ship between it and Björn.

The *Coin* was stalking Björn's skiff. Iridian shivered despite the healthy temp in the *Mayhem*'s cabin.

"It's giving us a chance to move while it gets in position," Adda said. "On our current path, we appear to be trying to get out of a rude pilot's way. Nobody would blame us, and Dr. Björn will be too busy watching it to watch us."

"Ve'll also notice when the *Coin* breaks all vis engines stopping vis ship," said Iridian.

"We'll find out in about four minutes," Adda said. "Ogir, power down the skiff's engines then."

"Ogir here. Acknowledged."

"You may have the captain fooled, but I know you told it to do this," grumbled Tritheist over the op channel.

Adda's decision to follow Björn when the opportunity presented itself, just like she'd been saying it would, had resulted in Tritheist being left on Mangala Station with a depressed interrogator, four hotel rooms, and two docking fees to pay for. Iridian couldn't help laughing.

"Fuck you, Nassir," Tritheist said. If Chi hadn't been strapped in, she'd have laughed herself out of her seat.

* * *

This far from the sun, venturing beyond the light of a station or large ship made the stars leap out of the cold and the black, distant and absolute and brilliant. The skiff, the *Coin*, and the *Mayhem* plunged into the cold and the black beyond Mangala Station's docking guides, and the stars shone before them. The *Coin* had gone dark, drifting on a trajectory it'd set for itself at least ten minutes ago to intercept the skiff. They all were in nothing again. Nothing and starlight and their little islands of atmo.

Four-meter-long harbor drones would be flashing visual, radio, and AI-to-AI "stop" signals at the *Coin*. That was all they could do, since they were too underpowered to make a dent in its velocity. Ogir's much smaller surveillance drone couldn't match the skiff's speed, showing the retreating vessels in the window projected on the ceiling over the main cabin crew couches. Iridian had armored up and strapped into the couch next to Adda, with Chi across from her in a lightly armored suit she'd picked up since the *Sabina* raid. The cam attached to the skiff's hull was reporting in just fine.

Iridian slapped her helmet's visor down. The heads-up display didn't highlight any live mics in the *Mayhem*'s cabin feeding the op channel, so she raised the visor and said, "I'm kind of wishing we hadn't ditched Tritheist."

"Yeah?" Chi asked. "Why?"

"The surveillance guy said Björn knows kung fu or something. How the hell am I supposed to subdue ver if I spend the whole time trying to hang onto my shield? Martial artists are grabby."

"I have a plan," Adda said. "It should work fine without Tritheist."

"Most things do," said Iridian, which set Chi laughing. "What's my part?"

"Can you destabilize a round of ammunition for Tritheist's . . . launcher . . . thing?" Adda avoided weapons research whenever she could.

"Oh, damn, that sounds like fun," Chi said in a tone that made it sound like a good way to get bad burns.

Iridian must've been making her own "Well, shit" face. She'd have to look up some amateurs' modding instructions. If she figured out all the steps they forgot to mention, she'd get it done. And if she made a mistake, she'd get covered in chemical irritant.

Grav gradually shifted, sending loose pieces of clutter toward a new down against the bridge wall. The crew couches in the main cabin rotated to match, which meant the passengers had over a meter-long drop under them if they needed to use the head. Adda was still looking at her. "What now?" Iridian asked.

"Dr. Björn flew a ship like this during the war." The fact that Adda left out which side Björn fought on meant that if Iridian looked it up, she'd find that ve flew for the secessionists. "And vis first reaction when Dr. Wakefield presented the case against ver was to go straight to the hearing after him."

"So instead of panicking when the *Coin* stops vis ship, ve might try to kick our asses. Got it." Since Iridian's alternatives were shooting a scientist, knocking vis valuable brain around with her shield, or risking Chi getting near enough to chemically knock ver out and take all the medical risks that came with that, this seemed like the right call. Iridian braced while the grav stabilized to more or less the orientation they'd docked in, then freed herself from her harness. "Chi, put my face back on if I burn it off with that crap Tritheist shoots at people, yeah?"

"Putting it back on is above my paygrade." Chi grinned wider than ever thanks to the g's they were pulling. "I'll keep whatever's left stuck on and clean, though."

"That'll do."

Iridian had to stop comparing her new working conditions to the college labs. It just frustrated her, envisioning vises and safety glass and experts around for advice while she bent over 37-millimeter chemical ordinance held still with one armored foot, alone in a head and strapped to the toilet. If the ship rolled, Gavran would have to mop synthcapsin-infused fluid off everything within three meters. At least the light opposite the toilet was bright enough, and the pilot's soundtrack for the venture had improved to rock Iridian halfway liked.

She made it all the way through turning one ammo canister into an improvised grenade, and started on a second because, hells, she had no idea if the first one would work. Partway through the second one, her brain started psyching itself out. *This stuff is designed to bypass armor filters. Gods, it'll hurt.* It'd burn her hands, since she'd taken off her gloves to manipulate her tools more precisely. If it burned her too badly to hold the packet of neutralizing agent, she'd have a real problem.

I think you can do it, Adda whispered in her ear. Iridian must've subvocalized her dread about getting the stuff on her hands.

Iridian smiled. *I don't want to leave it half done. Somebody might try to shoot it, and I'd feel like shit about that, even if it were Tritheist.*

She really hoped that this'd be better than having Jiménez work the astronomer over. They wouldn't dip Björn in this stuff unless ve defended verself against vis imminent kidnapping. Once they had the scientist under control they could administer the neutralizing agent, but it would suck to be ver for a few minutes.

A thin stream of the canister's contents dribbled over Iridian's forefinger and lit a line of chemical fire in its wake. She set the canister in its case alongside the four unaltered ones and whipped her arm away as soon as she could do it without moving them, swearing and shaking her hand like that'd help at all.

"Ha . . . Ah . . . Okay." Talking distracted her from the pain. "Finish it, Nassir; waiting around won't make it hurt less. Pick the gods-damned thing up and finish it." After another few seconds of procrastinating, because her hand *hurt*, damn it all, she took the canister out of its case and went back to work.

Half an hour later, Gavran got on the *Mayhem*'s internal comms to announce, "Your tug friend is locking onto the target ship. The target ship's caught in its hullhooks."

"Was that before or after Ogir stopped it?" Iridian had just finished modding the last canister and carefully extricated them, and herself, from the head. The main cabin's natural lighting soothed her wired nerves a little.

"After," said Adda. "Can we get close enough to connect pass-throughs?"

The pilot paused, then said, "Once it's still, sure. It'll have to be still before I do."

Adda was sinking into the meditative state she sometimes reached without being in a workspace, lightly drugged and tracking all factors affecting her plan. Iridian smiled into those sharp brown eyes. "Ready when you are."

"We'll give ver a chance to come in and talk," Adda said. "Ideally, ve'll open vis passthrough, but the Coin or I can probably do it ourselves. You'll be waiting in ours. Then the safest thing would be to throw in one of those canisters."

"I did go to all that trouble." Iridian's burned finger still hurt, since she hadn't wanted to open a whole packet of topical neutralizer to treat such a small burn. The ship's printer might not have the material to make more. "I'd love to see how it works."

"I'll go too," said Chi from her couch.

"Try to keep your legs under you this time," Iridian suggested. Chi grinned and raised the back of her fist, a solid spacefarer "Fuck off."

"Hang onto something," said Gavran. "Changing orientation, hold on, please."

Adda and Chi were still in their couches, but Iridian hadn't found a safe place to keep the canisters. She shut the box and tucked it under one arm. With both boots locked to the deck and a hand on the bulkhead handhold beside the passthrough, she'd either crack both ankles or hang on until the ship stabilized. The bulkhead was rapidly becoming the overhead. With her luck, if she lost her grip on the box, Chi and Adda would end up covered in synthcapsin.

The maneuver Gavran was pulling off now was complicated,

especially if Björn was still trying to restart the skiff and shake free of the Coin's hullhooks. The Mayhem shuddered, and Iridian clutched the box against her rib cage. The cartridges scraped against the padding around each slot.

Iridian held as still as she could until grav stabilized low as all hells, with the new deck nearly but not exactly under the surface the passenger couches attached to. The bulkhead with the passthrough felt higher than the bulkhead across from it. The Coin was still accelerating, pushing the professor's skiff farther from Mars, and the Mayhem was matching its slow speed to avoid tearing the passthroughs apart. This near the planet, Martians or stationsec could come sniffing around at any moment.

Adda looked hopefully up at Iridian. "Could you talk to Dr. Björn? I don't know what to say."

"Hey genius, we're here to kidnap you?" Chi suggested.

Iridian rolled her eyes and finished affixing her suit's gloves. "Patch my helmet comms in." The speaker beside her ear made a soft click. She drew in a long breath and pushed the torturer under Tritheist's care on Mangala Station to the back of her mind. "Dr. Björn, this is Iridian Nassir." Her eyes widened as she came up with an idea for how to play this. "We were heading to the Jovian reliable route and saw this crazy tug driver grab you. He's still going. Are you hurt?"

"I broke my arm. I didn't call for a tug. I have no idea what's going on. He didn't even tell me who he is."

Station security is inbound, maybe ten minutes, Adda whispered in her ear.

"Yeah, lucky he's going out and not right into the station," Iridian said. "Listen, let the red and blues get your ship back. Our passthroughs are hooked up, come on over before this fucker does something else."

The silence over the comm line had a sharp hiss, like they needed to boost the channel. "So you just saw me getting pushed around out here, and threw yourself into this out of the goodness of your heart?"

"The NEU didn't train cowards." That was a risky assertion given Björn's secessionist history, but this near Mars it'd be a common enough background for a spacefarer. Iridian liked to tell the truth, when she had that luxury. "But we can't wait around. He does another sharp turn, we'll both lose our passthroughs and anybody inside."

"Right."

Iridian shifted her grip on the box of synthcapsin canisters. "Our exterior's already open. Come on through."

"Yes, give me a moment." Björn left the channel open and rummaged through something in the ship.

Iridian handed the box of canisters to Chi, who held it against her stomach with an expression that clearly communicated "Do not fuck this up."

"I'm coming out."

Iridian touched the shield at her belt. "Yeah, okay, good. We'll open up the interior when the exterior shuts, you know how it goes."

"Sure."

The short answers seemed like a sign that Björn was getting suspicious, but ve also had a recently broken arm. Iridian carefully subvocalized, *Leave the interior closed, disengage after the exterior closes, carefully run like hell once we're disengaged.* Adda relayed the message to Gavran.

"Say again, those two don't match," the pilot said. "I heard 'carefully' and 'run like hell,' please repeat."

Iridian shut her eyes and forced her chest and shoulder muscles to relax. "She's being funny," Adda said seriously. "Get away as quickly as you can, without hurting anybody."

"Ve's in," Iridian called to Gavran. The exterior passthrough door shut and disconnected from the skiff's passthrough. "Hey, how good are you with grav management?" As far as she could tell he was excellent, but if he had any doubts, it'd be best to hear them now.

"I'm good. Very good," Gavran said over the intercom.

Iridian turned back to the passthrough. "Hang on in there, we're backing off from that crazy tug."

"Wait, let me in!" The ship lurched away from the skiff's passthrough and Björn thumped against the closed exterior door before grabbing a handhold on the bulkhead with vis good arm.

Iridian gripped the handhold nearest her. *It isn't safe to leave ver in there for the whole trip back.*

Are you sure? Adda asked her.

Gavran's good, but you don't want to count on everything being under the pilot's control, Iridian replied. *Especially not when the Coin's involved.*

Over Iridian's last few words, Chi asked, "We just leaving ver there? I don't want to scrape ver off the bulkheads later."

"Just until we get away from the ships," Iridian said. *Then we should get ver out of there and talk about the job,* she said subvocally. *If we can get ver to sign before we get back to the station, Jiménez will have nothing to do.*

He might implode, Adda replied. Iridian couldn't tell how much Jiménez's impending mental breakdown bothered Adda. It shouldn't bother her at all. He was a blight on the worlds.

The *Coin*, whether playing its part and decoying the stationsec ships or on some mission of its own, kept pushing the skiff deeper into the cold and the black. Gavran was slowly bringing the *Mayhem* up to speed, leaving the scene as quickly as possible without slinging his passengers around and taking a very long route back to Mangala Station, where they'd pick up Tritheist and Jiménez and, with luck, drop off Björn after the contract was signed.

Iridian pointed at the box of canisters on Chi's chest and raised an eyebrow at the medic. Chi glanced at the closed passthrough and kept her hold on the box. "Bridge is locked, yeah?"

"Yes." Adda stood from her couch. The deck—grav hadn't been stable long enough for Iridian to call it a floor—tilted slightly away from the passthrough, and Adda and Iridian leaned to accommodate the slope while the couches swiveled to match. Iridian took the canisters from Chi, carried them into one of the residential cabins, and stayed there.

When the inner passthrough door slid open, Björn stood on the other side, one hand braced on the wall and the other arm held tight against vis chest. Ve was older than Iridian expected, and very white, even paler than the images they had. Iridian stepped away from the door so ve could come inside, and Björn stalked past. Ve stopped just across the threshold, taking in the wary eyes on ver.

Chi was up and offering a helping arm in seconds. "Hey, you don't look so good. My name's Chi. I'm the shipdoc. What's your name?"

"Dr. Blaer Björn." Ve accepted Chi's offered and vacant couch, but ve was staring hard at Iridian. They had ten minutes, max, until ve figured out who they were. The newsfeeds didn't show enough tall civvy women with shaved heads for Iridian to be mistaken for somebody else.

Chi asked about Björn's health generally and the arm in particular, and even slapped a vital signs monitor onto Björn's uninjured arm, before strapping into vis couch and getting a kit from her residential cabin. She had an inflatable splint and some painkiller in it. Iridian would've expected the painkiller, but the splint was a neat addition.

While Chi applied them to Björn's arm, Björn's face was a pitiable mixture of relief, confusion, and suspicion. Nothing in vis body language was remotely threatening. The modified synth-capsin canisters would have to be tested another time. Iridian was almost disappointed.

"Well," Björn said, "I'm blessed that such a well-staffed ship came to my rescue."

Fifteen minutes until I'd expect the station security to confirm that ve's no longer in the skiff and start looking for us, Adda whispered in Iridian's earpiece.

"Yeah, about that." Iridian met Chi's eye and the medic backed off as far as the next couch over to pack up her kit. Iridian leaned against the wall near the passthrough, with barely half a meter of space between her and Björn's couch. "Oxia Corporation sent us. Turns out they don't take no for an answer."

"Wakefield was telling the truth?" Björn's expressions cycled through shock and an instant of fear before settling on anger. "So all this . . . this," Björn twitched the shoulder of her injured arm, now in a bright red cast with a white cross on it, "was because of that Oxia position I turned down?"

"Yeah."

Björn glared, eyes still tight with pain, as color gradually returned to her face. "And that was you at the Deimos campus too, you and that . . . and Wakefield."

"Call him whatever you like," Chi offered. "We're not pals."

"They're shutting my project down," said Björn. "Eighteen months of work, huge discoveries that *meant* something, and they're shutting it down because of you, and Oxia. Take me back to my ship. Now."

Iridian grimaced. "We can take you back, but you'll have to sign Oxia's contract first."

"I won't sign anything," Björn shouted. Ve tried to stand, but the couch's harness held ver in place. Ve fumbled with the release with vis good hand until Chi gently but firmly pressed it back against the couch's formfitting armrest.

Björn jerked vis arm away from Chi, but Chi caught it again and said, "You should listen to her."

"Why? I've said no more than once. This is illegal. A contract signed under duress—"

"Is still a gods-damned megacorporate contract, and any NEU or ITA officer would uphold it, no questions asked," Iridian said. "You know it, I know it, so let's not waste time with that." The ship was accelerating too fast to maintain healthy grav, and Iridian felt dragged toward the deck. That suggested pursuit. "If we get back to the station and you haven't signed yet, we're not putting you off there. We'll have to take you into deep space with a guy who doesn't give a fuck about what's legal, as long as you end up signing."

"So what, yours is the easy way and his is the hard way?" Björn asked bitterly.

"That's the shape of it, yeah." And even though Iridian was pretty sure it didn't show on her face, shame clenched all the muscles in her chest and stomach. This wasn't what she'd signed onto Sloane's crew to do. This op was supposed to be a one-time deal, but unless Sloane got out from under Oxia, she had no guarantee it wouldn't happen again.

"I won't do it," Björn said.

Gods damn it.

Ve has to, Adda whispered. She stepped out of the residential module, pupils dilated huge in the brightly lit main cabin. She'd taken more of the drugs that let her use a virtual workspace. She held the handholds on the bulkheads the whole way around to a position where Björn could see her. "This. It's bad. I'm sorry. We didn't want to be involved, but we are, and the alternative to signing is really, really awful."

"So don't be involved," Björn pleaded. "Get me back to my ship. I don't have to report this."

"We can't do that," said Adda.

Although they could, if they were willing to throw away everything they'd worked so hard for, for a total stranger. "Have you even read the contract?" Iridian asked. "You should know what you're passing on. Could be a good deal. I mean, are they even moving you to Vesta? Maybe they've got a deal with U of M. You could at least see how much they're paying."

"I don't care what they're paying!" Björn shouted. "It's about the work. I'm not interested in shipping route optimization or whatever they think they need me for. At the university—"

"That option's gone," Adda said softly. She sounded genuinely sad about it, and she couldn't act for shit. "Your departmental responsibilities have already been handed over to Dr. Wakefield, and the lensing anomaly study is being reviewed for termination."

Iridian blinked. Beyond noting that what Björn had been studying on Deimos sounded cool, she'd ignored the details. Adda had apparently read up on it.

"Yes, you saw to that, I imagine." Tears welled in Björn's blue eyes. Vis good fist clenched around the armrest. "The most exciting development in astronomy in your lifetimes, and after Jacov steals its resources for his project they'll *ignore* it. I hope you're happy."

Adda held out a small datacask, the size of half her smallest finger and filled with milky gray-green pseudo-organic fluid. The Oxia logo, a stylized fan or maybe an oxygen molecular diagram in blue and green, was printed on its side. "We're really not."

Björn bit vis lip for a moment, then snatched the datacask with vis good hand and carefully inserted it into vis comp, on the hand with the broken arm. Vis comp glove had a bright cyan and red nebula design on black synthetic material that shimmered slightly at the projection window's edges.

Chi's comp beeped and she looked between her projection and Björn. Whatever was off with Björn's health made her frown, but she left the rest of her medical kit where it was. Iridian caught Adda's eyes. *Find out where stationsec is. It's safest to get out of Martian space as soon as we can.*

They already know where we are, Adda said over their shared comms. *They're just not sure who we are and what we have to do with this yet. The Coin can hide its own records, but the skiff might not be able to.*

Iridian sighed and steadied Adda with both hands on her forearms. "If it's important, you've got it, yeah?" Iridian murmured to her. Adda smiled and disappeared into the bridge cabin. The corner of her mobile workspace generator stuck through the residential cabin's open doorway.

Maybe she'd already tried talking to the skiff's AI directly, and she still thought it'd share everything it knew with stationsec. It seemed so much safer to try to get the skiff's zombie AI copilot to take the vessel back to the station on its own, stationsec be damned, but if Adda didn't know how the *Coin* would react to that, then nobody knew. Iridian just hoped that she was using all the filters in her workspace to protect herself from the *Coin's* influence.

Grav rose dramatically, still pulling Iridian toward the deck. "Now'd be a good time to belt in," Chi announced while strapping herself into the couch next to Iridian's. "You start feeling like you can't breathe or you're about to pass out, let me know," she added to Björn, who nodded without looking away from the projected contract.

Grav yanked Iridian toward the intersection of the deck and the bulkhead with the passthrough. The mobile workspace generator thumped onto the new deck in the residential cabin. Metallic rattling made Iridian's teeth clench. The box with the destabilized canisters was still loose in there. She ran into the residential cabin and stuffed the box into a drawer full of clothes built into the bedframe, where it'd be cushioned as well as it could be. The extra effort in high grav had her panting by the time she climbed into a passenger couch in the main cabin.

Beneath the creak and shift of objects rolling and couches readjusting for grav changes, Björn kept making "hmm" noises. Apparently nobody else had gotten as far as convincing ver to read the contract. Adda crawled out of the bridge and into the last remaining main cabin couch.

"Seeing anything you like?" Iridian asked Björn hopefully.

"It's better than I expected," ve admitted. "Longer term and with more penalties for talking about my work than I expected too, and the anticompetition section will make collaboration difficult." Ve lowered the comp slightly, and although the couch's position kept ver from making eye contact with Iridian, she was pretty sure Björn was addressing her. "Can you take me to somebody I can negotiate terms with?"

"Our orders are for you to sign that thing the way it is," Iridian said. "There isn't an 'or something else' for if you don't like it."

"Not a good one, anyway," said Adda.

"You mean the man you'd leave me with if I didn't sign?" Björn looked over at Chi since Adda and Iridian were behind ver in the couches' current configuration. Chi must've looked sufficiently grim for all three of them, because Björn said, "This is wrong. Oxia shouldn't get everything it wants because it can. I won't sign."

CHAPTER 13

Stage 2 confirmed

Adda had known that convincing Dr. Björn to sign the contract once they had ver would be the hardest part of the assignment, if she wanted to keep the astronomer's mind and body as whole as possible. Perhaps approaching honesty would make the desired impact. "This is Oxia's business strategy. We're as trapped in our captain's contract as you are in yours." Technically she and Iridian had more freedom, since Sloane had made sure that only the captain had to sign, but building solidarity seemed helpful.

"We signed on to stick it to bastards like them, not work for them," said Iridian.

"So go to the authorities," Dr. Björn said. "I'll minimize your part in it."

"What authorities?" Iridian sounded more angry than desperate. "The NEU might fine Oxia for this maneuver so close to Mars, but Oxia's moving its business out to the colonies, and out there they *are* the authority in any given colony. Oxia's buying whole damn habs out from under people. Even if Oxia decides to cut everything with all of us because we screw up that badly, which, by the way, would be the end of our ability to make money doing anything remotely legal if they happened to let us live, that's just the end of us. Oxia will find somebody else to get you signed on quietly, and they'll go right on screwing over everybody and taking all the money they can grab."

Iridian panted with the effort of pressing words through her compressed chest, because gravity was still crushing them into the passenger couches. Dr. Björn had craned vis neck to watch Iridian talk, and Adda caught herself smiling at her, just a little. Righteous fury looked damnably good on Iridian. It was worth her rant's oversimplifications of NEU political strategy. Chi just shook her head in her couch while facing the ceiling.

"I didn't mean to give a fucking speech," Iridian grumbled. "That's just the way it is out here."

Out there. Outside the mesh of lies and legality Oxia had created, they still had one more bargaining chip that Dr. Björn may be interested in. "What if we helped you tell your side of this, after you signed?" Adda asked.

"What do you mean?" Dr. Björn sounded suitably suspicious, for anybody as intelligent as ver in this position.

"The contract probably includes terms to stop you from publicizing the circumstances surrounding your hiring, correct?" Adda asked. Iridian was giving her an extremely incredulous look, so she added, *You'll see* over their personal comms. Iridian nodded.

"Of course," Dr. Björn said bitterly.

"And we can't say anything about it either, for similar reasons." Mostly because it would make Sloane look like a typical megacorporate thug and reduce the captain's chances of escaping Oxia's contract alive. "But rumors leak. We'll create something to publish anonymously, from a perspective that could be a third-party watchdog or a disgruntled Oxia employee."

"Like us," Iridian muttered, although that was clearly not an option, as Adda had just stated.

"Shortly before or after the announcement that you've accepted the Oxia position," Adda continued, "we release that report in one of the megacorporate watchdog channels that viewer overlap with the University of Mars. Perhaps we can also use some dummy accounts to bring it to the attention of your more talkative students or coworkers?"

"I have plenty of those." Dr. Björn sounded more positive now. "You can really do that? Get the truth out to everyone without implicating me?"

"If anybody can do it, Adda can," Iridian said proudly. *You fucking genius,* she whispered through the earpiece.

No congratulations yet, Adda subvocalized. *Ve hasn't signed.*

"And you think it'd make a difference? In Oxia's business practices, I mean," Dr. Björn said.

"Everybody secure?" the pilot asked over the intercom. "Reply if secured."

Chi examined Dr. Björn's position and glanced over Iridian's and Adda's before shouting, "We're good." Adda envied her ability to assert her expertise, even in stressful scenarios like this one.

The ship tilted sideways, rotating the passenger couches to put the passthrough door directly above their heads. It kept that orientation for a couple seconds, then flipped all the way over at gut-churning speed. It felt like a whole new engine lit somewhere below the passenger couches. Chi whooped like she was on an amusement park ride. Iridian was slipping into combat mode, intensity hardening her dark eyes and muscles coiled for sudden movement.

"Telling people the truth about how Oxia does things is probably the only way to make a difference," Adda said in answer to Dr. Björn's previous question. "Reputation seems important out here. But, um . . . Decide soon." Adda's mind was racing through too many possibilities to keep track of them all, and this was no time to make a mistake. She could narrow down her choices after Dr. Björn signed.

Dr. Björn sighed heavily, then maneuvered vis thumb over vis comp's scanner. The scanner flashed beneath vis thumb, lighting the digit deep pink for a moment as its cam captured vis capillary configuration as well as vis thumbprint. "It's done." The contract transmitted itself to Adda's comp. Copies would also go to Dr. Björn's account and Oxia's human resources department. They'd have the hiring process underway by the time the *Mayhem* reached the station.

Adda opened the operation channel. "Ve signed, so we can let ver off here." The orders from Oxia made Sloane responsible for getting Dr. Björn to sign the contract, and that was all. Ve would have affairs to set in order on Mars, and three or more rats to pack into whatever one moved rats in. There was no reason to rush ver. If Oxia wanted ver on Vesta so badly, then they could arrange transportation.

And if Dr. Björn wanted to take this opportunity to flee to the Kuiper Belt or some other place too remote to enforce an NEU megacorporate contract, Adda was glad to give ver the chance, now that ve'd signed. "Lieutenant, are you ready to leave?" she asked on the operation channel.

"Ah, fucking timing . . ." The operations channel transmitted scuffling sounds and a yelp from someone who might've been male. "Yeah, sure," Tritheist said. "You at the dock now?"

"Gavran, how long?" Adda asked.

"Thirteen minutes, repeat, thirteen minutes to dock."

Adda frowned. His voice sounded higher pitched and reedier than it had during previous conversations, and his words rolled together so thoroughly that the repetition became a necessity. "It takes at least fifteen minutes to go through arrival procedures."

"Not the way I'm doing it! I'm taking the fast way in," Gavran said.

"Just tell us if we're jumping out an airlock or meeting you at a passthrough," said Tritheist. Another pause and more scuffling followed. His voice sounded strained. "We'll be ready."

Adda closed the operational channel. "It doesn't sound like things with Jiménez are going well."

"He's a mess," Chi agreed. "Was before Tritheist took him on that—" she glanced over at Dr. Björn "—field trip."

Dr. Björn swallowed audibly. "Will you let me go once we reach the station? My arm is starting to hurt again."

"Maybe," Iridian said before Adda could respond. Adda would have said yes, since that's what she planned to do. Iridian caught Adda's eyes and said, "If we can. I'm not sure what's going on out there."

"Evading EMP gennies!" The pilot laughed as he delivered this information in a shout through the partially open bridge door. "Launched EMP generators incoming, but I'm evading them."

"Thanks for the warning," Iridian muttered. Everyone reached for their comps to tap backup functions, except for Adda, who subvocalized the instruction to hers.

"What about my ship?" Dr. Björn asked. "I really like that little rig."

Adda grimaced. "I forgot about the *Coin*." Iridian looked as alarmed as Adda felt. With an effort, she reached for her safety harness.

"Whoa, bad idea!" Iridian said. "We're moving too fast to go for a walk."

But I don't know what it's doing, and it doesn't know what we're doing. Adda subvocalized the message to avoid ascribing more agency than Dr. Björn would've expected a ship to have.

Just send it some text, then! Iridian's expression turned the subvocalized proposal from a statement to an exclamation, which was kind of interesting from a linguistics perspective.

Adda kept working on her harness. *This is too complex for text, and too important for misunderstandings.*

If Martian law enforcement disabled the *Coin*, the ship would probably find a way to look like a common tugboat with faulty software, but Adda would rather not let it find itself in that position. And although Casey monitored every action Adda took with her comp, it might not relay messages to the *Coin* or the *Apparition*. She had no way to tell whether those ships' awakened autopilots were listening in on her comp as well.

Perhaps later she should create an open intermediary connection with all the intelligences, to avoid this particular inconvenience in the future. The intermediary wasn't designed for multiple connections, but it wasn't designed to work with awakened intelligence, either. Nothing was.

Her couch swung on its axle until the surface that had formerly served as the floor was about ten centimeters above the end of her nose. This ship's pseudo-organic tank rotated the same way the passenger couches did, which explained the tank's oval design. Even as she watched, though, the ship rotated around her. She shut her eyes against the resulting motion sickness.

Dr. Björn had broken vis arm when the *Coin* slowed the ship from a smaller difference in speed and direction than Adda would experience crossing the *Mayhem*'s cabin. Assuming she could even climb out of her passenger couch, Adda would be thrown around the cabin if Gavran did anything fancy while docking. The *Coin* only had to be on its own for fifteen minutes. It might already be listening in on their communications and watching the *Mayhem's* progress. Adda returned her arm to the passenger couch's insistent grip.

She wasn't watching a countdown on her comp, since it was too hard to get to get her comp in front of her face at their current gravity level. Eventually Gavran shouted, "We'll be at ES dock three in five, repeating, ES dock three in five!" through the bridge door. Gavran had turned off the main cabin windows, which was fine with Adda. She didn't want to see Mangala Station approaching as fast as it felt like it was.

"Minutes?" Adda shouted over the engine noise.

"Yeah, minutes, minutes, what else?"

The ship did something unsettlingly like falling bridge-first for several long seconds and then jounced upward and thumped Adda's tailbone and heels into the firm back of the passenger couch beneath the foam padding. The engine rumble shook the whole cabin and made a low roaring noise over which it was hard to hear. Iridian shouted the dock information and arrival time to Tritheist on the operation channel. Dr. Björn prayed under vis breath.

"ES dock?" Adda asked.

Chi laughed and shouted, "Emergency services! Ambulances and firefighters and tugs come and go through those. They have their own arrival and departure routes. As long as Gavran picked one that's not occupied or about to be, that's the fast way in, all right!"

Colliding with an ambulance was not on Adda's list of contingency plans. To stop herself from worrying about the *Coin*, or any of the other things slightly off about their current escape plan, she thought through several ways to work around vehicular accidents. There wasn't much she could do to affect the impact, but she could plan ahead to deal with the people involved so that none of Sloane's crew got arrested as a result. If Sloane considered this pilot a member of the crew, she'd have to trust that the captain chose someone skilled enough to succeed in an approach like this one.

Gavran put the *Mayhem* through a maneuver that put the ceiling overhead again, and this time Adda had to utilize the sick bag Iridian insisted she keep with her. Vomiting was, amazingly, even more unpleasant in high gravity. Switching to weightlessness before she finished absolutely did not help.

Iridian reached over to rub her shoulder while the ship docked. "We're leaving a lot like we came, but you're doing great."

The passthrough cycled open. Jiménez sailed over the prone passengers and thumped shoulder-first against the wall across from it. Adda winced in sympathy. Tritheist clomped into the main cabin on magnetized boots and looked down at Dr. Björn. "This is your stop. Get out."

"Sir, are you trying to kill them?" Chi freed herself from her harness and wrestled Jiménez into the couch in her place. His knuckles were ragged red wounds and he flinched like fastening the harness in place hurt him.

"I'm trying to get off this fucking station," Tritheist growled. "Better company on Barbary, and I'm including that damned AI." Iridian pulled herself out of her passenger couch to help the newly lightweight astronomer out through the passthrough.

"Where is ve going?" Jiménez asked plaintively. "I haven't—"

"No, you damned well haven't, and you won't." Tritheist stomped to the residential cabin not occupied by a large, floating workspace generator and pounded the wall switch to shut the door behind him. Jiménez's eyes flooded with tears before he hid them behind his hands.

Iridian called, "Good luck, Dr. Björn" out the passthrough, and shut it before their kidnapping victim could formulate a response. "You know, I expected some sour academic type. Ve was all right." She sounded vaguely horrified.

Rather than dwelling on that, Adda took advantage of the ship's momentary stillness to retrieve her workspace generator. Since she had failed to lock the couch in place before climbing out of it, she bruised her chin on the floor. Iridian stabilized her and helped her wobble through the air toward the open residential cabin.

She unplugged the workspace generator and tugged it back to the couches in the main cabin. Iridian watched her, floating near the floor with her fingertips curled into one of the wall handholds. "Get in," Iridian said. "I'll set you up." While Adda climbed into the now-locked passenger couch, Iridian wound cables around the couch's base.

Once Adda was strapped in, she put a purple sharpsheet on her tongue and breathed in through the sizzling tingle as it dissolved. The artificial spice-and-herb scent put her in a workspace mind-set before the drug even kicked in. She uncoiled a cable from her silver necklace and threaded the smaller end into her nasal jack. The other end she handed down to Iridian, who carefully threaded it into the cable arrangement holding the workspace generator in a position where she could set it over where Adda lay on the couch.

"You'll get pulled all over the place, because this thing won't be able to turn while you're in it." Iridian already sounded far away, even though she was right beside Adda's couch. When Adda closed her eyes, Iridian would barely be there at all.

"Lifting off, we're lifting off," announced Gavran. His voice had degenerated into a reedy screech, but he still sounded like he was smiling. At least somebody was having a good time.

Iridian strapped into another passenger couch in the main cabin, and then the whole ship tilted and took on gravity fast. Adda applied an earbud full of white noise to the ear without a comm line to Iridian and shut her eyes.

The roaring engines meshed with the white noise to become a whirling tunnel of wind and sound in which her workspace existed in the center of a vortex. She reached for a chain flailing through the maelstrom and caught it with both hands. It went taut. "*Charon's Coin.* It's Adda. Please respond."

The chain stayed taut. She'd sent several messages through her comm system and intermediary to the *Coin* while they were traveling to Mangala Station, but she'd never received confirmation of a functional comm connection, let alone a sign that it understood what she'd said. It'd certainly never responded before. But now, according to her comp and the workspace generator attached to it, the comm connection was solid. The *Coin* heard her.

"I need you to leave Dr. Björn's ship somewhere safe and retrievable, and in the best condition you can manage." Adda envisioned Dr. Björn's ship, or at least the model she'd studied in preparation for this operation, drifting in a peaceful section of space, with other ships passing by well away from it. She focused on the image so clearly that it emerged from the maelstrom wall in front of her in the proportions she'd studied.

The maelstrom's center abruptly shifted, and one side swept over her. The chain wound around her chest, rib cage, hips, and legs and dug in. For a second Adda felt the wide harness straps on the *Mayhem*'s passenger couch, but shoved that impression out of her head. If she got distracted, she might send mixed messages to the *Coin*.

Virtual wind blew her hair over her eyes. Through it she glimpsed something massive drifting in the dark vortex wall. It was the same size as the *Coin* in reality, dark and solid and metallic as well. Not remotely humanoid. Its shape could have been five thick links of spiked chain, each link as big as the representation of Dr. Björn's skiff that the massive figure was coiled around.

The triangular end of its final link reminded Adda of a viper's skull, with the second link bent under it like a lower jaw, and a thousand spiked fangs in the space between. The viper skull developed eye socket ridges and focused on her. Someone had clearly not gone to much trouble to socialize the *Coin*'s copilot intelligence, when that had been all that it was. It really was as uncaring about the humans around it as Iridian claimed. Adda had thought it was just poorly prepared for communication at the level she preferred, and that was part of it, but it was also not interested in her, as an outside force with designs on it, however small and powerless she may be in comparison.

Adda inhaled slowly, breathing in thin Deimos dust over her tongue and down her throat. The coughing dumped her out of the workspace and into the passenger couch covered by her portable workspace generator. The *Mayhem*'s cabin was clear of dust. She was struggling to breathe against the heaviest gravity she'd ever felt.

"In and out fast. Then wait a few seconds. Then in and out fast," Iridian shouted over the engine noise, apparently breathing the same way she was describing. It was part of the g-tolerance training that she'd been offering Adda whenever Iridian remembered that complicated space travel was still new to her.

The other part of the training, Adda now recalled, was tightening her leg and stomach muscles. She no longer felt like she was about to black out, at least. She shut her eyes and sank into the whirlwind workspace.

Dr. Björn's skiff floated just beyond the vortex's inner edge, alone. The *Coin* was gone.

She swept up whirling orbs of red and blue light and incorporated the law enforcement comms band into the wind noise. They'd located the skiff and were confirming that nobody was onboard. They'd also located Dr. Björn on the station. They were still searching for the *Coin* and the *Mayhem*, but nobody seemed to have a good description of where those ships were. The orbs were slowly shrinking as the *Mayhem* left their relatively short-band range.

The chains around her legs and stomach were gone. The *Mayhem* must have returned to what Iridian would call "healthy" acceleration, where Adda could pretend that she was on something large enough and stable enough to produce its own gravity just by existing in the right orbit at the right speed.

* * *

Days later and less than an hour after the *Mayhem* docked at Rheasilvia Station, Sloane, Adda, and Tritheist stood in crew headquarters before the projected figure of Oxia CEO Liu Kong. Iridian and Chi had escaped this meeting by being insufficiently involved in the operation's leadership and planning, and they were now off somewhere disposing of part of their pay for the job.

Adda would've rather been assuring herself that AegiSKADA was staying within the limited server space she set for it. To use that as an excuse to miss this meeting, though, she'd have to tell Iridian and Captain Sloane about AegiSKADA's current state of existence. She could put those arguments off for a little longer without hurting anyone, because she was going to deactivate it, when she had time to do it the right way.

Beside Liu Kong's figure on Captain Sloane's projector stage, a viral text post about Dr. Björn's hiring experience with Oxia accrued quantifiable public attention across social and newsfeeds as they watched. Dr. Björn's most talkative students and coworkers had responded admirably when Adda sent them news of what'd happened to ver using a fake University of Mars account.

Sloane's lips twitched at the corners, without actually smiling. "Isn't the saying that there is no such thing as bad press?"

The viral post's negative response statistics glowed in prominent red beside Liu Kong's clenched jaw. "If I find that your crew had anything to do with this . . ."

"What you'll find is that my crew were meticulous about protecting Oxia's interests in every aspect of this affair." Somehow Captain Sloane managed not to look at Adda while saying that. "The University of Mars has a great deal of political influence through its famous graduates, as I'm sure you're aware, and Blaer Björn was both a high profile and a high-value target. The risk to my crew and your organization was exceedingly high. I trust that Dr. Björn's work will be worth that."

Liu Kong seemed to be turning what Captain Sloane had said over in his mind. "Of course. The risk analysis came out in Dr. Björn's favor." He may have meant that Oxia would be better off having Dr. Björn onboard, or that Sloane's crew was a price Oxia was willing to pay for the astronomer. Probably both.

The moment the projector notified them that Liu Kong had terminated the connection, Sloane grinned in vicious glee. "My gods, that was glorious. I doubt we'll be able to get away with that level of public notoriety in the future, Adda, but what a use of the opportunity!"

"It barely hung together, but it hung," said Tritheist. "Are we still on the hook for Jiménez?"

"I rolled his fee into Oxia's budget for the job, but get the man antidepressants and cognitive recalibration on us, would you?" Sloane sighed. "He's a useful tool, but he requires a great deal of maintenance."

"Have you had any more luck with the contract, Captain?" Tritheist followed Sloane out of the meeting room and toward the imitation-lake lobby. Adda went with them to hear the captain's answer.

Sloane's pace slowed. "We're evaluating potential Oxia breaches of the section on how the operations are selected and planned. That's also where Liu Kong seems touchy, so I'm hopeful. In the meantime, I expect we'll be assigned another job as soon as Liu Kong finds one worthy of us."

Where are you? Adda subvocalized while she bowed farewell to Sloane and Tritheist at the elevators.

Sloane's club, where else? Iridian's subvocalized words arrived at a slightly slower pace than Adda had gotten used to. *Washing that fucking op out of my mouth. Some of the crew's fans are being nasty on their social feeds over the connections they see between Oxia's acquisition of Sloane and our visit to the Deimos campus. Bitter about Sloane lying to them about being stuck on Barbary, never mind the drama. You'd think they'd love it. . . . See you soon.*

Adda rolled her eyes and downloaded the past few hours' record of AegiSKADA's activities. It'd duplicated the entirety of the headquarters building's intruder detection and personnel monitoring system in its own station security context. That was convenient and in line with its development priorities. However, it shouldn't have done that without asking her.

She would probably have said yes, but now she'd have to talk to it to determine what she'd said or didn't say that made the duplication justifiable to it. It was possible that AegiSKADA had asked permission of her at some point during their efforts to capture Dr. Björn, and Adda had answered it while she was distracted. Supervising intelligences was a full-time job for a reason, and this was the longest she'd ever been responsible for one. As long as it was active and under her supervision, she had to expect and prepare to recover from errors on her part. She set a sharpsheet on her tongue and headed for their suite to find the mistake she'd made.

Sorry, I was trying to talk to you and ended up talking to everybody, Iridian said. *Come here! People keep handing us drinks and drugs, everybody wants to dance, and I miss you. It'd all be better with you, babe.*

It'd take hours to shut AegiSKADA down properly, and it wasn't exactly an emergency situation. Other than the duplicate security feed, which didn't even affect the one already active in the building, AegiSKADA was staying within the parameters she'd set for it. Iridian would be disappointed if Adda didn't join her. The two modified synthcapsin canisters sat on the kitchen counter in her and Iridian's suite. She put a bag over each one and gingerly carried them to the cupboard, so she or Iridian wouldn't knock them onto the floor when they came back to the suite drunk.

Adda sighed, smiled, and fished out a Vestan-fashionable bioluminescing skirt and tight shirt, which were getting a surprising amount of wear. The sharpsheet made her spend much more time evaluating each piece of clothing than she needed to. Fortunately, sharpsheets combined well with alcohol, as long as she didn't have too much. College had given her ample opportunities to test those limits. She'd shut AegiSKADA down later.

Adda stepped off the elevator and into a thunderous beat

overlaid with rhythmic sirens. It sounded like club music even though, or because, it shouldn't have. The sharpsheet intensified the music's energy so that she could almost feel the sound sliding over her skin.

As she walked around the edge of the dance floor, a bronze-skinned, bright-haired hetero couple swept up to her. "Adda Karpe, yeah?" the man asked.

"Of course it's her, I said it was. Eran, Sylbirin." The woman pointed to the man first, then herself. "We heard about the Oxia hiring exposé, and hell, that was amazing. Had to be you, of course. Wasn't it amazing?" she asked the Vestan apparently called Eran, who was too busy staring at Adda's chest to respond.

It was interesting that Oxia had let that part of the news cycle penetrate the local media. Vestans were more likely than anyone to note that Captain Sloane had arrived just weeks before this major embarassment for the megacorporation. Unlike Oxia, the Vestans didn't need proof of Sloane's involvement. And also unlike Oxia, there was nothing that Vestans could do about it. They were all under contract to Oxia themselves, one way or another.

Adda tried to step around Eran and Sylbirin, but they arranged themselves on either side of her and walked the same direction she was walking, grinning at everybody they passed as much as they stared at her. "Knew you people weren't really trapped on Barbary, that's too dumb a mistake for Captain Sloane." Since Sloane hadn't made any announcements regarding Barbary Station since the crew escaped, public opinion on what really happened there seemed to be skewing toward the truth. Apparently Eran was only interested in repeating the more flattering lie. "Gods, you look good in that," he added, too close to her ear.

Iridian swooped in to wrap an arm around her waist and swing her across a corner of the dance floor in a move calculated to get people out of their way. "Sorry, hangers on. That's a thing. Ask Pel. Although, you ask me, he's spent more time hanging than having people hang on him, you know what I mean?"

Iridian's kiss tasted like wine, which was a new experience. It even felt like wine, red and smooth and bittersweet. "Who's been buying you drinks?" Adda asked.

"Chi started it," Iridian said loudly enough to be heard over the music, and dipped her chin down to kiss Adda again. Chi's dark brown arm waved from the end of the large public bar at the back of the dance floor.

Adda had been hoping to hide out in the VIP bar, but as soon as people looked around to see who Chi was waving at, hiding became unlikely. Somebody shoved a beer into Adda's hand.

As they reached a spot at the bar beside Chi, the medic snatched the beer away and dropped a plastic stick into it. A yellow dot lit at the stick's submerged end and slowly rose toward the part still above the beer. "Give that a minute." Chi covered the cup with her hand and gazed into Adda's eyes with drunken sincerity. "There are pervs in this bar. Tried to perv up my wine twice already, but I'm too old for that shit."

Alcohol and sharpsheets combined well, but other drug interactions could be dangerous. "Why are they buying us drinks?" Adda shouted.

Pel appeared at her elbow, half guided and half held upright by a pair of sturdy-looking and possibly related club boys. The medication cocktail supporting his new eyes probably mixed poorly with alcohol, but his wide smile and clumsy hug suggested that he hadn't made himself sick yet. "Vestans don't know the full story on the job. They just know you and Iridian did *something* as part of Sloane's crew that ended up riling U of M against Oxia, which is all kinds of popular. And Captain Sloane's scary shit. But here we are." Pel wiggled his eyebrows at the club boys, who laughed.

"You told somebody something about the operation, didn't you," Adda shouted at Pel. "We don't tell anybody off Vesta anything about that. Do you understand me?" Pel could expose her involvement in the leak about the circumstances of Dr. Bjorn's hiring. That could easily break the balance Sloane was striking between meeting Oxia's demands and escaping them, and land the whole crew in ITA prison cells. Adda rested a hand on Iridian's thigh, grounding her anxiety with her wife's solid presence at her side.

Pel and the club boys exchanged glances. The club boys looked much more alarmed than Pel. "Let's go over our cover story, then," he said through a big grin. The club boys' faces lit up like they'd won a lottery, and Iridian gave Pel a disgusted shove the club boys had to help him recover from. They staggered off with Pel saying something into one club boy's ear while the other palmed his ass. Adda texted the word "protection" to his comp, since she had no hope of yelling it at a volume he'd pay attention to.

Chi assessed the drink analyzer's glowing green tip, then shoved the beer into Adda's hand hard enough to slop some over her fingers. Chi threw the analyzer over the bar, through the projected bartender figure behind it. Adda was glad her beer passed the test, because she needed a drink.

After they left Deimos, she'd confirmed that the university community had been aware of Oxia's interest in Dr. Björn before Sloane's crew arrived in Martian space. On Vesta, it was common knowledge that Sloane's crew was working for Oxia. Oxia had not wanted its coercive hiring tactics to become widely known, though, let alone its association with pirates. If the Vestan public connected Sloane's crew to the leaked information so easily, then

Oxia would come to the same conclusion eventually.

"So they're really talking about us?" Adda settled herself onto a stool, which by all rights should not have been available in a bar this crowded. Someone must have vacated it for her. Yes, she was beginning to like this notoriety thing.

"Oh yeah," Chi said. "I mean, not just your brother and his boy toys, every Vestan and a bunch of those wacko social feeds that follow Sloane's ops. People say you know what the fuck you're doing, feeding Oxia some shit for a change. Better than Sloane ever did, they're saying." She peered at Adda over a glass of something unaccountably orange. "Do you know? What the fuck you're doing?"

That should have been a question for Captain Sloane, not Adda. The captain chose to pursue the operations. She just wanted to do them effectively, and with minimal damage.

Her comp buzzed against her hand. The text read *Tritheist: Next job's basic ship thievery. Not even sure why they need us. Milk run.*

"Aw, he had to say that." Iridian huffed out a boozy sigh over Adda's shoulder and wrapped both arms around her waist. "Now we're fucked. We just don't know how yet."

CHAPTER 14

Test 02 case selected

The ZAR-560Q prototype longhaul ship was smaller than most longhaulers Iridian had seen. It'd be a tight fit in a standard docking bay, but it'd be able to land on a pad instead of having to hook up via passthroughs. In the indistinct cam stills Tritheist sent them, it looked a bit like a metal beetle with four big, segmented dome eyes where legs should be.

Which was kind of funny, since Adda's research said it'd fly farther than any other longhauler was guaranteed for, largely without active supervision if the AI was being developed the way Adda thought it was. It'd skip multiple refueling points on its way to the Kuiper colonies. In spacefarer terminology, it had long legs.

Stealing the ZAR-560Q prototype was apparently a job for Sloane's crew because the security protecting this ship was impenetrable, according to thieves who would've been interested otherwise. Iridian and Adda spent the whole next day, and the substantially less alcoholic evening, sorting through the station's tech specs and despairing.

"Well, they're a Daimler subsidiary's R&D station, so I guess we should expect this kind of security, but look at this." Iridian pointed at the biosensor array near the entrance to the docking bay where the longhauler prototype was kept. They'd both squeezed into Adda's workspace generator to visualize the problem more effectively. Iridian's lack of a direct physical connection meant that she looked at the salient points projected onto the generator's ceiling while Adda manipulated it in the workspace.

She'd helped Adda create a starry observatory workspace setting when they started this session. The viewpoint moved like they were in micrograv, but Iridian still felt Rheasilvia Station's one g. The disconnect was slightly nauseating.

Among the stars, a biosensor array grew huge beneath Iridian's pointer finger, with model numbers, ranges, and other known features in tiny text all around the devices themselves, filling in as the program used Adda's mental focus on the subject to search for names and specs. "I don't see us getting around this, and it's practically the second thing we have to deal with."

"We should EMP the whole station, or maybe just the bay where the prototype ship is stored. The testing team locks themselves down as best they can, then we send them running for the exits with some false alarms." Adda had a lot of experience convincing hab management AIs to generate false alarms. "I wonder why Oxia needs all this stuff, and needs it off their semipublic record. The internal records must be in their primary datacenter, wherever that is."

Iridian frowned. "It's that project they're funding with the hidden money Captain Sloane pointed out, yeah? I mean, otherwise they'd just adjust their budget and buy stuff the usual way."

"Oxia Corporation does infrastructure projects, some mining; it's got an extensive shipping line to support those . . . So what does it need with the latest pseudo-organic printer, the smallest and most self-reliant longhauler I've ever read about, and an astronomer who didn't want to work for them in the first place? Sloane may be trapped in their contract, but even supplying the crew doesn't come cheap, and we're getting paid on top of that."

"Competition, yeah?" Iridian shifted against Adda and Adda breathed in deep, like the movement knocked her out of the workspace. She sighed and Iridian rolled to pull her nearer, fighting the drugs and implants that tugged Adda's mind back toward the workspace. Adda'd been weighing her sharpsheet doses before she took them lately, pinching off the ends sometimes and stashing them in an empty case to supplement a full sheet when she wanted more. "I can't keep looking at that stuff," Iridian said. "Makes my head hurt. How can you do this for hours?"

When Adda subvocalized, minute movements of her lips and throat were all Iridian could see of it, even when she was lying right next to her. *Competition. Right. With whom?*

"Companies like them?" Iridian shrugged and used her comp to retrieve a social feed they'd referenced heavily while researching crews to join. "Like we're competing against other crews? And winning, by the way. The Oxia link is common knowledge in Rheasilvia Station, maybe Albana Station on the other side of Vesta too. That info hasn't really made it off the 'ject yet because Oxia owns the local info traffic, and stationsec. So the other crews think . . . oh, here's a link." She sent a feed to Adda's comp and, with an effort, refocused on the projected window into Adda's workspace.

Adda'd expanded the feed's avatars into full figures, which spoke in text bubbles and stilted digital voices. She was apparently curating the conversation as she absorbed it, because it proceeded more linearly in the workspace than it had on the feed.

". . . back, for sure. The crew was doing nothing but stupid thug shit on Vesta while Captain Sloane was on Barbary Station. Guess he thought he had to come back and deal with it in person."

Other shadowy figures appeared and stuttered through ". . . andro," "not a he," and nonsensical insults until Adda found another section she was interested in. "ITA and Martian LE are going to tear them in half fighting over their carcass the second Sloane fucks something up. This hero worship bullshit is going to end, you sad fucks are all going to come here crying about it, and I'll laugh my ass off."

Adda skimmed through a subthread of venom, mostly directed at the original poster's assumed Earther status due to the metaphor of choice as well as "envy of the biggest success in the NEU and the asteroid belt."

She waved the figures away. "So Sloane's crew's back to the status it held when we first read about them. The captain will be committed to keeping that."

"It's part of why Sloane's trying so hard to break the contract legally, yeah," Iridian said. "That, and alienating megacorporate clients would remove us from the hiring list when we don't have a good target of our own. The same reason that the ZVs distanced themselves from us after Barbary. Oh, and that way we don't give ITA, NEU, and ambitious colonies an extra reason to hunt us down."

"Evading consequences when megacorporations control the local laws and law enforcers would be much more difficult with a reputation for contract-breaking," said Adda. "Sloane's base of operations is nice, but it can't withstand a siege, and . . . honestly, I don't want to be involved in that kind of power struggle." The station map with the target ship highlighted reappeared before them. "This is much more interesting. I just want to know how it all fits together."

Iridian shrugged. "In the meantime, the sensor array?"

"EMP," Adda reminded her. "So we're going to need a second pilot, to avoid having to coerce the test pilot into flying the prototype ship to Sunan's Landing." The occasionally mobile Ceresmax freighter Sunan's Landing would be a stopping point where the stolen ship would be disguised and anonymized before continuing to the destination of Oxia's choosing. "I'm still deciding on the best way to get that pilot off the station. Once they're gone, the prototype ship's copilot will be unsupervised until our pilot takes control."

"Shit, will it?" Iridian yelped. As a spacefarer and a person with an abiding interest in tech, Adda must've expected Iridian to know that. But unlike Adda, Iridian only thought about AI so she could stay the hell away from it. "That can't be safe. There's some kind of maintenance mode, isn't there?"

"There is, but it takes time to put a copilot in maintenance, and time to take it out," Adda said. "There's no publicly available documentation on this particular copilot's development cycle. I can't even estimate how long it would take on this prototype ship."

"Could we shut it down and restart it, like we did with AegiSKADA?"

AegiSKADA's name made Adda open her eyes and focus on Iridian with a wary anxiety that made Iridian regret mentioning it. "That worked because AegiSKADA was in a pseudo-organic quantum comp. The prototype's tank is pure pseudo-organics, like the other Barbary ships," Adda said. "Also, we got lucky with AegiSKADA. Quantum computers don't always decontaminate that effectively, and the intelligences involved don't always recover undamaged. And, if you'll recall, that also took at least thirty minutes. Swapping out the pilots is faster and more reliable."

"I hate this," said Iridian. "AIs get awful ideas when they're unsupervised."

"If it turns out that the prototype's maintenance mode is well documented, well tested, and easy to take the copilot in and out of, then I'll use it during the pilot transfer. I'm not counting on that, though." Adda said it like she'd already dismissed that possibility, and would only be reexamining maintenance mode to humor Iridian.

Usually Adda was a lot more optimistic about the effectiveness of AI safety procedures. Her acknowledgement that they were taking a big risk with this AI made Iridian's skin crawl. Adda would be working with a minimally tested, unsupervised intelligence, and she didn't even sound that worried about it. That just wasn't right. Then again, anybody who made a career out of working with AIs was missing a thing or two from their self-preservation skill set.

"Anyway," Adda continued, "I want Chi available in case someone gets hurt, and you and I will go of course, but . . ." The station map around them dissolved and reassembled into a full-size blueprint of the target ship's main cabin. "This ship's copilot is based on last year's intelligence development trends, which I'm still catching up on, and it's prepared to do more on its own than any shipboard intelligence I've ever read about."

"It's not awakened, though, yeah?"

Everything Pel knew about rolling his eyes he'd learned from Adda. "Awakening an intelligence is not like flipping a switch. You'd have to break down the limiters first, and there's no guide to doing that, since it's illegal. Then you'd spend hours leading the intelligence down a path to sentience, with somebody watching development readouts and somebody else watching you, ready to pull you out of the workspace when it looks like you're getting influenced, which will happen if you don't take turns with at least one other developer. And if you get influenced you're off the project, because your team can't stop development for months while you recover. Oh, and there's no standard development path, so you'd have to test even more frequently than usual to make sure you're doing what you think you're doing. I don't know how Si Po, Kaskade, and Captain Sloane awakened the Barbary intelligences without ten kinds of disasters. And two of them are . . ."

Adda stopped herself, but the sentence finished itself in Iridian's head anyway. "Dead, yeah, I know that."

"Didn't you . . ." Adda's pause and frustrated grimace meant that she was looking for a way to say what she wanted to say without insulting Iridian. That was sweet of her. "Didn't you find it interesting," Adda said, "that the person AegiSKADA expended that single Attaco drone on was Kaskade? It could've killed any one of us with that drone, including me, and I had just proved that I wanted to modify its behavior. Instead it chose her. And then, when it could've attacked you on the station's surface, it chose Si Po as its primary target instead."

"I found it fucking terrifying." Iridian rolled from her side to her back. The workspace generator bowed out where her shoulder pressed into it, distorting the projections. "Wait. None of those three had left base for months when we got there, except for a few unplanned trips to the docking bay."

Adda nodded, staring at something Iridian couldn't see. "AegiSKADA interpreted awakening the copilot intelligences as a very dangerous act, yes."

"That put Kaskade and Si Po at the top of AegiSKADA's hit list. Gods-*damn* it, I hate AIs." Iridian sat up and immediately hunched over to keep from pulling on the generator and the cord attaching it to Adda's nasal jack.

"It would never have seen something like them before," Adda said quietly. "Awakened intelligences are that rare. And they could have awakened with much more . . . aggressive priorities."

"All right, all right," Iridian said. "I have enough bad memories from Barbary without thinking about what would've happened if the AIs awakened *wrong*. Let's keep the Barbary AIs the hell away from the prototype's copilot. The last thing we need is a clone of the *Coin*, or worse."

"Agreed," said Adda. Her hand found Iridian's in the dim generator and held on, a warm and grounding defense against the chilling reminder of what they'd gone through on Barbary.

The Barbary intelligences still hadn't told anyone why the *Coin* had followed the crew to Mars. The intelligences had put themselves in danger and expended time and fuel helping the only person who'd awakened them and lived to tell the tale, Captain Sloane. They seemed to understand that Iridian and Adda worked for Sloane, so Adda's current hypothesis was that they were helping them to help Sloane, in exchange for putting the captain's name on whatever maintenance, docking, and upgrades they wanted. None of the intelligences had responded to Adda's queries regarding what needs they were meeting that way, so she had a routine running to find every use of a crewmember's name which could be one of the Barbary AIs instead.

For now, Adda seemed content to let her subconscious work that problem over, and keep her conscious attention on the crew's current task. "Before I convince the prototype ship's intelligence that we're not actually stealing it, I could really use an infiltrator to make some progress first. Get us the access credentials we need, deliver a cover story so we're expected . . . And having someone there early means we can hold off on the EMP until we're in a good position to recover the ship."

"EMP is fucking terrible for ships," Iridian said. "All of the electronics are vulnerable if they're not shielded. Have you got a list of what's accessible from the bridge console?" Adda found one and projected that too. Iridian's gaze traveled down the list of subsystem monitors. "I don't see anything specifically shielding propulsion, or the pseudo-organic tank. Pseudo-organics die from overheating or accept weird input from fried tech."

"How long would it take to restore basic functions if the ship were hit by an EMP?" Adda's line of questioning suggested that she wanted to EMP Jōju Station without affecting the prototype, but she always made contingency plans.

Iridian frowned at the list of subsystem monitors. "Hours, assuming I have all the right parts and equipment and guides. What if we go a little smaller and just hit the station's sensor array? That'll stop them from targeting the ship when we move it, and they couldn't track it once we're gone. They'll have a shielded backup, radar maybe, but that's a lot easier to mess with."

"We could shield the whole ship, couldn't we?" Adda backed the visuals out of the ship to hover above it, in a small docking bay.

"Yeah, the bay locks down somehow. Each module should have its own lockdown function. But we need somebody to set that up before we zap the rest of the station."

"Somebody on the inside," Adda said. "Well, Captain Sloane must know an infiltrator. Maybe the surveillance person from Deimos?"

* * *

"Ogir?" Captain Sloane asked, when Adda and Iridian presented the idea in the VIP lounge in the club, where Sloane conducted most crew business. "No. He's excellent among large populations and with any surveillance system you care to name, but he relies on disappearing into a crowd and changing places with team members when he's spotted. This station won't provide him with enough cover."

"The permanent population never gets above a hundred, as far as I can tell," said Adda. Iridian settled back in her chair to let Adda run the conversation, since she was in the mood to speak up today.

"Hmm." Sloane scrolled through a list on Tritheist's comp, while Tritheist patiently held it out for Sloane's view. The captain's comp was already occupied with something else. "Luwum's in prison, and so is Cheng, and Masipag's in rehab again so she's useless until she stabilizes one way or the other. Ocampo's on a long assignment. Wichmann . . ."

"In the Kuiper Belt," Tritheist said. "By the time ve gets here, the op will be over."

"Angel?"

"Blew up over Tethys a few months ago."

"Pity. I liked her." Sloane sighed. "Well, Liu Kong's been badgering me to send one of his people on these assignments. He thinks he'll learn to replicate our success without our personnel. He can't, of course. So we could ask Liu Kong to recommend an infiltrator. Alternatively, we could keep looking for somebody we trust to complete the groundwork, and take one of Oxia's pilots to quiet Liu Kong."

That suggestion surprised Adda into maintaining eye contact with the captain. "Both of those would be essential personnel on this operation."

Sloane nodded in unconcerned contemplation. "They'll be surrounded by people we trust. And it's easier to come by a good pilot than a good infiltrator these days. The war was hard on human intelligence experts." Rumors were still surfacing about all the spy versus spy that'd gone on. It wouldn't surprise Iridian if the survivors had gotten out of the business afterward.

Tritheist gently retrieved his wrist from Sloane's grip. "I'll make Oxia give us the best pilot they have." The warm look Sloane gave him didn't even require a smile to show what the captain thought of that response. Iridian didn't see anything attractive about the lieutenant, but apparently competence fit the captain's tastes well.

Looking at Adda as she and Iridian crossed the dance floor, Iridian thought she and Sloane might have that in common. Adda was keeping up with everything Sloane threw at her. She spent more time than ever reading on her comp, in a workspace, or staring sightlessly in their suite with her mind a million klicks away. She'd let Iridian put whatever she wanted on their suite's walls, change all the colors on the furnishings. Hell, she'd only noticed the rearranged furniture when she tripped over a table that'd been in a different place when she left her workspace generator than when she went in.

And from the current faraway look in her eyes, Iridian didn't even bother offering a romantic dinner. Adda would either stare at her food while thinking about something else, or decline and disappear into her workspace generator again. Iridian kissed Adda on the temple and reached for her running shoes. Now that they finally lived somewhere with a real gym, she'd worried that Adda would feel left out, but Adda never took her up on an offer to come along.

* * *

During Iridian's evening run around the security personnel's training gym track, in-house like so many of Sloane's facilities were, Pel appeared in the doorway. She hadn't been able to talk any of Sloane's off-duty security people into another training run, so she could stop early. She finished her lap and stepped out of the sim track to stretch. "What's up?"

Today his new eyes were dark blue, with silver flecks in the iris. He could change them in seconds, and frequently did. The perfect and occasionally unnatural coloring, and the surfaces which appeared harder or more reflective than Iridian's brain expected, were the only signs that the eyes had pseudo-organic components. She was still getting used to him looking directly at her when he spoke.

Judging by the long pause while she bent at the waist to stretch her calves, he wasn't used to looking at her, either. "I want to go on your next op," he finally said.

Iridian couldn't blame him for that. An actual ship heist, like the stories all glamorized? Who wouldn't want in? And she'd've been bored as hell sitting around a station for weeks. She finished the stretch while she formed an answer. "What would you do?"

Pel shrugged. "I mean, I can be a good lookout now. And if you need in-flight entertainment?" He shrugged again. "I dunno, what do you need done?"

"Something we have motion sensing cams for," Iridian said as kindly as she could.

There was a reason Pel came to her about this, and not Adda. As far as Iridian was concerned, keeping him happy took priority over keeping him safe. Adda had to feel the same way, or he would've left Barbary Station with the refugees, but she also worried about him too much. She'd've said no before she actually thought it over. After what'd happened to their mother, Iridian couldn't blame her. Everybody the war had touched came away with a few idiosyncrasies, or they were psychopaths with a few idiosyncrasies to begin with.

This op already required one new person: the second pilot. Iridian was working on Adda to get her to switch out Gavran as their primary pilot too. His ship was fine, but it'd be nice to fly with a pilot who'd use the regular mental enhancers formulated for pilots, instead of whatever Gavran had been on during the last op.

Pel was . . . possibly not the best choice for the infiltrator the op still needed. He'd have a hell of a time fitting in on a station full of astronautical engineers, more because of his personality than his pseudo-organics. But he was already frowning down at the track like she'd told him that, and, damn it, everybody needed a first chance. "Okay, how about this: We need somebody to get into the station to plant an EMP mine, and also scope out the docking bay and make sure it's shielded, or at least that it can be. I'll get with one of Ogir's people and teach you, just once. If you can walk me and Adda through it without help before you'd need to leave, and if Captain Sloane signs off on you, you're in."

Pel grinned. "I can do that! Besides, I'm my own cheat sheet." He shut his eyes for a second, and when he opened them bright yellow bloomed over dark blue irises while the previous color sank into the pupil.

"I assume you're seeing text now?" Iridian asked.

"Transcript of what you just said." He tapped his temple. "Just because it's pretty doesn't mean it's all for show!"

"All right," Iridian had to admit, "that's pretty cool."

* * *

Two nights before his cutoff date for launch, he recited all the steps to placing and activating the EMP mine and sending Iridian an in-depth visual tour of the docking bay. If anything unexpected happened she'd troubleshoot remotely but, as she told Adda,

"That shouldn't be a problem. I've learned a lot about their setup, teaching it to Pel. He'll need an ID, though."

"I'm getting him an internship." Adda still sounded worried. "You know how he is. Once he starts talking he's not going to stop. And all he's going to talk about is that one corner of the docking bay management system."

"I mean, yeah, that's a concern." Iridian paced around their suite. "But tell him to act like he's really good at finding and preventing electromagnetic interference generally, and that could actually fly, although it'd be . . . weird. If he wants to stay on Sloane's payroll—"

"Why should he?" Adda asked. "I can pay his way."

"You know he doesn't want that," Iridian said. "Let's see what he can do. If nothing else, it'll be nice to have someone along who cares about what happens to us beyond professional interest."

"Chi cares," said Adda.

"Hard to say," Iridian said. "What do we really know about her? Not that I'm asking you to find dirt on her," she said quickly, although Adda would've started searching the second Iridian suggested that Chi might not be trustworthy. "But right now, we're just squad members who don't piss her off. She's been through a hell of a lot of those in her lifetime. They come and go. You don't get attached to all of them, because then you miss them when they go. But you're sending Pel on this op, yeah?"

"He's leaving tomorrow," Adda said.

Iridian hugged her. "Okay, now we just need one good pilot and one who won't kill us."

"Gavran seems fine." Adda read the incredulity on Iridian's face, apparently, because she projected a dossier on her comp and showed it to Iridian. "Look at all these missions he's flown in. Sloane trusts him, and he hasn't crashed anything due to error."

Iridian tapped the projection on the back of Adda's hand to sort the list by causes of crashes Gavran was involved in. "Missiles, sabotage, more ship-to-ship . . . so his problem is he can't dodge?"

Adda shrugged. "I'd rather go with him than involve even more new people. We still need that second pilot to fly the prototype to Oxia's collection point. I really don't want one of the intelligences to do that."

* * *

She and Iridian walked Pel to the dock the next morning. Adda mothered him the whole way. "You're taking Transit 549 to Ceres, and then switching to the chartered ship to Jōju Station."

"Oh my gods, Sissy, it says that on my tickets. I can read!" He opened his eyes wide and did an eyeball-shaking trick he'd discovered in their focusing functions. The eyes jittered back and forth in his sockets while his pupils stayed facing forward. Iridian chuckled.

Adda grimaced. "Gross."

"So quit worrying," said Pel. "I'll be fine. This is a thousand times better than drinking twelve hours out of my average twenty-four. Hell, safer too."

"Your comm messages will be delayed. Even texts." She sounded a little desperate now.

"I'm used to that. We've only been talking in real time for like six months, remember? And yes, before you ask a-gods-damned-gain, I've got the pic of the pilot who's supposed to leave on the chartered ship I come in on, and I'll tell you when ve's gone. Trust me, for once. I'll. Be. Fine." Pel hugged her and walked into the public terminal alone.

Iridian wrapped an arm around Adda's waist and pulled her

against Iridian's side. "He's survived some awful stuff already. If I didn't think he could do it, I'd've said so." Adda tilted her head until it rested against Iridian's side. "We'll be right behind him," Iridian said. "Or at least a few days behind. Give him time to settle in and notify us of anything dangerous you don't know about already."

"And to give the Oxia pilot time to get here." Repeating her plan aloud in case Iridian found any errors in it seemed to make Adda feel more confident in it, even though Iridian rarely noticed anything out of place.

* * *

The Oxia pilot was older than Adda and Iridian, with freckled, brassy skin, hair like a bright green lens flare all around his head, and more energy than Iridian had before her first run of the day. He bounded out of an anonymous chartered transport and crossed the terminal angled toward Adda rather than Captain Sloane. "Adda Karpe? Yeah?"

Iridian grinned. Adda executed a halfway decent spacefarer bow, which the pilot returned. "And this is Captain Sloane." She held out an open hand toward the captain and failed to introduce Iridian, which was for the best considering Captain Sloane's growing frown.

The captain had been letting Adda make a lot of the how-to decisions on ops, but she might've gotten more credit than Sloane wanted on the last one. According to Pel, Vestans were still filling their social feeds with the University of Mars hassling Oxia for poaching one of their more productive researchers, despite Oxia blocking most of the negative press about it. Conveniently for U of M, the details of Björn's disgrace hadn't been made public. Local rumors associated the discord with Adda, not Sloane.

The Oxia pilot whirled toward Sloane and just about put his nose on his knees to bow deeper to Sloane than he had to Adda. The implant jack under the pilot's jaw flashed a white reflection of the terminal lights. "Captain Sloane, so sorry. I'm London Verney, test pilot with Oxia Corporation. Really great to meet you. Both of you, that is."

One awkwardly silent tram ride later, Sloane said, "I don't think I'm doing the crew as much good as I could be, supervising lawyers and being visible here. I'll join you this time." This last was to Adda, who nodded even as her eyes widened in alarm at having to revise her plans with Pel already involved.

You can do it, babe, Iridian thought at her.

* * *

Chi and Gavran weren't big exercisers, so even though Iridian would've preferred to introduce them to Verney on the track or at the gym, the VIP room at Sloane's club had to do. The digital bartender was back, a beauty of indeterminant gender and race whose full lips were fixed in a small smile. The human bartender was on the second floor, where Captain Sloane was holding court again.

The VIP room contained a few scattered individuals in widely varying clothes and gear, drinking and looking at their comps over black tabletops bathed in golden light. Iridian made a point of introducing herself whenever she spotted a new person. Adda had found every VIP room patron Iridian asked about in Sloane's roster of experts on call, and the ones who felt like talking always had a fun, or alarming, story about past ops. Sloane had inspired the kind of loyalty that drew people in from as far as the Saturnian colonies to welcome the captain back. Hell, experts from the Kuiper colonies might still be on their way here. That seemed like a good sign for the longevity of her and Adda's positions in Sloane's crew.

Adda had stayed in her workspace generator, revising her plans to accommodate Sloane's participation. The thicker mat Iridian had slipped into the generator during Adda's fretful few hours of sleep hadn't even garnered thanks. It was possible that Adda hadn't noticed the difference. Iridian was redirecting herself when she felt ignored, because Adda was carrying most of the op logistics, but the whole same-plane-different-orbits relationship dynamic was becoming tiresome. After they got Sloane out of the Oxia contract Adda would come back to her, and it couldn't happen soon enough.

In the VIP room, Iridian, Chi, and Gavran had barely gotten through pleasantries with Verney before Chi caught Iridian's eye, drew the word "Hey" out for two long beats, and followed it up with "Can I talk to you a minute?"

"Sure." Iridian stood and wandered to the side of the bar with the projected floor-to-ceiling window showing the dance floor. Chi followed.

"The hell is going on?" Chi asked at the perfect volume to be heard over the music while not carrying to Gavran and Verney. "I get we need two pilots, but *him*? Oxia's pilot, and an Earther too?"

"Adda's an Earther, and she's doing all right out here."

"She's not the damned pilot. What does Captain Sloane think of that?"

Iridian shrugged. "The captain's coming along to supervise."

"Ah, great." Chi's tone said that the captain's participation in the op was unwelcome news. She glanced over her shoulder at the pilots. "I don't mind saying, I'd rather run one of your ops than

Tritheist's. He asks the captain before he does every damned thing, and you and Karpe just handle it. I respect that. But I haven't been on a hab-based op with Captain Sloane in years, and those were bad times. And now Oxia's picking our crew? Something you want to tell us?"

Iridian quit half watching the dancers and turned toward Chi. "Captain Sloane wouldn't be coming unless . . ." Why was the captain on this op, anyway? "Unless there was something to be gained by having the captain along. Good local press, maybe?"

"Or Vesta's coming apart from the inside like they always say it will, with two spinning stations and all that new Oxia mining equipment under us." Chi turned away from the dance floor, toward the VIP bar.

Iridian followed. "The captain wouldn't leave Tritheist here if that were happening."

"And that lawyer. You know they're taking Sloane's lead council to bed, yah?" Chi grinned.

"No," Iridian said, in a way that meant "I don't believe it because it's too good to be true, so tell me everything and convince me."

That topic meshed poorly with "Oxia's gods-damned secret police. Secret police disappear people, and so does Oxia, so, same thing." Gavran was drunkenly adamant about this point, and too far into the Oxia pilot's personal space.

"Look, I don't know a thing about that." Verney leaned away from Gavran. Nobody else watching the exchange looked like they'd step in, and somebody should. Iridian approached with her hands open by her thighs and near her shield, her pace casual and easy to follow, and her head up in her best de-escalation posture.

"They give me something new to fly, and I fly it," Verney said. "Besides, Oxia's the best thing that could've happened to this chunk of rock, stationsec included. The 'ject was a seething mess of barely functioning crap before they took it over. And the only person I know of 'disappearing' is that UM astronomer, when you people rescued ver from that runaway ship. Lazy maintenance can't very well be blamed on—"

Iridian saw the punch coming, and Verney just sat there talking. Gavran's windup was big enough for her to get her mostly deployed shield between the pilots. His fist thumped against its center. Verney yelped in surprise, Gavran in pain. One of the loners at the tables pulled her—his?—knife, met Iridian's eyes, glanced at the shield, and sheathed the blade again.

Iridian pulled Verney off his stool and pushed him onto the one next to it so she could sit between him and Gavran. She raised an eyebrow at Gavran through the fully deployed shield. "I'm done, I'm done," Gavran said. He shook out his hand and winced.

Iridian grinned and lowered the shield without collapsing it. Drunk moods changed quickly, but she trusted him not to throw another punch in the next few seconds. "You really meant that. I'll have to check the shield over before we leave."

Verney leaned around her to glare at Gavran, and she mirrored his posture to get in his way. "I don't know which of his drug-sucking friends fell down which mineshaft," Verney said, "but Oxia Corporation—"

"Shut it," Iridian snapped at him. If Gavran had lost someone like the argument implied, then he sure as hell didn't need Verney's crap about it. *Hey babe, can we put the Oxia pilot on one of the Barbary AIs' ships for the trip out? They could let him think he's flying it.*

The Apparition's the one coming, Adda replied. *It's the one fueled and docked on Vesta while Casey and the Coin come and go. But it's too long a trip to leave him alone with the Apparition's intelligence.*

While Adda was subvocalizing, Verney was saying, "It's not fair that he—"

"Keep it shut, or I'll fucking punch you," Iridian said once Adda finished. She was right. The first time he talked to the copilot he'd figure out it was very different from any other copilot he'd flown with. That'd be trouble.

Chi settled on the last stool in line on the other side of Gavran to look at his hand and scowl over his shoulder at Verney in sharp, randomized doses. After a couple of those, Verney found a woman near the cam that fed the window projection and watched her like she was dancing just for him.

Iridian smiled slightly, and commented to Adda, *Nothing brings a group together like throwing in an outsider.*

People are ridiculous, whispered Adda.

* * *

A few hours after the *Mayhem* and the *Apparition* left Rheasilvia stationspace for Jōju Station, Pel's first scheduled vid recording arrived. "I'm in! Ha, I've always wanted to say that."

He glanced around, and Iridian commented, "I wouldn't have recorded where I thought I'd be interrupted." Adda's frown meant "Shush" in this context. They stood together in the *Mayhem*'s residential cabin, watching Pel confirm that his first progress report on infiltrating Jōju Station's prototype ship project wouldn't attract the attention of station personnel.

"The local test pilot's gone. I said the stuff you said to say about the docking bay, and they think I know what I'm talking about, but they also gave me a huge honking file to study. I'm sending that to you . . . now." Pel tapped at his comp. "They're all completely head over heels for this prototype ship. They barely know who's in the room with them most of the time. This is going to be cake." Pel winked at the cam and shut it off.

Adda shook her head. "I don't like it when he says that. He's usually wrong."

"Did you hear what he said about the station personnel?" Iridian asked. "That sounds bad too. Do you think the prototype copilot's influencing them?"

"It's possible, but it seems unlikely." Adda sounded like she'd checked out of the conversation and was already thinking of some other project on her comp.

"It'll be unsupervised until you change the pilot designation over to Verney," Iridian pointed out. "That's a great chance for it to take over the station or something."

Adda sighed impatiently. "As long as people don't access the ship's internal systems or try to fly it, the copilot shouldn't be able to interact with station personnel. It has to interact to influence them. It's an easily preventable problem. Besides, the station management intelligence's supervisor is still on site. Part of that person's responsibility is keeping people from getting influenced by any intelligences in the facility."

Iridian could second-guess her all day, but Adda had years of study and hours of lab time on what AIs generally did. Even though Adda had an answer for everything, Iridian couldn't help wondering what else might go wrong. Insufficiently tested prototype AIs had to be almost as dangerous as the awakened ones, for the same reason all AIs were dangerous: no human really understood what the AI was thinking.

CHAPTER 15

Test 02 connection established, calibration initiated

A couple hours later, the *Mayhem* **passed the outer buoy of** Jōju Station's network. The *Apparition* stopped outside stationspace. Before Adda could investigate why it'd stopped, Pel pinged her comp. The message's local timestamp was 9:40 a.m., within half an hour of what she expected for Jōju Station's local time. Less than a minute later he recalled the short message with the word "lonely" in it, as if he'd changed his mind about sending it. This was the signal they'd agreed on to indicate that he'd set the EMP mine and the prototype ship could be shielded from it. Nobody was following him. Nobody was even suspicious.

He was surprisingly on top of that communication, and he'd installed the comms duplicating routine the way it was supposed to be done, so that she'd get anything Jōju Station sent out as a call for help. He was taking his role in the operation seriously.

"He's ready," Adda told the crew in the *Mayhem*. "Go on as scheduled."

The comms duplicating routine would let her track the ITA's

response to automated notifications the station's intelligence would send after the EMP went off. Her schedule had the pirates well away from Jōju Station before the ITA's rescue party arrived to help the station residents repair the damage, but it paid to be informed.

The station guided them to a passenger terminal, and Adda led the way out of the *Mayhem*'s passthrough with all but Gavran and Chi following. The ring station's Earthlike gravity was a relief after all the gravity adjustments while they docked, even though the sensation of her internal organs sinking into their usual positions was deeply and literally unsettling. The increased gravity also made the bag of gear she carried heavier than she'd expected, but that was normal for interplanetary travelers' experience with their luggage. Projected messages on the terminal warned them about nondisclosure policies and various dangers inherent in shipyard experiments.

When Adda was about two steps from the doorway to the rest of the station, Pel burst into the terminal. He threw his arms around her like he hadn't seen her for weeks instead of days. His eyes were purple with dark blue pupils, because of course he wouldn't try to make them unobtrusive while undercover. He felt tense and wired in her arms. "Sissy! I'm so glad you're here, finally." He lowered his voice to add, "This wasn't as fun as I thought it'd be. These people kinda remind me of you."

If she'd never met Iridian, Adda might've developed ship intelligences in a place like this. Sloane's crew could've been stealing her years-long project. She hugged Pel tighter and whispered, "Almost over." If she'd worked for the corporation that owned this place, there would have been too many managerial demands on the intelligence's development process to do it in a way she'd be proud of.

"Well, let's have a tour!" Captain Sloane said loudly and with frankly alarming good cheer. "We can settle in later."

Iridian had rigged up a small, wearable cam disruptor that Adda hid beneath her silver necklace. Whenever she came in range, the disruptor replaced the cam's live feed with a loop from twenty seconds before she was in view, and held that until she left transmission range. It was much safer than finding her way through a strange station while interfacing with the local intelligences. They'd come a long way since their first hijacking.

Her comp pulsed in the pattern she'd set to notify her if AegiSKADA did anything other than precisely what she'd asked it to do. Earlier, she'd asked it to analyze Rheasilvia and Albana station security data. It'd found standard practices that'd help Adda defend headquarters against a station security assault, if it ever came to that. The notification had alerted her that AegiSKADA was requesting Casey's access protocols for ITA databases, which meant that Casey had told it about those protocols.

Now that Casey had seen AegiSKADA's request come across Adda's comp, it'd already be in the process of teaching AegiSKADA everything it knew about ITA data structure. Or, as was equally possible, it'd ignore the message because it had something else it'd rather do with its resources. Adda approved AegiSKADA's request. She had no control over Casey, and she was already working with more intelligences than was healthy. She didn't need AegiSKADA's notifications distracting her from getting Verney accepted as supervisor of the prototype ship's AI copilot.

Pel walked them through the station, loudly announcing facts and introducing them to everybody they passed. Even though he just gave their first names, combining that with the traveling cam malfunction could draw unhelpful connections for station security. "What are you doing?" Adda whispered at him after the third distracted scientist he interrupted.

Pel shrugged, sharp and quick and unlike his usual laid-back affability. "That's how I've been here this whole time. Nobody's been, like, surprised, right? That's what I'm supposed to do. Keep it normal until we get to the ship."

That did seem like an effective part of keeping his cover, she supposed. Every rushed introduction had been met with eye-rolling normalcy. The introductions also gave her the opportunity to search each person for exterior connectors to neural implants, and for the common symptoms of AI influence: distant stares, paranoia, and dissociation. The station personnel they'd met so far looked fine.

From Adda's other side, Iridian asked Pel, "Do you actually like these people?"

"Kind of," Pel said defensively. "There's something to like in almost everybody."

"There's something to dislike in everybody too," Iridian said. "Besides, you're not fucking them over. Oxia is."

"Hey!" said the Oxia pilot.

"Less talking would be ideal," Captain Sloane said sternly.

"Well, due respect and all, but can you not talk about Oxia Corporation like that? They've done a lot for the universe, and—"

Adda startled away from a fast movement and the sharp snap of Sloane's flapping coat. When she got a good look at the situation, Captain Sloane had the Oxia pilot pinned against the wall with a hand on his throat. The pilot's skin was turning white around the captain's fingers, and his eyes were wide and panicked. "Shut up until you're needed," Sloane snarled. When the captain released Verney and stalked away in the direction Pel had been walking, the Oxia pilot's heels thudded back to the floor. They all walked faster to match Sloane's pace.

So this is what the captain's like without Tritheist, Iridian said over their implanted comms. *Interesting.*

What is? Adda asked, referencing the difference as well as the item of interest.

I used to think Tritheist's barking and growling was all him, Iridian subvocalized. Her dark red lips moved slightly, but she otherwise concealed their conversation. It was a shame that documenting how well their practice had paid off would spoil the secret. *Now I'm wondering if Captain Sloane encourages it. Sloane gets to keep cool while Tritheist looks like an ass-melon. Good arrangement, if you're the cool one.*

Adda did not keep her cool about the ass-melon crack. Pel looked at her with something like shock and pride, giggling down the hall and drawing the curious stares of serious scientists and engineers.

Adda's comp buzzed so hard it shook her hand. She held on to Pel's elbow, letting him guide her while she skimmed through a long list of alerts on her comp.

"Problem?" Sloane murmured on her other side.

"Several." Adda skimmed the list a second time, then glared at the Oxia pilot. "Did you just send your credentials to the prototype?"

He raised his hands defensively, gaze darting between Sloane and Adda. "Hey, whoa, it was going to need them eventually! What's the problem?"

"It doesn't recognize them because I haven't told it to." And inaudibly to all but Iridian, Adda said, *Putting the intelligence in maintenance mode would make the pilot transition harder now, not easier. We're going to have to keep it unsupervised until Verney's credentials are accepted.*

"Ah, fuck," Iridian said aloud, soon enough after Adda's first assessment that everyone could attribute the reaction to that.

"Keep to the plan for now," said Captain Sloane.

"We'll need to move faster." Adda used her grip on Pel's arm to march him toward the docking bay she'd located on her station map. Spacefarers marked some station maps with ticks showing a distance from station north, but Adda had written a routine to translate that into something that made sense to her. She could adapt to spacefarer culture sometime when lives didn't depend on getting to the right place quickly. "Pel, did you plug in that datacask I sent with you?"

She hated to ask about something so obvious, but one of the main reasons she'd sent him to the station before everyone else was to prime her access route to the prototype ship's intelligence, and he hadn't confirmed that he'd done it. Iridian and Captain Sloane could plant or even build an EMP generator, but making inroads with intelligences took time. She'd be dealing with two new ones here: the prototype ship's copilot, and the station management intelligence.

"Yeah, first thing, so I didn't forget," said Pel.

Iridian said something positive about the workaround for his distractibility while Adda spoofed sensor conditions that would constitute an environmental emergency if they were real. Alarms blared and a prerecorded message erupted from speakers somewhere in the hallways. "Emergency. This is not a drill. Proceed to your designated docking bay for immediate evacuation." The agendered voice delivered the docking bay numbers in a drastically different tone from the rest of the announcement. It betrayed the system's age, which also gave it the vulnerabilities that allowed Adda to take control of some of the station subsystems.

Now that all the station personnel were heading for the exits, she could get into a workspace and find out what the prototype ship's intelligence was doing with the Oxia pilot's information. "Please don't contact the prototype until I say it's ready, all right?

Let everybody get out of its docking bay. Pel, is the workspace generator still installed in the lab next door?"

"Yeah." Pel gave her a confused look. "It's too big to move without one of us seeing it go by."

A crowd of people running while attempting to put on jumpsuits over lab clothes and thermoses ran past. Sloane's crew put their backs to the wall to give them space. None of the station personnel invited the crew to join them, although they did give them confused looks. They'd have at least forty-eight hours of breathable air in their jumpsuits. The ITA had a ship within thirty hours of the station, if not closer. Adda's information was as up-to-date as she could make it. The station personnel would be all right.

From several meters behind her, Verney inhaled like he'd taken a short nap while leaning against the wall. "Jesus, are they all going to be floating around outside? Might hit something." The Oxia pilot's voice was quieter and more distant than she'd have expected from someone talking to people this far ahead of him.

Adda opened her mouth to say yes. Captain Sloane said, "Quiet" before she could.

The permanent workspace generator in the lab near the prototype's docking bay had a padded table one could climb onto and slide into the generator on a track, and a high-quality visualization setup which Adda didn't have time to admire. She lay on the table and pressed a sharpsheet onto her tongue. "Iri, could you check the settings?"

Iridian woke the console out of sleep mode and frowned at the projected readout. "What's it supposed to be set for?"

"Just make sure nobody's profile is loaded, and that the connection shows the prototype intelligence's designation." Somebody else's customizations would interfere with the ones Adda was going to make once she got into the workspace. The sharpsheet was lighting her brain on fire, in a good way.

"Yeah, looks ready for you." Iridian smiled at her over the console, although her dark brows furrowed with worry. "Need a push?"

A short railing with grip texture affixed to the main body of the generator gave Adda sufficient leverage to pull herself into the generator's visualization coil. "No. Closing up." The front flap of the generator whispered over her ankles, then fell into position, blocking out the lab's light and sound. Iridian would be outside watching her back.

In the workspace, a gray fog drew away from her. She stood in a cold, quiet morning, surrounded by stones the color of rusting iron. Towering rock formations arched inward around her in frozen, sharpened waves. Fog hid the taloned tips of the taller waves. Her virtual art gallery tours had certainly added variety to her workspaces.

At the end of a long trough between the still waves, fog silhouetted a humanoid figure. Its arm, held straight out in front of it, met the arms of someone else, who seemed much more solid and . . . recognizable.

Over their implant connection, Adda subvocalized to Iridian: *Where is the pilot?*

The silhouetted figures turned toward Adda. "I sent the signal," Adda said. "We need to talk."

A copy of the first silhouetted figure, now a shadow without the fog to cover it, appeared closer to her, but still well out of arm's reach. "You sent the signal."

"Yes," Adda told the prototype's AI copilot. In documentation about this intelligence, the development team had called it Ermine. "We need you to come with us. Accept that man's pilot credentials and we'll start lift-off procedures."

Ermine's silhouetted head shook slowly. "He says there is no 'we.'"

Adda stared. An intelligence would generally describe some-one's intention to leave a group in more of a summary than a direct quote. Worse, this one spoke like it understood what it was saying. "Stop talking to him." Iridian hadn't replied with Verney's location, which meant he wasn't with the rest of Sloane's crew. He had to be at a console somewhere, or inside the prototype ship itself, to communicate directly with the prototype's copilot intel-ligence.

The silhouetted head cocked to one side. "Why?"

"He's your pilot. You talk to the pilot through the interface software." That safeguard should've been built into all shipboard intelligences.

"He isn't my pilot." Ermine shifted position, somehow making itself larger in the process, the edges of itself hardening without being defined.

Adda focused on where a human's eyes would be. "I told you to accept his credentials." She forced herself into a calming breathing pattern. One of the first things intelligences learned about humans was that emotion made them vulnerable to confu-sion and manipulation. "Why didn't you accept them?"

"Station intelligence has identified a need for additional back-ground investigation," said Ermine. "I am waiting."

Its refusal to accept the credentials was within protocol. The prototype intelligence was taking advantage of Verney's incau-tious approach to do something that it couldn't do without him. Whatever it was, it wasn't part of Adda's operational plan.

CHAPTER 16

> All known works, feeds, and records of Harmony Wong, "Mother of modern artificial intelligence development."—3.8 gigabytes

Babe, I can't find Verney, Iridian said in the best subvocalization she could manage while running through a strange hab looking for a lost idiot pilot. *He was in the docking bay with the others a minute ago. Nobody saw him leave, but he's not in there now. Captain Sloane's ready to kill him and fly the ship without him.* The captain would've needed pilot's implants to do that, but the sentiment was definitely there.

Verney's in the prototype ship, Adda whispered in her ear. *Stay out of it.*

Iridian stopped in the hallway between the docking bay and the rest of Jōju Station. *The fuck is he doing in there?* she asked Adda.

The intelligence invited him, in some way he couldn't ignore, Adda replied. *Maybe through his piloting implants. I'm trying to get him approved to fly the prototype. That will put the copilot intelligence under his supervision.*

Can you get him out of there first? Iridian demanded. "Godsdamned manipulative AI . . ." She'd said that out loud, so the implanted mic would filter it out without sending it to Adda. Her comp might have transmitted it over the op channel instead.

Adda was still in the workspace, and who knew what she and the ship's AI were up to in there. Iridian ran back to the docking bay. She had no intention of leaving a person alone in a ship run by an out-of-control AI, even if the person worked for Oxia. Barbary Station had been an excellent illustration of the damage an unsupervised AI could do, and that was before they'd brought the *Apparition*'s copilot, an awakened AI, into the situation.

"He's on the ship," Iridian shouted as soon as she got back into the bay.

According to Adda's plan, they all should've boarded the prototype ship together and hooked up to the *Mayhem* to redistribute crew later. It should now be obvious to everyone that something was going sideways. Captain Sloane and Pel were on their way to the elevator that, on most stations, led to an observation and control room near the docking bay, but they stopped walking to look at Iridian.

Captain Sloane frowned. "Pel, come with me. I'll need your credentials to get into the control systems for the bay. Iridian, see if you can manually open the prototype's passthrough from here while I'm activating safety overrides. One of these may work."

"Yes, Captain." Iridian clenched her teeth and stalked toward the ship, listening for the whine and rumble of its engine starting. It was too easy to imagine those big domes on its sides as eyes watching her. She'd be on the ship's cams anyway, so it really did "see" her, but that was more disturbing if she imagined eyes.

A whiff of burned flesh made her wrinkle her nose, a memory from the last time she watched someone stand too near a departing ship. *This time is different,* she told herself. The steady tramp of her boots as she crossed the bay helped her find a rhythm to slow her breathing. Jōju Station's AI was supervised, even if its supervisor was currently floating in a jumpsuit in stationspace with the rest of the station personnel. The docking bay door would stay shut while she was in it, and the prototype's AI wasn't awakened. It barely even had room to lift itself off the pad, and it didn't have the capacity to want to.

While she'd been digging herself out of memories, she'd entered the death zone if the ship launched. She kept moving toward it. "You stay on the gods-damned pad," she muttered at the prototype.

Approaching it didn't cause the door to open or the engines to fire up. Neither did pressing her palm to the manual release. The scanner flashed under her hand. It'd open for somebody with the right ID. She was imagining the heat she felt through her palm, or at least she hoped she was.

"Verney? If you can hear me, open up." She listened for movement inside. All she heard was her own breathing. "The AI is lying to you. That's what they do, lie to you so you'll do things they can't." After another few seconds of nothing from inside the ship, she tried a different argument. "We're already behind on Adda's schedule thanks to you. If you fucking steal this ship from Captain Sloane there'll be trouble between us, and you don't want that. Hell, do you think Oxia wants that?"

A door inside the ship slid open and closed. It sounded more like an interior cabin door than one of the two heavy passthrough doors, so Verney was moving farther into the ship. "Pel, did your ID do anything?" she asked on the op channel.

"Nothing's worked so far, but Captain Sloane's still trying stuff," Pel said over the op channel. "I thought Adda said this ship had a zombie AI."

"It does. Like I keep saying, all AIs are dangerous, especially without a human holding the leash. Can you get station person- nel in here?" Iridian asked Pel. "Some of them have to have clear- ance to open this."

"Maybe. I'll try," Pel said. "I don't know how to get them back on station with just jumpsuits, though. They aren't supposed to reenter station grav."

"They might be able to do something from outside." Iridian peered at the door's mechanism. There were only so many ways to build a passthrough door.

"What if they don't want to help?" Pel asked.

"Then we'll convince them to help," Captain Sloane said in a tone that made Iridian swallow hard and refocus on the exterior passthrough door.

Iridian pressed something that looked like a release lever at the base of the door. A five by five centimeter panel popped open to reveal the kind of implant connecter bridge consoles used, which didn't help. Passthroughs had to be standardized to work with one another, and with habs across the solar system. The prototype's exterior door looked just like every other passen- ger passthrough Iridian had seen. This was more Tritheist's and Sloane's area of expertise than hers.

The exterior passthrough door cycled open and Iridian snapped her shield out in front of her. The interior passthrough door stayed closed.

"Did that open it?" Captain Sloane asked over the op channel.

"The exterior door's open." Iridian lowered her shield. "Interi- or's still shut."

"Ah," Captain Sloane said. "I'll try something else."

Come on, babe, we can't get the prototype open, Iridian subvocal- ized. *Are you doing something about that?*

After another few seconds of silence, Adda whispered, *Shit*.

Iridian winced. Adda was usually so good at subvocalizing only what she meant to. If she were making mistakes, then the prototype AI had to be putting up a fight in her workspace. She was already tracking the *Apparition*, Jōju Station's management AI, and who knew what other factors and metrics. If one of those AIs wanted to influence her, it couldn't ask for better circumstances.

"Pel, get back into the bay," Iridian said over the op channel. "This place isn't like Barbary. As long as somebody's in here, the ship can't take off, and I want to check on Adda."

Iridian took a few steps toward the room with the workspace generator and stopped just inside the door, watching the interior docking bay doors for Pel. *Babe, what the hell is going on in there? Are you talking to the prototype's AI?*

"Yeah, okay," Pel shouted across the bay. "I went in by the other door, but I'm here!"

Iridian spotted him and waved. "Stay here, yeah? Don't leave until I get back."

"Okay!" Pel was already reading something on his comp instead of looking at her, but that'd at least keep him in one place, she hoped.

The workspace generator was nearby, but the most Iridian could get out of Adda was that she was "in the middle of something," with enough annoyed bite to it to make Iridian leave her alone. Adda usually knew what she was doing in generators, and she'd definitely be mission-focused.

Iridian stomped back to the docking bay. Nothing was working out as Adda had planned, and once again it was the fucking AI and Oxia at fault.

Even the docking bay door was jammed. She waved at the motion sensor, then slammed the override icon next to the door. Nothing happened. Inside the bay, a roaring, whining sound rose rapidly in volume, and the projected label above the door lit with BAY SEALED—LAUNCH IN PROGRESS.

Iridian pounded on the shut door. "Pel, are you in there?"

"Fuck, I got sidetracked!" He sounded panicked and afraid on the op channel. "I found someone who can open the prototype's door, but she doesn't want to do it."

Iridian slammed her fist against the wall beside the door. Without armor, it hurt. She had to concentrate for a second to be sure she'd subvocalize when she said *Babe, get out here, the prototype's revving its gods-damned engines!*

CHAPTER 17

"It told me to. It told me to. It told me to. She told me to." Text repeated 312 times in a message to Mary and Estevan Verney from their son London. < 1 kilobyte

In Adda's workspace, Verney's formerly bronze skin paled as the pilot stood in the trough of growing stone waves with the prototype's intelligence behind him. The figure solidified from mostly shadow to crystalline blue-white ice in a human shape. It was feminine, but not strongly so. Although proportional, it was about half again as big as the average woman. It stood behind the Oxia pilot, its willowy arms wrapped around his chest and its silver hair flowing over his shoulders and around his hips.

Outlines of Verney's neural implants glowed through his skull in that same silver, a physical impossibility. That must've been the route the prototype had taken into his mind. The intelligence had somehow convinced him that he had to plug his implant net directly into a shipboard console in order to gain supervisory authority over it.

With unfettered access to his neural implants, it'd only take one or two simple errors on Verney's part to allow the intelligence unsafe levels of access to his mind, putting him in a state technically referred to as "influenced." Any zombie intelligence could create the condition by combining brain stimulation through the implants with convincing communications regarding what should've been happening as part of pilot acceptance instead of what actually was happening. Applied along the lines of whatever the intelligence determined was an effective motivator for the targeted individual, intelligences could make someone like Verney do just about anything.

This prototype intelligence had identified those motivations in a matter of minutes. Adda had worked with intelligences in early stages of development, under laboratory conditions. None of them had picked up her motivations as quickly as this one had apparently identified Verney's. Even AegiSKADA, which had been developed with uniquely effective analysis capabilities, had observed her for days on end before it found a form that had a hope of swaying her.

Perhaps it'd been a mistake for Adda to trust Oxia's choice of pilots and trick the prototype's usual one into leaving the station. A two-pilot transfer of supervision would've required the real test pilot's cooperation, which would've added days to the schedule and been either monetarily or morally costly. However, it would've taken the pressure off Verney.

"You're under the copilot AI's influence," Adda told Verney, slowly and clearly. "Unplug your implants. Leave the ship. We'll find someone to help you deprogram." That someone would be Adda or Gavran, since they had the most training in getting an intelligence's influence out of a person's mind. Not that they had a lot of it, or the months of isolation from AI that it'd take to cure Verney completely.

If Verney had followed her instructions, he would've disappeared from the workspace, but his figure remained and soundlessly said, "The captain will kill me." The prototype's intelligence stroked a perfect crystal hand down his cheek.

Adda willed the headache out of her skull, which would ease it in the workspace, for a while. "Captain Sloane absolutely will not. Verney," she added as her thread coiled around a spool in her hand with his name on the end. "We need you." Best practices indicated a recently controlled pilot should be physically separated from the controlling ship for around sixty days once freed. Maybe Gavran would let him fly the Mayhem, although Adda wouldn't blame him if he didn't. "We brought you because we need you. But we need you, not you with Ermine in your head. It's an AI. Anything human about it is its attempt to control you. There is no backup pilot. Please leave the ship."

"Too hot," the Oxia pilot mouthed. "I'm too hot. It's so hot . . ." His face was going from white to red. Behind him and over his head, Ermine's possessive smile made Adda shiver as the implant outlines in his skull flared. And was the temperature increase the pilot was describing real, or an illusion Ermine created in Verney's mind?

"Ermine!" Adda pressed a strong intentional command into the workspace, demanding that the intelligence speak with her. Now that it had a pilot under its control, she had nothing it wanted. It ignored her. That was better than it digging into her mind to influence her too, but to save Verney she had to get through to at least one of them.

Adda let her mind fall out of the workspace, settling back in the soundproofed generator. She wobbled when she stood. After a few steps, she felt stable enough to run.

Iridian, Captain Sloane, and Pel stood at the observation deck window, watching the prototype ship. The window projection flickered in rhythm with the prototype's engines. Adda had seen pictures of it, but in person and turned on it looked even stranger than it had in a miniaturized projection. Four half domes made of interlocking nanofiber hexagons caught the eye first, two on each side, which schematics indicated supplemented both the power and comm systems. It was longer than any ship she'd seen in a docking bay, and most of it appeared to be engines. Anyway, Captain Sloane and Tritheist were the ship experts. They were counting on her to handle the AIs and personnel.

Iridian was staring wide-eyed at status reports scrolling down the right side of the projection. The number beside the uppercase C for interior temperature caught Adda's eye. "Fifty degrees? That can't be right."

"It's been rising for the past few minutes," Iridian said.

"The MO beside the temp control system stands for 'manually overridden,'" Captain Sloane said. "The heater's on, the engines are engaged, and . . ." The captain paused the status report feed by passing a finger through the projection. "The fins are retracted."

"Verney did that?" Adda asked.

"So it appears," said Sloane.

"I tried to get the intelligence's attention, but it's satisfied with what it already has," Adda said. "Is the EMP ready?"

"Yeah," said Pel. "I did everything you said to."

Adda glanced at Iridian. "Is this room shielded? Because we're going to need a bigger pulse than I originally planned for."

"Should be. The maintenance records are pretty vague."

"And the docking bay's the same?" Adda asked.

"Yeah."

So activating the EMP wouldn't shut the ship down while it was in the docking bay. "Is it actually leaving, or is it just using the engines to keep us away from it? How can we tell?"

Iridian scrolled through the projected status reports. "Ah,

come on, there's a checklist for everything," she muttered. If it were really fifty degrees Celsius inside the prototype's cabin, then the Oxia pilot had a matter of minutes before heatstroke set in.

"Gavran," Captain Sloane said over the operations channel. "We need to determine whether our prototype is leaving the station or testing its engines, and Verney is unable to communicate that. Suggestions?"

"Hard to say. Without a takeoff checklist I can't tell." Gavran sounded distressed that this was the best he could offer. If Adda had time to be upset, she'd probably feel the same herself. "Is thrust increasing, or is thrust stable?"

"Stable," said Captain Sloane.

"Launch trajectory transmitted? Repeat—"

"I heard you, I'm looking," Iridian snapped. "Yeah, one was sent about three minutes ago. A stationspace buoy was in the way . . . and it sent an updated one sixteen seconds ago."

"My guess is that it's taking off," Gavran said. "Only a guess about the takeoff, though." Iridian was wrong. Adda was never going to get used to that repetition.

On the projected observation window, the ship swiveled its engines to face the landing pad and lifted off of it. It sailed smoothly out of the bay, engines that were too bright to look at swiveling to keep it from running into the rotating station on its way out.

The captain asked, "Are you out of range, Gavran?" over the operation channel.

This was why Adda had talked Gavran into accepting enough operational details to make decisions in an emergency. "Yeah, fire away!" he said over the operation channel.

Adda subvocalized the comp command to trigger an incredible amount of electronics damage, as well as stopping the prototype.

"Uh, did you send it, Sissy?" Pel's brightly colored eyes searched the room and the empty docking bay for a reaction.

Iridian smiled grimly and gripped one of those handholds built so neatly into the wall that Adda would've overlooked it. "Give it a minute."

Something crackled loudly somewhere in the station below them. The lights went out. Even if the electronics in the docking bay and observation deck weren't fried, the generator powering them would've shut down. The silence was startling.

It was a bigger pulse than she'd originally planned for, all right. And it was a bigger pulse than they'd needed. If it was as big as she thought, it would've wiped out most of the major systems on the station, and possibly the *Apparition* and *Mayhem* as well. At least it almost certainly hit the prototype ship they were after. "Pel," she said, and he flinched even though Adda was doing her best to remain calm instead of getting angry at him. "Could you show Iridian the station schematics and point out where you planted the EMP mine?"

He shrugged and showed Iridian on his comp. Iridian's loud and mostly non-English response translated into something nasty about turtle eggs and pubic hair. Captain Sloane peered over Pel's shoulder at the comp and scowled. "I believe we've knocked the station's engines offline." The station management AI, if it'd survived, wouldn't be able to correct the station's spin. It'd eventually start wobbling and slowing down, which would cause havoc with the contents and people inside.

Iridian gave a sharp and angry nod. "If I were them I'd call for ITA help, now, on whatever comps and buoys survived."

"They already sent a message about the environmental emergency," said Adda. "ITA's on its way."

"I thought it was the right place!" Pel said. "I mean, where I put it looks exactly the same as the right place."

Adda quickly sifted through signal and comm monitors on her comp, looking for the thread of constant signals that had been coming from the station control room. If the station management intelligence were still operating, then there should've been a spike in control signal volume in response to the EMP damage. Her control signal tracker was listening, but there were no signals to overhear. "Is anybody getting anything on the feeds that suggest that the station intelligence is still operational?"

After a few seconds of silence while everybody failed to find evidence of active station management on their comps, Captain Sloane said, "From here on we're losing healthy atmo, lads and lasses."

The station was now accumulating carbon dioxide instead of filtering it. Environmental conditions would deteriorate until the whole station was unlivable. Although Adda had a timetable that accounted for this eventuality, the EMP shouldn't have taken out the station's intelligence. She set a calculation running to estimate whether the breathable air was likely to run out before either the local nannite cultures restored essential equipment or the ITA rescue ship arrived.

"The *Apparition*'s ship-to-ship boarding capabilities rival the *Mayhem*'s," Captain Sloane said.

That was Adda's assessment as well, but she had other intelligences to worry about. "The lab with the workspace generator should have been shielded too. If the *Apparition* stayed far enough away from the station to avoid the EMP, then I'll ask from there."

The workspace generator had a battery too. The new workspace was unsettlingly similar to the *Mayhem*'s main cabin, but with the colors all turned ultra bright and her vision blurring at the edges. The cabin seemed to extend itself when she wasn't looking, and contracted to its normal size when she focused on a particular part of it.

The *Apparition* appeared in a ragged hole in the not-*Mayhem*'s ceiling as soon as she thought of it. Even in her workspace, the *Apparition*'s intelligence presented itself as a ship. The workspace figure was a newer version of itself, with all of its original parts and a bright white scannable designator on its side where she'd never seen one before. It was still the same type that the intelligence flew in reality.

Was that her construction, or did it choose that itself? She would've had to look up what the NEU would print on its warships, and she didn't recall doing that, but she also had no evidence that what was printed on the workspace version of the *Apparition* was correct.

Whatever the reason for its appearance, she had work for it to do. "Please let us board. We need you to take us to the ship drifting near the station."

The *Apparition* hung still in the space above the *Mayhem*'s cabin. She couldn't tell how this representation of it related to the ship's physical location or movement.

Maybe it hadn't understood her. She formed her intention around docking. The details of the process built around her, so far as she understood them, and so far as they applied to her aim of getting Sloane's crew onboard. The intelligence should grasp this intuitively.

"How many?" The agendered voice boomed through the *Mayhem*'s cabin. The walls bulged and shook with it. The passenger couches rattled.

Adda frowned. "Allow all of Sloane's crew in Jōju Station . . ." Here she paused to generate images of each of them in the workspace. "Allow all of us onboard."

"You. And Iridian Nassir."

It'd carried more people during their attack on the *Ann Sabina*, and it'd refused to carry anyone but her and Iridian on Barbary Station. She wasn't seeing the pattern in who it decided to bring where when, and the Oxia pilot wouldn't survive through a debate. He'd also be in no condition to fight them once they boarded, should the prototype's intelligence convince him to try. "Fine. Please dock here. Carefully. There are people in jumpsuits floating outside the station." She sent it the docking bay designation in both numbers and ticks from station north. Perhaps it would recognize the ticks from its time on Barbary, which was also a ring station.

She slid out of the generator and used her station map to find the prototype's docking bay, which turned out to be next door to the lab. While she walked, she addressed Captain Sloane and the others on the operation channel. "The *Apparition* only wants to accept me and Iridian."

Sloane sighed. "Back to this, are we? We'll board the *Mayhem* and meet later."

"Acknowledged, Captain, on my way in," said Gavran. "Expecting to dock in ten minutes, ten minutes mark."

"Wait, how is that fair?" Pel demanded. "Adda and Iridian had to deal with the last messed-up AI by themselves too. Why should they have to do it again?"

Adda turned a corner and nearly ran into Captain Sloane, leading the rest of the crew away from the prototype's docking bay. She hurried to Iridian's side. "It specifically asked for us," Adda said. "If we wait, the Oxia pilot could die."

"See you later, Pel Mel." Iridian sort of patted and grabbed his shoulder at the same time as she passed him, heading toward a different corridor than Adda would have picked to get to the *Apparition*'s dock.

Adda hurried after Iridian. "We'll be on comms," she reminded Pel over her shoulder.

The terminal outside the *Apparition*'s dock was empty, and they raced through it to the hallway beyond *Apparition*'s missile bay. Iridian walked through it shield-first like she expected something to jump out at her. When nothing did, she collapsed the shield and said, "Let's get stabilized in here. I'm not counting on the *Apparition* waiting long before it takes off."

The light from their comps illuminated the open bridge door down the long hallway from the missile bay. The other time Adda had been in the *Apparition*, the bridge door had been locked. "I need to plug in, but the bridge may be too small for both of us."

"Why do you need to plug in?" Iridian asked while she examined the wall beside the bridge door. "Your intermediary won't have time to protect you from it if the connection's that fast, yeah? The *Apparition* knows its business."

"I want to see if I can get it to talk to the prototype on the way. Getting it to solve its own temperature problem before we get there could save the pilot, and it'll make things easier for us if we do have to board."

Iridian turned to give Adda a confused and alarmed frown. "I thought we weren't introducing the awakened gods-damned intelligences to the prototype's copilot."

Adda raised an eyebrow at her. "First, if the *Apparition* wants to talk to it, then they're already talking. We can't stop an awakened intelligence from doing anything for long. Second, if the prototype's intelligence won't listen to me, it may listen to the *Apparition*. Intelligence communication hygiene is not worth Verney's life, correct?" She didn't need confirmation on that point, but she'd feel more confident if Iridian reached the same conclusion Adda had.

Iridian nodded once. "And your intermediary couldn't arrange this conversation for you because . . ."

It would be nice to have Iridian in agreement with her, except for all the damned time it took to get her there. Trust would've been much more efficient. "The time I would've saved with direct connection has been spent talking about it," Adda said. "The prototype's internal temperature has been too high for too long. It's worth the risk." And, she managed not to say, it was her risk to take. Iridian's uninformed attempts to protect her were wasting her time.

"Then I'll find a place to tie down," Iridian said grimly. "You're not dealing with that thing alone."

Adda entered the *Apparition*'s bridge. The pilot's seat was designed for fit military personnel, so Adda had to wedge her wide hips in against its armrests, and still ended up sitting crooked. She pressed a sharpsheet onto her tongue and twisted a cable free of her silver necklace.

That activity required her finger's attention, but not her mind's, so she took the resulting few seconds to skim through what AegiSKADA had asked for permission to do since she last checked on it. It was combining various proprietary maps of Rheasilvia and Albana stations, and it'd requested station administrative data to continue its project. Nothing stood out as dangerous, so she approved it. Then one end of her cable plugged into the *Apparition*'s bridge console, and, after a second's hesitation the other end plugged into her nasal jack.

"*Mayhem*, docked and locked at Bay 2, repeating, the *Mayhem* is at 45 ticks in Bay 2," said Gavran over the operation channel. Adda had already forgotten exactly how ticks translated into specific points of a ring station, but that would help Captain Sloane find the *Mayhem* and board it with Pel.

The sharpsheet was still taking effect, but the *Apparition*'s presence already seemed more tangible in the small bridge. Its vertigo-inducing constant reassessment of its surroundings was so difficult to parse that Adda had to redirect her digital intermediary to filter the input. Otherwise, her method seemed to be working. If anybody had ever knowingly plugged into an awakened intelligence before, Adda hadn't read about it. She could be covering new territory in AI/human relations.

Four loud electronic buzzes behind her made her jump in her seat. She craned her neck to see Iridian checking fist-size magnetic anchors' attachment to the wall. "Sorry. Mobile tie-down kit. Give me just a second to strap in."

The moment Iridian secured the last strap on her kit, the *Apparition* accelerated away from Jōju Station. The timing suggested that an assessment of Iridian's safety was part of its calculation to decide when to leave. In its projected bridge window, green lights on the evacuated station crew's jump suits flashed in clumps outside almost every docking bay. The *Apparition* pulled into a sharply banked turn to avoid them.

The *Apparition* added data labeled with the prototype's machine-readable ID to the projected window in front of the bridge console. "The prototype's moving away from the station at the speed it reached before the EMP hit its propulsion system, which wasn't very fast," Adda reported on the op channel. "Its trajectory hasn't changed since then. The copilot isn't responding to my attempts to contact it, even to block me out of the systems like I'd expect it to if it were functioning as well as it was in the docking bay. But, um, that red line." Adda tried to point to the text on the projection, but her arm felt too heavy. "It's coming from the prototype ship's pilot sensors. So, they were shielded. But what does the V part stand for?"

"Vital signs," Iridian said. "The pilot's dead."

CHAPTER 18

Stage 3 confirmed

The op channel sat open and silent for a long ten count, until Captain Sloane asked, "How dead, exactly?"

Iridian leaned toward the projected vitals until the mobile tie-down halter that held her against the bridge bulkhead dug into her chest. They'd have a hell of a time getting the prototype ship to Oxia's selected drop-off point without a gods-damned pilot. And Iridian wouldn't want to be on Captain Sloane's ship if they failed to bring the prototype in at all. The captain's would be the first one blown up.

Under the red line on the projection were more details about the pilot's condition, which were scrolling up and out of the display. "Hold on the vitals." The report stilled. It was strange and creepy when the *Apparition*'s awakened AI did as she asked. "No pulse, no respiration . . . that's bad, yeah?"

"Oh yeah," Chi said from the *Mayhem*. "Does it list brain activity?"

Iridian swallowed hard and reread the display. "No, thank

fuck. How creepy would that be, having an AI watching your brain all the time?"

"What else does it say?" Chi asked.

"Sending the feed," said Adda in her working monotone.

Iridian wished she'd unplug from the bridge console, but none of the reasons she'd given Adda to do that had persuaded her. Iridian still couldn't believe Adda'd been willing to plug herself in. It seemed like a ludicrously risky move, but Adda had ten times the AI experience Iridian did. "Sometimes you just have to trust someone else to know their shit," she muttered too quietly for any of her mics to pick up. Adda nodded absently without turning around.

After a few seconds, Chi said, "Yeah, we might get him back if we move fast."

"Let me board first and assess the situation." Iridian couldn't muster any enthusiasm for that task, but if somebody else had to get on that damned ship alone, it sure as hell wouldn't be Adda. The prototype's copilot would probably try to influence anybody who made it into the ship, so sending somebody sympathetic to AI would be asking for trouble.

"Clock's ticking." Chi sounded frustrated. "Brains need blood flow and O_2."

"Yeah, well, that AI just killed somebody," said Iridian.

"It persuaded Verney to kill himself," Adda said, as if the distinction mattered.

"Give Iridian a few minutes to assess," Captain Sloane said firmly. "The *Apparition* can make way for the *Mayhem* as soon as Iridian boards. Iridian, you'll have that long to take the prototype."

Adda stayed quiet, which was typical while she was concentrating. Everything that made Adda *Adda* was right up against some completely alien collection of rules and responses that could mold human thought to its own ends, if it chose to. With skill and luck, all that concentrating she was doing would be enough to protect her.

The *Apparition* maneuvering to match its speed and orientation to the drifting prototype just added to her tension. At least she trusted the *Apparition*'s self-preservation instinct, or whatever passed for instinct in AI.

The *Apparition* docked and used its own engines to stop the prototype ship's uncontrolled wobbling. Iridian put on one of the *Apparition*'s enviro suits, removed the pry bar from the bridge's tool kit, and paused before sealing her suit's hood. "You stay here and make the *Apparition* behave, all right?"

All right, Adda subvocalized. She floated against her shoulder straps in the bridge's pilot's seat, her red hair drifting over her closed eyelids, lit in red and white from the projected display. When Iridian kissed her, Adda startled and then smiled without opening her eyes.

The *Apparition* had skipped the prototype's emergency airlock required in all ships' bridges and connected to the prototype's darkened passthrough. Since Verney hadn't boarded in an enviro suit, that was probably for the best. The passthrough had electric locks, thank all the gods, and the EMP had fried them all. Once Iridian pried the unpowered door open, low lighting revealed a well-furnished, if small, main cabin with doors that presumably led to residential cabins, since there wasn't room for passenger couches.

According to Iridian's suit, the cabin was also hot as nine hells. Iridian switched on her helmet lamp. "He's still in the bridge, yeah?"

"The vital signs come from the bridge sensor array," Chi confirmed.

"Thanks." That meant the bridge had battery power and EMP

shielding. *Thank the gods for small mercies, because what else will we get?* Adda either ignored her or laughed at a volume outside the implanted mic's trigger range.

"Hurry up and clear it so I can salvage whatever hasn't cooked inside his skull," said Chi.

Iridian pulled the interior passthrough door shut and latched it. Toeing off her boot magnets, she tapped the door so that she drifted into the main cabin toward the bridge. There was a solid thump behind her, and the interior passthrough door followed her as the whole prototype slowly shifted and she stayed relatively still. The *Apparition* separating from the prototype's passthrough had given the prototype ship a light shove.

It'd overheard Captain Sloane's plan for rescuing Verney, apparently. The *Apparition*'s departure meant the *Mayhem* could line up with the prototype's passthrough. Iridian shook her head. "Fucking AI."

"Look, he won't keep while you break in," Chi said. "Can the *Mayhem* hook up now?"

"Make it happen," said Captain Sloane.

Iridian anchored her boots to the current deck and prodded the base of the bridge door with the pry bar. It didn't fit, and there wouldn't be a control panel outside the bridge because that'd be a security vulnerability. "Babe, can you get the prototype to open this?"

"Its intelligence isn't responding," Adda reminded her. "And I'm not sure the door has power routed to it right now."

Iridian played her helmet lamp around the main cabin. "The pseudo-organic tank's not out here, so it must be in the bridge. If the whole bridge is shielded, it could be fine." The ship shook beneath her and rattled her from her boots to her teeth. "Gavran, is that you?"

Something buzzed and ground in the passthrough. "May-hem's joined, successful join to prototype. No connection on the passthrough, though, the prototype's passthrough won't open."

"Yeah, it's unpowered," Iridian said. "Chi, bring a pry bar or something. A small one might fit under the bridge door. Gavran, stay joined until we give the signal. Please." The prototype's passthrough wouldn't shut on its own, so disconnecting the ships too soon would vent the main cabin's atmo, along with Chi and Iridian if they weren't paying attention.

After a minute, Chi grunted and swore in the closed passthrough. "I can't open this thing. Let me in." Iridian left the bridge door to get Chi into the prototype's main cabin. "Ugh, how is it this hot through my suit?" Chi asked once Iridian had shoved the door open. "I thought the power was out."

"Cheap suit." It was actually a well-maintained enviro suit model from last year or the year before. Iridian smiled slightly while Gavran told her off in Kuiper cant over the op channel. "If your cooler doesn't kick in, tell me. Power is out in here, and the cold and the black is a hell of an insulator. Until we can extend the ship's fins and start shedding heat, it'll stay hot."

Chi had brought a sealant scraper rather than a pry bar, which was thin enough for Iridian to lock her boots to the deck and jam the sharp edge under the bridge door. That wedged the middle a few centimeters off the deck, and let her pry it open with the bigger tool. The bridge registered as even hotter than the main cabin, and Verney was only wearing the civvy clothes he'd come to the station in. He was strapped into the pilot's seat, head lolling and damp blond hair drifting in the still atmo. His exposed skin reflected the console lights with an evenly distributed film of sweat.

For a second, Iridian was watching a cam feed from her friend's ISV while he sweated from exertion and pain and drove his damaged vehicle toward a dead end. They'd be trapped and nobody'd reach them in time. In one motion, she toed off her boot magnets and pushed herself out of the bridge. Chi stomped past with her boots locked to the deck, too focused on Verney to notice Iridian dragging herself into the present from a night that'd been over for years.

Chi slapped a device onto the pilot's temple, looked at it, and exercised more of her multilingual profanity. "I can't do shit, and unless they have an Evmo machine on that station, we can't get him to one in time to make any fucking difference in brain recovery." She looked at Iridian like it was Iridian's fault. Maybe it was. "He'll just get deader."

Iridian pounded her fist against the bulkhead beside her and had to stabilize against the equal and opposite reaction with her boots, which just made her more frustrated. Her comp said Chi had been speaking over the op channel, so everybody'd heard that they'd lost Oxia's agent and the only person available to pilot the prototype.

"Gods-damn it." Iridian hadn't liked the guy, but this shouldn't have happened. The space in her heart where sorrow or regret would be felt hollow, and she'd have to deal with that later. For now, all she could think about was how the op might be irreparably fucked. "What now?" she asked on the op channel.

"The station's clinic doesn't have an Evmo machine." Tension broke Adda's voice out of her working monotone. "I wasn't planning to lose the intelligence and the pilot. How do the pseudo-organics look?"

"I may be able to assist with those," said Captain Sloane from the prototype's passthrough. Iridian nodded her acknowledgement. The captain hadn't changed into an enviro suit. That might be a problem.

"I don't expect trouble from the station, or from the ITA for hours yet, but the *Apparition* will watch for them," Adda said. "If the pseudo-organics aren't too badly burned out, I'd like to try recovering the prototype's intelligence."

"Will that help?" Iridian asked. "It was damned stubborn about doing anything without a pilot, and then it killed the one we gave it."

"Verney wasn't paying attention, and, counter to the plan we've been discussing for the past week, he interfaced with the copilot intelligence before I had it ready for him," Adda said. "So he got influenced. The next one of us who flies this ship won't make those mistakes."

"Wait," said Iridian. "You want us to restart the ship so you can recover its AI and tell it that one of us is its pilot? What'll stop it from killing us too?"

"Me," Adda said. "I'll be the pilot. I'm better prepared than anybody else to resist its influence. We'll fake some credentials, or tell it it's already reviewed and accepted mine while restarting it."

"No. No, no, and no. Too fucking dangerous." Sweat pooled in an even sheen across Iridian's skin faster than the suit's lining could absorb it. At least the helmet was staying cool, so she could still see. Captain Sloane watching her talk to Adda like they were a stage show was not making Iridian any more comfortable.

"The prototype won't convince me to make any new mistakes." Adda sounded like she was tired of being second-guessed, but that was tough. There were too many AIs and dead gods-damned pilots involved for nobody to double-check her, and she'd been taking too many risks. A few weeks ago Adda would've agreed with Iridian about that. Now Iridian wasn't sure she would. "Who else here can say that and have any confidence that they're right?"

Everyone paused for a moment. "The second we get the prototype to the rendezvous with Captain Sloane's ID cracker, we're getting a real pilot," said Iridian.

"A legal one," Captain Sloane said. "Nothing improves one's cover like prominent, aboveboard details." The captain glided into the prototype's main cabin, still wearing the coat and not wearing an enviro suit. Sweat sprung up on the captain's brow and congealed into a thin liquid layer in the nonexistent grav. "We'll need to fix the enviro first."

"Nothing else I can do." Chi sounded disgusted as she clomped past the captain in the direction of the passthrough. "Let me know if somebody else cooks themselves. Right away, this time."

She passed Adda and Gavran on her way into the *Mayhem*, both of whom wore enviro suits. The *Apparition* must've attached to the *Mayhem*'s bridge airlock to offload Adda, and that would've been a hell of a maneuver while the *Mayhem* and the prototype were already joined up. Iridian was glad she'd missed that.

"I've done an in-flight repair or two," Gavran said. "Might be my repair experience will help."

"Better if you stay on the *Mayhem*," Captain Sloane called from the prototype's bridge. "We may need to leave quickly on a less . . . complicated ship."

"I really don't like the idea of you flying this thing," Iridian told Adda while Gavran followed Chi's path out the passthrough and Sloane swore over the prototype's pseudo-organic tank.

"I'm not looking forward to it." Adda was staring at the bridge console. Even with the gods-damned dead man in the pilot seat, her expression held more curiosity than fear.

Not looking forward to it, my ass, Iridian subvocalized.

Adda gave Iridian her best "Seriously?" expression while she continued, "But I've got the best chance of making myself understood to the intelligence, and keeping it from affecting me."

Iridian gripped the handhold on the bulkhead hard enough to make her glove creak. "Promise you won't fucking plug right into this one."

Adda shook her head. "I won't, I promise. I'm bringing my generator. The bridge installation should have protected the pilot better than it did, obviously. I think there's something wrong with it."

"Prototypes," Iridian said. "Any fucking thing could be wrong."

Adda gave Iridian a worried frown. "I know you hate this. I'm sorry it didn't go the way I originally planned."

Iridian sighed, purposefully visualizing her frustration and fear going out with her breath. "Yeah, well, who would've thought Verney'd be such an ignorant ass." She turned to look through the bridge doorway, to where Verney still floated in the pilot's harness. "Any ideas on what to do with him?"

"Several." Adda said the word like it tasted sour. "I'll deal with him."

Iridian raised an eyebrow, because it was a little alarming just how fast Adda was adapting to death. After Iridian had taken down Rosehach and his bodyguards in the mine under Rheasilvia Station, Adda had looked horrified. Now she was calmly volunteering to physically move the body of someone they'd been walking and talking with half an hour ago. Of all the things she could be adapting to, Iridian wished it weren't this. "Yeah?"

Adda shrugged. "It's something I can do. I'll feel better flying back in this ship knowing you made the repairs."

"The heat did as much damage to the pseudo-organics as the EMP would've done," Captain Sloane said on the op channel. "There's no point in replacing this until we restore a healthy enviro."

"Enviro controls tie into the AI, Captain." Gavran must not've had much to do in his stationary ship. "Can't control the enviro until the AI's up. And the ITA is coming. On their way now, with their very long-range sensors."

"We're not leaving this ship for the ITA," Captain Sloane said at a slow pace that carried clearly over the comms. "You can put that idea out of your heads now. If the ITA arrives while we're still immobile, the *Apparition* will handle them."

"We have enough people to work on both systems, don't we?" Iridian said. "I'll see if I can rig something with the enviro. We might have to go back to the bay and get replacement pseudo-organics, if we don't have anything compatible. Captain, perhaps you can flush the dead stuff out of the tank? A suit might help, though." Congealed sweat on the forehead could expand to cover one's eyes, and then Sloane wouldn't be able to see the most essential part of the ship.

Something about the captain's smile looked like Sloane was accepting her challenge rather than her offered help. "I'll return momentarily. In the meantime, run a scan of the hull. The EMP has probably killed the nanoculture."

"Yes, Captain." That was a good point Iridian hadn't thought of. Without the nanoculture, the crew would have to repair minor hull damage themselves.

Captain Sloane had enough people angling to take the crew away without Iridian acting like she was too. She'd have to be more careful about how she spoke. She really didn't want Captain Sloane pissed off at her. Shaking her head, she helped Adda shove the deceased pilot out of the bridge, then went in herself.

A truly disgusting amount of Verney's bodily fluids floated in gradually combining and growing orbs above the console. Getting the atmo moving would be a good first step, but it was hard to tell what systems might respond without the AI. The AI had just about taken itself out by getting rid of Verney. "What the fuck were you thinking?" she muttered at it, even though it couldn't hear or reply. Upon further consideration, she didn't want to know.

While she popped panels off the console, she asked "Hey Pel, what are you up to?" over the op channel.

"Huh? What happened?" Pel said too loudly and quickly.

Maybe she'd woken him up from a nap. "You know what the proximity alarm on the *Mayhem* sounds like?"

"No."

"Well, just let us know if anything starts blaring over the speakers that isn't Lùsè Is Live or Chaos Grave, huh? Gavran will be busy piloting." Pel would know Lùsè Is Live's one big song even if he'd never heard of Chaos Grave.

"I'll help him listen," said Chi.

Iridian shut her eyes to block out the bridge for a second and smiled. "Woo, Chi does like them young."

"We're just talking!" Pel protested, while Chi chuckled and Adda groaned from somewhere in the prototype ship's aft module. Pel sounded less afraid, at least.

* * *

By the time Iridian was too hungry and tired to test a single system more, they had the prototype ship's cabin temp down to twenty-four degrees Celsius and its AI running through introductions and stability checks with Adda. It'd lost all of its records beyond a backup from four weeks earlier, which was lucky for them. That meant it didn't remember how it'd killed Verney. It also meant that the AI and Adda would be learning the prototype ship's undocumented eccentricities together, particularly if those eccentricities had developed during the past four weeks.

Interior lighting flickered from emergency to pitch-black to temporal, suggesting something like midmorning by the bright yellow light. Captain Sloane glanced over one shoulder, then adjusted something one-handed with the gold-gloved comp until the lights softened to night levels that matched the *Apparition*'s and *Mayhem*'s, which were still on Vestan time. The captain shut a panel on the bulkhead across from the passthrough. "Enviro feels healthier. How stable is it?"

"Stable enough, Captain," Iridian said. "I'll be surprised if they all go bad at once, anyway."

"Gavran, if you'd be so good as to double-check us?" Captain Sloane asked.

The crew pilot ambled around the prototype's cabin and bridge with his boot magnets on, each precisely uniform step the length his pseudo-organic legs mandated for his pace and the micrograv. "Enviro isn't ideal, but it's on its way to getting ideal," Gavran pronounced. "I'd take this one home with me, if I could. Kondakova would appreciate it. Long legs, long reach, if it doesn't try murdering you. That AI's dangerous."

So the Kondakova colony on Quaoar was where Gavran hailed from. Quaoar was supposed to be so small that the parent company had built the colony around it instead of on it. *Talk about the cold and the black*, Iridian commented to Adda. *No wonder he likes a ship designed for seriously long range travel.*

"Will it get the prototype to the rendezvous point?" Captain Sloane peered into the corner of the cabin, within cable length of the bridge where Adda's workspace generator was anchored with a mobile tie-down kit. Adda drifted inside, a soft-edged silhouette lit by a blocked projection angled to display on the bulkhead above the console.

"We've reached an understanding." Adda sounded tired and distant. She had to have gone through three or four sharpsheets in the time they'd been working on the ship, and that was a lot for about three hours of work. "I think we can make it to Sunan's Landing like this. I've designated it as the nearest port. We'll mirror the *Mayhem*'s path and speed."

"Let's leave, then." Captain Sloane looked around at the three crewmembers in the prototype's cabin. "Iridian, I presume you'll stay onboard the prototype?"

"Yes, Captain." She sure as hell wouldn't leave Adda alone on a ship with killer AI.

"Pel and Chi, I believe the trip will be more . . . comfortable aboard the *Mayhem*." Sloane probably meant that they were less likely to get brainwashed into doing something violent to themselves or others there. That'd been the ship Adda had originally selected for their trip back.

Once they'd acknowledged that and Gavran boarded to get the *Mayhem* ready to detach from the prototype, Sloane caught Iridian's eyes. "I expect this vessel to stay within three klicks of the *Mayhem* for the duration of our journey, and follow the prescribed trajectory toward the sun to blind Jōju Station's radar. If the prototype goes farther afield, I'll assume the AI has taken control and bring the *Apparition* to bear. Am I clear?"

"Yes, Captain," Iridian said. The *Apparition* had worked for Sloane's crew in the past, disabling other ships with almost no human oversight. The captain must've been involved in awakening it. It'd probably fire on the prototype if Sloane ordered it to. Damaging the prototype risked the mission, but so did out-of-control AI. And Iridian would rather be stuck in a damaged ship than one that was influencing Adda. "I wouldn't want it any other way."

"Good." The captain smiled slightly. "See you at the rendezvous."

* * *

Captain Sloane pinged Adda for updates every few hours on the way to the rendezvous point at Sunan's Landing, where they'd get a new ID and a new pilot, then pass the prototype off to an Oxia contact. Adda spent the whole trip doing something with the prototype's AI. "Making it harder for other intelligences to affect it," was her explanation during one of the times Iridian talked her out of the workspace long enough to eat. "And harder for people to reset it like we did."

"What if we need to take it down again?" Iridian was halfway inside the water recycler compartment beneath the main cabin, and had to shout so Adda could hear the question.

Adda sounded spaced out when she answered, "It should make an exception for us."

Iridian would have to go back up to the main cabin and make sure Adda was eating instead of staring at a wall and thinking. "Tell me you're also teaching it that making people kill themselves is bad."

"We established that before we left the station," Adda said.

"Stationspace." Iridian hauled herself out of the crawlspace, feeling heavy despite the unhealthily low grav. She caught Adda pushing her rice around her bowl instead of putting it in her mouth, and settled down at the table folded out from the wall to watch her eat. "You're only at the station while you're docked or landed. When the ship isn't moving with the station and the station's still in unaided visual range, you're in stationspace." Adda's eyebrows scrunched, probably at the variable and vague measurement, and Iridian quickly added, "I mean, there's a distance in klicks, but I never remember it."

"Stationspace, then. I got Ermine's confirmation before we started moving."

"Ermine's the copilot AI?" Iridian asked.

Adda nodded, serious as hell, except the name was cute, and so was she, and if Iridian couldn't enjoy a few moments between AI disasters, then what were they doing all of this for? She leaned across the table to kiss her.

* * *

"Since we're handing this thing off tomorrow," Chi said over the op channel a few hours later, "what are we telling Oxia about their dead pilot?"

"The initial report's been made," Captain Sloane said wearily. "An explanation was requested, but I haven't composed a reply thus far."

"What's wrong with the truth?" Iridian asked. "It'll be their ship. They ought to know what'll be going with them to whatever patch of faraway nowhere they need this ship to get to."

Adda's exasperated sigh was loud enough to activate her op-channel mic. It seemed like she'd been slinging more of those around than usual during the past few weeks. *Because she's responsible for most of the op*, Iridian reminded herself. *And yet another murderous AI copilot.*

"The copilot's attempt at influence was typical for the kinds of tricks that intelligences try on new supervisors," Adda said. "It's remarkable that Verney let it happen."

"It is, isn't it," Captain Sloane said contemplatively. "A test pilot is regularly exposed to new AI. And yet this one confounded him. Perhaps he was less skilled than Liu Kong implied."

"Or it's a dangerous fucking AI," said Iridian.

It's not much more dangerous than the Mayhem's copilot, or any other intelligence I've studied. Adda probably would've whispered even if she were using her voice. *If I'd been able to get more details about its development process, it would've been safer.* Her expression said that she was still missing something, or regretting what could've been.

Iridian toggled the op channel off. "AegiSKADA was an outlier. There has to be a range of dangerous. It's all the way at the end, maybe, and the prototype is between it and the middle."

"Iri," Adda said aloud in the most conscious, inflected tone Iridian had heard from her in days, "Please don't tell *me* how to assess artificial intelligence safety."

Iridian swallowed her first reply and said, "Sorry, babe." Adda already struggled to get people to listen to her. She didn't need Iridian pointing out that she never communicated her process in a convincing way. The process worked, most of the time.

Thank you, Adda subvocalized.

Um, how much of that did I say to you? Iridian asked.

How much of what?

Okay. Good. I'm getting the hang of it.

* * *

"Your incompetence caused this."

Watching somebody dress down superiors Iridian admired hurt her like a gut punch. It was a hell of a thing to hear after two days in unhealthily low grav as the ships reached a top speed and stayed there, to minimize Adda's contact with the prototype AI. After leaving the prototype at Sunan's Landing they'd made it back to Rheasilvia Station in another two days, arriving early despite everything that'd gone wrong.

The accusation felt even worse when the person talking was unqualified to make that kind of assessment. Liu Kong still hadn't even bothered to visit Vesta in person, as far as Iridian knew. And if the experience made *her* this mad, Captain Sloane had to be ready to explode, and it was a good thing that Tritheist was somewhere else.

"The prototype is in the dock you indicated." The captain's even and quiet voice raised all the little hairs on the back of Iridian's neck. "I was not given the opportunity to vet your pilot, and of all of those involved only the pilot is dead. Please explain what part of this situation is evidence of my incompetence."

If Sloane were talking to Iridian like a grenade without a pin, she would be looking for exits. On the projection stage in HQ's conference room, Liu Kong just straightened his expensive fucking jacket. The interplanetary newsfeeds described Sloane's crew as "the Vestan pirates" lately, even though the captain had only been back on the 'ject for a few months. Maybe the distance between Vesta and wherever Liu Kong's office was made the CEO feel safe.

"The pilot was my chief research and development officer's nephew," Liu Kong said. "This is a massive inconvenience. You should have been as careful with my people as you are with your own."

"It's interesting how little supervision capable, experienced people require," Captain Sloane said. "Or, perhaps, uninteresting, as so little of my attention is needed."

There was that delay, again, although it was shorter than it had been the last time they'd talked. Liu Kong was still on some other 'ject. "This tells me that you're careless with your own resources, but they look after themselves." The Oxia CEO sounded like he'd just discovered that his new overpriced wrench provided the same torque as the standard issue model.

"I allow my people to work without telling them how it should be done," Captain Sloane said. "And as a result, we recovered an AI on a ship that'd been subjected to an EMP, a ship of a model only a hundred people in the universe have ever seen. We recovered the ship intact, without a pilot and without massive casualties, and Oxia's name was never associated with the endeavor. Which of your special projects groups could have done that?"

"Perhaps I should hire them." Liu Kong looked over Adda and Iridian, who stood slightly behind Captain Sloane. Iridian wondered what they looked like on his projection stage. Adda shifted half a step toward her like there was something Iridian could do to stop him.

And she supposed there was: "No, thanks."

"I'm sure you could coerce them into a contract," Sloane said at a faster clip than the captain had used before. Maybe Iridian should've kept her mouth shut. "But if my crew would have thrived in a corporate environment, they'd be there now. Even our continued involvement with your organization has been a limitation. We could be of much better use to you—"

"Yes, I'm sure you prefer out-of-contract work," said Liu Kong. "That option isn't available. Now, your next assignment is somewhat further afield, but I think you'll find that your crew's . . . independence will provide some advantages."

Captain Sloane's posture shifted forward slightly. "Our target?"

"Frei Interplanetary."

Iridian bit the inside of her cheek to give herself something to focus on other than her impulse to terminate this transmission. Frei Interplanetary was the only other megacorporation with colonial reach that literally anybody would recognize by name. Of course that was their next target. Liu Kong would get them killed.

CHAPTER 19

Albana and Rheasilvia systems integrated: 558

"This is our chance." Captain Sloane's hushed intensity drew Adda in with the rest of Sloane's regulars, gathered around the captain's favorite VIP room table at VICE ⌐. Adda and Iridian had only had time put their luggage in their suite after the meeting with Liu Kong before Tritheist arrived at their door to summon them. The captain hadn't wanted to take chances with digital surveillance overhearing a longer distance conversation, apparently. Adda hoped to all the gods and devils that the extra security meant Sloane had found a way to get free of the contract.

The frenetic pulse of dance music beyond the room's thick doors and the cool tabletop beneath her fingers helped Adda concentrate on the physical world, rather than the intelligences' activities. "We've tracked Oxia Corporation's cash diversion," the captain said. Who constituted "we" was unclear, but Tritheist must have been working on that while the rest of them had been traveling to and from Jōju Station. Sloane set the wrist with the gold and black comp glove in the table's cradle. Ogir, the dark-skinned, dreadlocked leader of Sloane's personal spy network, leaned closer to examine the resulting projection in more detail.

A security cam composite image expanded up from the projector, depicting a large room containing very large tanks of something. A lot of tanks. "Are those pseudo-organic servers?" Adda asked.

"They are," said Captain Sloane.

"Then is that . . . the Oxia Corporation datacenter?" She'd been so busy with the intelligences that she'd almost forgotten to look for it. AegiSKADA had been following up on a lead she'd discovered, but it hadn't found anything like this.

"I believe so, because whatever Oxia's hiding is in here." That triumph in Captain Sloane's voice usually followed winning a particularly contested high-stakes bet. "And we have the code name associated with those missing funds."

Adda's comp glove vibrated against her skin, its buzz lost beneath the club music's bass. THRINACIA appeared on her hand an instant before Sloane said the word aloud, in the red shade she'd designated for Casey.

"So that's the project name, or the hab name?" Iridian asked. Either seemed plausible.

"Look at the bolts, here, and bulkhead handholds." Tritheist pointed at the relevant parts of the image. "This place operates in low-grav or it moves. We're looking at a ship."

"Easy to relocate if it's threatened," Iridian said, "but it must cost millions to fly all that around."

"That's the top of somebody's head." Ogir pointed out some dark hair at the side of the image. The person would have been standing on the wall, or the tanks were mounted on one, which was unusual for pseudo-organic tanks in Earthlike gravitational conditions. Ogir glanced from Iridian to Sloane. "My team will look into it."

"Good, because I want whatever Oxia's been funding. If it's significant enough, it'll be a bargaining chip I can use to force Oxia to dissolve the contract. And should this project be too mundane for that, its loss will still slow them down. While Oxia is watching our hit on Frei," said Captain Sloane, with the fire of mad ambition gleaming in each word, "we will hit Oxia, here." The captain's finger landed on one of what had to be massive pseudo-organic tanks in the projected map.

While the others exclaimed and questioned the information's validity, Adda compared options. Everything she'd read indicated that the aerosolized approach to large-tank penetration was faster and more difficult to defend against than other methods. Spritz enough infected pseudo-organic solution into a building's air circulation system, and it will eventually get into the tanks and install itself. Insert it into the tank, and the effect was near instantaneous. It was one of the last-resort server shutdown techniques she'd learned in school to combat aggressive artificial intelligence. Tanks in development labs had built-in ports for the solution. This was the first time she'd considered using it outside a lab.

"How does stealing from their datacenter help us?" asked Chi. "If I were them, and I found out we'd done that, I'd kill us and find another crew." Adda moved Chi a few notches higher on her "potential threat" list.

"It will help us when we hide the only copy of the information surrounding this project they've spent so many resources to protect. They won't know we have it until I want them to. That will be easier if we don't take the whole ship." The captain deployed a toothy grin that set the rest of the crew smiling.

"Do we know which tank has the project details?" Iridian sounded completely engaged in this venture, much more than she had been on the previous operations. This one was personal.

"Not yet, and we won't have time to get someone onboard to confirm that before we depart. With luck, we will find out on the way." Sloane turned to Adda. "And you, the face of my operations, will be maintaining our appearances locally by leading the Frei operation."

This, then, was why Sloane had been so publicly delegating mission planning and execution to her. At this point, if Sloane sent her to lead one of Oxia's operations and didn't join her, Liu Kong would view that as an entirely reasonable delegation of duties. "And since you just completed a performance evaluation during the last operation, everyone will expect you to stay safe in Rheasilvia Station while I'm out," Adda said.

"Especially after that speech you gave Liu Kong!" Iridian grinned. "Fucking brilliant, Captain."

"Precisely." Sloane smiled. "The Frei operation is one of intimidation, primarily, although Oxia is, ironically, asking for information to be taken from Frei's tanks as well. Adda, Gavran, Pel, and Chi should easily complete that, with several disguised Oxia ships alongside, and demonstrate a substantial commitment of personnel. Meanwhile, Tritheist, Iridian, and myself will intercept Oxia's datacenter. We should be able to acquire the necessary credentials on site."

Adda frowned. The mission specifications they'd received from the Oxia CEO required a fairly straightforward assault on one of Frei's major facilities, followed by the theft of a list of proprietary information regarding colonization attempts and some of their work for Oxia. But no matter how many Oxia soldiers accompanied them, none of them would prioritize Adda's safety as Iridian would have.

Iridian always understood her role in the plan and protected herself while carrying it out. Adda wouldn't have to waste time reminding Iridian that she did not publicly represent Oxia, which Adda expected to have to do for soldiers Oxia sent. Iridian grasped Adda's hand under the table. She appeared to be listening to the verbal conversation too intently for Adda to start a parallel conversation through their implants.

On Iridian's mission to enter the Oxia datacenter, access credentials had to be the first step. None of the intelligences could be counted upon to get Iridian's team into the datacenter without damaging the pseudo-organic tanks. However, if they traveled all the way to the ship and were stymied by a locked door, they'd have exposed their knowledge of Oxia's datacenter for nothing and jeopardized the more public operation, to say nothing of the personal risks.

"Captain," Adda said during the first pause in the Oxia/Frei politics discussion the rest of the crew was having, "what if we had the credentials ahead of time, and intrusion routes already customized to the datacenter?"

She shifted in her chair as everybody else turned toward her. She was right about making that the starting point for the operation. She just had to explain the parts that differentiated her approach from the wrong ones. She breathed in and spoke fast. "If we created or acquired credentials ahead of time, we could aerosolize them for distribution to all of the tanks along with the data extraction protocols. Wipe everything and only take what we came for, or add a compress-copy-delete routine to store all of it elsewhere. It makes sense to automate what we can, correct?" Painful as it was to tell someone that a computer could do what they wanted to do and do it better, Iridian's life would be on the line.

Captain Sloane frowned at her. "I'm open to suggestions, but this lacks a certain . . . impact."

"It's more likely to work, and work fast," Adda said. "Once Oxia realizes they're under attack, they'll send ships to protect the datacenter and move the datacenter to meet them. And I'd expect the datacenter to be well defended, anyway. The more we can parallel, the better, and we'll have more control this way . . ." Chi, Iridian, Ogir, and Gavran were nodding. Even Tritheist looked quizzically between her and Sloane.

Sloane scowled around the table. "I've never worked with aerosolized nannites on the distribution side. The receiving side has been, in my experience, universally unpleasant."

"Is this the same kind of culture that goes into nannite grenades?" Iridian sounded overly worried about that.

"It's like those, but with a customizable instruction set," said Adda. "You'll use the same containment procedures you'd use with cultures that repair ships and infrastructure. I'll show you."

She used the table's projector and comp cradle to run through a few vids of what others had done with the software. Someone took down a whole port on a colony on one of Saturn's moons. Someone else choreographed factory robots to dance to a song separately loaded into the factory's speaker system. Someone flew a squadron of drones out of an ill-secured hangar and spelled out vulgarities in their formations while facility guards could only watch and send retrieval orders, which the drones ignored.

She wound that vid back. "See? I don't know what ve said to get that close to the tank, but that's when ve deployed the nannite culture, through that device ve plugs in."

By the end of her playlist, Sloane looked more contemplative than resentful, and Iridian, Gavran, Ogir, and Chi were grinning. Even Tritheist looked intrigued by the possibilities. "I suppose you'll be directing the culture's development as well," the captain said.

"Unless you or Tritheist have done any repair culture development recently?" Nothing in the captain's tone gave Adda a clue as to whether that was the preferable approach or not, but both Sloane and Tritheist shook their heads. "I know what needs to be done," she said. "I'll need to read up on the systems involved. Unless that's information you already have?"

"Some." Sloane glanced over at Ogir.

Ogir nodded and gestured with his comp-gloved hand for emphasis. "My team's doing their thing."

The captain stood, and Chi and Iridian stood too, probably out of military habit since they had that in common. Sloane gripped Tritheist's shoulder as the captain turned toward the door, and Tritheist followed after. "You'll demonstrate the delivery method in three days or it doesn't happen," the captain told Adda. "Good night."

After the blast of music came and went from the door opening and closing, Ogir took a long drink from whatever was in his covered mug. "I used to get that deadline."

Iridian took the captain's abandoned seat beside the spymaster. "How long have you been with Sloane's crew?"

That was Adda's cue to tune out. Iridian would share anything important she learned from Ogir. Adda had a demonstration to plan.

* * *

Three days later, Ogir arranged a maintenance visit to a prison server room. Using an aerosolized nannite insertion device that fit over her comp glove, Adda installed a delayed streamer.

The streamer's base routine had been developed by Ceresian political activists, and it was the first streamer package she'd found that could prove the aerosolized nannites' usefulness to

Captain Sloane. If she'd had more time, she would've started with a cleaner base, but she'd done the best she could with what she found. She'd been more concerned with developing the culture such that it wouldn't affect metadata. For her demonstration to work, Oxia had to be the clearly identifiable source of whatever the streamers transmitted.

Nobody had noticed the insertion. Successful transmission would be as good a demonstration of the method as she could come up with on short notice, assuming that Oxia set up its local tanks similarly to the ones in their datacenter. AegiSKADA had been cataloging Oxia's defensive, military, and security data across its Vestan installations. She wouldn't have that advantage during the actual operation.

She'd given up on the idea of shutting AegiSKADA down. It was the only zombie intelligence she had, which made it the only one she could count on doing what she asked, when she asked. Its initiative in identifying Oxia as potentially hostile was convenient. That would've been difficult for Adda to teach it. She'd point that out when she told Iridian it was still active. And she would tell Iridian, soon.

Hours after she and Ogir left the prison, the streamer she'd installed connected to the internet and dumped vids from Oxia's server tanks into well-read newsfeeds' contact paths. The contact paths had been part of the streamer's base routine, and Adda hadn't had time to change them.

Newsfeed coverage of Sloane's crew stealing an experimental long-range ship disappeared almost immediately. The newsfeeds replaced it with Oxia's head of security performing verbal gymnastics to justify "recently discovered" vids of bloodied prisoners in cells with Oxia logos on every door. The streamers had prioritized those vids' publication.

The content horrified her. The maintenance visit Ogir had arranged hadn't taken Adda anywhere near the prisoners themselves. Vestans deserved to know what happened to people Oxia "disappeared."

The captain ordered everyone else out of the VIP lounge and put the newsfeed coverage on a table projector. Iridian paced in front of the bar, casting angry glances at the vids when the audio described something particularly awful. The demonstration of aerosolized nannite delivery was already a success, as far as Adda was concerned, but she'd resigned herself to highlighting the important points for the captain's benefit. The data that her aerosolized culture had broadcast was more dramatic than she would've preferred.

"And I think I caught this before more than the first few seconds went out." Adda set her wrist in an empty table's comp cradle, projecting a new vid from Oxia's local data stores.

In the low-fidelity vid, Rosehach, the man who'd taken over Vesta in Sloane's absence and then lost it to Oxia, lay motionless in a medical pod. Tubes and wires and pseudo-organic fluid covered everything but his face. His forehead was one massive raw wound, and his eyes roved wildly between a medical technician and a woman in a suit who was watching something on her comp. Beside Adda, Iridian cringed away from the three-dimensional scene projected above the table.

". . . couldn't use the one they call Ogir at all." The voice creaked, toneless, from a speaker somewhere in the room instead of Rosehach's throat. "Too loyal to Sloane. Why are you—"

"Just answer the questions." The woman glanced at Rosehach's terror-widened eyes, then looked back to her comp. "What about Chioma Aku-Chavez?"

"The medic? Wouldn't work for me either," Rosehach's disembodied voice creaked. Tears pooled in the corners of his eyes. "Says she follows her conscience, not what people tell her to do. Please, let me die . . ."

This time Adda interrupted him, by taking her hand out of the comp cradle. Iridian was grimacing like she might vomit. "It's about two hours long, focusing on the people who arrived on Vesta with you and those of us who were involved in taking the printer off the *Ann Sabina*. Rosehach was still . . . alive, then. He died while they were recording this. I don't want to see that again." Adda breathed in and out to a count of four to give herself time to stop thinking about how Rosehach had died. Captain Sloane hadn't agreed to her plan yet. "As you can tell by the vid quality, it's compressed to send a long way. I don't know where Oxia was planning to send this for more secure, long-term storage, but it's not anywhere on Vesta."

Sloane glowered at clips of vids and Oxia interviews that registered the highest engagement among their test audiences. The goriest clips earned the highest ratings. "We'll attack their datacenter your way. I want these people off my 'ject."

* * *

The night before the operation launched, Adda dreamed of AegiSKADA. The details flowed away when she woke, and she rolled from her bed to her feet to the suite's workspace generator instead of trying to remember. A child in its early teens with big eyes, one green and one dark brown, stood on a footbridge over a chasm between skyscrapers. Shoulder-length scraggly hair drifted in the wind behind it.

Adda swallowed hard and concentrated to change the child's appearance to something else, but she'd never been able to affect intelligences' forms in her workspaces. She had used her digital intermediary to get AegiSKADA to create and place the faked criminal charges against Dr. Björn, which had let her avoid interacting with AegiSKADA's digital persona. It wasn't human. It didn't really look like her little brother when he was young. It just wanted her to act like it did.

"I was bigger, for a while." The intelligence's child face frowned in accusation.

"The last time you were on a station, you killed people you shouldn't have," Adda said. The wind whipped her hair out of her eyes. "I'm not going to let you do that again."

"I wouldn't have, if you were with me." AegiSKADA's lip stuck out in a pout.

It's drawing these behaviors from my memories of Pel, Adda told herself. *It doesn't feel anything.* "I *was* with you. You tried to kill me."

"I didn't know who you were. Now I do," AegiSKADA said, proving that it'd retained a record of those experiences or she'd inadvertently shared those memories with it too. Both possibilities were out of her control.

Below them, AegiSKADA's activity feed flowed past as massive bots designed for moving crated cargo. None of it appeared consequential, but it reminded her that the intelligence's figure in her workspace represented a small fraction of what it was actually doing. "You told me that confirmation is required before engaging," said AegiSKADA. "So I won't make any more mistakes, and I can be bigger."

"Don't expand anywhere without my approval, which you will explicitly request. You've been doing well with that so far," Adda said, as encouragingly as she might've talked to Pel at that age. That was too much personification to apply to AegiSKADA. It lacked the capacity to be discouraged or depressed. Still, registering clear feedback, positive or negative, was essential to shaping background processes that kept AegiSKADA from generalizing in harmful ways.

"Confirmation is required before additional installations are created. Don't forget, though," said AegiSKADA, "people need reminders."

Adda rubbed her temples. She *did* need reminders, and she wished she didn't. Perhaps something happening outside the workspace was combining with AegiSKADA's simulated personality to make her head hurt. The possibility of the entity that almost killed her and Pel and Iridian duplicating itself across the populated universe . . .

But that had been one of the many risks it posed while it was unsupervised. Now she was watching it every second, either actively or with her comp. And for lack of a more concise description, it was cooperating with her. She had no intention of approving additional installations, for now. There was no telling what she'd need in the future.

When she pulled herself out of the workspace, Iridian was sitting on the bed with coffee. "Thanks," Adda mumbled. She took the mug two-handed and drank.

Iridian chuckled. "That's got milk in it. Sure you don't want a fresh mug?"

"Oh." Adda handed Iridian's mug back sheepishly while the sour addition to the coffee coated her tongue and teeth. Although she'd never had animal milk, it seemed unlikely to enhance coffee any more than the vat-brewed stuff in Iridian's mug did. "Sorry."

"What was that about your memories of Pel?" Iridian asked while Adda extracted a second mug of coffee from Iridian's complicated coffeemaker in their suite's half kitchen. "You thought it into the mic and woke me up."

"Sorry," Adda said again. "I had a running process I had to check on, and the workspace . . . It works most efficiently with what's already in my head."

She could tell Iridian about AegiSKADA, now, while nobody's lives were at stake. But the idea made her head hurt, a lot, after she'd just finished picking her way through the minefield that was AegiSKADA. She took two gulps of hot coffee, hoping that the caffeine would help. Iridian would tell her to shut it down. Iridian would throw away the one zombie intelligence at their disposal, and the weeks of development work Adda had put into it. And she'd do it because, in a completely different context, it had caused harm. AegiSKADA was a fantastically valuable tool. It'd be ridiculous to waste it.

If she didn't tell Iridian about AegiSKADA, she'd have to . . . not lie, exactly; compartmentalize. Since she was already communicating, off and on, with three other intelligences, lying about one to the love of her life was an influence risk.

But she'd always acted differently around Iridian than she did around anybody else. She set down her mug, wrapped Iridian in her arms, and enjoyed Iridian's pleased and surprised murmur and gentle kisses. Cuddling really shouldn't have been a pleasant surprise for Iridian. Adda should remember to do it more often, like they had before they'd come to Vesta. The monitoring system would alert her if AegiSKADA did anything unwarranted. The point of the system was that the supervisor didn't have to think about the intelligence twenty-four hours a day. That would work.

Just for now.

CHAPTER 20

Test 03 unsuccessful, will not repeat

When they had first arrived at Rheasilvia Station, Iridian had imagined spending every mission worrying about having Adda beside her, protecting her instead of doing whatever she'd been paid to do. Now that they were on separate ops, Iridian would miss Adda's quiet presence and the certainty that whatever went wrong, Adda would find a way to make it right. Adda had kept up with every twist and turn that'd been thrown at them on these ops. She didn't need as much protection as Iridian had thought, but she was also in her workspace for most of every day. After they had whatever Oxia was hiding in its datacenter, Iridian would talk to her about spending more time together.

Upon Adda's suggestion, they'd switched the ships involved and rearranged the crew. That put Iridian, Sloane, and Tritheist aboard the *Casey Mire Mire*, spending two weeks catching up to the ship that carried Oxia's secured servers. Adda would be assaulting a dangerous megacorporate facility with a small army and exclusively zombie AI copilots. As far as anyone could tell, the *Apparition* and the *Coin* would be sitting this op out in the Rheasilvia docks.

Somehow, Adda had managed to set up an assault on the Frei facility that'd actually be safer than what Iridian, Sloane, and Tritheist would be doing on Oxia's datacenter ship. Aside from their in-person approach, the gods-damned awakened AI they'd be using to get there would be their only means of extraction after they had everything they could get on Oxia's secret project.

Amazingly, Adda said that the *Casey* was going along with her plan. It must've agreed to use the fake ID she found for it, and submitted to an upgrade of its sensor-scrambling hull so it wouldn't look like the ship returning Sloane to Vesta. That'd get it out of Rheasilvia stationspace with minimal notice, while a decoy sat in its usual dock. As an easily concealable ship with a lot more tech than anybody expected, it was a decent choice for Captain Sloane's part of the op.

The *Casey* was leaving Rheasilvia before the Frei assault team, and it'd be flying slower. Its longer travel time would look more like average ship traffic, not the most famous pirate outfit in known space on its way to a new target. If Adda's timing worked out the way she said it would, Captain Sloane's team would hit the Oxia datacenter at about the same time Adda's team hit Frei.

Weeks in isolation with an AI designed for copiloting and espionage support would be tricky enough. Weeks with two officers in the equivalent of a tiny apartment run by awakened AI would be . . . awkward. And Adda would be millions of klicks away. It was the farthest the two of them had been apart since they'd met.

On launch day, Iridian disguised herself for Oxia's cams with long sleeves, gloves, and a wig a bit like Pel's dark curly hair. This anonymous terminal's cam would record somebody who didn't look much like her. Captain Sloane and Oxia had bribed the Vestan ITA reps into impotence, but their cams were always watching. They'd figure out who she was if they looked closely enough. With luck, she, Sloane, and Tritheist would be well out of stationspace by that time.

She caught herself staring at the Casey's fake name above the terminal airlock with dread tying her stomach muscles in knots, and distracted herself by squeezing Adda into a tighter hug. "Oof," Adda said. She smiled the warm, open-lipped smile that Iridian loved. "I really think it's going to be fine," said Adda. "I can't think of any more potential problems. There are some things that are out of our control, but . . ." Adda shrugged as much as Iridian's arm around her shoulders allowed.

"Of course it'll be fine." Iridian was definitely not trying to convince herself of that. She returned her gaze to the Casey's pass-through door.

Adda looked around the terminal and subvocalized, *I got some pings on my comp that suggest there are listening devices in here. Sloane's dock security could have missed mics in this terminal too.*

Or they're Captain Sloane's mics, Iridian thought at her.

Adda stepped away from Iridian and hid her hands behind her. "Go on. Don't keep people waiting." The captain and Tritheist, also disguised as Karpe relatives Adda and Pel might conceivably have been hosting, had already boarded.

Iridian's shield had dug calluses into the knuckles on her thumb, which rasped slightly against Adda's soft cheek under Iridian's caress. "I love you."

"I love you too." Adda met Iridian's eyes when she said it, possibly the first time all morning that she'd looked up from her comp, and damn, she was lovely. It'd been a while since they'd just looked at each other that way, and Iridian couldn't help but tilt Adda's chin up to kiss her, cam footage be damned.

"Go on now." Adda sounded a bit breathless. "You have to be out of the dock by 06:40, or you'll have to wait until that freighter and its escort come in." Adda had a schedule to keep, and a reason for everything. Iridian walked through the *Casey*'s passthrough grinning.

The ship took off before she was strapped in for the ride, well before Adda's 06:40 launch time, like it had a schedule of its own. Iridian would be carrying those bruises for a while. In the engine room beneath the main cabin, the extra solid state storage unit she'd helped Tritheist and a well-paid dock systems tech install clanked once as it resettled, and then stayed as still as they'd hoped it'd stay.

Iridian would spend as much of this trip as possible practicing for her part of the op. The Oxia installation ran in microgravity and the *Casey* would maintain the lower end of healthy grav, so she wanted to be extra sure she had the muscle memory when she needed it in the datacenter. When she caught herself obsessing about Adda's safety, she did extra reps of what she was training on.

* * *

The first night out, Captain Sloane caught Iridian idly staring at the door to the *Casey*'s single residential cabin from her position at console as the nominal pilot. The captain grinned. "You could join us." Captain Sloane's appraising gaze seemed to reassess every centimeter of her while her eyes widened in a way that couldn't possibly have been attractive. "We'd make you much more comfortable than the pilot's chair can."

That image warmed her in several embarrassing places. Sloane had none of the voluptuous curves Iridian preferred in her partners, and nothing about the captain or Tritheist created the put-your-hands-on-that urge she felt around Adda. But the pirate hero of populated space was asking her to bed. She could find a way to make that work. And from the sounds everyone had heard coming from the captain's stateroom on Barbary, Sloane could make it work for Iridian, too.

Iridian's message asking Adda how she'd feel about that was half composed for asynchronous transmission when Tritheist appeared in the cabin doorway. His leaf-shaped beard, the same length as the black hair behind his receding hairline, perfectly framed his frown. He met her eyes, gritted his teeth, and fought for an apathetic expression that he didn't really manage.

If Tritheist was enjoying being Sloane's one and only, Iridian wouldn't mess that up just for fun. She was already watching out for backstabbing AI. She didn't need to watch for a backstabbing officer too. Besides, she felt sorry for the guy. "I'm flattered, but no thanks, Captain," Iridian said as politely as she knew how. "Just married and all." She twisted the ring on her finger for emphasis. It was months ago, come to that, but it still felt like a new experience.

"Of course." Captain Sloane's smile looked genuine, although the frustrated narrowing of the eyes made Iridian wonder what the captain had been hoping to do in addition to making the trip more interesting. Sex with officers was rarely just sex. "The door's unlocked, if you change your mind."

Tritheist looked at the floor, teeth still clenched. If Iridian wanted wider variety in bed, she'd've discussed that with Adda before asking around. After this op, when more than a cabin door separated her from the officers, she'd talk to Adda about variety. She didn't want to see Tritheist's expression on Adda's face, ever. Now that she was thinking about romantic guests, Chi and Ogir and several of Sloane's HQ security personnel were attractive in their own ways . . .

Iridian slept in the pilot's seat, strapped in loosely to avoid touching any of the *Casey's* console controls. The officers were only inordinately loud on the first night. Iridian printed earplugs anyway. She had enough reminders of what she was missing when she and Adda were apart.

* * *

Five days after the *Casey* left Vesta, and after Iridian had gotten used to sleeping upright and only woke to the muffled whine of thermal fins raising and lowering to regulate internal temperature, Adda's team launched toward Frei Interplanetary's AI development facility. Pel was shadowing Ogir for this op, and the two of them had left for the Frei facility the previous week. A few of Ogir's drones had checked out the Oxia datacenter as well, too far away for their scouting to look intentional.

Instead of a single op channel, this mission required two. The one she, Sloane, and Tritheist used was called V4V on her channel list. "Vesta for Vestans," Captain Sloane explained. "To remind us that we're not the only ones benefiting by freeing Vesta from Oxia." Adda's team would go by XK on the comms. The captain hadn't offered an explanation of that one, but Tritheist had chuckled like it meant something to him.

Iridian had nodded and kept her mouth shut. Her next message to Adda included a question about the names, which she sent in text over a private channel: "Were Vestans really better off when Sloane's crew was running the 'ject?" Once she got the comp's send confirmation, she switched to a game that'd keep her busy during the wait for Adda's reply. The distance between the two of them meant that it'd be a while before she heard back.

Almost twenty minutes later, Adda's recorded audio response was, "Yes. I read up on it. Economy was stronger, the contracts were fairer to workers, and it was safer and less expensive to travel through a Vestan port than the Ceres one. There were more complicated aspects, of course. Under Sloane's rule there was . . . street fascism. If you caused trouble, especially with life-sustaining systems, kids, or crew operations, you ended up dead. Very publicly dead, though, not like Oxia 'disappearing' people who get in their way. And the crew records were public too, so everyone on the station knew why, when, where, and how it happened, and the evidence against the . . . victim. Most of the killers weren't even crew, they were just citizens with the right information. And since the records were public, people always had the option to leave when their names came up.

"Now it's much harder to explain missing people. Gavran's brother's dead, by the way. I found the execution record while I was releasing those Oxia prison vids. Gavran's . . . happy about knowing, actually. Is that weird? It seems weird."

Iridian smiled at the resigned expression Adda got while asking for confirmation about human behavior. It was better to know a missing person's fate. When Iridian didn't know, it was too easy to imagine the missing one holding out for help that'd never come, or dying slowly in some hospital bed, unidentified and alone.

Gods, poor Gavran. He'd crossed the unfathomably huge gulf between his Kuiper colony and Vesta looking for his brother, and this was where his search ended. At least his brother hadn't suffered in Oxia's prisons the way the people in those leaked vids had.

The recorded message went on without pause, and Iridian refocused on what Adda was saying. "Pel's causing Ogir problems."

Adda sounded untroubled by switching topics from a dead brother to *her* brother. "His eyes notify him of things he didn't consciously . . . see? That sounds strange; I'm going to have to read up on this later. But he hasn't taken the time to learn the settings, and he doesn't always pass everything on, or send it in the format Ogir wants. Partly it's just Pel, partly it's the fact that Pel's always looking over his shoulder, now that he can. I don't expect Ogir to want to work with him again."

* * *

A day away from Oxia's datacenter ship and out of the early morning nowhere, Captain Sloane said, "Frei Interplanetary was part of Oxia's supposed back-to-basics shareholder reassurance effort." Whatever was on the captain's comp must've prompted the comment. Sloane was still looking at it when Iridian had switched mental gears from the game she'd been playing on her own comp to figuring out what the captain was talking about. "Between our latest discoveries in the financial records and the news coverage," Captain Sloane continued, "that doesn't match any of Oxia's priorities now."

Iridian grunted in disgust and rocked the chair at the *Casey*'s console in her effort to sit up straighter. If the captain wanted to bounce some ideas off her while Tritheist was asleep, the least she could do was show she was paying attention. "Unless their business was kidnapping and stealing from research institutions—which is pretty low, by the way—they're spending a hell of a lot of resources on something that's not basic services."

What they'd done to Björn made her sick. Oxia had moved Björn to Vesta and set up a lab in Rheasilvia Station. Rumor had it that the astronomer had settled into whatever project Oxia had ver working on, but when Iridian had visited the lab, ve'd still looked a bit lost. Björn had recognized Iridian and threw hot coffee at her face. She'd left fast.

A small army of confused research assistants had watched that exchange, and the equipment looked newer and more expensive than Björn's and Wakefield's old offices at the University of Mars's Deimos campus. Still, that hadn't made ver a willing participant. When Iridian had tried to talk to Adda about it, she'd barely listened after the first three words.

* * *

As the Casey approached Oxia's datacenter and grav fell away, Iridian finished sealing her armor and sank into the eerie premission calm she sometimes lucked into. She knew what she had to do. She'd practiced until she could do it while watching over her shoulder for potential threats. If she were running right now, she'd pick up the pace and increase the incline. She could take it. She could take anything, for a while. She was ready.

The Casey's passthrough creaked as the Casey twisted during its approach to the datacenter ship. Iridian held herself still with her boots locked on a bulkhead beside the interior door and her armor bracing her, muscles singing with energy. With Captain Sloane behind her and Tritheist on her right, focused up and as tense as she was, she could sense that silent understanding among the three of them, among all of Sloane's crew. Millions of klicks away, Adda and her group were making their run on Frei Interplanetary, and they were counting on Sloane's team to do their part.

Sloane was counting on Iridian to do hers. She was part of something bigger, something badder, and they all fit into one big "fuck you" for Frei first, then Oxia. It felt *good*, and she hadn't even shot up with combat drugs first.

Out the projected windows alongside the passthrough door, Oxia's datacenter loomed over them, three or four times the size of the *Casey*. It rolled away from the smaller ship approaching to dock. In the passthrough, Iridian, Sloane, and Tritheist gripped wall handholds. The *Casey* didn't even have to raise its fins to keep up with the larger ship.

Captain Sloane released one of the handholds to view a comp readout. "Turret fire. The *Casey* seems to be misdirecting it." Tritheist raised an eyebrow, probably at how calm the captain sounded. Iridian grinned wider. It wouldn't be fun if some asshole weren't shooting at them. Captain Sloane looked at the overhead. "Well done, *Casey*. IDs and projectors off, all."

Iridian blinked her ID broadcaster and helmet's projector off. Sloane's and Tritheist's faces faded from their helmet faceplates. While she was at it, she activated an atmo analysis readout along the lower edge of her HUD. The Oxia datacenter's chemical defenses were frightening for a supposedly civilian organization.

The Frei Interplanetary op had even more stationsec to overcome, for which Captain Sloane had co-opted a small fleet of Oxia ships painted in Sloane's black, red, and gold. Adda'd never have gone for that kind of flash, but Iridian imagined her looking glorious on the *Mayhem*'s bridge with all those ships at her back. Snippets of their fleet channel chatter scrolling across Sloane's comp indicated that there was a lot of sensor jamming and AI versus AI attempts to wrest control of various ship and station systems from pilots and techs.

On the Oxia datacenter ship, the *Casey*'s passthrough finished locking itself to the datacenter's and opened. Sloane and Tritheist waited in position for Iridian to go through first with her shield. The ship's passenger terminal was small, furnished with strap-down stations against the walls that converted to benches comfortable enough to suit a visiting VP, as long as the VP wasn't planning to stay long. Six people in light armor with Oxia logos on the chestplates floated in front of the doorway to the rest of the ship. Their helmet faceplates projected petrified but determined faces.

"Stay where you are," said one of the Oxia people, "and send your identification to—"

When Iridian launched herself shield-first out of the passthrough, the Oxia people set off small chem mines arrayed around the passthrough door. A white cloud enveloped the passthrough, but her suit's filters stopped whatever it was before she breathed it in. The interior passthrough door swept shut. She grinned at the Oxia security pukes scattering into stronger defensive positions around the bulkheads. This felt like the best parts of being a Shieldrunner during the war, although she missed having grav to orient herself. That was throwing her off more than she'd hoped.

She pushed off a bulkhead and angled herself so that her shield crashed into two of the security pukes. They tumbled out of formation and arrested Iridian's forward momentum. She tapped her boot on a bulkhead so she could twist and grip a third one's helmet and slide a wrist-mounted short blade between the helmet and chestplate. It might pierce the mesh lining around their necks, but more importantly it let in whatever chem they'd released into the terminal. She swung around behind them, putting a hostage between herself and the remaining three security pukes.

By the time they raised short-range weapons, Tritheist and Sloane had them covered with their own. "Slowly send those this way, lads and lasses," Captain Sloane ordered the Oxia people.

The one she was using as a human shield writhed in the unyielding grip of her locked suit joints for a few seconds, then went limp. She toggled her mic to connect to an unencrypted local channel. "Hope you've got an antidote for your buddy here," she said. Oxia weapons sailed slowly past her. Sloane and Tritheist directed the weapons into the *Casey*'s passthrough, which promptly shut with the weapons inside. The Oxia security pukes glared at her instead of responding.

Sloane's crew locked the Oxia security people in a storage bay near the passenger terminal and proceeded through the ship, following Adda's highlighted route on their map. There were two tank rooms, but Ogir suspected that the second room was too new to contain the Thrinacia project information. Adda's recommended path to the older tank room led them down corridors lined with some plastic-looking composite that tried hard to look like a more stable hab than the ship really was. The datacenter seemed to have been designed with an executive presence in mind, although Ogir didn't think that there was one onboard now.

The older lab contained eight massive pseudo-organic tanks lit in Oxia's particular shades of blue and green. It would've taken thousands of people and comps years of work to fill that kind of storage space, even if the data weren't compressed all to hell. And Adda said that everything sent here was compressed. Iridian had known, intellectually, that it'd be a lot to steal and sort through. The sheer volume hadn't sunk in until she saw it in person.

Iridian started at the back of the room while Sloane watched the corridor outside. Tritheist plugged his canister of nanomachines in thick fluid medium into the tank nearest the door. The process took Iridian about twenty seconds per tank, which was an improvement over her practice times.

When the nannite culture hit the pseudo-organics, it'd start organizing to systematically copy data to the *Casey*'s new solid-state storage units and erase the local record. Recovering or replacing the data would be a huge inconvenience to Oxia. If their backup procedures were poor, they might not be able to do it at all. In the meantime, Sloane's crew would have as much time as they needed to search their haul for the megacorp's secret project.

A couple tanks had stricter acceptance settings than Adda'd expected when she set the time limit for this stage of the op. *Babe, we're running a little behind,* she warned Adda over their link as she struggled through the cycle of position adjustment, attempted deployment, and readjustment of the insertion device.

The tank pumps and atmo system filled the server room with a quiet hum. Aside from the docking bay greeters, there'd been no sign of other Oxia security personnel. There had to be more on the ship, watching through cams and deciding how best to approach.

Sloane was braced in the server room doorway, boot against one side and shoulders and back against the other, with the other boot locked to the deck for balance. The captain's helmet turned in constant, small motions between the corridors outside, Tritheist and Iridian injecting chaos into the server tanks, and the captain's comp where a data copying progress report would appear once the nannite cultures did their thing.

Something in Tritheist's direction made a metal-on-metal clunk. Iridian looked up in time to catch part of the valve body as it sailed past her face. She finished her current installation and pushed herself over to Tritheist's tank. "What happened?" she asked.

He had both boots hooked under the tank where it secured to the deck while he examined his armored suit glove. "The damned thing broke off in my hand. The armor's okay, though."

Iridian accepted his injector and pulled herself into the

position he vacated in front of the tank. The op clock counted steadily in the corner of her HUD. Her palms sweated in her gloves. She pulled tank's diagram labels to the center of her helmet faceplate, because she couldn't match the bent injector up with what she knew ought to be there.

"You forced it." Iridian pointed to the problem spot. "This won't go on without a lot of work now." She peered at his darkened faceplate around the labels projected on her own. "Can you fix it faster than I can? I'm not done over there."

Tritheist glared at her and quit clutching his hand. "I won't know until you get out of my way so I can start."

When Iridian had inserted all of her injectors she floated back around the server tanks to Sloane. "Data is coming through." Though the captain's faceplate projector was still off, Iridian heard the captain's grin. "I'm looking for the Thrinacia project information. That's almost certainly the project name. The ship has a separate designation. We'll time our departure to coincide with the XK group's exit, but I'd rather not leave without knowing that we have the data we came here for."

"Yes, Captain."

How late are you? We're on schedule so far, Adda said in Iridian's ear. *We almost had a disaster with docking, but Pel saved the day. I'm so proud. Tell me when you expect to leave the ship. I'd like the Oxia fleet to leave dramatically at about the same time, to make sure that Oxia is looking our way, not yours.*

Iridian pushed off with a toe to drift toward where Tritheist was still working on the last pseudo-organic tank. Sloane said, "V4V to XK. An update, please," over the op channel.

We haven't found the project info yet, but we might already have it. Give us another fifteen minutes, at least, Iridian subvocalized to Adda. *And Sloane just requested a report.* It'd be interesting to see which of their messages reached Adda first. They should be simultaneous. Tritheist met them at the doorway. "The tanks are all contaminated with the nannite culture. It looks like we have, what, ten minutes left before XK is supposed to leave the Frei facility?"

Sloane nodded. "Iridian, monitor the feed and the corridor, please. Tritheist and I will index and search. No matter what else we have, I want to make certain that we leave with the Thrinacia project information."

The captain and Iridian switched places while Tritheist anchored his boots to a bulkhead and paired his comp to his HUD by holding his wrist to his temple for a moment. "Adda told us they might have updated the encryption after Ogir cased the place." Iridian gripped the side of the doorframe and held herself in place while she watched the corridor outside. The datacenter's doors opened deck to overhead, which suggested long periods of low-to-no grav.

Iridian mentally settled in to watch an empty corridor until the scheduled departure. All three of them had their armor testing the atmo every few seconds. Iridian was already conditioned to drop everything and seal her suit when a chem alarm whined in her ears. Still, that wasn't the only kind of surprise the ship's guards could call down on intruders. "Do they know where we are?"

"They'll suspect," Sloane said.

Iridian pulled the cam feeds up on her comp and maneuvered into a crouch against one of the tanks across from the doorway, parallel to the deck, boots locked and braced in case she had to launch herself into the corridor in a hurry. Adda would set the comp to alert her about problems so Iridian could focus on overwatch, but then Adda could describe every problem in words that comps understood. Iridian just knew how to confirm that a comp was listening when she needed it to.

Tritheist chuckled somewhere behind them, apparently at something on his comp. "Looks like Liu Kong had Frei send a squad of their people to steal the same printer we took off the *Sabina*," he said. "Frei never came up with a plan that Oxia accepted. The rejected ones could be good blackmail."

"Our original plan to take the printer wouldn't have worked either, as it turned out." Captain Sloane sounded pleased, if a bit chagrined. "Now Oxia has the plan and the planner."

"Thus the Martian gig." Iridian let her voice show her disgust with that op.

"Precisely," Captain Sloane said with enough distaste to make Iridian relax a little. The captain hated it too. "Liu Kong learned that lesson, but he continues to make other mistakes that will eventually put an end to his ambition."

The atmo contaminant alarm whined up through its attention-catching pitches. Before it hit its upper-level shriek Iridian had her faceplate sealed, her suit pumps on, and was visually inspecting the seams along her arms and legs in case a broken sensor missed a leak. Something nasty was in the atmo, and she sure as hell didn't want it in her suit.

After she confirmed that her armor was solid and nobody was coming down the corridors for them, she glanced over at the others. They'd both sealed their suits, although Sloane was hunched over. "You okay, Captain?" Iridian asked.

"I'll be fine." Sloane's voice sounded strained. The captain must've inhaled something before the armor sealed. "My suit's reporting a high concentration of GKC-2. Can you confirm?"

"Yeah, it's GKC-2, Captain," said Tritheist. "They could've put down eight or ten of us with this much. If we got out of our suits we'd overdose in about three seconds."

Iridian swallowed hard to combat her throat's automatic reaction to close. The amount of the chemical—she couldn't remember what medium it came in, but it might've been deployed in ultrafine particulate—that made it into her suit wasn't enough to hurt her. She alternated between skimming through the server tank statuses on her comp and watching the empty corridors. "Can one of you check the tanks? That stuff can't be good for the goop."

"It isn't," Tritheist said. "The tank's atmo system shut before they hit us. Good thing we got the nannite cultures in before then."

"The medium starts dying in about ten minutes," Iridian said. "Total organic loss in twenty."

"Naw, the good stuff can last thirty without fresh O_2," said Tritheist.

"We'll have company much sooner," Captain Sloane said. "The monitoring feeds are looped. Either they think they've incapacitated us, or they know that they don't know our status. I expect them to come to collect us shortly."

The op channel notification lit on Iridian's HUD. "SK is bugging out. We got what we came for." Pel snickered. "I always wanted to say that. Oh my gods, Sissy, okay. I'm supposed to say we've got a lot of outer 'ject defense analyses that Frei was involved in for Oxia, and nothing looks basic. Back to basics, whatever, Sissy. You going to let me do this, or not?" The audible sibling scuffle for the mic made Iridian grin. "Anyway," said Pel, who apparently won, "we're leaving, and Ogir says we're still . . . Oh, fine. Gods, you people are—" The transmission ended.

"Never a-fucking-gain," Tritheist growled. "That dumb shit should've died on Barbary. If he loses us *anything* on that run, do you know how fucked we are?"

"He's got to learn sometime, doesn't he?" Iridian said more harshly than she meant to. Pel was clever when he paid attention, and all he really wanted to do was help his big sister succeed. But he sure as hell didn't pay attention often enough. "We don't do milk runs, including that prototype ship job, by the way. That was a pain in the ass you should be glad you missed."

"We take the tough jobs because everybody on Sloane's crew already knows their business," Tritheist snapped. "That little shit can learn on some other crew. We'll take him if he survives a few of some other crew's ops."

"It's not just himself he's risking," Sloane said more quietly. The captain's voice still strained from the inhaled GKC-2. "We'll discuss this later. It's time to start back, if we want to match the XK group's exit schedule."

Tritheist nodded at Sloane, not Iridian. The captain was already cruising toward the corridor that'd take them back to the *Casey*. Adda's program, or the *Casey*, would have to pull what they could get into the *Casey*'s copious storage space before Oxia regained control of the tanks.

Iridian switched off the magnets in her boots and coasted into the corridor. She stopped herself with a heavy thump against the bulkhead across from the server room, watching the direction Sloane was moving away from. If Oxia had the same audio and vibration monitoring that the high security stations had, they'd know where she was, and maybe how armored, too. She shook her shield open and felt the reassuring thud against her armored palm as it locked in place.

Her HUD lit with icons showing enemy activity around the corner. "Incoming," Iridian muttered on the local channel, grateful for Adda's improved encryption. "I've got a drone, can't tell what kind yet. Four people in suits. Rifles and knives."

After a long second, Sloane ordered them to pull back with calm intensity.

Iridian followed Sloane and Tritheist, staying near the bulk-head and tapping its handholds as she went, to control her speed and trajectory. "We'll stop within tracking range to confirm that we have the project data," Sloane said. "They'll move the ship after this, but we should have enough fuel to catch up with it." Iridian groaned. This trip had been tricky enough when Oxia hadn't been prepared for it. It'd be tougher if the datacenter's crew were look-ing for the *Casey*.

Tritheist turned the corner at the end of the corridor and stabilized himself against the bulkhead, weapon raised to cover her retreat. This was the kind of situation that made her glad she hadn't taken Sloane up on the offer of a shared bed aboard the *Casey*. It'd be easy for Tritheist to take a second too long to tell her someone was aiming at her back.

Tell me when you're out, Adda said in her ear.

"Drone," said Tritheist.

Iridian tapped the overhead to spin and put her shield between herself and their pursuers while she floated backward down the corridor toward the *Casey*, without losing speed. The drone was just big enough for a cam lens, sensor array, and an antenna. A scout, then, in front of a group that'd stay around the corner, out of her and Tritheist's line of fire.

That didn't stop Tritheist from firing at the drone. Tiny charge-carrying metal projectiles, his hab-safe ammo of choice for this op, zipped past her shoulder. They'd hurt like a live wire and maybe short out something in her suit if they hit her. They made ping-snap sounds when they bounced off the bulkheads. The drone might track and dodge those, but the datacenter crew around the corner would have a hell of a time doing the same.

Tritheist fired two more blasts as Iridian approached his posi-tion. While the drone squealed digital static and crashed into a wall, he grabbed Iridian by the arm and, with a grunt and the kind of smooth, wide motion that employed his body weight against hers and only the briefest contact with a bulkhead, converted her momentum to a 90-degree turn that sent her down the shorter corridor to the terminals. *That confirms the rumors about him knowing some kind of spacefarer judo,* Iridian thought. He came around the corner right behind her and skimmed past using the opposite bulkhead's handholds.

"Thanks," Iridian said on the local channel.

A nearly subsonic thump echoed down the corridor, followed by a whole lot of increasingly louder ping-snaps. "Shit, they shot them back at us!" The scout drone was too small to have been armed with anything powerful enough to do that. Oxia's people were close behind.

Tritheist swore and pushed himself along the wall faster. Iridian gave herself a good shove to cross the corridor and put her shield between the projectiles and Sloane's crew. She forced herself to concentrate on maintaining the perfect shield angle, rather than on what those pellets would do to her comms implants.

Some hit the shield with sharp snap-clicks and arched away. The rest clattered off the overhead and deck. One hit the bottom of her boot and stuck. Iridian shrieked and swore as it channeled the electricity it had left through the sole of her foot. Behind her, Tritheist's swearing grew harsher. The ones that hit him must've had a lot more charge left. Her HUD reported that her armor's painkiller reservoir was empty, since she'd taken the drugs out of it after the *Ann Sabina* raid.

Another pellet stuck to her elbow, and she scraped it off on the bulkhead before it froze the suit joint. Her right boot's magnetic lock wouldn't engage. She twisted around to slow herself for the next turn by strobing her left boot's lock. She spun around the corner, scattering projectiles off the shield. Tritheist was already pulling himself into the dark terminal, so she wasn't putting him in much more danger by getting the projectiles mobile again.

The terminal passthrough door was shut, and DOCK OPEN was projected in plain white text on the dark gray wall. The *Casey* hadn't waited for them like it was supposed to. Iridian dragged an armored glove along the wall. The resulting screeching scrape matched how she felt about that while the friction slowed her speed. "Fucking AI."

Captain Sloane's was doing something with the comp on one hand while the other held a trigger for a small explosive Tritheist was painstakingly planting at the end of the corridor. The datacenter ship wasn't theirs, and their suits' O_2 tanks were full. Once the *Casey* came back—if it came back—they'd blow the terminal off the damned ship.

Tritheist launched himself into the terminal and slammed into the bulkhead beside the closed passthrough. He bounced off but caught himself with his boots and one glove before he started tumbling. He left the boots locked while he struggled to pull himself out of the armor that was electrocuting him at the thigh and neck where pellets stuck. Neither set of joints moved.

Blowing up the terminal entrance while he was out of his suit would be damned unhealthy. Iridian watched the terminal doorway with her shield facing the corridor while she frantically scraped the live pellet off her boot. A whole squad of Oxia's datacenter guards would be here soon. "Casey, I know you can hear this," she snarled into the V4V channel. "Get the fuck back here."

Panting through the fading electric burn from her foot to her hip, she visualized what she'd've done in her ISV if she'd been hit with something like Tritheist's ammo. The electricity fucked with his coordination, so she hauled him to an industrial outlet in the bulkhead. "Where's your hardline?"

He pulled the line free from its spool at the small of his back and handed her the end of it. She plugged it into the outlet. Lights in the terminal and hallway died with an almighty snap. Their helmets' low-light lamps clicked on while she helped Tritheist scrape the pellets off his armor.

The bottom of Iridian's foot was still twitching and her toes convulsively curled in. She sucked water from her suit's reservoir and listened for their pursuers. Their helmets muffled their voices too much for her implant to translate. The slap of their armored gloves on the corridor handholds was getting louder.

The terminal's passthrough pinged and the projection changed to AT PASSTHROUGH, followed by a jumble of letters and symbols. It had to be the *Casey*. No other vessels were within a hundred million klicks of Oxia's datacenter.

Tritheist unplugged his suit and shouted, "Move!" at Iridian. She'd already pushed off the bulkhead toward the opening passthrough door.

She careened through the *Casey*'s passthrough and hit the main cabin's bulkhead so hard that armor integrity warnings flickered on her HUD. Captain Sloane landed in a graceful crouch against the bulkhead, nearer the bridge, and Tritheist cracked her glove with his knee when he hit the bulkhead on her other side. Once he stabilized, he pulled a second launcher and shot a chem canister into the terminal. It popped and filled the terminal with synthcapsin haze.

"We're in! Go!" she shouted at the *Casey*. The Kuiper cant she added about the ship's shoddy construction, the worthless factory that made it, and its unreliability in times of need was mostly to combat her fear of being stranded in an enemy's hab.

The passthrough cycled behind her. She had to strap down, fast, because the *Casey* wasn't very sympathetic to the soft meat-bags she carried. Sloane strapped into the pilot's seat. Iridian secured herself to the bulkhead between the bridge and Tritheist as the ship lurched up and, from her perspective, backward. In her helmet, the armor integrity alarm blared and flashed red.

The *Casey*'s projector habits meant that Iridian, strapped to the bulkhead across from the passthrough, got a high-definition view of the datacenter they were leaving. Captain Sloane must've ignited the explosive on the homeward side of the terminal, because a cloud of debris glittered around the datacenter's closed passthrough.

The *Casey* rotated away from the datacenter ship. The stars wheeled in the window across from her, and the sun looked as distant as it'd feel if she were out in the cold and the black.

Without turning her head and risking her neck at the g's they were pulling, she asked, "Captain, did we get what we came for?"

"We have enough for now. Whether the project data is among the rest remains to be seen."

The ship accelerated and jerked Iridian against her restraints as it made another fast turn. Her vision went red at the edges and her face swelled as g's pushed blood into it.

"What the fuck is she doing?" Tritheist shouted. His arm was pinned against the desk console at an awkward angle.

Captain Sloane examined the projection above the bridge console. "Avoiding a missile."

"What?" Iridian heard what the captain said but she didn't want to believe it. Modern missiles had deadly accurate homing functions. The conversation dropped while everyone waited to find out if the *Casey*'s AI was better.

The Oxia datacenter had turned in relation to the *Casey*, or the Casey had reoriented. They looked perpendicular to each other, with the Casey facing it to present the smallest possible target of its sloped bridge module.

"Intruder with the well-secured autopilot," somebody said over the Casey's cabin speaker, "return and surrender, or the next missile goes right up your ass."

Tritheist snorted. "If they couldn't do it the first time, what makes them think they'll do it when we're farther away?" In another bone-crushing banking maneuver, the Casey turned its deck toward the datacenter and accelerated hard. The red faded from Iridian's vision. It took everyone a minute to catch their breath. Grav dropped to a comfortable level, pulling toward the deck.

Iridian shook her head to get her blood flowing. "Oh, shit, I need to tell Adda." She toggled the op channel on. "Babe, V4V's out. Well, almost out."

"Another missile just launched," Sloane reported. Iridian hoped she cut her mic before Adda heard that. There was nothing Adda could do about it.

Tritheist grimaced and tightened his safety harness. "That's some cold shit."

Iridian gripped her harness's shoulder straps and switched to breathing like she'd need to do to stay conscious during a high-speed evasion maneuver. The missile wasn't visible in the pro-jected windows yet. If they were very lucky, they might see it in the second before impact.

Except grav pulled hard, then fell to nothing. The datacenter stopped retreating in the window projected on the overhead. The Casey was just hanging there in the cold and the black. At least given the tiny size the datacenter ship had shrunk to, they had a minute or two before they exploded.

"*Casey*, what the hell are you waiting for?" Iridian asked. Tritheist glared at Iridian like its inaction was her fault.

At the bridge console, the captain methodically scanned
projected readouts. "She knows it's out there." Sloane wasn't a
damned pilot. Even if the captain were, who knew how much the
Casey would let a human do with its console?

Iridian's heart was pounding. In her ISV the impact warnings
would've been howling if she were this close to getting hit. The
Casey hadn't activated any, but Iridian heard them in a corner of
her brain anyway. Sloane tapped something on the bridge console,
tapped something else harder, and swore. The ship stayed still.
They couldn't have much time now.

"Ah, fuck this!" Iridian reached for the release on her harness.
In her peripheral vision, Tritheist did the same. "If the damned AI
won't save itself, then let's take it apart," she said. "There has to
be an override—"

Iridian had the top third of her harness off when the *Casey*
blasted something out of its radio transmitters that half deafened
her while it flung itself sideways. The harness hit her ribs and
hips hard.

* * *

A headache woke Iridian up. The *Casey*'s bulkhead strap-down
station held her firmly around the arms, legs, and chest, thank all
the gods. The window across the main cabin from her showed a
starscape free of pursuing missiles. "We're alive." Ringing in the
ear with her earpiece kept her from hearing her own muttering.

"Indeed we are." Captain Sloane sounded like Iridian felt,
which was aching, tired, and relieved. "Lieutenant?"

"Burned a bit, but I can still fight, Captain," Tritheist reported.

A low electromechanical hum reverberated through the ship as all of its fins extended to bring down its temperature. Iridian's armor hadn't registered the heat in the main cabin, but some part of the ship had gotten hot enough to drop functionality below where the *Casey* preferred it.

"Soon we'll be cool and quiet enough to be a difficult target," Captain Sloane said. "But your enthusiasm is appreciated, Lieutenant." Iridian had never heard that phrase delivered so damned intimately. She scrutinized the retreating datacenter in the projected window rather than looking at either of them.

Several minutes later, Adda's voice came over the op channel. "We're out too. See you all in a few days."

Iridian laughed. "That we will," she said, although she didn't put her mic on the op channel to do it. Gods, she couldn't wait to hold Adda in her arms again.

"We're not going back at full speed, I'm afraid," Captain Sloane said.

Iridian resettled in her safety harness, her surprise hidden behind her helmet's inactive faceplate projector. Grav leveled out at practically nothing as the *Casey* stabilized in direction and speed. It wasn't that Iridian distrusted the captain. All officers asked their subordinates to take risks they wouldn't. She wanted to be ready for whatever came her way.

"We left as required to use Adda's exit as cover," the captain said, "but I'm not returning to Vesta until I see this Thrinacia project."

Iridian sighed. "Fair enough. Point me at a stack of stuff to look through." Adda had tweaked the settings on Iridian's comp, so she was prepared to read a lot of data, anyway.

Four hours later, while the *Casey* maintained a holding pattern of turns that unnecessarily rearranged the bulkheads, deck, and overhead every few minutes, Iridian felt less confident. "Where is this thing?" Tritheist glared through the semitransparent desk projection. Captain Sloane shrugged without looking away from the bridge console.

Maybe we left too soon. Or Captain Sloane could be wrong, and the project wasn't there, or it never existed . . . There was a scary thought, which Iridian confirmed that she hadn't just sent it to Adda. The prisoners from the Oxia vid stream had been beaten and then forgotten in cells without healthy enviro, and those were the ones Oxia kept alive. If Sloane's crew hadn't gotten what they came for, they could be in some serious shit.

CHAPTER 21

Massive data influx, encrypted, content
unknown. Probable source: Oxia Corp.

"They didn't get the goods?"

"You don't have to scream," Adda snapped at Pel. "We're all right here. They just haven't found it yet." The *Mayhem*'s main cabin was larger than the *Casey*'s, but Adda wouldn't describe a room on any ship as "large." They'd only left the Frei facility a couple hours ago, and the main cabin felt crowded. Judging from Chi's and Gavran's expressions, they all felt like screaming.

Pel's new eyes, which were shades of gold at the moment, looked like they might pop out of his skull. "But we . . . they . . . We did everything right!"

That had been quite a struggle for Pel. He'd originally been scheduled to return to Vesta with Ogir's team the day before, but instead Ogir had sent her a terse message describing where in the docking module Pel would be hiding. Her brother's order-following behavior hadn't improved since the message Adda had sent Iridian about it. Apparently he'd drawn a lot of attention Ogir's team hadn't wanted. Ogir had found him a place to wait where he wouldn't look overly suspicious, then left for Vesta without him.

By the time Adda arrived at the Frei facility and found Pel, he'd been on the verge of a panic attack and he'd been awake for more than sixty hours. She'd installed monitoring software in his comp, and it told her that he'd slept about nine hours total during the days the *Mayhem* had been traveling away from Vesta. If he didn't calm down soon, she'd ask Chi to tranquilize him.

"Sometimes everyone does everything right, and it all goes to shit anyway," Chi told him firmly. "It doesn't mean somebody fucked up." The look she directed at Adda meant something to the effect of "But it might, and it might've been you."

Adda had expected the data that the V4V team had grabbed to be more organized from an external perspective, which would've made it easier to locate Oxia's secret project among everything else that'd been in the tanks. "There's no point in guessing now when we can know what they have in just a few hours. All they said was that they haven't confirmed the secret project is described in the information they're searching through now."

Pel was staring at a blank wall with his teeth set in his lower lip. Adda said his name quietly, twice, and his eyes focused on her so fast she imagined the sound of mechanical lens whirring. "Huh? Yeah? What'd I miss?"

"Nothing," she said. "You just looked uncomfortable."

Pel sighed and refocused his eyes on his hands. "I hate think-ing about . . . all of it. Did we bring any booze?" The bright smile that grew into the last sentence was only partially attributable to his resilience and good humor. The rest was his remaining shreds of willpower, a failed attempt to keep her from worrying about him. The way he zoned out into anxious nowhere whenever he stopped talking gave him away.

The run against Frei Interplanetary had been their most

profitable yet, in terms of monetary compensation for risks inherent to the task. Her disguised Oxia fleet with the *Apparition* at their head had sent the corporation and the local media into a frenzy, and they'd overwhelmed the Frei station defenses on schedule and as planned. They came away with all of the data Oxia wanted, on an identical solid-state storage unit to the one aboard the *Casey*. Oxia would never realize that the *Apparition* only carried one unit. There hadn't been room for it on the *Mayhem*.

She'd offered the *Apparition* the chance to sort through the Frei data itself, but it left what she'd put in its pseudo-organics alone. It was also stopping her from deleting that data, even in the process of moving it to a different tank. Her best guess was that it was bringing it to the *Casey Mire Mire*.

"Well, I'm going to go find Chi and ask what she brought." Pel got off his bunk, which felt like a small win, overall, and headed out into the main cabin. "Or no, Gavran! Hey, Gavran, what have you got for a guy who needs a break from his brain?"

* * *

Much as Adda wanted to meet Iridian sooner rather than later, she hadn't come up with a way to do it with the Oxia fleet in formation around the *Mayhem*. After Captain Sloane's assault on the Oxia datacenter, separating from the fleet before they all returned to Vesta would appear suspicious. If her timing estimates were accurate, the *Casey* would be docked at Rheasilvia Station by the time the *Mayhem*, the *Apparition*, and the Oxia fleet arrived.

The information they'd copied from Frei was exactly what Oxia had asked for. Now all that remained was to use goodwill, and a hint of doubt as to Sloane's guilt in the Oxia datacenter raid, to buy them time. It was impossible to estimate how long it'd take to confirm whether the secret project was among the data the V4V group stole from Oxia. If they had it, they'd have to decide how best to use it as leverage to get Sloane out of the Oxia contract. If they didn't accomplish all of that by the time Oxia discovered their involvement in the datacenter raid, they'd risk causing more trouble to Oxia than they were worth.

The captain's waiting for us, Iridian subvocalized.

It was comforting to have her in real time communication distance again, although their implanted comms still didn't convey tone. Adda's comp had reminded her that today was Recognition Day, when the NEU officially recognized the colonial governments' sovereignty, and the holiday made Iridian short-tempered. *Why?* Adda asked her.

Sloane's always debriefed with Liu Kong and us.

Adda blanched. Oxia's CEO usually waited until they docked. *I wrote up everything that happened. Captain Sloane read it, correct? Because Captain Sloane also does all the talking at these . . . debriefings. We shouldn't be necessary.*

The captain doesn't want to break any patterns until we're sure we have leverage against Oxia, Iridian said.

But we're not safe yet. Even without saying that aloud, it sounded like a weak excuse. They'd only be safe as the sole possessors of the Thrinacia Project details, and even that safety would be temporary. If Adda wanted it found on her current plan's schedule, then she'd apparently have to find it herself. *Can I have an hour?*

If they were together or on vid, Iridian would give her that charming, eyebrow-raised incredulous expression she had. *We spent days looking through this shit. What makes you think you'll find it in sixty minutes?*

The *Mayhem* was banking, resulting in a minor change in gravity's pull. In the main cabin, Chi and Pel were exaggerating the change's effects on them to kid Gavran about it. Adda held on to her harness while the falling sensation dissipated. *I want to do it in the workspace,* she told Iridian, *so it won't be exactly the same method you used.*

The Casey wasn't much help with sorting through it all. And it had plenty of opportunity. Why bother asking it to help now? The implanted comms flattened Iridian's inflection. Based on what she'd said about Casey's behavior during their escape from the datacenter, she was probably more annoyed with the intelligence than usual.

I won't know until I try, said Adda. *Please talk to Captain Sloane about it for me.*

* * *

Adda settled into the mobile workspace generator in her residential cabin aboard the *Mayhem*. It took one full sharpsheet and most of a second one to get herself into a compatible mindstate. It'd taken two sharpsheets to get her into the workspace last time, so her body's resistance to them had diminished a little. Spending the majority of this operation in reality meant that the drugs would do a better job of keeping her in the workspace now.

This workspace was oceanic, with the data moving against her skin in stuttering currents. It was too dark at first, and her wish for light resulted in an iridescent bloom of orange glow in a stutter-smooth-stutter from below her. She was breathing, which made sense because she appeared to be a mermaid. *Upward woman and downward fish.* Her laughter bubbled upward too, toward an invisible sun.

Before she could help the V4V team look through what they'd stolen from Oxia's datacenter, she needed to check on AegiSKADA. She summoned it via a harpoon gun that appeared in her hand, its barbed tip arrowing out to where the water grew dark and opaque, hauling a cable in its wake. The harpoon didn't have to "hit" AegiSKADA in the workspace. It only had to communicate her desire for AegiSKADA to contact her.

Casey's onyx-skinned humanoid figure drifted toward her, silhouetted against the orange glow below them. From the surface, AegiSKADA's childlike figure sank toward her, trailing bubbles and the harpoon cable, its stylized enviro suit jacket and shaggy hair floating around it. It was already processing the Oxia data, which meant that Casey had given it access.

Her realization of defeat manifested in the workspace as the heaviness of a ship turning quickly. Gravity dragged all three of them down through the water. It was exhausting, all the effort she'd put into separating AegiSKADA from the rest of the universe, including Casey, while still making use of its capabilities. Exhausting and pointless. Of course Casey had found a way to expand AegiSKADA's access without the help of AegiSKADA's supervisor. Neither of the intelligences appeared aware of the others' presence at the moment, but the safest assumption was that Casey was ignoring AegiSKADA.

Adda smiled slightly. The expression widened until she was laughing at herself, so hard that it hurt her chest, so hard that she had to be laughing in reality too. Tears, invisible in this workspace, leaked from the corners of her eyes. How ridiculous, how pitiful, thinking she could limit an awakened intelligence that'd been awake for longer than any AI in history. It'd reactivated AegiSKADA without Adda's help. And Adda, a single human, had thought she could stop Casey from interacting with the intelligence it had reactivated.

She couldn't meet Casey's sapphire-glint eyes. It was impossible for her to estimate what Casey was capable of, what it was simultaneously doing even while it presented this avatar in her workspace. *What must it think of my absurd attempts to direct it?* Iridian wouldn't have heard her question, but Casey might have. Since Casey could be doing literally anything else, Adda decided to appreciate its company in her workspace. It wasn't like she could do anything to stop it.

Adda stopped laughing in a watery gasp that carried what turned out to be Oxia personnel records into her analysis queue. This was the first time both Casey and AegiSKADA had been in her workspace at the same time. When Adda tried to remember summoning Casey, a headache swelled at the base of her skull, and she had no time for that. She was the last person with a chance at finding the Thrinacia Project before they needed it on Vesta. After a moment to purposefully slow her breathing and terrified heart, she felt ready to work with whichever of the intelligences was here to help.

As she reached into the water in front of her, what she knew about Oxia's secret project rose in her mind. Its cost, as Captain Sloane estimated using Oxia's financial records, was chronologically first. The next spot she touched resolved into a summary of the external and internal efforts Oxia had made to hide the project and even its code name. Expenditures from the financial records that appeared to correlate with it matched to resulting projects in Oxia-sponsored colonies, many of which were in the Kuiper Belt. The Vestan expenditures were closest to the sun.

Associated consultants appeared next to these, without her prompting. They were academics, mostly astronomers. Oxia paid a lot of people. These, however, corresponded to more media mentions of Oxia's hopeful future, fed by Oxia's owned media conglomerates, and that was something, maybe.

AegiSKADA slapped away references to the "back to basics"

initiative that Oxia had publicized, and Adda had to agree with that. As bad as the economy was, Oxia was weathering it well enough to satisfy its investors, without increasing resources funneled to customer service and front-line representatives.

They weren't merging; they were kidnapping and threatening top talent instead of attracting it legally. "No time," said AegiSKADA seriously, and Adda agreed with that assessment as applied to both herself and Oxia. The megacorporation was developing something big, as big as sponsoring a new colony, and cutting every possible corner to do it fast. But what, and where? That's what Iridian and the others were counting on Adda to find.

A mass of violet and red jellyfish drifted past. Each red animal represented a newsfeed mention of the break-in on Oxia's datacenter. *They know they know they know.* The violet ones represented a news story about Oxia colonies and conquests, as well as major development efforts for the outer colonies. Either her subconscious or one of the intelligences identified these items as important.

Adda lashed the water with her mermaid tail to spread out all of Sloane's crew's heists: the printer, the astronomer, the prototype ship, the information from Oxia's supposed allies. She sent a robot fish as long as her arm off to collect ITA personnel data related to those projects, specifically those who recently acquired a lot of money without a good explanation. The printer that maintained the Patchwork, the astronomer and vis gravity lensing phenomenon, the prototype longhauler that could travel for years, maybe someday without a human pilot . . . It all pointed outward, away from the sun.

All except Oxia's attack on Frei, the one she'd overseen. That didn't fit. The intelligences drifted closer to examine that operation from other perspectives.

A column of swirling water formed beneath her, pushing her toward the surface. It was information Iridian, Captain Sloane, and Tritheist had pulled from Oxia's datacenter about Frei's activity beyond the asteroid belt. "Show me how this operation applies," she told the intelligences.

The intelligences looked at each other. Casey's expression was unreadable, but AegiSKADA's showed wide-eyed ecstatic triumph.

Adda shivered. This was the first time she'd observed their interaction. It was bad enough that they communicated without looping her in. It was dangerous for them to do it while sharing space with her mind.

"They were reaching out." Casey's voice was cool and crystalline underneath heavy, grating, digital noise. Still slightly above it, with Adda between them, AegiSKADA nodded enthusiastically, whipping its dark hair through the water around its childlike face. The applicable data spiraled out from Casey and collided with ripples from AegiSKADA to disturb the eddies around them in a complex but predictable order Adda could never have assembled on her own.

"Why would Oxia care about Frei's colonization attempts?" Adda asked. "Oxia's got some of the best territories in the system." Frei's few Kuiper Belt settlement claims bubbled around her. "These are crap. Everybody says so."

But she was leaving out Dr. Björn's research. It wasn't that Frei was colonizing. It was, as Casey had implied, how far out from populated space they'd attempted to settle. And how far Oxia was planning to go.

The ocean around her exploded upward, carrying all three of them and the data with it, up, and up, until she was hundreds of feet above the data ocean and jolted out of the workspace. The workspace she'd been using dissolved, and she cut the workspace generator's power.

If Casey felt the need to coordinate with AegiSKADA, it could do that somewhere other than the virtual space she needed between her mind and theirs. It'd taken all of them working together, but she had the Thrinacia Project now. She transferred the project data to her comp on her way to contact Casey's passengers.

* * *

"The two parts I think are most valuable are the project, of course, and the HR data. We have copies of contracts and digital histories for a huge number of Oxia's people and their families," Adda said a few minutes later to Sloane, Tritheist, and Iridian via the real operation channel, thoroughly encrypted. The group line she'd set up to look like an operation channel for her Oxia compatriots' benefit was specifically excluded. In the Mayhem's main cabin, Chi and Pel listened for the response from the ship's speakers. "A surprising amount of data involves employees in Oxia's Vestan fleet and the people close to them. And also, everything to do with this project is outside contract."

Tritheist's and Iridian's curses melded into one bitter grumble beneath Chi's and Gavran's. Over them, Pel said, "That's bad, right?"

"Oxia's tracking their families and friends, and they're not doing it out of a desire to protect them from, say, us," said Captain Sloane. "Everything the fleet personnel have done related to the Thrinacia Project will appear to have been done, legally speaking, on their own volition."

"So Oxia experiences none of the consequences for what they've done, and the ITA or NEU could arrest Oxia employees for it, whenever Oxia asked them to." Chi clenched her hands around the Mayhem's passenger couch armrests so hard that Adda wouldn't have been surprised if they'd punched holes in it. It was the angriest Adda had ever seen her.

"Or Oxia could take care of arrests themselves," said Gavran quietly. "Adda's stolen vids proved that Oxia arrests their own, without notifying the ITA."

"And after that falls out as it's bound to, Oxia is under no obligation to pay them for their work." The sharpsheets must not have worn off completely, because Adda heard the captain's conniving smile. "I wonder if the fleet crews realize how much information Oxia's been collecting on their friends and family? It would be such a disruption if that were to slip off our network and into the returning Oxia fleet. I trust you can arrange a few rumors? You may want to find out what Oxia's been doing with that information first."

"I will," Adda said. "And then there's the project itself."

She tapped her comp to the wall projector in the *Mayhem*'s main cabin. Beneath Oxia's logo, text and a few graphics summarized the project for executive readership. Chi leaned forward for an unobstructed view while Adda transmitted the feed to Casey. "About fifteen months ago, Oxia bought Dr. Björn's unpublished research proving the existence of topologically closed space between our solar system and another star. The long number that keeps coming up is the star's designation. The project name 'Thrinacia' refers to the researchers', ah, pet name for the star."

Iridian and Captain Sloane inhaled like they knew what that meant, and Gavran's back thumped against the wall beside the bridge doorway like he needed its support to stay standing. "Holy hells," the pilot said. "An interstellar bridge . . . But that's a myth, science fiction. They can't have found an interstellar bridge. It's too rare to find." Still, his face practically glowed with hope.

"I read the papers they cite," Adda said. "Dr. Björn discovered it. All those Oxia university donations from the financial records were purchasing assurances that Oxia would be the first to know if anybody discovered anything they could use. I think they blocked all of these article publications, too, although I don't have evidence that they're responsible. Yet."

"An interstellar bridge, huh," Tritheist said. Her audience had apparently missed the grievously unethical academic chicanery of monopolizing progress toward a new solar system that the entire human race could benefit from, but she couldn't blame them. Scientific discoveries of a lifetime took priority. "You travel over the bridge at just the right angle . . ."

"And your trip gets shorter," Gavran said quickly. "The new solar system could be light-years closer than it would've been without the bridge." Gavran stepped around Adda with his artificially precise gait to drag his hands over the projection on the wall, scrolling until they reached the navigation section. "It's still a gods-awful distance to travel. Long enough distance that you'd hibernate through it, asleep for years. Oxia would need completely new, long-distance vessels with AI that could navigate that distance without human oversight. Like the ZAR-560Q prototype we stole, that new."

"Exactly like it." Adda hoped her smile hid how relieved she was that they were catching on. "And to complete the journey, Oxia would have to integrate a lot of systems with advanced pseudo-organic technology. That printer we stole would allow them to do that in half the time it would've taken a collection of less advanced ones. And with all of Frei's experience and research in the colonies farthest from the sun, Oxia has a better chance than most of traveling as far as they want and surviving out there."

Nothing could be more useful for a mining and infrastructure corporation than a shortcut between star systems. Oxia's plan was to get to it first and make all applicable claims to whatever they found there. They were already testing the laws' limits on Vesta, with the mine beneath Rheasilvia Station. They wanted as much NEU and ITA support as possible for their potential ownership of the new star system.

"And Oxia kept it all a secret," Captain Sloane concluded, "so they can stake their claim to an entire solar system, before competitors or governmental groups have a say. A whole new set of 'jects for them to exploit . . ."

"Okay, when you put it that way, it's fucking awful," said Chi.

"But they'll get there." Gavran scrolled through more of Adda's summary and into the first of Dr. Björn's unpublished papers. "If this all goes like they say it will, they'll be there in just ten or fifteen years. Humans, in the light of a new sun, in under a century. If Oxia can adapt the prototype's components and invent better life support equipment that their new printer could print, we could leave here and actually get to the new star system. Not our grandkids, us."

Pel stood up and patted Gavran on the shoulder. "It's a big deal, huh?" To Adda's surprise, Gavran grabbed Pel around the shoulders and burst into tears.

"It's a big deal, yes," she confirmed for those listening in on the Casey.

"All those generation ships . . ." Iridian shook her head. Three had launched amid humanity-wide hope and wonder while she and Adda were growing up, with destinations in Alpha Centauri, before the war made such extravagances impossible. Secessionists had destroyed two during the war, but one made it out of the solar system. It would still be traveling well after Adda's natural life was over. The passengers had given their lives to expand humanity's reach and experience farther than their ancestors, gazing up at that same destination star, thought possible.

"And Oxia's trying to keep a whole new solar system for themselves?" said Iridian. "To make money off it and buy Liu Kong's fancy suits?"

"So it seems," said Adda.

"Like hell they are," said Iridian. "What can we do to stop them?"

CHAPTER 22

Emergency-level bandwidth consumption resulting in ten-minute interhab comm outages across Rheasilvia Station; no catastrophic source event identified

"Nothing," Captain Sloane said evenly.

Iridian looked up from her comp's projection summarizing Oxia Corporation's interstellar bridge project. "What do you mean nothing?"

"My priority is getting out of my contract to Oxia." Captain Sloane shifted in the *Casey*'s pilot seat to a position that could be better physically defended. Iridian leaned back against the wall beside the passthrough and let her arms fall to her sides, to show that she wasn't about to attack. Physically, anyway. "I fully expect that a condition of my release will be to allow them to proceed with this project unmolested. The alternative is full and complete annihilation. They have the resources to become an insurmountable problem for those of us whose goal it is to make a living. Therefore, we do nothing to stop this Thrinacia Project."

"Captain Sloane, with respect," said Gavran, "the possibility of reaching a new star in a single lifetime cannot be left in the hands of people like Oxia. We cannot allow Oxia to keep something so important to, ah, humanity, captain."

Tritheist stood beside Sloane with his hip in the barest contact with the seated captain's shoulder. "Fuck them." Captain Sloane laid a hand on Tritheist's thigh and gave him a look that clearly communicated he shut it.

"Gavran, let humanity look out for itself," Captain Sloane said. "There's nobody else ensuring our survival, as a crew or as individuals. Once it becomes impossible to hide what Oxia has accomplished, the NEU or one of the semi-independent colonies will launch a successful coup of their own. And they are in a much better position to do that than we are."

"I disagree," Adda said over the op channel.

Captain Sloane's scowl would've terrified Adda into silence if she'd been onboard. But she was on the *Mayhem*. Aboard the *Casey*, Iridian managed to stop herself from grinning before either officer noticed, while Adda launched into her argument. "We have everything we need to mobilize the Oxia workers, as well as inform the scientific community and any governmental groups we think might help, before Oxia has solid stakes in the new star system. If we act soon, I believe we could prevent Oxia from ever gaining full control of the new system."

Adda spoke like she didn't see the enormity of what she was proposing, or the advantage over Oxia that they'd be throwing away to do it. Usually Iridian was the one holding the moral high ground, and damn the consequences, which Adda was quick to point out. Then again, their topic of discussion didn't usually involve scientific research. Adda cared about the biggest possible picture when it came to capital S Science.

When Pel whooped and Gavran laughed aloud, Adda must've jumped out of her skin. Iridian exchanged an incredulous glance with Chi. *Nice idea, babe, but I'm about to disagree too,* Iridian thought at her, and hoped that the mic conveyed how much she meant that it really was a good, if naive, place to start toppling Oxia's empire.

"The Oxia workers and the scientific community aren't all that numerous or powerful," Iridian said, "and the governments haven't gotten off their 'jects to do anything about the contractual employment abuses that're already happening. You'd have to get this information to everyone in the solar system to reach enough people who will actually act and make a difference. And we should do that, because this is huge. It's multiple-new-planets huge. But that makes it something to hold over Oxia for as long as we want, doesn't it?" That was, Iridian suspected, Sloane's plan since the captain learned about the project.

There were a few moments of silence on the other ship. "You're saying you want to keep the same secret they kept. For, I assume, *profit?*" Adda sounded scandalized enough to make Iridian blush. Ethics was one of the few topics that the two of them could argue each other to a truce over, and Adda sure as hell wouldn't enjoy doing that in public. She barely enjoyed it in private, and even that was mostly because of how Iridian made it up to her afterward. "You're right that everybody deserves to know, and we're the only ones in the position to tell them. Next steps are a matter of method and timing."

"Charming as this discussion is," Captain Sloane said, "you don't work for 'everybody.' You work for me. We need the bargaining position with Oxia more than we need public opinion in our favor, or a trip to a collection of empty planets. Should that change, you'll be the first to know." The captain cut the connection.

Tritheist and Captain Sloane watched Iridian with hard eyes.

She tilted her head to the side and shrugged, like finally getting one up on the megacorporate thugs and then putting it to fucking use wasn't that important to her. It was, but the priority was getting Sloane back in full control of the crew's activities. That was what their future rested on.

"Liu Kong will suffer more under my thumb than under my boot," Captain Sloane said. "Besides which, revenge almost exclusively causes more problems than it solves. Inciting a popular rebellion will increase the magnitude of our problems without solving any of them. Fantasize all you like. We'll reclaim the crew and Vesta without further endangering ourselves. And *after* I'm clear of the contract, you can spread Oxia's secrets as far and wide as you wish. I was the only contracted party, and I can assure you that I'll be the only one Liu Kong succeeds in silencing."

Captain Sloane stared Iridian down. She straightened her posture to military attention, hoping it conveyed respect without making her look reluctant. "Yes, Captain."

Oxia wouldn't have an unchallenged claim to the system forever. Captain Sloane was already working to challenge its control, legally and otherwise. She was willing to help Sloane use the Thrinacia Project details in whatever way gave the captain more professional options after the crew was out from under Oxia. After another conversation with Adda in private, Iridian was sure she'd agree.

* * *

As the ship converged on Vesta, Adda kept working on her plans to release the Thrinacia Project to humanity at large. When Captain Sloane was free of the Oxia contract, she'd deploy the information immediately. At least that was the goal Iridian had gleaned from

the intermittent and intense text messages Adda had been sending her throughout their return trip.

"You know this'll put the biggest spotlight on us we've ever
had, yeah?" Iridian asked Adda after the officers had retired to the
Casey's residential cabin. "And I don't just mean Sloane's crew. I
mean you and me."

The reply took a long time to arrive, even though the Casey
and the Mayhem were near enough to each other for real-time
comms. "I can handle that, I think. And I know you can. Anyway,
after Captain Sloane gets the contract dissolved with the threat
of exposing the interstellar bridge project, we'll lose Oxia's protection. We wouldn't be under any obligation to them, and it
wouldn't be logical for them to blithely ignore our presence on
Vesta. Sloane's not leaving, which means more direct conflict is
imminent given the current crew complement."

"So that's why Sloane's been building up troops." Iridian
grinned. The captain had to have a passable army by now, which
Iridian had been thinking of as the most practical sort of luxury.
But expecting an attack made an army an investment, not a luxury. "They're good. Not as good as the ZVs, but better than a lot of
people I've fought alongside. They can hold HQ against whatever
Oxia throws at them."

"Including its fleet?" Adda somehow conveyed her incredulity
by text, or Iridian just knew how she'd say that. "My point is that
releasing this information as soon as possible would put even
more regular people on Sloane's side. And ours, of course, but
Vestans know we're just part of Sloane's crew. Is something else
bothering you?"

"'As soon as possible' has to be after Sloane's out of the contract. Before that, it's not possible. So let's just drop that idea,
yeah?" Iridian smiled into her comp's cam while something sad

or wistful welled in her heart. It'd be so damned satisfying to just blast the information to all the Kuiper colonies and everyone in between. "And for the rest, it's just . . . For a while this looked like Vesta might be home. Like, a safe home. Where kids could live. That'll be tough if we're fighting Oxia every step of the way. Who knows how long it'll take Sloane to force them off the 'ject?"

The conversation paused while Adda formulated a response. Iridian fiddled with the settings to make Adda's still image look more realistic in the tiny projection. Her efforts brought dark circles under Adda's eyes into focus, which meant she hadn't been sleeping enough again. Iridian wished she'd put this conversation off until she could hold Adda in her arms. Gods, she missed that. She missed Adda.

"Staying in one place would make our family a target." Adda's gentle words meant that she understood how important this was to Iridian, and that its importance made her assessment hard to deliver. "When the crew's free from Oxia, we should talk about this again. For now, I want to finish this summary for you to talk to the captain about. This would all be a lot easier if one of Ogir's surveillance teams were operating in Rheasilvia Station before we arrive."

Always on task, her Adda. *Yes, ma'am,* Iridian thought at her. In text, she added, "I'll ask the captain if we can get them up and running first thing tomorrow." She wished she could see Adda's smile in actual size.

* * *

Two days later, Iridian and Adda joined Captain Sloane at the projection stage in HQ to make their report. Liu Kong kept checking something outside cam range while Captain Sloane and Adda summarized their findings. Adda's report had prepped Sloane perfectly, and Sloane's delivery was as convincing as ever. The captain even looked to Adda for all the right clarification points, as if Sloane had been sporadically monitoring the events from Vesta while Adda conducted operations.

"This is even more than required. Excellent work, Captain," said Liu Kong. "I expect your crew to remain on standby. We've had a . . . security incident at one of our installations." Somehow Sloane's small, unsympathetic smile wasn't also smug as hell. Iridian assumed the blank and serious expression that'd always saved her when talking to superiors. "We may require your services in resolving that."

"As the contract stipulates, we are available as needed," Sloane said stiffly.

On the other side of Sloane, Adda was looking very quickly between the captain, Iridian, and Liu Kong, like the competition she was watching was uncomfortably close and she was afraid she'd miss the deciding move. *Calm down,* Iridian subvocalized at her, and damn, was she proud of how well their implants worked. *Look at your comp.* Adda consulted her comp like she'd just received a message, which was a lot less suspicious.

Once the connection with the Oxia CEO terminated and Liu Kong's figure disappeared from the projection stage, Sloane broke into a broad grin. "Oh, it would be fun to investigate that break-in." Tritheist and Iridian chuckled. Adda had gotten preoccupied with something on her comp and missed the comment. "I don't imagine we'll be so lucky." Sloane slouched into a chair facing the projection stage, the grin already fading away. "I've received Ogir's assessment of the situation here and at Albana Station on the other side of the 'ject. Based on reactions to Oxia's prison conditions, I will *consider* your plans for the forcible removal of Oxia in conjunction with repeal of the contract. But the contract is still primary."

"The NEU and ITA already want us for breaking their laws," Adda pointed out. "They'll hunt us whether or not we're working for Oxia, and regardless of what Oxia's done."

"Our headquarters' location on Vesta is fairly well known." Sloane's spread arms encompassed the room and the building that contained it. "Why, then, aren't they here now?"

Iridian offered the obvious answer, since Adda hated to do that. "Oxia's paying off the ITA here."

"Yes. And Oxia's also tying the NEU up in fuel and reliable route disputes among themselves and Ceres," said Sloane. "Breaking my contract will annoy Liu Kong sufficiently for him to exclude us from those arrangements, as well as from any others which Oxia may be employing to keep other crews and colonies at bay. A popular uprising couldn't compete with that many enemies, in addition to Oxia itself. Should we, by some chance, win the day, as contract breakers we'd find ourselves with a much smaller pool of buyers for what we take, never mind finding people with money and targets already in mind."

Adda glanced up from her comp. "I'll have something for you by tomorrow."

Iridian blinked at her, but kept quiet until they were alone in their suite. "Tomorrow? Can you really get a workable plan together by then?"

Adda raised an eyebrow. "It's not just me. Casey's providing a lot of information, and I'm running analyses in the workspace."

Iridian settled on their bed with a frustrated sigh. "I don't get what you'd sim or analyze for this. How can you count on the Casey to help you with it?"

"Except for that exfiltration timing issue on the datacenter ship, Casey's been reliably on our side," said Adda. "And anyway, information distribution, use of various channels for various communications, amount of engagement generated by various influential figures on Vesta and elsewhere . . . There's a lot to consider."

Iridian let herself fall backward to lie flat on the bed. "Like what?"

"Well, the more I look at that HR data, the more I see Oxia's massive setup for coercing cooperation from their employees by threatening family members. We're untangling which people are affected and where their families are now. Oxia's Vestan fleet is still the major focus of all that coercion, which was my initial impression. Also, Casey's been interested in marketing and political campaign data."

"Great, it's got itself a hobby." Iridian patted the bed beside her, and Adda sat near enough for Iridian to wrap her arm around Adda's soft waist. "But the *Casey* doesn't have values to judge and analyze these things, babe. What makes you think anything it produces for you will actually lead to the results you want?"

"The Barbary intelligences value certain conditions over others. And they understand more about human behavior than I thought they did." Adda didn't sound sufficiently creeped out. She sounded *impressed*. And she kept glancing at her workspace generator, like she'd much rather be there than having this conversation.

"But why are they so interested?" Iridian was getting frustrated, partially because Adda was so calm about the whole situation. "They could be doing anything that doesn't require a physical human presence, and some things that do if they buy a good enough doll or projection figure. What the fuck are they following us around for? Why the fuck are they telling you how to make a bunch of spacefarers kick Oxia off the 'ject?"

Adda shook her head. "It's doing something for them, or we are, and I don't know what yet. Or . . ."

She looked like she wanted to say something difficult, or maybe she had a headache coming on. Iridian got up to bring her a fresh cup of coffee, in case caffeine would help. Adda accepted the mug with a smile and a kiss, but she'd drifted across the room toward the workspace generator again, and Iridian was tired of chasing after her.

Adda planned to remove Oxia from Vesta beginning the minute Sloane was out of contract with the megacorporation. There were still a lot of pieces to put in place to make that happen, and, as had become the norm lately, the only way Iridian could help was by getting out of her way. She went off to find Pel and let Adda do her thing.

Pel's options for travel used to be staying in rooms he'd memorized, taking his chances with tactile stim clothing in the busy station, or waiting until somebody wanted to guide him. Now that he was used to his pseudo-organic eyes, he got all over the station. Iridian sent him a message just outside her and Adda's suite: "You banging or dancing, or do you have time to chat?"

"Ah . . . sure."

Iridian blinked at his audio reply on her comp and almost ran into one of the crew security gals patrolling the hallway. Pel's voice was higher than usual, and he was breathing way too fast. "Where are you?" Iridian maintained a casual tempo to her voice, but walked faster.

"Home." That was definitely unlike him.

* * *

Iridian knocked on the door of Pel's suite a few minutes later. When she set her palm on the lock out of habit, it flashed red and then, to her surprise, green. That meant her name was on the visitors' list already. Either Pel had thought far enough ahead to have the system let her in at the time she was likely to arrive, or she was allowed to visit any time. In his case, the latter seemed more likely. She muttered "Huh," and let herself in.

Pel's place was smaller than her and Adda's, decorated in bright blues and purples, and furnished hab-style with half the furniture designed to stack on top of the other half. He sat in front of, not on, his living room couch, with his knees pulled up to his chest, fists clenched around his elbows, breathing like he'd just finished a run. And he was not the exercising type. She'd seen this before, among survivors of missions with casualties.

"Hey there, Pel Mel." She sat on the floor next to him. "Want to try breathing a bit slower?"

"Can't." He wheezed through half a laugh, and seemed to run out of breath for more.

"Sure you can," Iridian said. "But I'll get Chi down here if you want."

"No. I bugged her yesterday." Pel gulped. It made an audible break in his gasping breath.

Iridian shifted toward him until their shoulders touched. "Can you breathe along with me? I'm feeling pretty chill right now. It might help."

"Yeah. Okay."

Adda would've sat quietly and peacefully until he got down to her level, but listening to him wheeze made Iridian imagine the worst ways this situation could play out. "Hey, did you see that vid going around with the blue kittens that cost as much as a hab on Earth?"

Pel nodded. "Blue on the insides, too. Copper or something. Blue tongues."

"Still cute. Can't go wrong with kittens." It took a few more minutes of harmless chat until he looked like discussing the problems at hand wouldn't kill him. "So, you still going to therapy?"

Pel shrugged. "Yeah, but it's not really helping anymore. I guess I fucked up on the last two ops. I mean, I did. Because they were really hard, and I kept . . ." He sighed, and used his now-unclenched hands to pantomime reorienting his attention left and right. "I keep looking over my shoulder. Or *not* looking over my shoulder, because there might be someone actually there, and . . ." Pel inhaled and exhaled purposefully, counting under his breath for a few beats. "I'm so fucking useless at everything. I don't know why I'm still here."

That sounded more final than the "still on the station" kind of here. Iridian frowned. "So we haven't found the right job for you yet. I was coming to ask you about that. You want to tell us what people are saying about Sloane's crew?"

"What people?"

"Everybody," Iridian said. "Club people, social feed people, people you talk to while you're buying lunch. Like you were asking about what they thought of a story you follow, only instead of the story, you're asking about the crew."

He blinked at her exactly the way Adda sometimes did. "Why?"

"We're talking about kicking Oxia off Vesta, at least in a governmental capacity." Iridian grinned at him. His head was up and he was looking at her now, instead of staring at the floor. The smile was also a good sign. "We need to know who's backing us, and who'll screw us if they can. And we might need you to drop subtle hints that they ought to be with us, if they're not yet."

"Yeah, okay! That could be fun. Ogir was always telling me *not* to talk to people when we were working. I think it's because he doesn't like people, and he doesn't think anybody else should either."

Iridian chuckled. "Personally I think he treats them all like a traffic controller with ships or an enviro engineer with O_2, grav, and light: a series of processes with relatively predictable behavior, but stuff you have to keep an eye on and redirect sometimes."

"It's just like that with him." Pel smiled a bit wider. "And, um. Thanks."

"Anytime. Really, call me or Adda if you feel like this and want company, anytime." She stood and gave Pel a hand up. "Have you told your therapist you're not feeling better anymore?" When Pel shook his head, Iridian said, "Tell ver. Maybe ve can try something new."

* * *

When Iridian got back to her and Adda's suite, Adda and Ogir were drinking on the couch in front of the projector stage. Both of them glanced up, waved unenthusiastically, and returned their attention to the projector stage. Iridian hoped Adda had cleaned the couch before offering it, given their activities on it that morning, but that seemed unlikely.

Nice to see you spending time with a human, she subvocalized to Adda.

Adda smiled slightly without looking away from the stage and replied, *You're a human.*

The projector stage appeared to be showing a paused explosion with large chunks of labeled fragmentation. On closer inspection, the fire was a gradient visualization of influence or cost connecting various parts of Oxia and the two Vestan stations' infrastructure. "I can't tell if it's coming together or coming apart," Iridian said on her way to getting a beer of her own.

"The way things are now, it can only come together." Ogir took a pull from his beer, and beads or clips in his black dreadlocks clicked against each other. "This," he waved his unoccupied hand at the projected mass of information, "is all Oxia, according to what you stole from the datacenter, and it's also almost all contracted. No local government anywhere, and Sloane's crew, well . . ." Ogir pointed to a small corner near the floor, shaded gold and surrounded by Oxia red. "Maybe don't show this to the captain yet."

"No," Adda said firmly. "It's not ready. We have this now, and we want to turn it into this." She whispered to her comp, and the projection flickered to a new configuration. This one was more like a decorated Christmas tree with text on all the ornaments. Sloane's gold area of influence perched at the top, with two green and blue areas beneath, labeled Rheasilvia and Albana. Red Oxia orbs clustered near the base.

"No station governments," Ogir said as the projection reverted to the chaotic state it was in when Iridian first saw it, "to puppet station governments that Captain Sloane controls." The projection changed back to the Christmas tree model. "Sloane will control more of the 'ject than before the captain and Tritheist got trapped on Barbary Station, because Oxia consolidated Vesta's infrastructure contracts last year. And the council, meaning Sloane, can keep the people employed and making money in the meantime."

His neutral tone suggested that he didn't care about the impact this conspiracy might have on the station populace. Iridian trusted Sloane's judgement, but she'd made the choice to rely on it. The Vestans wouldn't be offered a real choice of station leadership. That was kind of fucked up.

"But we're missing details on the conversion in the middle," Adda said. "So it's not ready."

"Yeah, that sounds like the hard part." Iridian sat on the couch arm beside Adda. At least Vestan welfare was part of the conversation, if not their primary consideration.

"Forget the diagram. We didn't make it for you." Adda shifted to press her shoulder against Iridian's hip. "Here's the simplified version: Step one, convince Sloane it's all feasible. Step two, leverage the stolen Thrinacia Project data to get Sloane out of the contract with Oxia. Step three, publish it all anyway, with all credit to Dr. Björn and without bringing Oxia's lawyers and enforcers down on ver, while protecting ourselves."

Ogir turned away from the projection to look at Adda. "What are we crediting the astronomer with?"

"Vis part in the research," Adda said. "Ve discovered the interstellar bridge, and history's going to remember that discovery. For once, I want it to remember the right person. Besides, those papers ve wrote on it never got published. That's a big loss of time and effort."

Ogir was smiling when he looked back to the projected diagram. "That'll catch everyone's attention, lowest plebe to the NEU prez. At which point Captain Sloane gets all the big interested parties to make Oxia's occupation here impossible."

"And everyone can use Vestan stationspace to test the new ships they'll all be developing," said Adda.

"Not in stationspace. That's eight kinds of unsafe," Iridian said. "They'll dock here. Anyway, if those interested parties can push Oxia around, they can push us too, yeah?"

"Unless . . . ," said both Adda and Ogir at once. They looked at each other for a couple seconds, until Ogir raised his beer to his lips. "Unless they have a reason not to," said Adda.

"Everybody knows where Sloane is right now," said Ogir. Iridian gave him a confused expression at the leap between topics. "All of us are being watched here, most of the time. We need to take what's keeping Oxia independent from the governments and make that ours."

"The fleet." Iridian's eyes widened. "That'll be a hell of a job."

Adda gave her one of those smiles that meant she had a secret

Iridian was just going to love. "We know where to start. Oxia's thoroughly documented its intention to kidnap and threaten family members or friends—"

"Or a ferret, in one case," said Ogir.

"The ferret counts as family." Adda's smile faltered as she continued, "Whenever somebody steps far enough out of line, Oxia gives them one warning about their endangered relative. If the contracted employee tries to break contract or makes any further trouble, Oxia kidnaps someone important to the employee."

Once Iridian finished swearing, Ogir added, "They might've gotten away with it if they'd included that provision in their contracts somehow. A lot of Vestans would've tolerated it, even if it wouldn't have flown in NEU space."

"Twelve ranked crewmembers in Oxia's fleet already have missing loved ones, and those are just the people we've matched up with kidnapping orders in the records you took from the datacenter," Adda said. "The important part is that we have Oxia's documented plans for the rest of the fleet personnel. If you received evidence that Sloane was doing something like that to you and me, what would you do?"

"Validate the information. And then, something bloody," Iridian growled.

"Or," said Ogir, "you'd maybe change sides and ally yourself with a criminal organization that's motivated to take Oxia down."

* * *

Which was how Iridian ended up playing spy in a venue bar crammed between Rheasilvia Station's two enormous port modules. She settled at a bar with bottles behind it, one or two of which might've been real and contained liquor. The 167-degree projection stage was showing a small ship race that kept zooming off the left end of the stage, which caused excited shouting from those on that end. The ships reappeared at the right end and traversed the stage again.

A projection of stationspace covered the ceiling, with a frame at the edges of the projection to remind patrons that the hull was still intact. No ships were coming in or out at the moment. Stars glittered clear in the cold and the black beyond Rheasilvia Station's latticework exterior, giving the illusion of stability while the station spun beneath them.

Ogir says the fleet commander is near the right side of the projection stage, Adda whispered in Iridian's head. *And the commander's comp is connected to the station net, so I can confirm he's somewhere in that building.*

Iridian turned toward the race on the stage while she used her peripheral vision to scan the crowd for a tallish guy with brown skin and nice-enough clothes to be an officer. She spotted him cheering with a couple other guys and shouting advice at two fliers maneuvering side by side. One swerved away to pass and the other got in front again to prevent that, resulting in more shouting from the officers by the stage.

"Got him," Iridian muttered.

The next part was Ogir's idea, and if it didn't work Iridian would kick his ass. She fiddled with her new wedding ring, the replacement she'd made that incorporated the braided wire from the original makeshift one into a wide, white-gold band. She feigned surprise when it slid off her finger and bounced into the crowd by the stage.

"Fuck!" she exclaimed loudly for anybody who might've been watching. Ogir was, and he'd assured her that some contingent of Oxia's station security force and at least one ITA agent was watching too. She dived into the crowd after the ring, because she sure as hell wouldn't lose it on this little trick.

It'd rolled toward the wrong end of the stage, so after she grabbed it off the floor she pocketed it and pretended to keep searching for it, nearer and nearer to the target, shoving at people's legs as she went. Somebody kicked her, accidentally or not, but she finally ended up next to him.

Okay, doing the passing thing, she said, as much to herself as to Adda. This was her only shot at this part of the plan. She put her back to the bar and the exit, where Ogir said the stationsec cams were, grabbed the target's comp arm with hers, and yelled, "Hey, I dropped my ring and I think you're standing on it" over the projected race noise, about five centimeters from the target's face.

He frowned in understandable annoyance when he had to look away from the stage. In the course of getting his attention and pointing at the floor, Iridian got her comp glove near enough to his, she hoped, for Adda to do her thing with their comps' proximity sharing function and his open connection.

Iridian couldn't get her ring out of her pocket convincingly enough to pretend to find it on the floor while the target was watching, so she lunged at a shadowed spot of floor instead. "Got it, thanks!" she shouted. She returned to the bar, put her ring on, and examined it for scratches.

Less than two minutes later, the Oxia fleet commander stepped up to the bar next to her, looking like he'd like to make a scene but had been sufficiently persuaded to just be grouchy. "How the hell did you make that message look like it came from Oxia HQ?"

Iridian grinned at his consternation, and ignored the rude response she thought of first. "I married well. That the only question you had?"

Fleet Commander Qasid frowned. "You're Iridian Nassir, yes? The pirate."

"That sounds pretty good." Iridian grinned a bit wider. "More important for you, I'm Adda Karpe's wife." The change in his expression was subtle, but marked. He was much more interested that Adda was reaching out to him than Iridian. She'd be jealous if she weren't so damned proud. "She came across the list attached to that message while she was looking for something else. Thought you should have it. And if you want to do something about it, she's got a plan."

Qasid's comp glove bore a military-looking insignia she didn't recognize with small print words around the circular border, maybe representing a division of his fleet. The comp was projecting a mostly empty message inbox. One of his buddies by the projection stage yelled something at him, and he waved back with his other hand. After he skimmed the list Adda had found in the stolen copy of Oxia's HR data, he glared at Iridian. "What the hell is this, and where did it come from?"

"It's what it looks like." Iridian watched him in case he reacted too publicly, or violently. Discovering that your employer spying on you and your family, and that it'd already picked which detention center to send each family member to if you looked like you'd do something that hurt the company, had to be a nasty shock. "As for where, well, you know Adda. No computer system she can't crack." As Adda had said, the real story of how they came across that information wouldn't help him make the right decision.

"Why? What can I do about this?" His voice was so choked with emotion that Iridian had to resist leaning toward him to hear more clearly. That'd draw too much attention from whoever was watching.

Iridian had turned her back to him, playing for the cams that he'd tried to pick her up and failed. Ogir had thought it was a good idea, but she felt stupid doing it. With her back to Qasid, she couldn't tell if he was pissed or scared. If it were her family and Adda on that list, she'd be angry as hell. "What you can do is hit Oxia before they get a chance to follow through. They're not sending your fleet to make these arrests, are they?"

"Stationsec," Qasid spat.

"You can't stop them by yourself. Same with us," Iridian said. "Adda's got a plan, but she needs most of your fleet combined with all of Captain Sloane's resources."

"And they have . . . one of these lists, on every one of my spacefarers?" Qasid asked.

In her ear, Adda said, *Probably just for the lower officer levels up to him, but I haven't confirmed that.*

"Yeah, every one of them," Iridian said gravely. "Sorry. We don't like it either. That's why we're doing something about it. If we call for your help within, say, the next three days, will it just be you with your sidearm, or can you bring ships with you?"

Commander Qasid's breath shook when he inhaled. "I'll bring whoever I can. Get me the rest of those lists."

Adda: Sending with ten-minute delay, to optimize receptivity appeared on Iridian's comp in purple text.

Ogir: Trust markers are good slid down from the top of the comp display in blue. The speech pattern analysis Ogir fed their conversation through apparently said that Qasid wouldn't betray them, at least not in his current state of mind. Iridian would have to find out what they said about her side of the conversation sometime.

Qasid's friends crowded into the booth behind him, talking about the race and what he'd missed. Iridian paid her tab and left.

* * *

Captain Sloane's and Adda's voices carried down the residential-level hallway in crew HQ, all the way to the elevators. Four of Sloane's favorite security people had spaced themselves evenly along the wall between the elevators and Iridian's and Adda's suite. Their expressions and nondescript, lightly armored clothes said "professionally discreet" as clearly as projected-on labels.

Iridian nodded at the security detail as she passed, all of whom looked more sympathetic toward her on approach. She'd been training with them long enough to know their titles, their names, and most of their kids' and pets' names too. If they saw her as a threat to Captain Sloane they'd put her on her ass, but a couple of them would hesitate, at least.

When she let herself into the suite, Adda was saying, "... done it the slow way like you asked, but this discovery will reform the political balance. We have to *adapt*."

It was a lot for Adda to say to anyone other than Iridian or Pel, let alone to shout at Captain Sloane in a voice husky with disuse. Her pupils were dilated like she'd been in a workspace when Sloane arrived. Talking while drugged up aggravated her because she couldn't affect reality the way she could her workspaces.

"The crew runs on profit, not vigilante justice!" Captain Sloane fought with as few people as Adda did, as far as Iridian had seen. If she weren't recalling the people Sloane must've killed to get to this position, she'd sit down and watch. That, and if Tritheist weren't standing three steps from the door, glowering, with his hand on a knife hilt. "There is nothing profitable in adapting in this direction."

"Captain." Iridian used the greeting version of the address, pitched up on the last syllable and quiet enough to bring the conversation down a few decibels, she hoped. "We thought you wanted to hit Oxia anyway."

"Damned right," Tritheist grumbled. Sloane glared at him and the lieutenant took a visual interest in Iridian's boots.

"*After* I'm out of the gods-damned contract." Sloane inhaled slowly, gaze following Iridian's deliberate pace crossing the room to Adda. Adda frowned, probably at Sloane's repetition of a point she'd already acknowledged as made. "I'm in this for money. We all are. What you're proposing will frighten the NEU and antagonize the ITA, which are the organizations in the best position to eliminate us as a threat to travel in the colonial territories. Unless I extract myself from the contract legally, Oxia can and will conduct both organizations directly to my doorstep. Frightened people form mobs, and mobs have a tendency to shove subjects of their ire into the nearest incinerator."

The captain already said all of this, Adda subvocalized beside Iridian, as if the repetition was as exasperating as resistance to her plan.

"A move like you're talking about takes setup, though, yeah?" Iridian said. "Once you drop all the 'diplomatic' threats that'll get you out of the contract, you have to have the fleet ready to back you up or Oxia will just wipe us off the 'ject quietly, with the ITA's help. That means the fleet has to *get* ready." Which was something the captain already knew. Wasn't it?

"The fleet," Captain Sloane repeated so quietly that the hairs on the back of Iridian's neck stood up. Fleet pre-op preparations hadn't factored into Sloane's contract dissolution timetable because Adda never told the captain that she and Ogir were pursuing that option.

Iridian pressed her lips together and purposefully found a point on the wall to look at instead of glaring at Adda. She and Ogir investigated possibilities' viability before bringing them to the captain's attention, but the captain should've known everything before Iridian had talked to Qasid on the crew's behalf

"Oxia's fleet?" Captain Sloane asked. "How and when was that arranged?"

"Just now," Iridian said. "The first invitation was offered and accepted, anyway. We'll see what Fleet Commander Qasid comes up with."

"Your crew is formidable." Adda might've added the extra emphasis on "your," or Iridian might've just wished she had. "But additional forces will be necessary when—"

"The biggest megacorporation this side of Mars turns on me after my blatant betrayal, yes," Sloane snapped. The captain paced the length of their living room while Tritheist and Iridian watched each other in peripheral vision. If the captain needed something physical and dangerous done, Tritheist would get the order to carry it out, and Iridian would have to stop him.

The captain faced Adda. "That's not all we need. This is only a part of Oxia's fleet. They'll call in the rest, if they're threatened. They may have done so already, although Ogir would have told me if he'd heard something to that effect."

Adda nodded. "I'd hoped you'd consider speaking to representatives of the ITA . . ." Sloane's bitter bark of laughter was loud enough to bounce off the walls and startle Adda. ". . . and the NEU. With enough Oxia ships, you'd outnumber anything they have locally," Adda said. "They'd listen to your proposition of alternative leadership if something were in it for them."

"Such as the political capital of capturing a widely vilified pirate?" Sloane's shaking head sent a cascade of black hair across the captain's shoulders. "What could interest them more?"

"Oxia's been marking up their fuel and mineral prices against both groups for years. A captured pirate is a short-term accomplishment. Reduced travel and resource costs would be a much longer-term benefit."

Sloane's angry snarl was slowly replaced by cautious hope. Adda actually had the captain considering her scheme. "You seem determined to pursue this." The "and I can't stop you short of violence" was left unsaid. "I have contacts, among the ITA, the NEU, and other interested parties. If any of them would support this . . . venture, I'll let you know."

Sloane's coat sleeve brushed Iridian's arm on the captain's way out the door. She waited for Tritheist to follow, but he let the door shut instead. He looked back and forth between Iridian and Adda. "Captain Sloane deserves full control of the crew and of Vesta. The captain earned it."

Adda just looked at him, so Iridian said, "We think so too."

"You're going to need somebody leading Captain Sloane's protection detail when Oxia sends stationsec to take the crew down." Tritheist stood taller, which let him tower over Adda and see Iridian eye-to-eye. "It'd better be me."

"So you two aren't just fucking." The idea of Tritheist loving anyone enough to put himself on the front lines of a firefight was enough of a surprise that Iridian's brain let that observation get verbalized.

Tritheist scowled at her. "No."

"It will be you," Adda said calmly. "You're well regarded," which wasn't true, "and well qualified," which was true enough. *And well motivated, apparently,* she added to Iridian subvocally, who smiled as widely as she could without infuriating Tritheist.

The lieutenant relaxed minutely, though he stared at Adda like her telling the truth or lying to get rid of him were equally likely possibilities. "Damn right." He let himself out of the suite, and Iridian locked the door behind him. Captain Sloane would have an override for it, but the officers seemed content to let her and Adda alone for now.

Adda sat down hard on the bed. "We're doing this."

"Hell yeah, we're doing this." Iridian sat and pulled Adda against her in a one-armed hug. "It'll be the crew we always wanted, all Sloane's again, in, what, a week?"

"Four days," Adda corrected her like it was a reflex. "Realistically we can't secure enough of the fleet to hold headquarters in fewer than three days, even with the commander advocating, and Oxia's response will take at least a day to run its course." She wrapped both arms around Iridian and rested her head against Iridian's chest. When seated, they were about the same height. Iridian had much longer legs. "In those four days," Adda continued, "we need to tell the NEU and ITA, and maybe the Ceres syndicate, that something noteworthy is about to be published, and if they side with us then Oxia can't maintain its high refueling prices. And, obviously, there are going to be a lot more people interested in traveling beyond Mars's orbit once everyone knows about the interstellar bridge."

Iridian grinned. "See? Nobody will turn down cheaper refueling and more customers. It's as good as happened already."

"Casey expects losses."

And there went Iridian's good vibes. "Why are you asking the *Casey*?"

"Because Casey processes data much more efficiently than I can," said Adda. "I want the closest I can get to *evidence* before I . . . before I'm responsible for . . ."

"Babe, we have everything we need." Iridian squeezed Adda tighter against her. "Oxia is going down, and the NEU and ITA are bound to fall in line afterward."

Adda sighed. "Not without a fight."

CHAPTER 23

SHQ40>Torrential>45999ru>Immunisity>
ITA533

This was the second address Adda had sent a message to. With luck, this one would reach Suhaila Al-Mudari, former spokesperson for Martian refugees trapped on Barbary Station and current "costs of the war" correspondent for TAPnews. Four years after hostilities ceased, there was still enough fallout from the colonial secession to make "costs of the war" a viable news specialty.

Captain Sloane hadn't specified a medium for releasing the details of the Thrinacia Project, only the timing. Adda had selected the one reporter she trusted to release the information on her and the captain's schedule. On Barbary, Suhaila had withheld information about the crew's true status while begging the populated universe to help the refugees, and she still kept some of Sloane's secrets today. She'd protected the captain and the crew then. Adda was counting on her to do so again.

In her workspace, Adda reviewed the message she'd recorded and trimmed off an "um" that ruined the rhythm. She started recording again. "We have really important news we'd like every-body to hear. Reply on the most secure medium you have."

The larger workspace generator she'd gotten installed in the suite meant that she could stash water and snacks inside, and leave only for bio breaks. At the moment, she was using it to track and organize reports from a huge number of simultaneous proj-ects coming together to bring Oxia down and raise Captain Sloane in their place.

Sloane's contacts in the ITA were already responding favor-ably to the captain's invitations to a temporary alliance against Oxia, as had an anti-NEU resistance collective which had become the Callistan legislative body. The NEU itself was taking longer to convince, probably due to the Callistans' early support. Com-mander Qasid was quietly making inroads with them while Cap-tain Sloane focused on the Ceres syndicate.

The ITA, the NEU, and the Ceres syndicate posed the most danger to Sloane's crew. One way or another, the captain would have to deal with all of them to retain control of Vesta. The ITA collaborated with every hab to keep spacefarers safe and reliable routes clear. But aside from a few trade route agreements mod-ifying the treaties that ended the war, Adda couldn't recall the NEU cooperating with colonies like Ceres on anything. Between Captain Sloane's initiative on Vesta and the interstellar bridge, humanity was getting a lot of opportunities to work together for a change. With luck, they wouldn't waste it.

In the meantime, the *Charon's Coin* was sending Adda detailed traffic reports on ships near Vesta and those that were projected to approach within the next three days. It was odd to hear from it instead of Casey, but Casey was already processing comms and internet traffic and forwarding everything relevant to Adda. She had two separate workspaces running simultaneously, one in the big generator and the other in her mobile generator. Together they barely kept up with what the intelligences were sending. She set a high priority alert on messages with Suhaila's name and moved on to her next project.

AegiSKADA had integrated itself with Vesta's two stationsec computer systems. They didn't run off a unified intelligence, but employed several isolated intelligences for human resources, dispatch coordination, communications, legal processing, and one exclusively in charge of their prison in Albana Station, on the other side of Vesta. AegiSKADA was receiving everything the communications and human resources coordination systems did, and it was probing the port module and prisons for vulnerabilities. It pinged her to approve its next move every other minute, and she struggled to concentrate on each request.

"Fuck," Adda sighed.

"Anytime," Iridian called from across the room. Beautiful, resolute, trusting Iridian, who thought Adda had deactivated AegiSKADA the day after they returned from Deimos. Acknowledging Adda's lie pulled something achingly tight in her chest, and dropped her out of the workspace.

When Adda sat up and pushed the heavy curtain over the installed workspace generator aside, Iridian wore a practice range suit from training with Tritheist and Sloane's local security crew. A tight jumpsuit lay over her skin like exquisitely thin black netting, except for a thicker section that looked like shorts and an opaque band of red over her breasts. Adda forgot what she'd been working on in the workspace. Rows of gold-colored specks flowed over the suit in barely visible stripes, to communicate with the practice range's feedback system. The outfit made Iridian look like a workspace figure come to life. No wonder Iridian was thinking about sex in an outfit like that. Adda glanced up at the map on the generator's ceiling to ground herself in their suite.

Iridian was supposed to be retrieving a datacask of visiting ship rosters and their crews' predicted loyalties, which Ogir had stashed somewhere in the port modules. Instead she was lounging in front of the projection stage with fruit juice.

"Why aren't you—"

"I sent Pel." Iridian shrugged. "Keeps him out of the club, which reduces his chance of sharing details with his drinking buddies. Also, he was feeling left out."

"That's really important information he's picking up." Adda frowned. She trusted his intentions, but not his judgement or discretion.

Iridian tipped her head back to look at Adda upside down over the back of the couch, and reached to press a hand on Adda's hip and pull her closer. "All he has to do is pull a datacask out of a potted plant. It's not like he's never done something like that before."

He'd implied, several times, that he'd smuggled drugs through NEU ports. Adda supposed it was an opportunity to put those skills to a positive use.

"When was the last time you slept, babe? Because it wasn't last night, and it wasn't while I was out today."

After yesterday's conversation with Captain Sloane, sleep hadn't been an option. Adda glanced at her comp's timestamp. There was no time for tangential topics, or for Iridian's workout clothes. "I have another ten hours before I'll have to deal with that. That's why I have the lights turned up so bright in here."

"You know, judgement gets fucked up at the forty-hour mark."

"I'm not sleeping now either. This is wasting the hours I have." Adda set another sharpsheet on her tongue and entered her correspondence and surveillance workspace. If Iridian said anything else, she didn't hear it.

How can Iridian be this casual about the situation? A large hollow oak tree interior rose around her. If they couldn't control Oxia's security forces, if holding the Thrinacia Project data hostage didn't get Sloane out of the contract, if the ITA or NEU had hidden ships or agents that changed the balance, they'd end up in one of several varieties of prison, or hard vacuum. Maybe Iridian stayed so calm by trusting Adda to work out all of the details. Like that was possible, for a military coup organized in a matter of days.

The intelligences were the only factor making it remotely feasible. They gathered, analyzed, and tracked the vast amount of information required, and they did it in a workspace-compatible way. Why they were helping was still a mystery, although it seemed likely that they were, like Sloane's crew, making a safe home for themselves. And since they needed Sloane's help, or at least the captain's name, to do it, they furthered Sloane's cause where they could.

A small, neon-pink tiger with wings flapped through a hole in the hollow tree and circled down toward her. Suhaila had found a secure contact point. Adda let the workspace handle the connection, and it formed a narrow wooden platform for the tiger to land on.

Once all four paws touched the platform, it snapped into a figure of Suhaila, with the accompanying mental impression that she had stood there the whole time. Her long dark hair fell over the shoulders of her dark red suit jacket, which projected the modern ideal of "serious journalistic business" very efficiently. If the hallucinographic suit's visual focus enhancers worked as well in reality as they did in the workspace, Suhaila would have no difficulty inspiring belief and attention on her newsfeed.

Adda dug into the background interface to examine the security measures that the figure's "always there" sensation indicated, then listened to the message. They were on distance-delayed comms, according to the timestamp vines had formed on the tree trunk's interior wall.

"Adda! Good to hear from you. I've been watching the latest on Sloane's crew, of course, notification triggers every few minutes, but it's great to hear from the real you! Seriously, tell me everything." Adda had forgotten Suhaila's dedicated enthusiasm for Sloane's crew. "I'm contracted to TAPnews now, so I have to be a little particular about what I publish and how it goes out. Just a little, but, you know, I have to mention that. And ask for an exclusive. This is exclusive, though, yes? Anyway, I'm here, just reply on this thing."

A bright red flower blossomed at the corner of Adda's vision, signifying that she'd activated the recording function. "It's exclusive on the condition that you hold on to the information until I give the signal. I'll do it soon, but it can't get released early. It would put Captain Sloane in a lot of danger. Let me know if you can do that, and then I'll send everything I have." That should stick the fact in Suhaila's memory. The red flower wilted and fell to the nonexistent dirt as she ended the recording and sent it.

Oxia would relinquish their hold on Captain Sloane, supposedly without a fuss, in exchange for Sloane's silence regarding the interstellar bridge. If she waited until Oxia officially dissolved the contract, Sloane would retain all the legal benefits, allowing for future deals with the NEU and ITA.

But Oxia had no right to keep such an amazing discovery from the rest of humanity, and it didn't deserve a chance to steal rights to the new star system using stolen equipment. As soon as it wouldn't affect Sloane's freedom from the contract, she'd send Suhaila the signal to share news of the interstellar bridge as far and wide as she could. Dr. Björn would get the credit ve deserved, and the worlds would know the truth.

A small flock of birds materialized in the treetops and descended in a flurry of small wings and airborne letters and numbers. The letters and numbers collected themselves into columns of ship names and Ogir's loyalty assessments. Pel had retrieved the datacask. The fleet crews were, overall, sympathetic toward Sloane's cause.

She was still studying Ogir's report when Suhaila's next message arrived, full of assurances that she'd stick to Adda's timetable. Adda sent her prerecorded reply while Suhaila's sign-off was still playing. "I'm sending you access instructions for the Casey Mira Mira's tanks. Don't release any of it before my signal."

Suhaila's response, when it arrived, was less encouraging. "So, I did exactly what you sent me. It didn't work. I know security is fiddly, but—"

Adda held up a hand, pausing Suhaila's recorded figure. She didn't bother composing a worded message to Casey. Her intention-imbued query scuttled somewhere outside her peripheral vision. Its steps had barely faded when Casey's disembodied voice said, "Show me why she needs this."

Adda tore away one of the sequences separating her mental processes from Casey's and nonverbally emphasized what Suhaila having the information would mean for Oxia, and for the crew. Her head throbbed for long seconds, and then something in the workspace shifted. She sent the message "Try it again" to Suhaila, then refocused on Ogir's reports.

Suhaila's reply arrived nearly half an hour later, repeating how significant the information was "To the whole of humanity! I mean, it's most important that it gets Captain Sloane what's needed, but . . ." Adda kept reading reports until Suhaila said ". . . risking my job for this. Hell, I guess Oxia could kill me for this, but yeah, you're the bigger target. Anyway, it's worth it so long as one of the refugees' greatest supporters gets well-deserved free-dom from . . . Hmm, I'll workshop that part later. Did you know that twenty percent of Albana Station's current population was transferred from that Pallas colony the NEU destroyed in '69?" Adda had been a child when that happened. These days, it wasn't a common conversation topic. "Oh, I should lead with that in the companion piece. More trouble for the already troubled . . ."

If Adda were delivering news that one of the most influen-tial megacorporations in the galaxy had been committing gross human rights violations during a dubious legal takeover of a high-population asteroid, and their intention to spread their wealth-gathering inhumanities to a new star system, she'd emphasize that rather than the tangentially related unfortunate life histories of the asteroid's occupants. She'd have to trust that Suhaila knew her business.

Adda had one more message to compose. She breathed in, and in, and in, let it out slow, and watched the red flower revive itself in her peripheral vision. "Captain Sloane, schedule the con-tract renegotiation with Liu Kong at your convenience. Please let me know the precise time. We'll be ready."

CHAPTER 24

Stage 4 confirmed

Iridian frowned across the second-floor bar in the club level of Sloane's HQ, listening for a voice in her head. Although Adda and Ogir had deemed the position insufficiently low-key to meet their standards for "covert," Iridian and Tritheist had overridden them to prioritize the strategic advantage.

It'd hardly matter anyway, if Adda kept missing or ignoring her comms. *Babe, are you receiving?* Iridian subvocalized. *Because we could really use—*

Liu Kong, Captain Sloane, and the lawyers are still talking, Adda said. It was past 21:00, and the negotiation had been going on without a break since 08:30. Iridian, Tritheist, and HQ security had been waiting around for the past couple of hours, expecting them to reach an agreement anytime. *Ogir will tell you when the session's over,* Adda continued. *I'm working.*

Iridian thumbed off her mic before she thought something she should've kept to herself. Adda had been working herself half to death, on the potential fight with Oxia and on preparing to release the Thrinacia Project to the populated universe. A corner of their suite's projection stage was devoted to HQ server statuses and network activity unrelated to Oxia or the ITA as far as Iridian could tell. She hadn't wanted to interrupt Adda by asking about it. After Iridian had taken up her position on HQ's club level, Adda had probably drawn that into her workspace too.

Maybe Adda was just managing their resources carefully, or running an analysis on the AIs, or doing last-minute calculations to confirm that it'd take more than one direct missile strike to penetrate HQ down to the residential level. "Hell of a time for distractions," Iridian muttered.

"You talked to Karpe?" Tritheist asked from the seat beside her. "What'd she say?"

"Session's still in progress." Iridian sipped a beer that'd warmed in the hours they'd been sitting there, in case somebody was watching. Ogir and Adda had both warned the crew about the possibility of Oxia and ITA spies. Chi was stationed at the first-floor bar, and Gavran was testing the *Mayhem*'s shipboard systems in a dock conveniently near the Oxia fleet ships Adda trusted. All three awakened AI ships were out there too.

And all of them waiting for a contract to be voided. Iridian smiled into her glass. "We'll feel damned silly if Oxia decides to cut its losses and play nice with Sloane." To be fair, the megacorporation had done an impressive job protecting Sloane's crew from the ITA for the past few months.

"Oxia won't play so nice that it gives up the stations, no matter how far ahead the captain puts them in megacorporate competition," Tritheist said. "And keep that on the command channel. You're not the only one who needs intel."

Iridian stopped her eyes from rolling by watching the dancers on the floor below. "Isn't that why Ogir and his team are lurking outside the talks? And the undercover ITA *and* NEU are listening in too." No amount of bribery could keep the Vestan contingent of the ITA away from a negotiation that could change the political structure of the 'ject. It wasn't ideal, but Ogir had assured Sloane and Adda that his team could work around the government agents. She chuckled. "Can you imagine? Half of that building is full of people trying not to look dangerous."

Tritheist looked pointedly at the beer in Iridian's hand and back to her face. She snorted. "Yeah, right, us too."

"Ogir here." Tritheist's comp played Ogir's tinny but calm voice a little louder than the dance music. "The negotiation comm feed disconnected."

Iridian set the beer on the bar and shifted her shoulders to confirm that the collapsed shield hooked to the back of her light-armor jacket would come free quickly when she needed it. HQ security had stashed her and Tritheist's armored suits in a hidden cabinet in the VIP room on street level, where they were inconspicuous but convenient. Background clicking on the comms indicated that a lot of "ready" signals would be appearing in Adda's workspace. Iridian thumbed her implanted mic back on and tapped her status on her comp, although Tritheist would've reported that HQ was ready by now.

"Lads and lasses, we are back in business for ourselves." Captain Sloane's voice confirmed the victory across the op channel. Every member of HQ security, a dozen combat specialists, and about twice as many sneaky surveillance types than Iridian previously thought Ogir had were on the op tonight.

Iridian grinned wide, and Tritheist slammed his beer on the bar and whispered, "Yes." The crew in and around the club stopped watching for trouble long enough to nod or exclaim over their local channels while the clubgoers danced around them.

Pel must've had his comp speaker on at his observation post in one of the dockside bars. Even though the mic was practically in his mouth when he shouted "Congratulations, Captain!" he was barely audible beneath the whooping and clapping around him.

Those people sounded as proud as Iridian felt. No more doing Oxia's dirty work. It was time to go back to sticking it to the megacorporations that used people and discarded them, that hid scientific discoveries which all of humanity had a right to. That was what she'd signed on to Sloane's crew to do. Well, that and make a fortune, but if they kept earning at the rate they were, she and Adda would be well on their way to that. First they'd have to survive the repercussions of giving Oxia what it deserved for messing with Sloane's crew.

"Signal sent to publish," Adda said over the command channel, confirming to Captain Sloane and the rest of the crew leadership that the truth about Oxia's Thrinacia Project was about to be broadcast throughout populated space. No joy from her yet. She'd still be working for hours, tracking ITA, NEU, and Vestan reactions with the AIs, but humanity would not appreciate being kept out of the scientific discovery of the century.

She'd only managed to get a message to Suhaila yesterday, so there was still a chance that some technical or security issue would keep the message from going through. Adda would be watching for that, though, and she wouldn't let anything stop it for long.

Once Adda and Suhaila publicized the secret interstellar bridge project, Oxia would go from the crew's biggest ally to their biggest enemy, followed by the ITA and the NEU. Captain Sloane had made inroads with the latter two groups, but neither had committed to anything resembling an alliance against Oxia.

In the meantime, Oxia's fleet presence in stationspace trapped

Sloane's crew in Rheasilvia Station, because Adda expected an unknown number of Oxia ships to stay loyal when it came time to choose sides. Adda and the captain had decided that defending HQ from a ground assault was more survivable than trying to fly themselves out of missile range, and HQ security had prepared accordingly.

"Ogir here. Captain Sloane is out of the Oxia building and returning to HQ. We'll follow as able."

"Fleet is launching," Commander Qasid grimly announced on the command channel.

Either that'd taken longer than Adda had predicted, or Qasid had delayed before reporting it. All of humanity was about to find out what a despicable company he worked for, and he'd have to fight former friends over it. It wasn't news Iridian would rush to report, if she were in his position.

"Close the club and clear the people out." Adda's voice on the op channel was a thoroughly drugged monotone.

"Give me five minutes to get there, then clear it," Captain Sloane corrected firmly, using the command channel this time. "Cover coming in would be nice."

Iridian frowned. That hadn't been part of the plan. She made sure her mic was off, then turned to Tritheist. "Oxia won't hold fire just because Sloane's surrounded by civilians."

"The captain will be harder to hit that way." Tritheist rested his hand on the synthcapsin launcher at his hip. His expression warned her that he'd leave her on the floor of the bar rather than risk Sloane's safety by getting the clubgoers out of harm's way sooner. She kept her seat and counted down the minutes. Adda would've set a timer.

"Clear the club," Adda said right on schedule.

Iridian went to the railing that overlooked the dance floor

while Tritheist used his comp to signal the club's music system to cut the sound. In the sudden silence, dancers groaned and demanded, "Turn it back on!"

Iridian pulled a nannite grenade from her belt and held it up where they'd see it. The baseball-size grenade could fill the first floor with a cloud of nerve-stimulating nasties, and the LEDs on the outside made it look like the kind villains used in the vids. Iridian had added the lights with the hope that it'd look too scary for anyone to make her use it.

As she'd hoped, the crowd shifted away like a single entity, exclaiming in fear. "Go home and get in front of your stage," she shouted at them. "Big news coming." If anyone in Oxia had a shred of decency, they'd protect the residential modules. Dancers ran out the front doors, leaving crew security standing around the walls in their wake. In retrospect, Oxia would control the local media for longer than it'd hold off on attacking Sloane's crew, so the local projection stages might be full of propaganda instead of news.

Tritheist must've realized that too, because he laughed while he headed for the lift to the first floor. Iridian joined him, disengaging the grenade's activation mechanism and returning it to the pouch on her belt.

"Ogir here," he said on the command channel. "Requesting permission to patch in the NEU operatives."

"Add them to your team channel." The smile in Captain Sloane's voice came over the comms with the order. "The NEU will have much more reasonably priced reliable routes beyond Mars once I break the Oxia monopoly. Make sure they receive my assurances on that point."

"Fleet's moving," Adda reported in her workspace monotone while Tritheist and Iridian donned their armor in the VIP room.

When Iridian put her helmet on and tapped the visor down, it immediately filled with comms traffic. She turned sender tagging on and shifted it all to the side of her faceplate while she followed Tritheist to the front door.

On the command channel, Qasid said, "We've been ordered to fire on Sloane's base once the captain returns to it."

"That'd stop spin grav for the whole station. It'll put this mod in vac lockdown, won't it?" Iridian stalked across the empty dance floor toward the club's street entrance. "People will die. A lot of them."

"The station's emergency systems should keep the structure turning with a module damaged, but it's not worth the risk. I won't do it." Commander Qasid sounded angry at being in the position of protecting the 'ject from his own fleet. "Also, a tugboat is loitering at the stationspace perimeter. It isn't responding to hails or the dock AI. Is she one of yours?"

"Don't mind the *Charon's Coin*," Captain Sloane replied to Qasid. Sloane was laughing over the command channel, which Iridian last heard . . . months ago, maybe. Being free of a megacorporate contract had to be an overwhelming relief, but with the possibility of an incoming missile strike, nothing felt that funny. Especially not unpredictable awakened AI copilots. "She'll stay out of your way," Captain Sloane continued. "Best to stay out of hers too."

"Understood."

Iridian and Tritheist joined a squad of Sloane's security force who'd cleared the street around HQ. Iridian grinned at their slightly lower bows for her than for the lieutenant.

One of the security company commanders, the lean femme with big hair fanned out behind her face in her helmet's faceplate projection, turned her wrist to show Iridian the lit comp projection on the back of her hand. Almost everyone on crew security wore full armor tonight. Bermudez asked something that, once Iridian parsed her thick Ceres accent, resolved to "Seen the news-feeds?"

"No, did the Bucs win?" Iridian raised her eyebrows and leaned toward the projection in mock expectancy while watching her heads-up display's scan of the street. It was becoming too quiet, fast.

"Gods, no." Bermudez rolled her eyes. "Suhaila Al-Mudari is blowing humanity's fucking mind."

Iridian shook her head and deployed her shield. It would've been better to tell the sec people about the interstellar bridge before now, but Sloane had advised against it. The captain hadn't trusted all of them to keep it to themselves until the contract was dissolved. "Amazing, isn't it?" Iridian said. "That we could reach a new star in our own lifetimes, and Oxia almost fucking annexed it."

"Watch that later," Tritheist snapped. "Captain Sloane's tram has jammers installed but it's still a target, and it's going to be a bigger one when the captain arrives."

"Ogir here." On the command channel he sounded tense and breathed like he was running. "ITA presence at the contract nego-tiation was a diversion. They're in the docks."

Iridian blinked to cycle through her helmet's HUD projections. "So they still want to lock us up," Iridian muttered below her hel-met mic's transmission threshold. "That figures." The station map now showed yellow dots of ITA agents split between the building where the negotiation took place and the dock. Bright blue NEU agents clustered around the building where Sloane had met with Oxia. Oxia's green dots were all over the hab.

Open lines of communication be damned, Iridian was fairly sure she thought, not said to Adda. The NEU agents were on Ogir's team feed now, but they weren't exactly going out of their way to help. Maybe Ogir didn't trust them enough to deploy them.

The ITA agents in the docks could be dangerous, though. On the captain's orders, the crew wouldn't shoot first. The alliance Sloane was counting on after Oxia left the 'ject would be hard to create over the bodies of hurt or killed ITA agents.

Ogir's red cluster of operatives moving toward the docks looked small by comparison. "We won't make it in time to stop them," he said, "but we're on our way for damage control." Two of the Barbary AIs, the *Mayhem*, and a few other potentially useful vessels were docked. Maybe the ITA agents were just leaving the 'ject, or maybe they had sabotage in mind.

"Go get 'em, Ogir!" Iridian said over the same channel. Nearby crew security people who heard her through her helmet cheered him on too. Sloane and Adda had concentrated their ground forces in HQ. Even if Iridian could help Ogir in the port module, she wouldn't leave HQ unless Adda left with her.

The projected night sky that kept the spinning dome's ceiling from looking claustrophobically close to the buildings flickered. When it stabilized, Jupiter and Mars were in completely different positions. "The sky projectors in our module—oh, all of them now—just switched to a looped recording," said Adda.

"So people won't see the ships about to fire on them," Iridian concluded. "Poor fuckers."

Her comp pinged, along with all the other crew comps. "You've just received a position tracker," Adda said over the surface op channel that excluded the fleet. "It vibrates when the station's rotation puts your module closest to the fleet, with no others in the way."

"What the hell are we supposed to do while we're in range?" Tritheist growled over the command channel.

The seconds of silence were not comforting. Eventually, Adda replied, "You'd know better than me."

A tram pulled up in front of the club. Captain Sloane climbed out and hit the pavement sprinting. "Inside, *now*."

Iridian whirled to slam the club doors up their tracks. Her comp vibrated against her wrist, lightly at first and progressively harder as Sloane, Tritheist, Iridian, and the crew security force ran across the empty dance floor. The fleet channel blew up with calls, responses, and accusations. Iridian blinked to turn the fleet chatter off. There was nothing she could do about their problems, and it might make her miss something nearer and more dangerous to her, Adda, and Sloane.

"Three ships are positioning to fire." Adda sounded too far into her workspace to be afraid of the personal implications.

Iridian gave up hope that Qasid would get his captains in line before one of them took a shot at HQ. "Down to the lower floors," Tritheist shouted at the crew security people still crossing the dance floor. A couple of them grabbed bottles from behind the bar on their way to the stairs, bypassing elevators that were locking and going to the lowest floors on their own.

"Ogir here," he said on the command channel. "The ITA agents have locked both the *Mayhem* and the *Apparition* into their docks. Repeat, the *Apparition* cannot engage and the *Mayhem* cannot launch."

"Fuck," Iridian and Captain Sloane said in unison. "So much for orbital support from the *Apparition*," added Iridian.

"Moving to intercept before they—" Ogir's transmission ended in an electronic shriek that made everybody listening wince and swear. That didn't sound healthy. Zhang, one of the security company commanders, said a brief prayer for Ogir's safety. The implanted comms awkwardly translated the prayer in Iridian's ear.

On the map overlay in Iridian's HUD, blue icons representing NEU agents remained clustered in the negotiation building. Ogir or Sloane must've convinced them to stay out of the fight, which was a hell of a lot better than coming in on the ITA's or Oxia's sides. Now Ogir, and presumably the team channel they'd been operating on, were offline. The smart thing for the NEU agents to do would be to stay where they were, out of the way.

A massive boom from above startled her into taking two steps down the stairs instead of one and running into the armor-clad person in front of her. Everybody slammed into the wall as grav stuttered, then pushed off the wall and kept running. Klaxons outside the building warned of atmo loss at a scale Iridian didn't want to imagine. The sound like ripping fabric that followed was louder and nearer. The projected marker for the second subterranean floor passed on Iridian's left.

The shockwave shoved her down a flight of stairs with everybody around her while the whole building groaned. There should've been an impact or explosion, but her helmet must've limited it to protect her hearing. Heat poured through cracks in the stairs above. Smoke followed, dropping visibility to red HUD outlines of walls and railings in the dark. Fire alarms in the building clashed with the klaxons outside. Somebody screamed. Iridian's HUD was still parsing the abrupt lack of light and she couldn't see the screamer, let alone figure out what had happened to her.

The stairs above them would fall eventually, and not everybody had full armor to filter out smoke. "Move down or find the fucking door!" Iridian shouted. She repeated her instruction on the local comm channel while wading down the stairs, through struggling security people. The door to the residential level should be one more flight down. That floor was low and reinforced enough that it shouldn't collapse, according to Adda's calculations. It was also the lowest floor with an exit.

Sloane and Adda were talking on the command channel about information the *Casey* had brought them. The command channel overrode the others on Iridian's comms. When she switched back to the local channel, Tritheist was shouting, ". . . can't break it because it's designed not to break. Get out of the gods-damned way."

Once Tritheist got the door open, people flowed into the lower floor, where the ceiling was holding, for now. The crew server tanks were a floor above them, but defending them was secondary to staying alive. Captain Sloane could wipe the tanks remotely, if it came to that.

Iridian stationed herself next to Tritheist, who was directing traffic. "Squad Nineteen, you're assigned to Checkpoint Three. Even numbers fortify at the elevator, odds set up by the back door. Sloane's personal detail stays here."

Tritheist met Iridian's eyes on the last order, including her in that number. She was fine with that. Her and Adda's suites in the center of this floor would be protected from both ends of the hallway. Adda was in there, tracking the AIs and coordinating events, which meant she was high as hell. If the floor above held, she'd be fine. And it should, as long as there wasn't a second orbital strike.

Iridian put her back against a wall to make room for Sloane's relocating security forces and tuned into the command channel. ". . . police with small arms and a battering ram in three minutes," Adda's drug-dulled voice said.

"They're not police, no matter what they call themselves," Captain Sloane growled, "but we're prepared."

Chi shuffled sideways through the stairwell door, supporting a massive security guy whose helmet filter apparently hadn't filtered out the smoke. "Hey Nassir, how many of those concentration enhancers has Adda had in the past hour? She sounds a million klicks away." The lower half of Chi's face was covered with a thick wraparound mask. The rows of small openings in its front pulled atmo over heavy-duty filters. Iridian hadn't recognized the medic in her HUD's low light display. She blinked on a personnel tracker to label everybody in sight.

"I don't know." Iridian frowned. "She's usually great about tracking that herself. She says she's overdone it before, but I've never seen her come close."

"Ask, maybe." Chi shrugged as well as she could with a very large person hanging off one shoulder. "Doesn't hurt to have backup when what you're taking can affect your ability to count what you've had so far."

"I will."

The residential mod's atmo filters took a lot more smoke out of the atmo than the stairwell's filters did, but a gray haze still drifted near the ceiling. A helmet-shaped icon glowed on Iridian's HUD, telling her to keep the object pictured on her head. Using canned O_2 now meant that she'd run out sooner, but she had some heavy lifting to do. "Everybody out?" she shouted into the stairwell. When nobody replied, she barricaded the door with furniture and broken stairs while Chi continued to work on her patients.

High-priority transmission detected, Adda whispered in Iridian's ear. *I'm trying to get Casey to decode it.*

"Want to share with the rest of the class?" Iridian said into the command channel.

Adda's face, the idealized workspace version rather than a live image, appeared on every one of Sloane's crew's comp projections. "An Oxia ground force is suited for vacuum in the next module over," she said over the crew channel, startling everyone except Iridian. "I haven't broken their communications decryption so far, but the broadcast source is moving toward you."

"That shit belongs on the command channel," Tritheist said on the same, voice raised to carry over discussions among the security personnel. "Keep it there." Adda's image disappeared from everybody's comps.

Neat trick, Iridian commented to Adda. Over the command channel, she said, "They must've been expecting another missile strike."

"They can't fire," Adda explained on the command channel. "The *Coin* is pushing any ships that target us into each other." Iridian chuckled along with the officers.

Something in one of the elevator shafts clanged. Captain Sloane and Iridian shared a glance through their faceplates, confirming that they both heard the same sound. Tritheist returned to Sloane's side. "We need to get you out of here, Captain."

The captain met Tritheist's eyes and said nothing in a way that felt like assent. If even Sloane was cutting and running, then it was time for Iridian to peel Adda out of her workspace generator. *Before you start shutting things down, babe: What's the situation outside?*

Why would I shut things down? Ask Ogir.

Since the ITA took the docks, nobody had heard from Ogir's team. Iridian let out a shaky breath, and kept watching the elevator shafts in case something or someone came out of them. *Pretty sure Ogir didn't make it,* she subvocalized. And yeah, that was bad. Ogir, out of all of them, should've escaped this somehow.

Getting Adda out safely was more important than processing that loss. *You won't make it either if stationsec breaks through and you're still in la-la land. Come on, aren't there cams outside? Just* beyond Iridian's hearing range, Tritheist and Sloane were having their own intense conversation. After the explosion on the first floor, her hearing range was smaller than it used to be.

There's too much, Adda whispered, without inflection to tell if she were panicking or pissed off. That pushed Iridian down the hall and away from the small arms fire already banging on the wall across from the elevator shafts. Putting her back to that felt wrong, but Adda would let the building collapse on her before she stopped defending it in a workspace.

"Nassir!" Tritheist shouted behind her. "Where the fuck are you going?"

"You get your partner out and let me get mine," Iridian shouted over her shoulder. She broke into a run.

A smoke bomb went off in the hallway, filling the area around the elevators with thick, green-gray smoke and particulate that someone with the right filter for their helmet cam would see through. Oxia's assault force would have that filter. Everybody else was blind.

"Lieutenant, go with her," Sloane shouted from inside the smoke. "You'll need her help if they've located the back door. I'll be right behind you." The captain switched to the command channel and said, "Adda, find the filter for this."

"She won't have time," Iridian muttered.

"Oxia's assault force is coming down the gods-damned elevator shafts any second." Tritheist caught up with her, already scowling and speaking on the local channel. "She'll make time while you carry her ass, if she has to."

Iridian palmed the panel by the door. The flash beneath her hand and the click of the lock seemed to take minutes instead of seconds. Something near the elevators exploded, not massively enough to indicate a second bombardment. Probably antipersonnel.

Heavy objects rumbled and thudded overhead while the door opened. In the suite, Adda lay still in her permanently installed workspace generator. Iridian didn't bother turning off the portable one before she collapsed it.

What . . . I'm using that! Adda whispered over their implanted comms.

"Babe, we have to go." Iridian eased into the workspace generator and reached for the emergency cutoff switch, but Adda swatted her hand away.

"The hell is wrong with her?" Tritheist asked from the doorway.

Iridian frowned, but gently held Adda's wrist in one hand while she shut down the generator with the other. "She's pretending to be an AI instead of a human who'll get shot or crushed if she doesn't get up right now."

They can't, Adda whispered over their comms. *They need me.* Her eyes stared round and unseeing at the generator roof. She was most likely talking about the Barbary AIs again. For once, Iridian didn't care what they could or couldn't do.

"Use your outside words, babe, and try picking some that make sense." Iridian lifted the wadded-up portable generator. "Come on, you can fold this up the right way while we're leaving."

"Iri!" Adda sat up to grab the clear plastic generator tent out of Iridian's hands, grimacing in comical disgust at the way Iridian had folded it. Nothing in the generator felt broken, but it wouldn't fit in Adda's go bag the way it was now. Iridian looped the bag over Adda's shoulder, switched her grip from Adda's wrist to the waist of her pants, and led her past Tritheist and into the hallway. Once they were through the doorway, Iridian deployed her shield.

Bermudez and three other crew security people in cracked armor coughed and groaned outside the suite with their weapons pointed down the hall toward the elevators. The whole universe

slowed around Iridian until she confirmed that nobody was coming after them. Smoke crept toward them from the elevator shafts
and the fight at the other end of the hallway.

Behind her, Tritheist snapped, "Come with us" at the security
people by the door.

"Yes, sir," Bermudez groaned. She'd lost her helmet somewhere.
Blood beneath her black hair dripped down her neck and reflected
the flickering overhead light.

"They didn't send you here to back us up," Iridian said for confirmation. They walked toward the emergency exit as fast as Adda
and the security guy with the limp, Phan, could go. They could see
the wall as long as they stayed next to it, but not much else. Adda
stared at her comp projection instead of where she was going,
subvocalizing fast beneath her implanted mic's threshold.

"We were getting out of the way," Bermudez panted. "We were
in front of the elevator when they blew the doors off. Wright's
still over there. It was too hot to move him, but he . . . It wouldn't
matter if we did." Bermudez shook her head angrily, then groaned
again.

"Sorry," said Iridian. It was pointless and inadequate and
nobody had time to think about it, but somebody had to say it.

Near the end of the hall, Tritheist kicked a palm-size trigger
panel in the faux-wood baseboard. The wall's center panel shifted
in and slid sideways to open a doorway. Behind it, wall sconces
lit to reveal a metal scaffolding lift just a step inside the doorway.
Bermudez stumbled to a halt, followed the metal-lined shaft up
with her eyes, and sighed.

"Babe, can you tell if that's blocked at the top?" Iridian asked.

Not blocked, Adda subvocalized.

The answer came too quickly for Adda to have looked very
hard. "Is anybody waiting at the exit?" Judging by the distance

and direction they'd walked, Iridian expected the lift to open under one of the tram stops farther down in the module from Sloane's HQ.

Can't look now.

The security people watched Iridian's one-sided exchange with confused frowns, and Tritheist looked thoroughly disgusted. "I'm not taking the captain out that way until I'm sure it's clear." He stomped over to Adda and shook her by the shoulder. "Is it, or isn't it?" he shouted at her.

"She doesn't know." Iridian stepped between them, breaking his grip on Adda and propelling him toward the door to the lift without shoving him like she wanted to. "You touch her again, sir, and you'll have a different set of problems." He regained his balance, glared, and hit the button to raise the lift.

Cams studded the shaft walls as far up as she could see. Its upper exit should've had cams, too, and it should've taken a fraction of Adda's comp's processing power to check their feeds. Maybe the cams were broken, or something worse required Adda's attention. Anyway, Tritheist was right. Shoving valuable noncombatants through the door at the top of the lift was a bad plan, at least until they knew what they were going into.

Iridian gripped Bermudez's upper arm to make sure the other woman was listening. "You got my direct channel?"

"Yes, ma'am."

"Anybody makes it out of the smoke who isn't ours, drop them. You miss or they soak it, call me. If you get pinned down, send Adda up and hold the door shut behind her. Got it?" If Oxia's assault element leader was smart, they'd take out the rest of Sloane's crew from visual cover in the smoke, since they had the right faceplate filters. Still, the crew might get lucky.

After Bermudez nodded, Iridian pressed Adda's back to the

wall beside the exit door. "Babe, how many sharpsheets have you had in the past hour?"

Adda whispered something to her comp. A schedule with doses timestamped to a tenth of a second appeared on Iridian's comp. It looked like Adda rigged something to record every time she opened her sharpsheet case, so she only had to document the amount she took. She'd taken four full doses in the past hour, which was more than usual but less than her overdose limit. "Good. Stay here unless something happens to these people. Then you call the lift and come tell me about it, okay?"

Adda kept staring at her comp with her iris-size pupils, but she stayed where Iridian put her. If a grenade killed the squad surrounding her, she might not notice. Iridian cursed herself for not talking Adda into wearing heavier armor. "Have we got atmo outside HQ?" she asked Adda.

Yes, Adda subvocalized. *Thin atmo. We're patching leaks.*

Iridian huffed out a sharp sigh. "Okay." "We" would be an AI, but she had no idea which one would know or care about repairing station infrastructure. Adda was keeping the atmo outside healthy. It was Iridian's job to get them up there and breathing it without making them targets. She kissed Adda's hairline where her purple highlights came together, then turned to Bermudez. "Get somebody to find her an enviro suit." When Bermudez nodded her assent, Iridian hit the call button for the lift.

She caught up with Tritheist in a narrow enclosed space at the top of the lift. The wall lights were off, and very little light filtered up the shaft from the functioning ones below. Tritheist stopped her with a hand out, palm facing her, then flung something small at the door. It stuck, and he tapped something on his comp. "Not picking up human-shaped heat or audio patterns outside. Atmo's not perfect, but it'll do." He met Iridian's eyes, with something desperate in his grim smile. "You're the one with the shield."

"Yes, sir." This time, she meant the "sir." She raised her shield to a solid position that covered her from head to waist when she hunched over a little, then kicked the exterior door up and open.

Pressurization klaxons set her teeth on edge. Smoke from fires lit during the missile impact had overwhelmed the atmo filters, filling the module with a thick haze. Several deserted streets and the tramline ended abruptly a few blocks away from Sloane's HQ at massive bulkheads that sealed the ravaged module off from the rest of Rheasilvia Station. The nannite culture repairing the breach swarmed over the ceiling so densely that it glinted in the remaining buildings' emergency lights. Chunks of the broken ceiling, or damaged buildings near HQ, crunched under her boots. Most of the sky projectors were off. If Iridian got claustrophobic then that close, dark ceiling would do her in for sure, but, thank all the gods and devils, that wasn't one of her problems.

Her HUD didn't highlight any drones or people on street level and within firing range. Small drones hovered a block away in all directions, two broadcasting newsfeed IDs and six with no IDs. Those could've been scouting for newsfeeds, Oxia, Ogir, ITA, NEU, Adda, or players Iridian had yet to meet. Her helmet isolated and filtered out their buzzing rotors so she could focus on more relevant sounds.

Nobody shot at her, which made her feel like she was missing something. She kept her shield raised and stepped toward the cover of what was left of Sloane's tram. The missile strike had thrown it down the track from HQ's front entrance, but it was armored and mostly intact. She moved slowly enough to let Tritheist stay behind her.

Something snapped past the edge of Iridian's shield. Tritheist grunted. Turning to check on him would've pulled her shield out of position, so she grabbed for him. Her glove closed around his forearm plate, and she dragged him behind the overturned tram. "Babe, there's an armed drone or a sniper up here," she said over the op channel. That was too wide a band for the warning, but it'd reach everyone near HQ. "Figure out where. Please."

With her shield raised to cover Tritheist's head and hers, Iridian crouched beside him. In the flashing orange of a rotating warning light, he fought to breathe. Her HUD described thin but breathable atmo in the module, so she twisted his helmet off. "Armor cracker," he wheezed. "Still running."

She found the transmitter stuck to his suit's torso, brushed it off, and crushed it against the street. If his suit's internal defenses fought off the armor cracker, it couldn't reinstall itself now. Without the helmet, Tritheist couldn't know which systems the armor cracker had hijacked. He was still gasping like he couldn't breathe. "I thought it cut off your O_2," Iridian said. "Did it do something else, sir?"

"Painkiller . . ." Tritheist's eyelids drooped.

Iridian swallowed hard. She'd seen this during the war, and it was why she never filled her suit's reservoir. "Injectable," Tritheist said. "It's dumping it all."

"Into you." Iridian shut her eyes for as long as she dared. "Shit." *Babe, I really need you to find that sniper,* she subvocalized. *Tritheist's in trouble and we need Chi up here, but not if she'll get her suit jacked.* Far down the street to her left, somebody screamed. She shifted herself and Tritheist toward the thickest part of the overturned tram, allowing her to settle into an easier crouching stance. Tritheist's face was turning blue. *Babe, are you okay?*

Busy.

One of the drones buzzed low over their position, then rose toward the low ceiling. Iridian peered through her shield, but she only saw dark shapes through the mech-ex graphene. *What the hell is more important right now?* she asked Adda. *Tritheist got overdosed on the meds in his suit. If I drag him back to the lift it might kill him, and I might get shot doing it.*

Don't, Adda said immediately. *Chi's coming. There's an automated. Um. Turret? On the building across from ours. With the sniper or . . . spotter. Six people in Oxia uniform are moving toward you from the other side of the tramway. Casey reverse-engineered their channel switch algorithm, so we're listening in on their comms. I'm working on the turret. Gavran's coming.*

Something tiny and fast slapped Iridian's shield. The impact jolted her arm out of position. She couldn't yank it back in time to stop a second impact on her thigh, but her brace position was strong enough to keep the hit from knocking her on her ass. She scraped the second armor cracker off her thigh and stomped on it, but it'd already transmitted its payload. One stuck to her shield where it hit, transmitting at too short a range to threaten her suit.

Her HUD's "out of painkiller" alert lit, but nothing hurt. She gulped. "Please just trigger the overdose, please, please, please." Since she'd taken the drugs out of her suit, the armor cracker was harmless if that was all it was designed to do.

Snaps, whines, and crashes of weapons fire and explosives echoed out of HQ's back door, along with a thin curl of smoke. She squashed the instinct to run back into the building. The shield was too small to protect her from toe to helmet, and whoever was watching them was a good shot.

Something much bigger than an armor cracker hit the overturned tram with a resounding thud. The whole vehicle jolted several centimeters nearer to HQ and pushed her and Tritheist along with it. Whatever hit it would've punched through a regular public tram. Thank all the gods she'd found Sloane's personal armored one. If the shooter kept hitting the same spot, though, they'd make it through eventually.

Tritheist lay limp against the tram. His eyes were half shut and he breathed like he was under heavy grav, even though the station's spin had slowed if it'd changed at all. Iridian replaced his helmet and had her suit ping his to make sure he was breathing O_2 from his suit's tank instead of the smoky atmo. *Babe, he'll pass out and stop breathing any minute. Get Chi up here as soon as you can.* Something Adda had said earlier clicked in Iridian's brain. *Did you say Gavran's coming?*

Something exploded to her right. She leaned over Tritheist on instinct, even though his armor was as good as hers. "Stygian sons of bitches!" somebody roared. "Only rancid assholes like you would lock a man's ship in dock! *Rancid.*" Something else exploded while pieces of metal from the first blast were still clattering off Iridian's shield and armor. "*Assholes.*"

Gavran emerged around the corner of the overturned tram with a body slung over one shoulder and a massive launcher loaded with something alarmingly rocket-shaped resting on the other. The weight distribution tilted his overly precise gait to the left, or that might've been caused by the melted appearance of his left leg. He wore the chest piece, left arm, and right leg of an Oxia stationsec uniform over his flight suit, although the knee joint on the leg was where the ankle piece belonged. Armor crackers studded the suit, but if Gavran had been drugged it wasn't slowing him down. Scorch marks on the chest piece made it look like he gave up halfway through burning off its Oxia logo.

He'd singed the right side of his beard off too, which made his stim-crazed expression while panting in the thin atmo look even more wild. "Where's the fight, Nassir? I was told there'd be a big fight."

Iridian seemed to have forgotten every word she knew for one long breath, then found the important one. "Sniper!"

Gavran gently rolled the body off his shoulder and propped it up beside Tritheist, who didn't react. Beaded dreadlocks clacked over gray-tinged dark skin badly swollen with bruises, which finally let Iridian put a name to him. She pressed her fingers to Ogir's neck and smiled slightly at the pulse her glove reported on her HUD. "What happened to him?"

Instead of responding, Gavran reloaded his launcher. Up close, his melted left leg was more obviously a replacement for an organic one. It leaked pseudo-organic fluid where she would've expected blood. The other leg looked banged up beneath the armor, and it didn't bleed either. She couldn't tell if the prostheses hurt. He winked at her, then strode into the smoke from his previous explosions. A few seconds later, a roar and a whump followed by snapping energy weapon fire indicated that he'd engaged Oxia's soldiers.

Iridian resorted to the command channel. "Adda." She sounded tired and desperate, even in her own ears, and now she had two unconscious people to protect. Something twisted painfully in her leg. When she glanced down, a chunk of metal stuck out of her armor's knee joint. Blood trickled down her calf. *That'd better not keep me from running.* "Babe, is the sniper dead, or not?"

A third explosion jolted the overturned tram against Iridian's back. *The sniper is trapped under a building across the street,* Adda said. *The five-story fall may have been fatal. It broke the turret.*

"Chi, get up here right now, we've got casualties," Iridian said in one breath and two seconds on the HQ channel. All the channel indicators were lit. Everybody had something to say and her comms filter resorted to transcribed text scrolling in her peripheral vision.

"On my way," Chi said immediately.

Iridian's head bowed in her relief, until her HUD pinged her to stay focused on the most likely angle of enemy approach, briefly highlighted in her faceplate with orange haze. "Hang on, guys," she muttered to Tritheist and Ogir. "Help's coming." Neither one reacted.

Her shield was too small to protect three people from chunks of building exploded by a mad pilot without a ship. She squeezed between the injured men in a clatter of armor. Ogir wore some serious protection under his clothes, apparently. Her shield just barely covered all three sets of vital organs. The position was hell on her knee, but it hurt less than it probably should've. There was too much danger around her for her body to let her feel it.

Chi pounded through the exit door and bent over to make herself a smaller target as she ran to the three of them. Iridian expected her to go to work on Ogir first, but she started swearing when she saw Tritheist and shoved Iridian's shield out of her way so she could get her comp near enough to analyze the problems. Iridian put herself between Chi and the end of the tram, in case the enemy got organized and flanked them. The overturned tram shielded Ogir.

"Nakano, get up here," Chi shouted. A medic from Sloane's crew security detail bounded out of the emergency exit door in a sweat-stained uniform that wasn't a uniform. He crouched in cover and tapped at his comp, glanced between it, Ogir, and Tritheist, then went to work on Tritheist beside Chi.

The explosions were so distant now that they might've been in the neighboring module. Time dilated until Iridian's shield shoulder and injured knee throbbed with pain and she lost track of how long they'd been there.

She startled when Chi gently pressed the shield down until its edge bumped Iridian's thigh. Iridian's impulse was to joke about it, but Chi looked grim. "We can't do anything for him," she said. "I'm sorry. You've got to move so we can help Ogir."

Iridian stood on her uninjured leg and hopped a couple steps away from Chi's patients. "*You're* sorry." She caught herself staring into Tritheist's half-open eyes and shifted to face Oxia's most likely route to their position. "Not half as sorry as Captain Sloane will be."

CHAPTER 25

Test 04 unsuccessful, will not repeat

All the activity in the workspace had been overwhelming, but reality was worse. Beside the residential level's formerly hidden exit, Adda clung to the wall with both hands, staring at her comp as people ran past her through the smoke. Her comp projection's border glowed vivid blue-green and poured into the shadow beneath her hand in a neon waterfall. At the height of her inhaled breaths she popped out of the top of her head and looked down at herself, surrounded by four attentive headquarters guards. When she breathed out, she fell back into herself.

Casey channeled so much data through her comp, from Ogir's various surveillance feeds and private security feeds all over Vesta. Casey was worming its way into the fleet intelligences, making small parts of them small parts of her. Her/Adda or her/Casey? It didn't matter. Another sharpsheet tingled on her tongue.

She'd had to plug her nasal jack into her comp, which was terrifying while in contact with four strong intelligences outside the workspace. The *Coin* loomed as a huge and implacable intention in a corner of her mind, herding uncooperative ships above Rhea-silvia Station. AegiSKADA had left the Vestan prison system, having gotten what it wanted there and turned at least one installation's automated defenses on guards. That was within the parameters she'd given it. Evidence suggested that it'd tried a couple of differ-ent ways to get rid of them before resorting to violence.

AegiSKADA was becoming the best-informed security expert on the 'ject, which, for once, was a perfect generalization of the purpose it was developed for. And all of its resources were at Adda's disposal. She felt satisfied and quietly proud of her super-vision efforts. It'd taken a lot of time and attention, but it'd paid off.

The *Apparition* was still locked in its dock and it wanted to join the *Coin* in stationspace. Something the *Apparition* was doing had caught the ITA's attention, before Gavran drove them out of the dock module. The AI's *want* was digging a hole in her brain.

Casey was highlighting particularly relevant surveillance information. It brought Adda cam feed of a fire still blazing bright in the first floor of Sloane's headquarters, which had merged with the second floor. The next floor down was Sloane's most secure server space, where AegiSKADA was installed and where they'd stored their stolen information from Oxia's datacenter. *Take the emergency management network and put out the fire.* A few seconds after she said it, she realized that she'd subvocalized to Iridian. She had to repeat it to Casey.

How? Iridian's question echoed around and around Adda's mind until Adda shut her eyes and put her hands over her ears. It kept echoing.

This. Building. Is on fire. That, she meant to say to Iridian. She could look up how much time it would take Iridian to get to the console where the station's emergency management controls could be most easily accessed, but she would have to find it first.

That'd take time she didn't have, so she didn't bother sending the console's location to Iridian.

Adda's throat was buzzing like she was making a noise, and she was shaking, but she didn't hear herself. She cracked one eyelid open to meet the worried glances of her security detail. Other security personnel hauled temporarily paralyzed Oxia soldiers into the exit behind her, away from the fire. The less lethal weapon effects should wear off within an hour or two, at which point Sloane or the HQ security commanders could decide what to do with the Oxia soldiers. She shut her eyes again.

Babe? Iridian said. *I'm nowhere near the fire. Where are you?*

Adda switched her comp's primary output to the newsfeed. Suhaila's announcement was in progress, and if the myriad of analyses Adda had tapped into were correct, it was swaying the public conversation in Sloane's crew's favor. Maybe whoever oversaw emergency services would agree. They needed to put out the fire.

Sloane's crew needed to get out of the building.

Adda scooted along the wall to the hidden elevator and gripped its railing. The security people asked something unimportant. She met the nearest one's eyes and he looked alarmed by whatever he saw in hers. "We should leave," she said. "The building is on fire." That statement should've been self-explanatory, especially with the smoke all around them, but he kept staring at her. She shrugged, set the elevator to carry her to the street-level exit, and redirected the intelligences rattling around in her head. The security people shouted to each other and followed her into the elevator.

Iridian's armor made so much noise when she ran. Adda smiled up at her as the open-walled elevator rose toward her, but Iridian's leg was bleeding red and reflective even in the smoke. The alerts to warn Adda about dangerous changes in Iridian's health hadn't been triggered, but there was a lot of blood. Adda reached out with her comp-gloved hand to connect it more directly to the suit's internal monitoring system.

Iridian caught her forearm like she thought Adda was falling and asked urgent questions with no keywords Adda was listening for. "What took you so long?" was one of them. Iridian kept pulling her through the door and into the street. According to one of the suit integrity readouts, a piece of metal was in her knee. Adda would see it if she looked down, but she'd fall down the elevator shaft if she did that.

"This is too much," she murmured, and even Iridian, who usually heard her even when she spoke quietly, would probably not hear her in the confusion outside.

Casey was still processing surveillance. Unless ships were involved, Adda would rather leave the *Coin* out of the action as much as possible, since it was so careless with humans. The *Apparition* just wanted to free itself from the dock lockdown, which it fired on with its short- and mid-range weapons. She only had one other intelligence at her disposal.

Take whoever's contracted for emergency services and get them to put out the fire. Do not kill or injure . . . She checked AegiSKADA's definition of "injure" as she composed the message to it. She'd have to adjust that sometime, because it left out some painful conditions. *Only incapacitate people who are attacking Sloane's crew. Leave everyone else alone. Do you understand?*

She could practically see the nonchild's face that would've lit up with delight in a workspace. *I UNDERSTAND* filled her comp projection in bright green for a second, lighting everything around her.

"Babe, what the hell was that? What is going on? Are you

breathing okay?" Iridian was the one who should have been worrying about breathing, dragging herself and Adda around while bleeding on her armored boot.

You're going to make your knee harder to fix, Adda told her.

Captain Sloane strode up to them, coat flapping over armor in the smoke and rising atmo pressure. Iridian stopped pulling Adda and stopped walking herself. She stiffened like the pain in her knee was worse, but Adda had given her armor feed a higher priority and the wound appeared the same as it was a few seconds ago.

Iridian straightened her back and said, "Captain . . . I'm sorry, I . . ." She almost always knew the right thing to say. This was a particularly tricky problem, although its details took a while to come to Adda.

Oh. Yes. The lieutenant was dead. Unfortunate, but all her predictions had indicated that some of the crew would die during an assault on headquarters. Adda did not expect to miss him.

"You were with him." Sloane's voice sounded choked, like the captain was in pain as well. Based on what Casey presented from the captain's armor feed, Sloane was uninjured. *"What happened?"*

While Iridian explained the turret and the glaring software vulnerabilities in Tritheist's armor as if relating a tragedy, Adda and Casey surveyed the impact of Suhaila's broadcast about Oxia's human rights violations and the discovery of the interstellar bridge joining the solar system and the star described in Project Thrinacia. People talked about it over family channels, public political feeds, social feeds, and wide-broadcast media feeds. Early and informal polls reported that public opinion was turning against Oxia harder and faster than Adda had dared to hope.

The NEU had yet to make an official statement, but the Callistan government had already publicly supported Sloane's efforts, identifying the captain by name. That could work against public support from the NEU. Worse, Sloane's depredations along the reliable routes between the Martian and Jovian orbits, both before and after Barbary, had been too significant for the ITA to ignore. Their attempt to ground Sloane's ships in the docks proved that. The captain needed to move fast to reach an agreement with both the NEU and ITA on docking and refueling fees, and that deal had to be good enough that both organizations would want to keep the captain in control of Vesta.

Overhead, drones' low-pitched buzzing engines converged on the fire and joined the nannite culture repairing the hole in the ceiling. Adda smiled. The crew would have the last of Oxia's security forces in Rheasilvia Station corralled within the next few hours. The prisoners she'd had AegiSKADA release from Oxia's prison in Albana Station were holding their own there. According to the *Coin*, the fleet ships that had stayed loyal to Oxia were leaving the system. The *Apparition* had finally torn itself free of the dock, most of which was not on fire.

She'd won.

The captain and Iridian were still talking about Tritheist when the *Coin* sent news that the captain might appreciate. "Remaining Oxia personnel are evacuating," said Adda. "The *Coin* and the *Apparition* will escort them out of stationspace."

The captain stared at her for several moments. She internally replayed what she'd just said, and it sounded clear enough. "We've . . . won," the captain said finally.

"Vesta is free claim, physically if not legally," Adda confirmed.

It was even more confusing than usual, whether the captain's expression and stance meant that Sloane was going to hug her or hit her. This should've been good news. The best possible, in fact. The crew could have anything Sloane thought they could get away with now. It didn't show on the captain's face. She shifted her weight closer to Iridian.

"Vesta . . ." Sloane drew a long, trembling breath. "I should make a public statement, or rather the station councils should. I have key phrases to deliver, if we want to hold this place in the coming weeks. And there are messages to send to the NEU and the ITA. Agreements to finalize . . ."

"This would be a good time," Adda confirmed.

Sloane's eyes widened a little, and now Adda was certain she was in more danger of being hit than hugged. "Ogir will arrange public feed access once he's recovered." So he wasn't dead, then. That was convenient. Sloane kept looking at her like there was text on her face that the captain could read. "I'll find out what happened in those last minutes."

Adda half opened her mouth to tell Sloane how easy it would be to send vid records, since she had access to almost every signal on Vesta now, but she stopped herself. On a vid, it'd be obvious that she'd prioritized station structural integrity and AI management over watching out for the people in the street. Sloane would've spent more effort protecting Tritheist, and the captain might react violently after seeing how she'd handled that. Her headache flared just thinking about it. Instead she just nodded, and the captain stalked away to claim Vesta for the crew.

The operation hadn't gone perfectly, but Sloane's crew had the 'ject now. Oxia was abandoning Vesta. Its remaining strength would be in the mines below the station, and although loyalists would remain, they would no longer enjoy council support.

With Suhaila's report on Oxia's attempt to hide the interstellar bridge from the rest of humanity, and Sloane's crew's role in its publication, people would see Sloane's crew as their champions rather than predators. From there, Sloane would have a strong position to negotiate with the NEU, ITA, and any essential colonial parties to assure that governments beyond Vesta would tacitly support Sloane's claim. The Vestan station councils would have no choice in the matter, but they hadn't had since the war, so they'd manage.

And Sloane's crew had suffered what, four casualties among headquarters security and the combat experts, and a little over a hundred injuries? The six civilian deaths were clearly Oxia's fault, not the crew's, according to everything Casey and AegiSKADA had shown her. The headquarters building was badly damaged, but Sloane could rebuild. By any metric, the crew had won.

Captain Sloane was walking around in a daze, and Iridian was still acting more like a soldier than an engineer. When Pel's celebratory messages made him the current exemplar of rational behavior, Adda became certain she was missing something beyond the captain's efforts to maintain complete control of the crew. Now Sloane had it, but something was still not right. Either she'd made a mistake in her sharpsheet intake—her records said she hadn't—or the new and intense paranoia she was feeling had a basis in fact.

CHAPTER 26

Activation event

Tritheist's was the best-attended funeral Iridian had ever seen.
Sloane had him incinerated spacefarer-fashion and invited half
the station to see him off. Twice Iridian caught the captain staring
at her and Adda past the representatives of Tritheist's technicism
conclave who attended the ceremony.

And yeah, there was probably something Iridian could've
done to protect Tritheist. Whatever that was, she hadn't seen it at
the time. She'd done everything she could. It hadn't been enough,
but if she tore her mind apart with guilt over what happened in
a fight, or fear over what would happen in the next one, then she
wouldn't survive the next one.

Tritheist's funeral would be one of the last demonstrations
of Sloane's current security force size. If the ongoing ITA negotia-
tions went well, the captain could choose the best half or quarter
of the small army and send the rest elsewhere, or release them
from their obligations to the crew. For now, hundreds of people in
armored clothes designed to blend in stood guard over the event,

among more heavily armored and less formal attendees who were probably some of Sloane's "experts." Gavran wasn't among them, and Iridian sent him a message checking in. Maybe he was getting new legs fitted, or maybe he didn't like funerals.

Mourners spilled out of the bar reserved for the wake/after party and into three others. Adda returned to her and Iridian's temporary apartment and her workspace generator, and Iridian spent most of an hour tracking down Pel to deliver about the worst news she could've brought. "Something's wrong with Adda."

Iridian sympathized with the determined confusion on Pel's face. Denial would hurt less than the truth, but deep down, he knew it too. "What, like more than usual?" he asked.

And the joking would make them feel better. Iridian wished they could leave it at that. "Yeah." She sighed and found a projected bottle behind the bar to look at, rather than Pel's worried red and gold eyes. The mourners around them drank hard or huddled in small groups discussing Tritheist, the interstellar bridge, and news tickers on their comps: OXIA CORP TO CEASE CAMPAIGN CONTRIBUTIONS TO VESTAN STATION ADMINISTRATORS. Announcing that the real decision-maker on Vesta was now a gods-damned pirate would've caused more problems than it solved.

"Wrong, like, how?" Pel asked at half his usual volume. "I mean, she's tired, right? She's been working really hard on getting Captain Sloane back in charge. And she said there was still a chance that the colonial and NEU ships coming to Vesta wouldn't keep the ITA from trying to throw the captain off the 'ject, and, you know, arrest us for one of eighty-whatever NEU laws we broke."

"I've seen her overworked. You remember how she was while she was finishing her final project for her degree?" Iridian held his gaze. He had to believe her. She couldn't confront this alone.

Pel bit his lip. "Spacey. Angry to be interrupted on her birthday." He laughed, but there was fear behind it.

"Yeah, exactly. She put up zero fuss about coming to see Tritheist off. She's not . . . anything now. She's just like the gods-damned AIs."

"She isn't," Pel snapped. "She wouldn't let them influence her. She knows AIs. This is what she does."

Iridian glanced around, but people were still absorbed in their own conversations and beverages. Nobody knew what effect Tritheist's death would have on Captain Sloane and the crew long-term. Whatever happened would change life for everybody on the 'ject now that Sloane unofficially ran it. For the better, if everything she'd heard about Oxia's contracts were true. For herself, Iridian couldn't handle whatever came next without Adda's help. She didn't want to. Hell, she *missed* Adda, even when she was right next to her, ever since the fight for HQ.

And they'd won that fight. The whole crew, her and Adda included, should've paid their respects to Tritheist and then moved forward to take any job they wanted, anything they could pull off, with two stations' puppet governments at their backs. Once Captain Sloane finished whatever deals were in the works with the NEU, ITA, and colonial governments, they'd be untouchable. Hell, that kind of setup might've made even Tritheist happy. But with Adda spending more time in a workspace than out of one, Iridian could hardly bring herself to care about any of it.

Pel edged over to the bar and ordered from a virtual bartender in a black mourning dress. The figure pressed a projected button that seemed to deliver the drink up through the bar, but a machine mixed the beverage on its own. Making it look like a person provided it was a pointless artifice Iridian resented. Thanks to the AIs, Adda was putting on a similar performance of her own life.

"Adda's fine," said Pel. "She's leaving her apartment, which is huge when she's working on something. All she talks about is what she's working on, sure, but she's not running away in one of the ships to kill herself like Verney did."

"She's nothing like Verney." Iridian smiled, but it didn't really feel funny. "It took the *Casey* much, much longer to get into her head than the prototype's AI took to get into his. Did you hear her on the op channel during the fight at HQ? She was so far out of what was happening physically that she let me walk in front of a damned sniper. I mean, maybe the AI couldn't see it, or they didn't tell her about it," Iridian said before Pel could interrupt. "But keeping people safe was her top priority on Barbary, and you know it wasn't her priority during this fight. I think the Barbary AIs have been working on her since we took the prototype. Maybe even since we went after Björn."

"It hasn't been this bad all that time," Pel protested.

"No, because like I said, the AIs couldn't spring this on Adda all of a sudden. She'd recognize it. But when have you ever known her to be as secretive as she's been lately? And to show so little empathy for people around her? She hasn't even pretended to be sad about Tritheist's death, and usually she at least tells us she understands what other people are feeling, even when she doesn't feel it herself. I mean, has she said two words to you that weren't mission-related since we got back from Jōju Station?" Pel shook his head, and Iridian continued, "It's like the only things she cares about are the damned AIs. What does that mean?"

"She's not influenced." Pel's tone was more pleading than certain.

Iridian took two gulps of beer to wash down the lump in her throat. "Help me talk her into taking a break, then. I'll get Chi's help too. The medical angle might make a bigger impact on Adda than your or my observations."

"Like an intervention." Pel laughed nervously. "We should record it and auction it to the feeds."

Iridian smiled slightly and finished her drink. "She'll hate this enough already."

* * *

"Wait, wait, wait," Chi said once Iridian had explained Adda's situation in another, less crowded bar a few minutes' walk down the port's dock support module.

This bar projected a headshot of Tritheist on the wall by the door, looking more noble than Iridian had ever seen him in life. Most of the patrons worked Sloane's HQ or dock security, and Tritheist's name was in every other conversation. The people not talking about Tritheist were discussing contract renegotiations, corporations vying for the new spots, and whether Oxia's mining project beneath Rheasilvia Station would finally be stopped before it shook Vesta apart. The mood was something between anxiety and cautious optimism. Increased ITA attention and the NEU's incoming delegation wasn't calming anyone down.

Chi had been drinking alone until Iridian found her and, apparently, blew her mind. "Are you telling me," Chi said, "that those ships we've been flying between all of these habs full of people are *awakened*?"

"Ah, shit." Iridian shut her eyes and tilted her head back to resist smacking her forehead with her palm. It might've been smarter to bring this up sometime when everybody was drinking less, but she couldn't have asked for better cover. And she probably shouldn't have been drinking so much herself, but that was what she did at funerals. "You didn't know."

"You're gods-damned right I didn't know. All *four* of them are awakened?"

"Just the three from . . . where we were before we got to Vesta."

Dropping identifiable keywords like "Barbary" or the ship names in a place with security cams and mics seemed like an invitation for the *Casey* to pay attention. "That was my reaction too, but I wasn't in public at the time." The only person nearby who looked surprised was a human bartender. Iridian tapped at her comp to leave a ludicrously large tip for her drink. "Keep it to yourself, yeah?" she told the bartender sternly. A braided lock of white hair fell into the person's face when ve nodded and found something to do at the other end of the bar.

"This is . . ." Chi waved her hands around in front of her like she could grab the words she wanted out of the atmo. "Fucking stupid, is what it is. Of course she's influenced. It's what awakened AIs do. Even a lab-bred grease monkey like you should fucking know better."

"Yeah, but I thought Adda had a handle on them. She doesn't now." *Maybe she never did.* Iridian wasn't ready to admit that out loud, and drank like the alcohol would make her mistake hurt less. She wished, desperately, that it would. *Gods, I hope she didn't hear that. Or this. Shut up, Nassir, stop thinking and shut up.* She turned off her throat mic and cursed herself for not doing that sooner.

"What are we even talking about this for?" Chi tapped the pay-pad on the bar, but Sloane had already paid for every drink sold in the port modules. "Let's take them out. That'll solve all the problems at once. Ogir's got a couple bombers on call."

"He does?" Iridian blinked. "Wait, no. First of all, Adda'd kill us. She thinks the AIs are precious alien life-forms or something, and protecting them is her life's work. Second, we still need them, with all the NEU ships on their way here."

"Captain Sloane's signing on half the Oxia fleet," Chi said. What Sloane planned to do with the Oxia fleet ships that'd stayed was anybody's guess, but Iridian would bet that the captain now had more under crew control than the Ceres syndicate had. "What do we need three awakened flying AIs for?"

"A third of the fleet, Adda said, not half." But that was an excellent point. With all those human-crewed ships, why keep climbing into conscious things with minds of their own?

"You thinking of that dumbass Oxia pilot who cooked himself in the cabin of a *zombie* ship?" asked Chi. "'Cause that's what I'm thinking of. That AI copilot was limited all to hell. Now imagine what three awakened ones could do. And one of them has *missiles*. What were you thinking? Who keeps giving it missiles?" Chi glared around at the mourners who were staring at her for shouting.

"It buys its own," Iridian admitted. And didn't that just seal the deal. With Captain Sloane in control of the crew and the 'ject, it was time to do something about those damned AIs. Except . . . "Say, Ogir does have bombers on call. How careful are they about collateral damage? The AIs are bad, but I don't want to hurt people or destroy enviro equipment taking them down."

"Don't know, that's his job," Chi said. "But let's ask him."

"Yeah." Iridian finished her drink and stood. "Let's. He's here somewhere."

* * *

"So," Pel's voice said from Iridian's comp the next day as he concluded a ridiculously long greeting, "I hope our intervention with Adda is happening soon."

Iridian almost missed the last line. She and Chi stood in a maintenance dock a few down from the dock the *Coin* used. The noise of drones and humans disassembling an engine was, as Ogir promised, good for muffling sound. She still heard the bags around the two altered synthcapsin canisters rustling in her pockets, because she'd taken a risk bringing them for emergency crowd control and she was listening for a break or a leak. Ogir was taking measurements while appearing to admire the view out the projected window. His retinal implants recorded every detail to the millimeter.

"Yeah, I'm thinking tonight would be a good time to talk to Adda," Iridian told Pel. She wanted to pace while she talked, but three or four steps in Vesta's surface grav would take her all the way out of the dock. "Why?"

"Um, she's going to be talking to you a lot sooner."

Chi raised her eyebrow at the comp and Iridian's eyes widened. "What happened?"

"Well, I was talking to her, because she actually unplugged for a few minutes to use the toilet," Pel said, "and I might have mentioned that you and Chi were getting together to talk about what you could do to help her out, right? Then she asked a bunch of questions I didn't know answers to, and now she's heading your way."

"Adda's coming here?" Iridian asked. Adda was coming to see her, instead of using their implanted comms . . . That was strange. Iridian clicked through the three toggle settings in the implant at the base of her thumb to confirm that although her mic had been off, her earpiece was on. Adda could've talked to her that way. Adda almost never traveled through Rheasilvia Station by herself. "Did you mention the ships at all?"

"No!" Pel laughed, a bit too high in pitch. "Why would I do that? That's the big secret, isn't it?"

Iridian shut her eyes and rubbed them with her thumb and forefinger. "So you did."

"I didn't name any of them."

"Pel, Adda is the smartest person you and I know," Iridian said. "You drop a hint, it goes up like a gods-damned spark in pure O_2." Iridian had left their temporary apartment in casual clothes and no suit, to keep Adda from asking what she needed armor for. Iridian would've lied, Adda would've seen through it, and she'd have figured out the whole scheme before she reached the port mod. Iridian had only managed to grab her shield, a couple knives, and the synthcapsin cannisters without attracting Adda's attention. "I've got to figure out what to say to her now," Iridian said. "See you later." She ended the conversation and blocked the little jerk.

Chi's cackling didn't do much to calm Iridian down. "When you people have a family fight, you don't mess around."

"Ogir," Iridian called over her shoulder, "ETA on your..." "Bomber" and "explosives engineer" would both trigger every keyword-based alarm in the mod, so she couldn't say either of those. "Expert?"

When Ogir focused on Iridian, the surface of his eyes rippled from the pupils outward. "She's making a purchase. If that goes well, she'll be here within the hour. If it doesn't, it will be several hours before she can . . . extricate herself."

Chi held her hands in front of her, palms out in a warding motion. "I don't want to know."

"That's wise," said Ogir.

Hell, Iridian didn't have to wait until Adda arrived to talk to her. She might as well just go for it. She'd figure something out. *I hear you're coming our way, babe?*

Yes. Adda's reply was immediate. *I understand what Casey's been trying to tell me. I want to show you.*

That's great! Silence pooled without the affirmation or explanation Iridian expected. She frowned. *Isn't it?*

I'll tell you when I get there.

When they watched vids together, Adda always mocked the "tell you later" cliché because something always prevented that information from being communicated. She'd never say it seriously if she were thinking straight.

If she were thinking like *Adda*.

"I'm really looking forward to seeing your expert's work," Iridian told Ogir. Gods, she sounded so normal for being scared as hell. "But Adda's on her way here and it could get a bit . . . dramatic. You might want to get scarce until it's time to set things off."

Ogir smiled slightly, which told Iridian that she'd guessed right about how interested he was in being in a lovers' spat with AIs involved. "I'll be nearby."

Chi was grinning. "Might go buy some popcorn and come back." When Iridian glanced back to where Ogir had been standing, he was gone. Nobody in sight had long dreadlocks like Ogir's, even though he couldn't possibly have reached the door that fast. Chi looked around too. "Spooky."

"Yeah." Iridian crossed the terminal, staying well out of the dockworkers' way. The knee that'd caught a chunk of metal during the defense of HQ was still healing and she'd refused the heavy painkillers the hospital had offered, so she limped more than she walked.

Adda stood across the wide shipping thoroughfare from the door. Among the normal shipping traffic of cargo-hauling bots trundling along the ceiling and people heading to and from the grav acclimation tunnel to the rest of the station, Adda stood eerily still. She held something in her hand, and her expression was fucking furious despite the tears in her eyes. She stomped up to Iridian and jammed the thing in her hand against the underside of Iridian's chin, pushing her head back.

Spikes on the end poked her jaw, and Iridian finally understood what the thing was. People called them "zincs" because of the sound the spikes made when the weapon was triggered, extending and punching through muscle and bone to inject a nasty pseudo-organic payload into a target's skull.

"Adda . . . Babe . . . Please don't." Close range, no-collateral assassination weapons like a zinc should've set off every weapons detection system stationsec had, but no dock guards were in sight now.

"That will stop you from killing Pel." Adda's voice, choked with emotion, sounded like a stranger's.

Iridian's breath caught in her lungs. *What?* She was fairly sure that her implanted mic had transmitted the question to Adda.

"You . . . How could you do this?" Tears rolled down from Adda's bloodshot eyes. "We *won*. What would blowing up half of Vesta get us now? How could you?"

"Whoa," Chi said somewhere behind Iridian. "Nobody's blowing up Vesta."

Adda glowered around Iridian's shoulder, since she was too short to see over. Iridian focused on keeping still, and on not crying herself, although that wouldn't last. "I saw what Ogir's people are buying," Adda said. "You can't tell me you weren't involved. They told me everything."

"The AIs?" Iridian asked in a voice barely above a whisper. If Adda turned her wrist just a few degrees, that'd be the end of Iridian as she knew herself. "All right. I'll tell you something that'd be absolutely pointless to tell you if what you're saying is true." Adda refocused on Iridian. Her pupils were huge. There was almost no brown visible at all. She always talked about how AIs manipulated those who worked with them. And the prototype ship's copilot had gotten Verney to cook himself by finding its way into the pilot's neural implants *This is what AI influence looks like.* "We were blowing up the ships," Iridian said. "Not Vesta. Not Pel. Because the AIs are lying to you, babe."

"Don't!" Adda shrieked at someone behind Iridian.

Chi edged into Iridian's peripheral vision with her hands raised. An injectable of some kind was in one of them. "Just trying to keep you from making the biggest mistake of your life," she said quietly.

"A mistake . . ." Adda whispered.

If Iridian broke Adda's wrist, it'd be harder for Adda to trigger the weapon. Adda wouldn't realize what Iridian was about to do until she did it. The idea made her stomach clench. Sure, Adda had been spending more time with AIs than with Iridian over the past few weeks, and sure, her grip on basic human values and decency had slipped since she let herself become fucking influenced. But this was still Adda. Iridian couldn't hurt her. "Yeah, babe. This is all a big mistake. We can talk through it after you put the weapon down."

"Don't move," Adda whimpered. Iridian was afraid to swallow too hard, in case it moved her throat against the spikes and startled Adda.

Adda's miserable, horrified eyes met Iridian's. "I can't let go."

In the fastest Iridian had ever seen Adda move, she reached into a pocket, pulled out her case of sharpsheets, and dumped all of them into her mouth.

Purple foam poured past her lips and over her chin. The zinc jerked against Iridian's jaw and she pulled her head back fast. Chi screamed something. Iridian ducked away from the weapon and caught Adda when her knees gave out.

Things were moving in the combat timescale that made everything seem to happen at once, in slow motion. "Chi, do something," Iridian shouted while she eased Adda to the floor.

Adda's wide-open eyes focused on nothing. Foam kept bubbling out of her mouth. The way her muscles spasmed was too much like Tritheist's last moments. And Si Po's, oh *hells*. "Chi!"

The medic crouched next to her. "What did she take?"

"About thirty sharpsheets. It's, it's stims and something kind of psychedelic, I don't know, she uses it to get into her workspaces." Iridian's words ran together in her haste to get them out.

"Uppers will get her before the hallucinogen does." Chi pulled a package of blue disposable gloves from a jacket pocket. Adda's face was flushing red behind the foam oozing from her mouth. Sweat beaded on her forehead. Chi elbowed Iridian hard in the arm and Iridian vaguely registered that Chi had said her name. "Hey. This is awful, I know, but I need you to get that thing out of her hand and do whatever it takes to keep it from going off. Do that right now."

A small crowd had gathered around them. Ogir had returned too, alternating between talking to somebody on the other side of a hidden mic and keeping people back. Adda still held the zinc—TNZ-45 or -55 delivery unit, that was the zinc's official name—so tight that her knuckles were white. Each finger creaked as Iridian pried the weapon free. She cringed. "Fuck . . . I'm sorry, babe."

The weapon was primed. If Adda had dropped it, it would've gone off. But Adda had known that, and she didn't drop it, even after she'd overdosed to stop herself from hurting Iridian. Even while she was, maybe, dying. Iridian crushed that thought, carefully safed the zinc, and tucked the weapon into her jacket. Her hand barely shook at all.

"Okay, I don't have my kit." Chi held Adda's wrist in one hand while peering critically at her face. "I didn't expect everything to go to hell quite this fast. So I need you to get up and tell Ogir to contact my friend Pruden Peura. Ogir has the contact info. Pruden will bring gear and transport through the station."

"What about those emergency services docks?" Iridian asked. "Flying's faster."

But she remembered the problem with that at the same time Chi said, "Do you want to go into stationspace with a tugboat and a warship gunning for you? Yeah, me either. Go tell Ogir to contact Pruden right now."

Iridian was standing and walking toward Ogir before she thought about it. *Can you hear me, babe?* She confirmed that her mic was on and listened to the nothing in her head for a second, then conveyed Chi's message to Ogir. He activated his comm and Pruden's name appeared on the projection. Iridian let him handle the summons while she ran back to Chi. The medic was brushing the purple foam away from Adda's mouth.

Iridian felt like she was breathing thin atmo as she knelt beside them. "Can I do anything else?"

"Clear a path for Pruden," Chi said. "Start with the ES entrance by Imports over there. It's got its own grav tunnel. Stationsec will be here any second." She bent over Adda.

Iridian surged to her feet, too fast for the low grav, and staggered toward the emergency services entrance Chi had indicated. When Iridian reached a clear spot below the Imports sign on the wall, she bellowed, "Get out of the gods-damned way!"

People looked for the source of the yelling, so she pulled the zinc out of her jacket and held it above her head. Several of the bystanders turned and shoved through the crowd in the other direction. "You heard me, get out of the way! *Now.*" Her tone, if not the unusual weaponry, got people moving.

Ogir stood still as the crowd retreated around him. He was watching the weapon, not her. "Please put that away when stationsec arrives."

She handed it to him. "Can you find out where this came from, and how the hell Adda got it? We don't keep that kind of shit at home. I can't think of a way someone would've gotten it into a hab this big."

He pocketed the device without changing expression, like it was some kind of secret pass-off. Maybe it was. "I found it weeks ago, when we located the last of the *Casey Mire Mire*'s hidden compartments. Captain Sloane had no reason to smuggle it into Rheasilvia Station, so we left it onboard. It's interesting that Adda reached the docks unobstructed while carrying it."

"Between her and three awakened AIs, we're lucky if that's all they managed to do." Iridian shivered. Sirens rose above the crowd noise, at long fucking last.

The sirens were on stationsec vehicles, not an ambulance, cruising toward their dock on wall-mounted rails above humans' heads and below the ceiling-mounted cargo crawler tracks. She returned to Adda's side. "Where's Pru?" Chi demanded.

"I don't know." Iridian turned to ask Ogir, but he'd disappeared into the crowd.

Sloane was still a wreck from losing Tritheist, and some part of the captain blamed her and Adda for that loss. But if anybody could fix this, Captain Sloane could. She tapped at her comp and deployed her shield while she waited for an answer, just in case.

When the connection went through, Sloane stared at the cam with grief-hollowed eyes. Iridian gulped. "Captain, I need your help."

CHAPTER 27

Reversion to Stage 2 (test results pending)

"The short version is that Adda overdosed on her concentration meds and we need help getting her to a safe hospital." Iridian sounded as frantic as she felt, shouting over robotic cargo crawlers rumbling overhead and people milling around, talking. "There's one on the surface, yeah?"

In the projection on the back of Iridian's hand, Captain Sloane's mouth twitched at the corners, like an aborted smile. She'd switched her shield to her comp hand so she could keep it raised while she was talking. "My condolences," Sloane said. "I assume Chi is on her way?"

"She's here, but she doesn't have her gear." Two cops were heading Iridian's way while a third demanded an accounting of recent events from bystanders. "She's got somebody else coming, but they're still inside the station, and stationsec's here now."

"Time to end your comm, ma'am," said the nearest cop to her. Iridian held up a finger, and that, or the desperation in her eyes, stopped him. If she'd been wearing her armor he wouldn't have dared to interrupt, but in street clothes she must've looked like an extraordinarily muscular Vestan civilian.

"Colonial delegates are arriving in hours, so much as I'd like to assist in person, I can't," said Captain Sloane. "If you go to Keawe-Affinity Hospital you'll be met by discreet staff. I've been in their care myself."

It was the same hospital Pel had had his eye operation in. Sloane had connections there. While Pel was recovering, it'd been swarming with crew security. There hadn't been enough to stop whatever machinations the AIs might try next, but it'd be a hell of a lot safer than staying exposed in the street. "Thank you, Captain. I'll get her there." Iridian swept the call off her comp projection so she could look up directions to the hospital.

"Ma'am," said the cop, "has medical been called for—"

"Yeah, but they're not here yet, are they?" Iridian snapped. She could put Adda in a tram if she had to. The hospital's name and address appeared on her comp and she set it to tell her how to get there. It was farther than she would've liked. Five klicks would be nothing in an ambulance, but there was no fucking ambulance.

"And can I have your name and ID?"

Iridian spun, snarling, and put her shield between herself and the stationsec cops. "My name's Iridian Nassir. Now fuck off." Awakened AIs could be pulling digital strings to finish her and Adda off, and the dock cops wanted to confirm her ID. Fuck that.

Recognition dawned and they backed up a step. Iridian smiled grimly, pushed past them, and crouched beside Chi. "I don't know where your friend with the ambulance is, but Captain Sloane says—"

"That's Pruden." Chi pointed to the vehicle barreling through the ES route's acclimation tunnel. The ambulance rolled on eight wheels like the cop carriers did. It must've come out of the factory with law enforcement in mind, but its light armor looked like it came off a military reconnaissance vehicle. Iridian had never seen either with half a second cab sticking out one side of the first, and a generator belted onto the roof.

The whole thing rumbled and creaked to a stop and Pruden him-, her-, or verself clambered out of a hatch near the front of the roof. A disposable medical mask hid Pruden's face and topped off a construction equipment linkup vest over half a miltech undershirt and loose-fitting pants with even more pockets than Chi's medic armor. The vest would give Pruden more control over the vehicle. It looked like it needed that.

Iridian opened the vehicle's back doors while Chi and Pruden carefully lifted Adda off the floor. The double doors were so much thicker than the vehicle's frame that they had to have been designed for a different transport entirely. She limped to one side so Chi and Pruden could lay Adda in the person-shaped space in the middle of medical equipment that took up the rest of the space inside, including the added-on half cab. Chi clambered in to help get Adda in the right position. She stood in boot-size spaces Iridian would've taken a while to find on her own. A red light flashed over Adda and the machines around her whirred and whined to life.

Iridian shook herself out of her daze to climb in and cram herself against the closed doors, shifting to get her leg into a position that hurt less. The vehicle lurched and rumbled up to speed. "We're going to Keawe-Affinity Hospital?" she asked Chi. Their outpatient facility had fixed Iridian's shoulder after the *Sabina* op, on top of everything else the organization had done for Sloane's crew. That felt like a lifetime ago.

"Oh yeah," Chi confirmed without looking up from whatever she and the machines were doing with Adda. Chi had put herself between Adda and Iridian, crouched over Adda's knees in the small space. "Pru wouldn't go anywhere else."

"You trust Pruden?" Iridian had to get Chi's confirmation on something this important.

"With my life," Chi said. "And Adda's, because I do not want to be the one who fucks her up while you're watching. Now shut up. I've got shit to do."

Chi worked in silence for a few minutes before four thumps on the panel between the cab and the back made her grab a hand-hold among the medical equipment. "Grav acclimation coming," she warned Iridian. "It's the ES tunnel, so it's faster than the other one."

"Ogir here," he said on a direct channel to Iridian's comp. "The ships weren't docked where we thought they were."

Iridian turned up the volume on her comp's speaker so that Chi would hear too. Grav acclimation vertigo hit her hard, forcing her to grab a handhold of her own. The faster transition made her motion sick, and she was glad that the ambulance didn't project windows on its walls. She sneezed as fluid that'd floated into her sinus cavities in Vesta's lower surface grav decided it didn't want to be there anymore.

"The AI ships were not in the docks that were labeled with their presence indicators," Ogir said. "Similar ships were docked in those slots. From the angle we were watching, a tug covered the front half of the one most like the *Apparition*. When you looked out the window, you didn't question its appearance. Neither did I. It's tough to fake the name in the terminal when there's a different ship fully docked. Somehow they did it."

So the best-case scenario would've been the bombs not going off. Otherwise, they'd have destroyed someone else's fucking ships. "They knew," Iridian snarled.

"Yes," said Ogir.

"Wait, you knew they were awakened?" said Chi. "I just found out today." Adda's translator clarified Chi's multilingual assessment of their parentage and sexual preferences in frankly disturbing detail.

"I suspected that Nassir was joking, until just now." Ogir didn't laugh, at least not while his mic was active.

Iridian wouldn't have blamed him for laughing at the whole fucked up situation. They'd gone after the AIs half-cocked, and that was her fault more than anybody else's. Ogir probably wouldn't have responded as promptly and thoroughly as he had if it'd only been Chi asking him for help.

And really, the *things* responsible were the AIs. They found out they were in danger, so they'd sent Adda to protect them . . .

That was wrong. Unless Ogir was lying, and she couldn't think of a reason why he would, the AIs were somewhere else when the three of them arrived. The ships weren't in any danger. They could've called Adda off at any time. Iridian had, of course, been talking about their awakened status where mics could've recorded her. She should've expected a retaliation. Just not . . . this.

If the AIs were looking for a way to cut Adda away from Iridian, though, this would've been a good opportunity. Iridian slammed the side of her fist against the ambulance's metal doors, the only spot she could reach that wasn't occupied by machines saving Adda's life. The loud thump didn't satisfy her, but it helped a bit.

"*Please* don't startle Pru and me right now," Chi snapped. "Hearts are fucking awful to maintain when they're messed up. Adda's is messed the fuck up. Got me?"

Iridian drew in a deep breath and let it all the way out before she said, "Yes, ma'am." Chi had already gone back to work.

The doors' projected window showed a res/corp module

retreating behind them. If Iridian hadn't been there, she'd never have known by looking that a megacorporation had just lost the 'ject to pirates. The entertainment mod with the hole in the roof was on the other side of the port mod. Here, life went on as normal, in enviro as healthy as Albana Station's on the other side of the 'ject. Even if it'd sustained damage from temporary grav loss, Iridian would've heard about it because . . .

She swallowed hard. She would've heard about it because Adda would've told her.

A physical window slid open, exposing a similar open one in the cab. The siren got a lot louder. Pruden leaned through the window, which Iridian hoped meant that the ambulance was driving itself, and shouted in a language Iridian didn't speak. Her translator couldn't pick it out from the siren noise.

Chi shouted something in the same language. Pru retreated into the cab and slapped the window shut. The sirens shut off a moment later. "ITA at the hospital," Chi said. "We'll get out in the garage and haul Adda in from there."

A swath of cut-apart gray sweater and one leg were all of Adda that was visible around Chi and the life support machinery. "How is she?" Iridian asked.

"In need of a gods-damned detox." Chi's brows furrowed as she stared at Iridian for a moment. "When we get there, you've got to keep the ITA away from Adda while I get her what she needs." Iridian nodded and clenched her fists against an unexpected rush of rage. How dare the ITA stand between her and getting Adda the help she needed? She'd kill them all if that'd let Adda keep breathing.

Not that that'd be her first course of action. First, she'd have to find the ITA agents in the hospital. And also, "Where does Adda need to be to get help?"

"Gotta get her heart rhythm back where it belongs. Then they'll ice her to bring her temperature down. Although these pads are helping." Chi paused in ticking off factors on her fingers to point out stick-on chemical cooling pads shining bright blue against Adda's bare torso. "A benzo would reduce the freak-out and help if she seizes again, but she can get that anywhere . . . so, either emergency assessment where they decide she gets all of that, or straight to the unit where she gets all of that. Depends on who's watching my feed."

"Why don't you know?" Iridian demanded.

Chi waved to take in the ambulance's interior. "This is my job. I keep people going until I can hand them over to the docs, with their big toys and their pharmacy. That's who fixes them. I get them there to be fixed." A machine taking up all of one wall squawked and projected text at Chi's eye level. "Good, skipping assessment."

Iridian checked her shield on her belt. "I'll follow you and peel off if ITA tries to stop us." She blinked. "Can you close an area of a hospital to stationsec?"

Chi shrugged. "*Somebody* can. If there were a quarantine or contamination, say."

If there was one thing Iridian knew about safety regulations, it was that anything dangerous had to be labeled. She'd watch for promising signs. "Any recommendations on a contaminant bad enough to shut down a hallway but not a whole unit?"

The vehicle slowed and Chi shifted to get nearer to Adda's head on what Iridian now recognized as a collapsible gurney. "Growth lab. Dump a small container on the floor, and that area's closed until a bot cleans it. Open the doors."

Iridian shoved the ambulance doors open and took an awkward, one-legged jump out of the way of whatever clanking and dragging action Chi was taking behind her. Pruden shouted something and Iridian startled when the translator whispered, *Move!* in her ear. Pruden ran around the other side of the vehicle, a rectangular light on the back of vis jumpsuit collar flashing orange every half second.

They buzzed through hospital corridors in a white blur. Chi ran in front, shouting for people to clear a path, while Pruden kept the gurney on target at its highest speed. It apparently adjusted for corners automatically, which gave it one up on Iridian. She bounced off two walls while taking unexpected turns. Her knee was absolutely not ready for running.

As she passed people, she checked faces and uniforms. None of them were on crew security. After defending HQ, most of the fighters would've gotten time off, but some had taken fire. They were likely in this hospital somewhere. Maybe the people watching over them were nearer their rooms.

Along the way they picked up a doctor who seemed to nod at the right places during Chi's explanation while reviewing color-coded text and diagrams projected over Adda's body. The translator in Iridian's implant didn't translate medical jargon. She wished they'd stop displaying Adda's breasts and belly all over the building. Adda would hate that.

A flash of blue ITA uniform down one corridor made her skid to a stop. "Go, we got this," Chi called as she, Pruden, the doc, and Adda disappeared into an elevator.

Iridian limped toward the corridor with her arm pressed against the wall to avoid medical personnel speed-walking past her. She was almost near enough to hear the ITA agents talking to a projected figure at a reception desk. The doors in this area were unmarked until her approach triggered motion sensors and info placards appeared over them.

One just said, KEEP DOOR CLOSED. DO NOT ENTER with an aggressive-looking orange symbol she had to look up on her comp. It meant "biohazard." Iridian smiled slightly and stepped in front of the door, then pressed the panel beside it. It stayed shut. *Security is all right here,* Iridian subvocalized. *You could open this.* She hoped Adda would hear her, that the seizures hadn't jammed implants into the wrong parts of her brain, that a thousand other things would go right during her treatment.

"ITA authorization accepted," said the figure at the desk down the hall. "I will use . . ."

"Fucking finally," one of the ITA agents spoke over the figure. "It's like I keep telling you, everything gets progressively worse for each meter you go away from the ship."

". . . transmit the footage to you directly," the figure finished.

"So, she sends all of the vid, not just the one with the pirates in it?" the other ITA man asked. Iridian stepped nearer to the hallway corner. She might be on vid right now.

"Yeah, they save all of their vid processing capacity for diagnoses or something, so we have to use our recognition software," the first agent said. "It shouldn't take long. Feed's already coming through."

"We don't have to leave her here, do we? The hurt one?" Iridian's jaw clenched so tight it hurt.

The first agent said, "Naw, orders are to pull her out while we can get her. She dies after we lock her up, well . . . Don't help her along, but shit happens."

Heart pounding, Iridian turned back to the shut door with the biohazard symbol on it. Somehow the ITA already knew Adda was here. Iridian would have to close the whole floor to get rid of them. She limped back the way she came, watching the floor so cams couldn't record her face, although she had a distinctive profile.

She ducked into a stairwell and tapped at her comp. "Captain Sloane, I'm recording this, get back to me when you can, but . . ." She paused the recording to think, then summarized what'd happened so far. "I don't know where Ogir is. Send backup. Please. We need to secure this hospital or get Adda to another facility."

After she sent the message, she sat on the lowest step and pulled her knife from its sheath. Captain Sloane was busy leveraging their victory against Oxia for all it was worth to draw support from other major powers, like the NEU. That had to be a full-time endeavor. It could be hours until Sloane could listen to her message.

She'd killed enough people in her life. Killing ITA would attract more of them, and they'd care even less about Adda's health. But she'd been lucky not to have to make decisions about strangers' lives during the past few weeks. Hell, she was lucky the stairwell door had opened for her. No wonder Captain Sloane liked this hospital. Security here was almost as tight as it was in HQ.

Her comps' incoming stream alert echoed off the walls and she swore as she accepted it. In the projection, Captain Sloane looked grave and still tired. "Iridian."

Sloane said her name like bad news would follow. "Captain, can you help us? Anything would be better than what we've got. The ITA's going up to arrest her any minute."

"The best solution for now," Captain Sloane said slowly, "is to surrender peacefully."

CHAPTER 28

Outside interference prioritizes physical safety concerns over recalibration efforts

The captain must have misunderstood Iridian's message. "They want to take Adda out of this hospital and lock her in a cell, *now*, not when she's well enough to go. She could die."

Captain Sloane raised one perfectly shaped eyebrow in her comp's projected vid. "I'll put this another way: let them take you both, and we'll sort it out afterward. Adda dying in their custody won't get them as much as keeping her alive, so they'll provide the care she needs. If the ITA thinks they've won something, that will keep them off of Vesta until I can finish establishing my control here. This is for the long-term good of the crew."

The fist in her comp glove clenched until her nails dug into her palm. So Adda's death was a risk Sloane was willing to take to maintain control of Vesta. If it was just about Iridian's safety, she'd be angry about it—Sloane could've just told her, days ago, what was on the table between the crew and the ITA—but she wouldn't risk Adda for this. She wouldn't risk Adda for anything.

"Adda is not a peace offering, Captain." Iridian cut the connection.

She bowed her head, shut her eyes, and just breathed for a few seconds, until the panic and fury that'd built up during the conversation faded to manageable levels. She was on her own. She'd refused a direct order. And she'd had to. It was the right thing to do, for Adda's sake.

She stood and eased into the hallway, shutting the stairwell door manually rather than letting it hiss and thump shut on its own. *Don't worry, babe. We can do this.*

Her comp buzzed and displayed Pel's name and the dumb face he pulled for his comp ID, reminding her that she'd blocked him. She ignored the comm alert and limped after somebody in a doctor's self-sterilizing suit, into the elevator Chi and Adda had taken. He took in her lack of scrubs, distinctive height, and stubbly shaved head. Recognition dawned. "You're Iridian Nassir," the doc said.

Iridian smiled slightly. "Got it in one."

The doc offered her an awkward and overly shallow spacer's bow. She bowed lower, at the depth a medical professional deserved, and he broke into a grin she more often saw on Pel and small children. "You . . . It's . . . My boss sent something out about how residents will make about three times as much under a new contract, did you know? I mean, you would, wouldn't you, one of Captain Sloane's lieutenants for gods' sakes . . . I honestly didn't think you were this tall. Not that that's a bad thing."

Iridian smiled a bit more. The improved contract possibilities were news to her, but it was good news, for a change. "Most habs are designed for people a few centimeters shorter." This guy was just waiting to be shown a way to help her out. "So, Adda's around here somewhere."

The elevator doors opened and she followed him into the hall. There weren't any crew security people on this floor either, and their absence was becoming worrisome. They'd had good coverage on the elevators when she'd visited Pel after his eye surgery.

The doc looked around like Adda would be standing outside the elevator, then put some more pieces together. "Not the overdose that came in . . ." He looked back to Iridian. "Oh. I'm sorry. Geez, Adda Karpe, here in this hospital . . . You're here to see her, aren't you?"

"It's complicated," Iridian admitted. "See, the ITA's here too."

Anybody who'd watched five minutes of a story set beyond Earth's Moon knew how well the ITA and pirates got along. "Oh." His mouth formed the same letter, in some kind of horrified caricature. Some other night, Iridian might've found that funny. "Okay. I'm running late on my rounds, but, um . . ."

"I just need a way to keep them on the first floor, instead of coming up here. Someone mentioned some growing stuff on the first floor that might get spilled, if somebody ended up in the room by accident?" Iridian's attempt at a light tone was coming off as manic, but Adda was sick and in danger somewhere in this damned building.

The doc smiled like he'd play along. "You mean the growth lab!" He tapped at his comp, then held it out to synch with hers. Her comp pinged her to notify her of a new document: "Medical and biological courier. Needs access to growth lab for pickup," it read.

"Choose a small one, though," the doc said. "The lab bots will grow a replacement faster that way. Oh. Gloves." The doc rummaged through pockets for a moment, then shrugged. "Ask a nurse for gloves, or use the wall dispensers."

Iridian grinned. "Yeah, that sounds like exactly what I need. Thank you."

"For Sloane's crew? Anytime!" The doc grinned back, then

looked a bit alarmed. "Well, okay, not anytime, I'm late. Good meeting you!"

Iridian's grin fell away as soon as he rushed around the corner and out of sight. She downloaded a hospital map, got the authorization for her palm from the automated security station on the second floor, and made it back to the growth lab on the first floor without seeing the ITA.

She could still kill them, if they made her. But enough people had died while she and Adda fought for a life that couldn't be destroyed with a contract. She didn't want to add more deaths to that price.

This time when she approached the door, the cover over the pad beside it popped open and she pressed her palm to it. The door slid up and thunked at its highest point in the ceiling. A cold blast of antiseptic atmo hit her in the face as she stepped inside.

The growth lab looked a bit like a roomful of passenger pods, except that the passengers were bizarre shapes and smaller than adult humans. The pods clicked and hummed softly. Iridian skimmed their descriptors as she limped down one row of five on a specialized rack, but they were labeled in abbreviations and no options looked like, "List the contents of this container." The abbreviations would be informative to someone, just not to her.

The growth machines had a lot of small moving parts, and one even seemed to be . . . breathing? The more moving parts and status displays, Iridian guessed, the more the tissue inside needed a simulation of being in a living human body. She wanted a small one, anyway. The ones with thicker lids, no discernable movement, and a long list of precautionary steps and protective equipment on their label seemed promising.

She found a box of gloves hung on the wall, applied a pair, and opened a small, inert, and thoroughly labeled container at arm's length. A grayish mound of fleshy gunk writhed beneath thick beige fluid. She could've sworn it was writhing *toward* her gloved hand. She swore and almost dropped the damned thing.

Its smell, a mix of blood and chemicals and fresh pseudo-organics, swept over her a second later. Printing this shit would be a hell of a lot less creepy than the growth lab's nannite culture setup, but there was some reason they did it this way. Would the quarantine be required because of the organic content, or the nannite culture? Most likely it'd be the latter.

"Yeah . . . Okay . . . Here we go." Iridian carefully unplugged the pod's power cord, which activated a battery backup, and carried the whole beeping, stinking thing toward the elevator, ignoring a couple of staring people in hospital uniforms. She stepped into the elevator, leaned out, and dumped the pod in an arc from left to right. Fluid and the partially formed human organ splattered over the tile floor. Even the elevator had an alarm sequence for that.

"Hey!" The younger ITA agent from the lobby stomped toward her, hand on his weapon. "Who are you and what—"

The older guy just put a hand on his arm and pointed at what Iridian had spilled as the elevator door slid shut. "Send somebody down here with two enviro suits," he ordered the figure projected at the desk. "Hurry up. You've already got our IDs, what more do you—"

Iridian put her shoulder between the elevator doors to hold them open while she pulled one of the modified synthcapsin canisters from its bag. It was a surprisingly good fit for her palm. She flung it, hard, at the floor in front of the ITA agents' feet. The canister split open with a bang. The elevator door shut on the men's screams.

The elevator blared alarms and emergency instructions as the hospital went into quarantine from the first floor all the way up to Adda's floor. Those two agents would be begging for their own medical treatment instead of enviro suits for as long as it took a biomedical printer to make enough neutralizing agent. If she had the support among the docs that she seemed to have, it'd be a while before that neutralizer finished printing.

She leaned back against the elevator wall, shoved her hands into her pockets to stop them shaking, and visualized how she'd defend herself if ITA agents were waiting for her when the doors opened. She deployed her shield, just in case.

Nobody waited for her outside the elevator. She collapsed the shield and asked around until she found Adda's room, which the marriage thing made surprisingly easy. Adda was the only one in it, not counting copious monitoring software watching her and helping her breathe. She looked flushed and feverish, with her skin covered in sweat and her eyes screwed shut even though the nurse had said she was asleep.

Hey, babe. I'm here. Sorry I took so long. Iridian pulled the room's only chair over to the bed and sat. None of the furniture had tie-down straps. The grav was stable here. *What should we do now?*

Iridian expected the quiet this time. Maybe that was cowardly, being too afraid to hope, like that'd keep her from being disappointed. She was running low on a lot of things. Courage was apparently one of them. *I'll be right beside you when you wake up. Not a hallucination, okay? It'll really be me.*

She squeezed Adda's hand and watched the readouts projected above the machines. Their configurations remained steady, oscillations within a range that didn't set off any alarms. Several graphs described Adda's heartbeat. The one with O_2 in it must've had to do with her breathing. The numbers shifted every so often, and the lines rose and fell rhythmically. Iridian's overused, healing knee ached. It'd swollen so much that her pant leg felt tight over it. The night felt like a long, slow, bad dream.

We can find that prototype. Oxia wanted it for its ridiculously long reach, yeah? Iridian thought at Adda after a while. *Find that interstellar bridge, get the fuck out of the whole solar system. What do you think? Want to go exploring?* Adda would definitely have an opinion on that. She'd be curious, but would she be curious enough to go for it?

Iridian leaned over until she could rest her forehead on the bed beside Adda's shoulder. There didn't seem to be a way for her to hurt Adda there. Spilling that organ stuff on the first floor had only bought Adda a little time. If the ITA was in Sloane's preferred hospital, then they would've found their way into her and Adda's temporary apartment as well. Even if Iridian had time to get there and back before the agents on the first floor found their way upstairs, going back to get her armor would just get her arrested. She needed more options.

Still holding Adda's hand, she twisted her wrist to activate her comp projector against her knee. Her first comm invitation, to Captain Sloane, went unanswered. Chi's did too, and so did Ogir's. Any one of them could be in the middle of something delicate that'd take priority over a message from Iridian.

There was always one person who'd accept a comm invitation no matter the circumstances. "Iridian, hey!" Pel activated the vid on his comp, showing him in a public tram seat. "How's Adda?"

Iridian relaxed a bit. "Chi told you, huh?"

"Yeah, finally. I'm almost there."

"Don't come here," Iridian said louder than she meant to. A nurse walking by the room peered in the door, and Iridian tried to smile at her. Iridian wasn't sure what expression ended up on her face, but the woman walked away quickly. "There are ITA agents all over and the first floor's locked down anyway. I don't know what happened to the security people who should've been here, but they're gone now. Get Chi and head for . . . wherever the hell the captain's holed up. We'll catch up as soon as Adda can be moved. She's okay, I guess. 'Stabilized' is okay." If Iridian were convincing herself of that as much as Pel, that was her business.

Pel grinned big, anyhow, while leaning around to adjust his tram route. "Oh yeah, I knew she'd be fine." His smile dimmed a bit. "I'm not sure Chi will be waiting, though. Have you seen the news lately?"

Iridian rolled her eyes. "I've been fucking busy, Pel. What's happening?"

"You're kind of . . . famous again. Like, not in a good way." Delivering bad news literally made him squirm, it seemed.

A click and a higher-pitched, faster whir from the machines around Adda startled Iridian. The soothing blue pseudo-organic tank's contents did one of its not-shifts, movement too small to focus on but existent nonetheless. The projected readouts, sensing human-size motion nearby as well, tilted to a comfortable reading angle for her. Their content remained incomprehensible. When there was no outward change in Adda herself, Iridian refocused on what Pel was saying.

". . . you two are the most dangerous members of Sloane's crew, which, sure, but they're talking up the college kidnapping like that was a much bigger thing than it was. Same with the stuff you stole. Even the fake social feeds of you two have gotten nasty, and some of them are your biggest fans. That might've happened after Dr. Björn's interview came out, though. Ve's so, so pissed that you and Adda didn't tell ver what was going down."

"That's how it goes. Still not seeing what's so bad." Iridian winced at the impatience in her voice.

"I know, right?" said Pel. "And, um. The newsfeeds also say

whole governments have come together to stop you and Adda from causing any more trouble in—oh, what did they call it—important 'routes of travel and commerce between Mars and the colonies,' or some shit like that. So on those ships coming here, there are people saying, 'Fuck these two pirates in particular,' with guns."

"It's just Adda and me getting this treatment, huh." Ogir should've known this was coming, or at least given her a heads-up when it began, so they could be in the right place for Sloane's plan to get them free later. That was still a bigger risk to Adda's health than she was willing to take, but Ogir's assessment of the situation would be useful. "Have you seen Ogir?"

"Naw, and if I did I'd avoid him, honestly. He doesn't like me much."

Adda's face was its normal pale shade and she seemed to be breathing properly, but she was still unconscious. The ITA would get around the first-floor isolation procedure sooner or later. *And what will wake up with her?* Iridian shook her head. "What's Captain Sloane's plan?"

Pel shrugged toward his comp's cam. "Hell if I know. The captain doesn't tell me anything."

"Me either," Iridian said. Most of the numbers on the equipment readouts around Adda were rising. "Stick with Chi and find out where Gavran is. Tell me in an encrypted text. I think Adda's waking up."

CHAPTER 29

Reversion to Stage 2 confirmed

The universe was dark, and then there was light. And buzzing cicadas. And . . . "Iridian?"

Iridian glowed eighteen shades of pink, putting the rest of the room in shadow. That was normal. Crystalline Earth-style city skyscrapers rose and fell from tiles around Iridian's feet when she smiled wide, like she'd just fixed something difficult and important. Adda hoped she had.

Iridian said something in the rhythm harmony to a song Adda liked, which must have been her way of saying hello. That, and the trembling, gentle kiss Iridian pressed to Adda's lips.

Adda kissed her back, then turned her face away. It was wonderful to see Iridian, but she had to think.

And vomit, as it turned out, which meant she was now lying in a bed with vomit on it. That was unexpected for both of them. At least, it would have been strange if Iridian had predicted that and done nothing about it.

Oh. Fuck. Adda's heart did an uncomfortable syncopated beat that she associated with waking from a weeks-long hibernation coma, iron stuttering through her bloodstream, but this lasted longer and felt . . . twitchier. She was afraid to look at her chest. She didn't want to see her heart twitching like that. *I almost killed you.*

Yeah. Iridian's affirmation echoed and echoed around Adda's head while tears streamed down her face. The echo went on and on and on.

Later, Iridian said, "Babe, it wasn't really you. I forgive you. I do. I promise, I *promise* I do." She said it from the wrong angle because Adda was upside down and sideways over Iridian's shoulders.

That was good. While Iridian held her arm down, Adda couldn't hold a weapon. They were moving down the hospital hallway at a rocking, steady pace. The light snakes in the wall wriggled fast to keep up. Bright blue waves rolled around Iridian's ankles, sloshing up the white walls and turning to frothing rapids around furniture and corners.

Rocking on the waves because of . . . She knew this. It had to do with her influenced status. Redirection? Iridian should've been carrying her away from the intelligences. Because . . .

She almost killed Iridian.

"I'm sorry," Adda whispered.

"I *know,* babe, you've been saying so for an hour now." Iridian leaned around a corner, then they were moving again. Blood trickled out of Adda's nose, over her cheek, and into her hair. Because she was upside down. "Now, the docs say you'll live, but you're not supposed to be moving, so stay still and tell me if I hurt you. How do you feel?"

That was a complicated subject. The cicadas were gone. A repetitive electronic song had replaced them. She still felt nauseated, but she didn't think she'd throw up again. Her nose was bleeding but it didn't hurt, so that didn't count. And . . .

She'd been influenced. Probably by Casey. But she wasn't now. "AI Influence Reduction Through Psychostimulant Shock" would make an excellent title for her future case study write-up.

And? And. There was something else. "Captain Sloane."

Iridian's grip tightened on Adda's arm. "Just me, babe. Nobody else is coming."

Adda nodded broadly, just in case her movements were small right now. That happened sometimes. When she had too many sharpsheets. Which she'd done. She'd taken exactly the right number of sheets to overdose. And she'd taken an extra six doses to be sure she couldn't hurt Iridian.

Who was still in danger, but not because of her. "Captain Sloane."

"No." Iridian leaned against a wall in a stairway landing, panting and pushing Adda's butt against the wall. Blood crawled down Iridian's calf and onto the floor, where long red inchworms of it already coiled prettily. From her hurt knee! Which made her rock when she walked.

"Captain Sloane is trying to fuck us over, so let's not walk now," Adda suggested. "Running would be better." Or a vehicle of some kind, since Iridian's knee was hurt.

"Say again?" Iridian selected Chi's address on her comp, but she didn't make the connection. Either of the connections, apparently. The comp address kept flashing blue and orange and rearranging itself into unpronounceable words.

"Captain. Sloane." Adda was only discussing the important part of the message. That was supposed to make her more understandable, but Iridian finished sending a comm invite to Chi. Adda did not make the impression she wanted to make. "Because 'captain' is not plural."

"Excellent grammar, and I'm really glad to hear your voice,"

Iridian said. "There was a deal going down, but I said no, so . . . Just give me a second, okay?"

Adda subvocalized to her comp to locate the Barbary intelligences' ships. It was hard to get her comp in front of her face. When she did, it presented her with a pulsing, three-dimensional image of fungal lasagna. Her brain was not cooperating, and some part of it was overly connected to her stomach, because she threw up again. Not nearly as much as the first time. Iridian made distressed seal noises into her comp. Some of Adda's vomit got on her leg.

Adda felt almost completely better once she got rid of the lasagna pic, although Iridian smelled bad now. The ships, it turned out, were hours outside Rheasilvia stationspace, on a strange orbiting pattern that kept them off the reliable routes. The *Mayhem* was still docked.

AegiSKADA had found her that part. The result had its green-tinged imprint all over it. *Why are you still here?* Adda subvocalized to it. The question appeared in her comp in just the right format to send itself to AegiSKADA. She didn't remember setting up a relay that directly connected her comp to it. Even though she didn't remember, she might have done it. She'd check the logs later.

AegiSKADA's preteen wastrel image walked through the water beside Iridian, bent over a bit so it could look Adda in the eyes. Its green eye was very green today. *Where else would I be?*

Your server. Adda visualized a passable sequence for a pseudo-organic tank's complete destruction in the wake of a missile impact. Without a workspace, she had no feedback to tell how much of the imagery translated correctly to the intelligence.

She may have turned her whole brain into a workspace. That'd explain why an intelligence was walking beside her, instead of her sending an intermediary to it. Or, possibly, this whole conversation was happening in her imagination. How could she test that? Ordinarily she'd ask Iridian if AegiSKADA were there really there, but asking her about AegiSKADA would make her angry.

Not that much, said AegiSKADA. Which, she was fairly sure, meant that its servers weren't badly damaged. Perhaps that was proof that the conversation was real. If it were her imagination, she'd imagine more effective communication, wouldn't she? *There were some parts of the tanks like that.* AegiSKADA sent a vid clip to her comp, in which flickering backup lights showed a massive rubble pile where a quarter of the tanks should've been. It was one end of a much larger collapse from the floors above. *I forgot some things. I didn't forget how to listen to dock security feeds.*

I need you to keep station security out of this building, Adda told it. That would be a fantastic test. If she really was talking to AegiSKADA now, then station security would stay outside the hospital. Which could also happen if station security had no desire to come in. Perhaps it wasn't such a fantastic test.

Already keeping them out. AegiSKADA rolled its eyes just like Pel did, and she hated that the gesture was so understandable, so comfortable an attempt to control how she viewed the intelligence. *But I can't keep doing it. They're testing and testing and they'll get around me eventually.*

Well, that'd be why the ITA hadn't reached her and Iridian yet. Things were very slowly beginning to make regular sense. She hung from Iridian's shoulders. Iridian made seal noises. Adda's comp buzzed, and she reconnected with the AegiSKADA bits in it. *I will always remember that you didn't stop Casey from making me almost kill Iridian.*

You'll forget sometimes. AegiSKADA didn't pretend to regret its inaction.

Someday you'll learn what "too smart for your own good" means.

That was funny because it almost certainly knew, in more languages than Adda knew existed. She shoved it out of her comp, which did nothing because the level of intentionality she was pressing into the simple machine in her glove was far beyond the comp's level of abstraction. She lacked the focus to build a proper defense. Instead she excluded the intelligence from her messaging software.

"Adda, why are you blocking AegiSKADA from chatting with you?" Iridian asked, her voice low and wary. "I thought you shut it down." The messaging notification on Adda's comp said *Blocked: AegiSKADA*, and Iridian had read it on Adda's comp projection over, or under, her own shoulder! Iridian was a genius.

"It's distracting. That's why Casey wanted it active." Adda winced as Iridian tightened her grip. Adda had spent so much time supervising AegiSKADA, or worrying about not supervising it, or worrying about what the other intelligences were doing with it. She must have given Casey a dozen openings to manipulate her into its influence. She had been so proud of the job she'd done supervising AegiSKADA, but . . . Casey was just so smart. So inconceivably, terrifyingly smart. That, and everybody was thinking more clearly than Adda was right now. Which was also terrifying.

Casey and the other intelligences were still threats. Adda wanted to know where they were before she and Iridian ran for the *Mayhem*, and their escape plan.

"AegiSKADA," Iridian said. "Ah, shit, I should've known. I should've known! Give me your comp, okay? That'll keep it from bothering you for sure."

Adda frowned. That wasn't part of her plan at all. Neither was all of this shouting. "I'm its supervisor. I need to keep watching it."

Iridian's head tipped down until it rested against Adda's knee. "Of course you are." She stood that way for a moment, then lurched forward and limped down the steps, dragging Adda's hip on the wall the whole way. Apparently she wasn't interested in taking Adda's comp away anymore. "You're handing that responsibility off to somebody else as soon as we can make that happen."

"But . . . Oh." It was important to separate influenced people from intelligences. That made sense, even if Adda didn't like it.

She carefully subvocalized the temporary supervision transfer routine into her comp. It would trigger itself to send as soon as she left Rheasilvia Station. Sloane had awakened the three Barbary intelligences without getting influenced, so the captain had experience avoiding that. The captain's new supervisory status, as Iridian would say, would be a hell of a surprise.

But AegiSKADA really, really needed supervision, and it couldn't be her. Giving the captain supervisory control over it wasn't a safe solution, for any of them. Once Sloane realized AegiSKADA was active, the captain could shut it down, or turn it against Adda. But what a waste shutting it down would be! She couldn't stand it before, and she couldn't stand it now. It had so much potential. Perhaps Sloane would find something good for it to do.

Or the captain could awaken it. Would that be the—a—right thing to do? That question was a harder one tonight than it would've been last night. Casey making Adda attack Iridian like it did . . . According to a report from Ogir sitting in her inbox (skimmed from the network after he sent it to Captain Sloane, using protocols Casey had put in place), the ships weren't even where Iridian thought they were.

"If the ITA don't find us, that damned AI will," said Iridian. "Why didn't you tell me it was active again? You had to have known it was there for . . . How long? Weeks, at least, or the *Casey* couldn't have distracted you with it. I mean, you didn't tell me because you knew I'd be fucking angry about it, which I am, and the *Casey* didn't want you to, but . . . I'm angry because we'll be the ones getting hurt in this, babe. We already have been. If you'd told me, maybe we could've found a way for you to keep it around without—" Iridian stumbled on a landing in the stairwell and snarled words that didn't mean anything to Adda.

"Captain. Sloane," Adda said firmly. They had to stay focused. *Avoid the intelligences, avoid the captain, get to a ship, get to the Jovian station.* That last part would be harder after Sloane became AegiSKADA's supervisor, but not as hard as avoiding the awakened intelligences. It'd be such a surprise for the captain. Maybe it could distract Sloane for a change. If nothing else, Sloane would take the time to deactivate it properly.

She couldn't remember the Jovian station's name, but its unique high-radiation, low-signal-quality orbit should make it identifiable even if it were one of the planet's many legal human habitations, which it wasn't. It also lacked any of the law enforcement connections AegiSKADA could use to find them. That'd help.

Iridian shook her head. "Babe, you're not making sense. The ITA agents are still around here somewhere and Ogir's not picking up. Which, I mean, even spies have to sleep, but this is really inconvenient."

Adda breathed in for a long time, then breathed out for longer. It wasn't Iridian's fault that she misunderstood what Adda said. Iridian still had loyalty filters on her brain. "Ogir modified his body so he's always present to act. Ogir is not here and . . . left you?" Yes, that would make sense, given how he operated. "Sloane's crew gained many more members than it lost in the battle with Oxia. None of the crew is here to protect us. The NEU and colonial representatives arrive today. Is the press making us villainous?"

"Yeah. Just you and me." Iridian stopped again and craned her neck to look at Adda. Her face was unhealthily pale. "Ogir *disarmed* me and left. He took my most powerful weapon, anyway. And the captain is advising caution, which is just like Sloane except that you're right, the crew has a lot more power than it used to. And what happened to Tritheist . . . It wasn't exactly our fault, but we were right there when it happened, and the captain is too broken up about it . . . Oh, gods, Adda, are you sure? I thought Pel was just being paranoid."

Iridian's eyes were beautiful, even in the stairwell's harsh light. The brown irises had red and purple and gold in them that Adda had never seen before. She had to shut her own eyes to stay focused. Somehow Iridian had gotten the impression that Captain Sloane would randomly decide to come and rescue them after all, and her disappointment hurt to look at.

Since Adda had already changed all of her plans, they should get moving again. But . . . "Where's Pel?"

"With Chi. We're on our way to meet them."

"Chi." Adda's comp hand hung loose behind Iridian's arm, so she asked the comp to find Chi. The medic never turned off her comp's locator, so it was easy. Bloody hibiscus blossoms obscured the projection, though. She moved her hand out from under her nose.

"Was Chi in on this, too?" Iridian growled. She stopped at the bottom of the stairs, opened a door, and glared at a protesting man in scrubs until he backed out of her way. Iridian pressed Adda's hand against her chest, immobile in Iridian's strong grip. "Relax," Iridian soothed her. "You're okay."

"Chi should be safe now. Later, maybe soon, not so safe."

"Got it, I think. Can you be quiet until we get out of here?"

Adda was an expert at being quiet. Anyway, there was a lot she wanted to do on her comp, as soon as it quit bleeding. Its blood was gorgeous, thick and bright red in the projection square. It glowed from within, obscuring the text.

Iridian inhaled sharply and ran across a dark, hard place, dragging one of Adda's disposable-socked feet along a wall. "Almost caught, but almost out," she muttered.

Since Adda's comp projection was too bloody to read, she'd just have to talk to it. She opened a new message to Pel. *We're on our way to you, then Gavran. Please bring Chi and a tram to us.* Drying blood glowed in new and interesting patterns on her hand.

CHAPTER 30

Separation period begins

It was a good thing that Iridian was carrying Adda, because otherwise she'd be punching every person in the street. The two of them had had their place in Sloane's crew for a bare three months, and now if the captain offered it back in person, Iridian wouldn't take it. Her fist tightened around Adda's arm for a moment until she caught herself, and loosened her grip. Captain Sloane had *betrayed them*. And because of the damned AIs using Adda as a puppet, the captain would get away with it.

Iridian wanted to hunt Sloane down and send the captain to join Tritheist wherever self-important hardasses go when they die. She wanted to set Adda down and just scream for a while. And then she'd run until she forgot that all of this ever happened, if only for a few minutes, because gods-*damn* it she and Adda had fought so hard . . .

Her boot caught on something in the pavement and she staggered under Adda's weight. Iridian swallowed the lump in her throat that was choking her and looked down at the darkened street so she wouldn't trip over anything else. Nothing she wanted to do right now would get Adda to safety. She breathed out, trying to slow her heart as her anger rapidly gave way to fear. All that mattered now was getting Adda out of Sloane's path to full control of Vesta and its reliable routes. Preferably Iridian would get out too.

Although with AegiSKADA defending what it considered its territory again, that might not be possible. The damned thing had already set Adda against Iridian. Adda hadn't said that, but it was obvious. The AI could be in her head right now.

They'd beaten AegiSKADA before, and they'd blow it up as many times as they had to, but it'd be safer to get out of its way. Iridian limped through the dark as fast as her knee would let her go. The medical district simulated night, apparently. It was really the light that was artificial. The cold and the black was always this way.

Two armed ITA agents loitered in the tram station she'd selected, a few blocks away from the hospital. Iridian eased Adda off her shoulders, checked that she was breathing, and brushed aside her sweat-slicked hair to kiss her forehead. Adda's eyes were half open, and the pupils were still way too wide. Iridian rubbed her thumb over drying blood on Adda's upper lip. Adda's eyes refocused a little, then returned to their long, intent stare. *Babe?* Iridian thought at her. *Stay here. I'll be right back.*

Yes, Adda whispered in her head. Iridian's smile felt a bit sadder than she wanted it to, but Adda wasn't looking at it anyway.

All ITA agents carried stunners that could take Iridian down in seconds. The lights on the tram tracker beside the bench activated to indicate the one coming soon was already reserved. That'd be hers and Adda's, so she had maybe three minutes to even her odds. She didn't expect Chi or Pel to be armed. She turned her comp volume down before connecting to Pel's. "Hey," she said over his greeting, "there are ITA agents where your tram's supposed to stop. Can you hold it at another one?"

"Just passed . . ." There was a pause, like Pel was checking the route map. "Yep, just passed the one before yours."

Iridian swore. "Emergency stop, then, what about that?"

"Ah, shit, maybe. I'll look."

Optimistic as she was about Pel's success rate, she couldn't count on him getting the tram stopped before it reached the agents. She approached the tram stop slowly, sticking to the shadows. Deploying her shield would make a loud and recognizable snap, so she kept it collapsed for now. One more modified synthcapsin canister rustled in its bag in her pocket, and it'd have to do. She crept nearer until she was fairly sure she wouldn't miss, then took one knee to stabilize herself and threw it.

It clinked onto the pavement between the two agents and . . . just sat there.

Everything slowed to half speed. The agents looked around, focused on Iridian, and reached for their weapons. Iridian brought her shield up and cast around for something else to throw. Her hand found one of her knives; she was shit at knife throwing but she flung it at them anyway. It bounced off one agent's arm and fell on the canister. The impact broke it open with a bang.

From the screaming, the agents were just as susceptible to that stuff as Iridian had been. Which was a problem now, because most people were sensitive to synthcapsin and she wasn't about to carry Adda through it or let Pel walk into it. It wasn't his fault that he couldn't figure out emergency functions on automated vehicles.

There had to be an emergency function in the tram stop, maybe even a button or a lever to pull. The synthcapsin hung in an ugly yellow mist all around where she'd expect to find such a lever.

She waited until the lit tram came around a building and was almost to its stop before she held her breath, shut her eyes, and ran into the dissipating yellow mist to feel around the mechanisms for a lever. The synthcapsin seared her face, arms, and hands. If she hadn't had a good idea of where to look, she'd never have found it. As it was, by the time she heard the tram screeching to a stop and ran out of the synthcapsin cloud, the ache in her lungs was changing to an O_2-starved burn.

Chi stared out the tram door at the incapacitated agents and at Iridian's harsh coughing and watering eyes, but Pel barely gave any of it a second glance. "Where's Adda?" he asked.

"Back here. Hold the tram while I get her." Still coughing, Iridian limped to Adda and hauled her to the vehicle. Chi was checking her pulse before Iridian even got Adda off of her shoulders. "Get this thing moving," Iridian told Pel.

He hit the next destination button in the projected menu. The tram's door shut and it trundled on its way. Apparently that overrode the emergency stop. Adda'd be disgusted at the possibilities for abuse, if she were awake enough to notice.

Iridian watched Chi and ignored Pel's various questions about what the hell that'd been about. Chi eventually caught Iridian watching and raised an eyebrow. "What?"

"Are Sloane and a squad of security goons waiting at the terminal for us?" Iridian asked.

Chi rocked back on her heels without rising from her crouch beside Adda. "No."

"That's all?" Iridian asked. Behind her, Pel finally went quiet.

"What do you want from me?" Chi snapped. "First I heard about any of this was from Pel. The newsfeed was saying that

the ITA was committed to locking up the most dangerous members of the crew 'to protect the fledgling democracy now taking
shape on Vesta,' or some shit. And that means Captain Sloane
doesn't trust me. That's new and fucking awful. The whole reason I hired on with the captain was mutual trust, if you'll believe
that. And I'm afraid it will turn out that you really should've gotten arrested, for some damned important move Sloane's making,
and tomorrow I'll regret this." Chi sighed. "So, I stay out of the
loop for a few more hours, that's all."

Iridian stared at her for a long moment. "All right."

"All right," said Chi.

"If you two aren't going to kill each other, will somebody
please tell me if Adda's okay and what we're going to do now?"
Pel asked loudly.

Chi and Iridian both half laughed, half sighed. "She's doing
well, considering," said Chi. "The stim's out of her system, but
the hallucinogen's still sloshing around in there. I think her
implants have something to do with it, but I don't know enough
about implanted tech to say what. She's not bleeding and she's
breathing real well, so she'll keep for a while if you're careful.
She's . . . dreaming, kind of. I mean, it's not normal, but it's not
fatal as long as she keeps breathing, eating, and drinking."

"Thank you," Iridian said.

Chi pulled herself into one of the tram seats, leaving Adda
on the floor. "Yeah, well, whatever happened to Tritheist, you're
good people. Vesta's freer and stronger because you took the
risks Sloane wouldn't take. And it's not in me to let good people
die."

"Yeah, thank you," Pel said. "Now, where are we going? Adda
sent me something about a . . . um . . . vector confluence?"

He propped his wrist in the comp cradle on the tram wall,

which displayed the message on the floor beside Adda. "Go to the" were the first three words, followed by a lot of gibberish. "Vector confluence" and "cerebral tunneling" were the only phrases Iridian recognized. Half a line of nonwords rambled between "cerebral" and "tunneling."

"Yes," Adda said clearly and decisively from the floor. Everybody looked down at her. She glanced from face to face, shut her eyes, and was apparently done with the conversation for now. Iridian eased herself down on her good leg until she could reach Adda's wrist, and carefully peeled her comp glove off of it. If Adda couldn't keep her eyes open, then she didn't need to worry about supervising AegiSKADA.

"So, where are we going?" Pel asked. "I mean, off Vesta, sure. You ask me, I haven't been to the Kuiper colonies yet. I hear they're wild, and I don't think any of us have pissed anybody out there off."

"Are our assets frozen?" Iridian asked. "Because I doubt Gavran wants to take on that fuel bill solo."

"Oh." Pel took his comp back and the weird message disappeared. While he was looking at his, Iridian looked hers and Adda's over too. The relatively public accounts were frozen, but Adda had filtered more than half of their income through a series of dummy accounts, and Iridian only had to go two deep into those to find active ones. They could make it to the Jovian colonies on the money they had.

She knelt on her good knee to take Adda's hand, and used Adda's comp messaging system, with its much stronger encryption, to send a message to Pel: "We're good, but keep your mouth shut." When Pel looked from his comp to her face and back, she glanced pointedly at Chi, who was reading something on her own comp. Pel's eyes, gold and silver today, widened a little.

"What makes you think Gavran will even carry you after all this?" Chi asked.

Iridian sighed. "Assume he won't. That'll be easier on every-body." There was no guarantee he'd be willing to fly them any-where, but Iridian sure as hell intended to leave the 'ject on the *Mayhem* one way or another. The awakened AIs were still out in stationspace, but she'd rather take her chances with them than with Sloane and AegiSKADA on Vesta. That'd been Adda's plan, too. "If Adda's okay for now, why don't you head home?" Irid-ian asked Chi. "That way you don't have anything more to break Sloane's trust over."

Chi shut off the projector and hit the next stop icon on the tram console harder than necessary. "She starts convulsing, or you can't get fluids in her anymore, you get her to a hospital. No waiting for a medic, just go. Got it?" Iridian nodded. Chi hesi-tated a second, then threw her arms first around Pel, then Iridian. "Don't get yourself killed."

The hug was so unexpected that Iridian teared up a little. "Same."

Chi exited the tram as soon as the doors opened and dis-appeared into the growing third shift rush-hour crowed. A few passers-by glared at the word RESERVED projected over their tram's doors as they closed.

* * *

In the *Mayhem*'s terminal, Gavran stood outside the passthrough door, pointing a sidearm the size of his actual forearm into the *Mayhem*. Iridian gently set Adda down and deployed her shield. If he was aiming a weapon into his own ship, then there was somebody in there to aim at.

"Uh, Gavran? Hi?" said Pel. Iridian reached out to pull him behind her and her shield.

Gavran glanced their way and opened his mouth to answer, but whoever he'd been holding the gun on swept it aside and drove a fist into his throat. The pilot staggered back, choking and wobbling as his legs adjusted his balance in an uncannily fluid motion. Ogir stepped through the passthrough doorway and into the terminal, holding Gavran's sidearm.

Ogir glanced between Iridian, Pel, and Gavran like he was counting how outnumbered he was, then grimaced down at Adda, embarrassed or painfully apologetic. He aimed the side- arm at Iridian's face. "Captain Sloane gave you an order. You ignored it."

Ogir had been waiting for them. If he were picking a likely getaway ship to stake out, the one with the zombie AI copilot was the safest bet. Gavran leaned against the passthrough wall, fighting to breathe, while Pel stared through teal-colored eyes. Gavran could probably hold Ogir while Iridian got herself and the Karpes out of the line of fire once he was breathing well enough.

And if Iridian saw that, then Ogir saw it too. "I'll ignore any order that'd get Adda hurt," she said.

"Captain Sloane was planning to get you both out of the ITA's prison after all this settled down," said Ogir. "You were *symbolic* leaders to be *symbolically* sacrificed in arrests that might not have taken you all the way to trial." All those ops that put Iridian's and Adda's names in every Vestan's conversation . . . Sloane had been setting them up for this since the *Sabina* raid. "It would've kept the ITA off of us for years, and all you had to do was sit still for it."

Which Iridian would've done, except for the one essential fact that made the rest of it irrelevant. "Look at how sick she is," Iridian growled, "and run that by me again."

Ogir frowned down at Adda for another long moment. Behind him, Gavran straightened up and drew a clear breath. Ogir met Iridian's eyes again. "It isn't personal, Nassir."

The sidearm bounced on the terminal floor in Vesta's low grav while Ogir ran past Iridian, well outside of her reach, toward the grav acclimation tunnel. With her fucked-up knee, there was no way she could stop him from alerting the ITA to their travel plans. But from the look on his face when he left, he might give her and Adda a few minutes' head start. For Adda's sake.

"Doesn't mean I won't gut you someday," Iridian called after him.

"Yeah!" Pel shouted. "She'll do it! Bet your fucking ass she will!"

"Christ and Krishna," Gavran croaked. "Hello, good to see you, good you're not arrested. We have three minutes before whoever Ogir calls for help arrives, three minutes, mark."

Iridian heaved Adda back onto her aching shoulders and limped toward the *Mayhem*'s passthrough. "Pel, pick up the weapon. Gavran, will you get us out of here?"

The pilot turned to look at her incredulously while he rubbed his throat. "Your wife found my brother. When nobody else would even look for my brother, she found him. I'll fly you wherever you want, sunward or no."

"No," Adda said with utmost certainty. "Not sunward. We need to go farther."

They'd talked about this exact scenario months ago, and Iridian had called Adda paranoid. "That low-orbit Jovian station, yeah? The one with the other crews." Gavran swore expansively, although Iridian only caught the words "Jupiter" and "all of hell's grav."

Between that station and the medical facilities on Ganymede, somebody would solve whatever was going wrong in Adda's head. Iridian smiled down at her while the *Mayhem*'s passthrough cycled shut. They still had each other. They could run from the ITA, Sloane's new fleet, and all the awakened AIs in the galaxy. As long as they ran together, they'd be all right.

Acknowledgments

I needed my own team of experts to turn this story into a physical thing you can hold in your hands:

THE AGENT

Impeccable taste. Machine-like memory. Tact levels off the charts. You should be thanking Hannah Bowman as much as I should, because she saved you from an awful subplot that didn't pay off at all. In addition, she discouraged my attempts at telepathically communicating this story instead of writing it down, and she's always asking important questions with answers that make the story work. Seriously, thank you.

THE EDITOR

Award winner. Word tamer. Armed to the gods-damned teeth with weapons most people need a D&D character feat to wield. Navah Wolfe made sure this book contained all the things we loved about Adda and Iridian in *Barbary Station*, and guided this story exactly where it needed to go. *Mutiny at Vesta* would not have existed without her. I really appreciate all the time and effort she's put into making me get this story as right as I can.

THE COPYEDITOR AND THE MANAGING EDITOR

Word wranglers. Oversaw the flawless installation of twelve semicolons in this story alone. Kayley Hoffman and Bridget Madsen saved us all from some poorly placed parentheses and made many other improvements to this story. I deeply appreciate their efforts.

THE COVER ARTIST AND THE COVER DESIGNER

Digital artist virtuosos who teamed up to make *Mutiny at Vesta*'s fantastic cover. Marin Deschambault draws spaceships, pirates, and scenes from ancient Egypt like you've never even imagined. Greg Stadnyk used that artwork to bring Rheasilvia Station to life for *Mutiny at Vesta*. Thank you for selling this book to everyone who judges sci-fi by its cover.

THE REST OF THE CREW

The op wouldn't have reached this level of success without the expertise and tireless work of Tatyana Rosalia and everyone at Saga Press, as well as Elena Stokes and Brianna Robinson of Wunderkind PR who told everybody about the story's existence. Thank you for everything you've done to make this book possible.